YAMA'S LIEUTENANT

ANUJA
CHANDRAMOULI

YAMA'S LIEUTENANT

EBURY
PRESS
An imprint of Penguin Random House

EBURY PRESS

USA | Canada | UK | Ireland | Australia
New Zealand | India | South Africa | China | Singapore

Ebury Press is part of the Penguin Random House group of companies
whose addresses can be found at global.penguinrandomhouse.com

Published by Penguin Random House India Pvt. Ltd
4th Floor, Capital Tower 1, MG Road,
Gurugram 122 002, Haryana, India

Penguin Random House India

First published by Random House India 2016

10 9 8 7 6 5 4 3 2

ISBN 9788184007398

Typeset in Adobe Garamond Pro by Manipal Digital Systems, Manipal

Printed at Manipal Technologies Limited, India

www.penguin.co.in

FSC www.fsc.org MIX Paper | Supporting responsible forestry FSC® C043100

This is a legitimate digitally printed version of the book and therefore might not have certain extra finishing on the cover.

For Daddy, aka Mr Ramesh Rajah, my favourite superhero.
Always.

Contents

1

The Dead Goldfish

Six-year-old Varuna was inconsolable and had been so ever since she had discovered her goldfish floating belly-up and truly dead to the world in its very own glass house, early that morning. Her twin brother, Agni, was equally crushed—partly because he was not himself till he chugged down his glass of Bournvita, but mostly because he could not bear to see his sibling in so much pain. Manfully ignoring the hunger pangs, he focused on making her feel better.

Their mother had named her children after the Vedic deities of fire and water, but it was Varuna who was the raging inferno to Agni's still-water-like temperament. When runaway emotions spewed forth like a bout of virulent diarrhoea, her twin was the only one who could calm her with his seemingly infinite calm, as if by osmosis.

The goldfish had been a birthday present from a cool aunt who had possessed the rare good sense to not buy them boring clothes or toys designed to sharpen their intellect. Mother had been less than thrilled. 'I am not particularly fond of fish. They are so smelly—' she began but Varu broke in with a shriek of protest while Agni murmured his own remonstration out of sheer habit.

'You like fish well enough when it is grilled to perfection or deep-fried till it is nice and crisp!' their father helpfully pitched in, always game to play the hero to her villain.

Mother shot him a warning look. 'I am not sure about this! Fish tend to stink up the place and it is never a good idea for a home to smell like the fishmonger's!'

Varu wasted no time in turning on the charm. '*Please*, Ma . . .' she began, her palms pressed together beseechingly, and Father joined his voice to hers. Ma still looked uncertain but she was starting to cave and, right on cue, Agni said his piece, 'We'll take care of them. You don't have to worry about a thing. We'll feed them and clean the bowl twice a week. It won't be any trouble, I promise!'

There was little resistance to be mounted against a three-pronged attack of this magnitude, and Mother had no choice but to retreat with all the grace her misgivings allowed her. She did not give voice to her thoughts, but hoped the slippery nuisances would not die on them, for her little girl would be inconsolable, and something of a nuisance, when she believed herself traumatized.

Later that night, looking at the fish that had been granted a place of honour on the windowsill—right next to the Glo Worms that Varuna had placed next to them so that they need not fear the dark—they argued over names. It was a momentous decision, and they ruminated on it with suitable gravity, even if they were inclined to make farting noises every time an unsuitable name presented itself.

After a lengthy deliberation occasionally interrupted by thrown pillows, Agni had settled on the names Batman and Robin, whereas his twin had cast her vote in favour of Aurora and Prince. 'We need to have a boy name and a girl name, silly!' she whispered to him, kicking off her Tom-and-Jerry bedcovers and clambering on to his bed. 'Batman and Robin is a dumb idea!'

'Robin is unisex,' he informed her, smug in the superiority of his own knowledge. 'Remember the time Ma got Dad a yellow shirt for his birthday and he refused to wear it because it was too girlie? Ma insisted that yellow was a unisex colour, which means both girls and boys can wear it . . . Robin is exactly the same. Mother's pen pal is called Robin and she is a girl. Ma showed me the photo. Robin Hood, on the other hand, is a boy. So we should just call them Batman and Robin.'

'How come Mother did not show me anything? It is not fair! And I still think Batman and Robin is stupid! Besides, you can't call a fish "Bat*man*" . . .'

They would have spent the rest of the night in enjoyable argument, pausing only to admire their new friends, had Agni not had the brainwave to christen them Zan and Jayna after the beloved Wonder Twins whom the twins adored for obvious reasons. Varu was mildly annoyed that she had not thought of it herself, but she magnanimously let the matter slide.

Nearly two months of excessive love and care later, Jayna was dead and Varu was beside herself with grief. Agni could not tell them apart, but Varuna seemed confident and that was that. 'We should give her a proper burial,' he intoned solemnly and, meeting no resistance from his sister, the little child used the net to lift the dead fish with a gentleness that was unusual in boys his age. He deposited it carefully in the shiny red bucket that was part of a beach set that had been yet another of the good birthday presents. Taking the matching spade along, he led the way to the garden, followed closely by Varu with her own beach equipment.

Working in silence, he dug a little grave just below the slide while Varu gathered flowers. Varu placed Jayna in her final resting place, sniffling a little and wiping her nose on the sleeve of her printed pink pyjamas; they had moons and stars all over it so as to assure anyone with a smidgen of doubt as to its intended usage, that it was most certainly nightwear. Agni had exactly the same pyjamas; only his, not surprisingly, were blue.

The little girl looked at poor Jayna in her final resting place and burst into a fit of theatrical weeping so intense that her brother was alarmed. 'What can I do to make you feel better?' he asked her helplessly.

She did not answer at first, enjoying the feel of the tears coursing down her cheeks and dripping on to the garden bed, wishing Jayna could appreciate how devastated she was by her passing. 'I am crying for Zan also,' she told him finally, hiccups interrupting the steady stream of tears. 'What will he do without his twin? He will be so lonely! What would I do if you were to die? It would be horrible!' Varu stamped her feet for added emphasis and cried a little harder.

'Wait here!' Agni told her and, grabbing his red bucket, rushed back to their room. When he returned, Zan was with him. He was still flopping around when they placed him over Jayna and shovelled the loose dirt over the ill-fated creatures. Varu arranged the flowers over the grave and stepped back to admire her handiwork. She took her brother's hand in hers and they stood there for a few moments, revelling a little in the macabre enjoyment that their first brush with death had given them.

Varu broke the silence first, anxious to get him to confront her fear and make it go away, 'Promise me you won't ever die and leave me! You must never ever do it!'

'Neither of us will die!' came the reply with the weight of the worldly wisdom that was his right to confer as the firstborn, having preceded her entry into the world by exactly thirteen minutes. 'I will never leave you! I promise!'

'Good!' Varu replied, smiling at last, her anxiety stilled for the conceivable present. 'Now let us go in and find Ma, so you can drink your Bournvita. I'll let you have my share as well because you have been good today!'

• • •

Twenty-four years later, Agni still remembered bloody Zan and Jayna, thanks to his moronic memory, which insisted on giving his thoughts the gravitas of a presidential assassination or the loss of his virginity. Almost everything else from that time, which included sharing a nearly perfect childhood as well as adulthood with Varu, had since been banished from his consciousness, almost to the point of no return. Back then, they might as well have been Siamese twins joined at the hip, for even when distance separated them their spirits remained so closely entwined they may well have been a single entity. A lot had changed since then.

Yet, from a sea of forgotten memories, this was the one that turned up on the shore of his thoughts most often. What was even more surprising was the remarkable detail with which he remembered it. He could still recollect how it had felt when Varu's knees had dug gently into his side, when she had clambered on to his bed to explain why his names were stupid, the pattern on her pink pyjamas when she had bent down to arrange the flowers on the grave of their departed friend, the softness of her fingers as they clung to his, Zan flopping around in vain and his gills working frantically to snatch some air while they buried him alive.

The montage played itself in his head over and over again until he could scarcely stand it. He gnashed his teeth in fury when the words of his foolish promise from a long time ago reverberated in his skull, taunting him for his failure to honour his words. Mostly, he cursed himself for failing to protect Varu, but on some days, when his memories tortured him more than he could bear, he was furious with her for leaving him behind and taking off to regions unknown, having appropriated for herself half of the single heart, soul and spirit they had always shared.

2

The DCP's Dilemma

Agni Prakash took in the evidence of his handiwork with a quick glance backwards, pausing in the act of lowering his limber frame into the driver's seat of his silver-grey Innova, which was no longer as spiffy as it had once been. Its driver was in marginally better shape, or at least had been until a few short moments ago.

Agni was tall and his height was enhanced by his leanness. One of those people who lived in their jeans, he came across as debonair, usually pairing them with a white tee under full-sleeved shirts. At thirty—though Agni felt closer to three hundred—the grey was just starting to show, and his eyes had the dreamy cast of an opium user, although they could suddenly adapt to laser-sharp focus when something arrested his attention.

As his eyes scanned the scene, he seemed to be looking into the future. It wasn't pretty. On an extremely busy road in the city of Maduram, a school bus had been set on fire. A lot of screaming people swarmed around the place, the scene reminiscent of biblical locusts descending on Egypt, leaving nothing but destruction in their wake. Even those who wanted to help merely seemed to get in the way and make everything worse.

The ferocity of the flames as they licked lasciviously at the vehicle stung his eyes afresh and made them water, though he had taken care to park his car a good distance away from the scene of the crime. An unpleasant odour assailed his nostrils as the smell of burning oil, perspiration and, inexplicably, frying bhajis mingled freely and wafted through the air.

Red spots danced in front of Agni's eyes and the knife wound he had sustained just below the ribcage wept in silence as he fumbled with the keys and started the car, which lurched forward drunkenly as he fought to bring it under control. He did not look back again. Doing what he did, it was important not to spend too much time looking at the past or squinting too hard, hoping to discern the future. The present was where all of it was, and Agni concentrated on putting as much distance as possible between himself and the burning wreckage, hoping that this would be the last time he would have to deal with the nonsense of a world that he was sick to death of.

The cops had arrived on the scene and, unlike in the movies, where they were lamentably ineffectual and hopelessly tardy, the boys in khaki did their job with a modicum of competence over the blare of wailing sirens and flashing lights. Firefighters were all over the place, and the ambulances had already begun pulling out, loaded with those who required medical attention. Mostly these were children, although a few rough-looking individuals could also be spotted, sporting hastily attached bandages.

The deputy commissioner of police (law and order), Maduram city, Kiran Raj, was there to stop things from spiralling out of control. Under a quick-fire fusillade of his instructions, the cops had organized themselves efficiently and cordoned off the area surrounding the burning bus, rounded up the injured—quickly packing them off into the ambulances—and chased down most of the rioters who had made a belated attempt to escape.

Currently, they were in the process of gathering intelligence pertaining to the events that had led to such a complete breakdown of law and order. The firemen had succeeded in bringing the flames under control before the fuel tank burst and blasted them all to kingdom come.

Had he stayed, Agni would have been relieved to note that the police had the situation well under control, which almost always wasn't the case. The crowd was now almost eerily silent. The chief suspects had been cuffed and dragged off to the police station. Local politicos, their ranks supplemented by the group of Harjas—agitating over the unfair treatment that was their lot on account of their lower-caste status—had been inclined to be noisome and make nuisances of themselves over the arrests. A couple of blows from the lathis, dealt out on the order of the DCP, had encouraged them to be a little more docile and cooperative, although they could not resist muttering veiled threats under their breaths.

The parents of the children on the bus who had escaped death by a hair's breadth had rushed off with them in the ambulances. However, a few relatives and neighbours still hung around, glaring at the Harjas; but the lathis did not discriminate between troublemakers on the basis of their caste, and they had also become mostly passive.

Kiran looked around, grateful that things were not worse. He had to suppress a shudder when he contemplated a what-if scenario wherein the rioters had succeeded in their maniacal endeavour to burn down the bus with the students inside. Fortunately, each one of the children had survived and, barring a few broken bones and other assorted injuries sustained by members of the mob, which were mostly deserved, nothing untoward had happened. If the DCP had been a praying man, he would have thanked every one of the gods in the pantheon.

Ideally, Kiran should have been quite satisfied with the efforts of his men, but he wasn't. He could not get over the niggling feeling that he was missing a crucial piece of the puzzle, and it would drive him to distraction if he did not figure it out. Rubbing the balding patch on his pate, a trademark gesture which was a residual habit from his younger days when he had tried in vain to smooth down an unruly mop of hair, Kiran made eye contact with his inspector and Raghavan rushed to his side. 'Sum up the details of this mess for me as succinctly as possible and leave nothing out, even if you deem it trivial. Start at the very beginning.'

Raghavan was a short, compact man who was almost the exact same colour of his shabby but neat khaki uniform. He did as he was asked with the air of one who was born to take orders. 'The problem began with the Harja boy who was found hanging from the ceiling fan in his room. It was ruled a suicide since all the evidence pointed to the same. There was no suicide note, however, and except the bruising on his throat, which was consistent with strangulation, there was no other sign of foul play.

'Nobody suspicious has been seen leaving the house. For all intents and purposes the boy had been holed up in his room all day and had not even gone to school, claiming he was unwell. He was a class twelve student of Government Boys' School. There was no one else at home, since his parents had left town for a relative's wedding. A neighbour had taken some food to him but the boy had refused it, and that was the last time anybody saw him alive. Upon being questioned, the neighbour insisted that she had noticed nothing untoward, adding that sick or not, the boy should have had the decency to consume the food she had prepared for him at his mother's request and not shut the door in her face.'

The DCP nodded, noting with irritation the beads of perspiration that were flowing down his back in rivulets and pooling at his armpits. It seemed to be a straightforward case, but there were a few intriguing aspects that demanded further examination.

'Apparently, the boy had been in love . . .' The inspector pronounced the word as 'louve', saying it disdainfully, as though it was something foul that needed to be spat out. At a younger age, he had kept his nose clean except for the occasional cigarette or pornographic video, but had been sensible enough to steer clear of real girls, who he firmly believed were more trouble than drugs, booze and gambling together.

Allowing himself a little harrumph, Raghavan continued hurriedly, 'The girl in question is in class eleven, belonging to one of the forward castes, and studies in a nearby school run by nuns. The two used to sneak out of school and meet in secret. The nuns discovered the affair and informed the girl's parents, who promptly arranged for her to transfer to a boarding school and kept her under house arrest in the interim. Unable to see or even talk to his lover, the boy must have taken this fatal step.

'That is the general idea but his parents are having none of it. They're insisting that the girl's parents and relatives must have hired a professional to bump him off and make it look like suicide. The boy had, on a previous occasion, foolishly gone to the girl's house and made quite the racket outside, causing the affair to become common knowledge. This had led to more than a little rancour, and he had been roughed up for his trouble by the elderly watchman and drivers employed by the girl's father; though, to hear his parents tell it, it would seem like a group of hired goons assaulted him and almost killed him on the spot . . .' said Raghavan.

'So far it is not different from a thousand other cases of post-pubescent puppy love . . .' the DCP pronounced, rubbing his bald spot vigorously. 'Teenagers go around looking for kicks because their brains have been turned to rice pudding from all their television viewing, Internet browsing and what have you. Needless to say, mummy and daddy refuse to get on board with their nonsense so they elope, only to get chased down and killed in the name of honour, or the boy pours acid on the girl's face for listening to her parents and dumping him in order to marry the more suitable NRI groom they have lined up.

'An alternative scenario in these unions is that the couple gets an annulment, either willingly or under duress, and they are married off quickly to the first schmuck the parents can scrounge up. And yet, this case has a few interesting elements that make it unique. Do go on.'

Raghavan was nodding his head in agreement, although it was equally probable that it was out of sheer habit. 'In this case, the duo did not get an opportunity to elope. The girl is from a wealthy family who are very particular about their reputation. They seem respectable folk too, with their old-fashioned values intact, and the father is your typical stern patriarch. All they seem concerned about is drawing as little attention as possible to this unfortunate business so that it does not affect the girl's marriage prospects. It would not be in character for them to actually harm the boy.

'Following the midnight altercation with Romeo, Juliet and her mother were packed off without further ado to her maternal grandmother's house in Chennai. The boy may have given in to despair and killed himself, but his relatives swear that this is cold-blooded murder.

'Joining hands with some of the infamous rabble-rousers in these parts, they gathered to protest outside the police station as well as the girl's house. By this time, even the girl's father had flown the coop and, after rounding up his entire family, taken off to visit relatives in Dubai. Thwarted, the mob had no outlet to vent its fury, especially after your order to freely employ water cannons.

'Ordinarily, the thing should have ended then and there, except it didn't. Somehow, the miscreants were incited to believe that justice would be served only if the rich girls who lure the hapless males of their caste are taught a lesson for good. They believe that these girls use treacherous snares to make their victims blow money on costly gifts and fancy meals they can ill afford and then discard these men shamelessly like garbage.

'Consequently, they attacked the school bus, which the girl was known to take, before it could leave the bus stop at about 8.30 a.m., intending to burn it down. They had come armed with petrol bombs. The alarm was sounded within a few minutes of the bus catching fire and we were able to respond quickly and undo the worst of the damage those hot-headed fools had sought to inflict.'

Kiran nodded as Raghavan summed up the situation, not at all surprised that he seemed to be in agreement with the main principles of the mob, if not their methods. The DCP stared at the blackened hull of the bus long and hard before he spoke, 'The fire chief and I had a little chat about the blaze. Witnesses swear that they saw the bus going up in flames at about 8.35 a.m., and the alarm was raised. Parents and many onlookers rushed to the scene to help the girls trapped inside. The rioters tried to stop them but even though they were armed with knives, bicycle chains and soda bottles they could not prevail over the rescuers who had nothing. Before the first police jeep or fire truck arrived on the scene at around 9 a.m., every one of the girls had been saved from the burning wreckage.

Kiran said, 'The bus was on fire, but the fire chief swore that, given the ease with which they managed to put out the flames, there was no way it could have been burning for half an hour. Ten minutes was his estimate. We took a look at the girls as well. All the witnesses agree that the bus was well and truly on fire, yet none of them, even the ones who had been pulled out last, had sustained burns or got even a little soot on their uniforms. They were all in shock and had a few cuts and bruises from being pulled out of the windows after the glass had been shattered, but the damage from a raging blaze could not be seen.

'Moreover, there are many among the witnesses who swear that the bus caught on fire suddenly while the rioters were still gathered around the bus engaged in a yelling match, just after they had stood in front of it to prevent the driver from pulling away. People have confirmed that they saw the home-made bombs lit and released and thrown on the bus only after the sirens were heard approaching. It is consistent with the chief's report, and our own men have discovered the remains of the incendiary devices on the ground, where many of the rioters had simply let them fall—'

'It is a good thing, isn't it, sir?' Raghavan interrupted hesitantly, not liking where this was headed. He was a simple man and a slogger, but his brain invariably shrieked in protest when taxed thus about impossible phenomena. 'God works in mysterious ways . . .' he added but allowed the words to trail off when he saw the look on his superior officer's face.

'That is not all . . .' the DCP paused, unwilling to go on, because he knew what it would sound like. On being questioned, there were a few people who had claimed that the fire was reddish, and that it showed them their future, leaving them ululating with superstitious dread. Ordinarily, he would have dismissed it as drunken natter but under the present circumstances it had made him pause.

As if that were not enough, one witness claimed repeatedly that a complete stranger had set fire to his companion and left him to burn. He swore that he had tried his best to put out the flames but could not save his friend, who was burnt so thoroughly that not even the ashes remained. But nobody could verify this story, although some agreed that this man had been friends with a newcomer to the city. The witness also insisted that he could not get close enough to help his friend and was repeatedly knocked to the floor each time he tried. Some of the witnesses confirmed his statement and agreed that they saw a few of the rioters fall to the ground.

The DCP supposed it was a good thing as Raghavan had said, that the whole situation had not spiralled out of control, but even so, it would have been nice if the damned circumstances had made sense. But then again, in his line of work, the only thing worse than unanswered questions were the unpalatable, soul-crushing answers. So, there were times when you had to take your victories where you could find them and learn to live with your doubts. Otherwise, dementia and a padded cell were just around the corner.

Taking one last look at the scene, he walked away.

3

Yama's Lieutenant

Had he been around for the conversation, Agni would have sympathized with the DCP's puzzlement. After all, none knew the paralysing effects of doubt and fear better than him. In the early days, the two had pulverized his brain and left him almost incapable of the Herculean task required of him. Out of necessity and due to the paucity of time he faced to master the fine art of meditation, Agni taught himself to still his mind, which had been like a monkey hopped up on steroids, and calm the chaotic senses that had bombarded the equanimity he needed to keep himself from bouncing off the walls.

Agni had trouble articulating exactly what it was that he had been chosen to do, not that there was anybody with whom he could talk these things over. There were days when he was almost positive that he was a raging schizophrenic with no idea of how to demarcate between reality and the delusions conjured up by a fevered imagination. Given his medical history, the odds of this assessment being correct were high.

Mostly, he tried not to think about the things he was expected to do. The things he had done ensured that he would never know a good night's rest, free from the nightmares, the shrieks in his head fit to bust his eardrums or the visions drenched in blood. But stray tendrils of thought were hard to keep pinned down.

They escaped their prison and Agni saw the *arakshas*, the creatures that had once been human, who bore the marks of the torture of the flesh and spirit they had sustained in Yama's hells. It was not so much the grotesqueness of their forms that got to him as much as the bitter hatred and corrosive rage that spilled out of their eyes and turned to jelly, from when the rot had set in. No force could ever prevail over them forever. But it was what Agni did, and he could feel the unstoppable power that had been bestowed upon him to wield, like a drug that he wanted to be high on all the damn time.

Over and over again, Agni, who had been chosen to be Yama's lieutenant, summoned the force of the lord of the damned to send the accursed ones back to the torture chambers of hell. But when the after-effects of the magic drained away to regions unknown, the only things that remained were the emptiness and self-loathing.

It was the sort of thing that, if said aloud, could earn one permanent membership to a mental institution. But it was what Agni did, armed with weapons from Yama's own arsenal, which were his to summon and use as he saw fit. The incident with the burning bus was a typical day in his life, but it would be nigh impossible to explain the damn thing to a fellow human.

It had all begun in the recent past. Agni knew from long experience as to when the fit was almost upon him and he had collapsed on to the nearest chair in the miserable excuse of a hotel in Brunalore where he was shacked up. His entire body went taut and rigid as though stretched out by wires. His eyes were blank and became scarier when the balls rolled back into his skull, leaving only the whites showing. His neck muscles clenched as his head whipped back. His fingers closed tight in a white-knuckled grip on the armrest as his knees jerked ceaselessly in a clacket-y rhythm, and Agni gnashed his teeth together, keeping time to it.

•••

Everything disappeared around him, plunging him into another dimension. Agni saw the araksha. It had not bothered with a disguise, discarding its corporeal form. The marks of Yama's hells were upon it, telltale evidence of the tortures of the spirit and flesh it had endured. This one had no hair, and its skin, or what remained of it, hung loosely over the partially exposed skeleton as though it had been poured over the framework.

He had seen this before; Yama's fires did not burn the way Agni's (his divine namesake's) did. That would have been too quick, for the god of fire did a thorough job and endeavoured to leave nothing behind. The fires of hell burnt their victims but did not consume them entirely, merely melting the flesh, so that in its softened form it could be moulded into indistinguishable shapes and left to cool for when the torture began again.

Through the gaps in the mutilated flesh, Agni could see parts of the windpipe which showed up starkly white against the garish redness of the muscles, tissues, entrails and even the heart that pulsed as though still alive. Arakshas wore their deformity with pride, believing that it justified the course of action they had decided to pursue. Mortals could not see arakshas in their natural state, which was for the best, since the sight would have driven them to madness or stopped their own hearts. But their presence could be felt, and it would feel like the brush of death preceding a descent to hell.

The fiend wrapped its fingers, which oozed slime, around the neck of an unsuspecting boy who was slumped over a small table, lifting him up with its supernatural strength. Its victim never had a chance. A few brief kicks marked the futility of his meagre resistance, and then he was dead. Leisurely, the thing fashioned a noose from his bed sheet and hung him up from the ceiling fan.

The next thing Agni saw was a burning bus. Rioters torched the vehicle and fought off the frantic attempts of rescuers to save the students. The police arrived but by then the situation had escalated into a full-blown war. The cops opened fire, shooting madly into the crowd, and the aggressors responded with more petrol bombs, which were flung into the melee. Cars were blown up, police jeeps were overturned, and trucks careened into adjacent streets to avoid the battle. Severed limbs and burning bodies festooned the place, and the wails of the injured competed with the sounds of fighting and killing.

Fire raged over everything, consuming everything in its path, and spread to the next scene where every single house in a sheltered community had been set ablaze. Many were trapped in their homes and watched everything they cared for, from their children to their possessions, go up in flames.

The araksha was in the thick of things and had once again discarded its human disguise. Suddenly, it turned, as though it knew that someone was watching, and looked directly into Agni's eyes. It did not have lips, but the bony jaw opened in a grotesque smile . . .

•••

Agni did not know how long he was unconscious. When he came to, he was in a puddle of his own urine. Swearing softly to himself, he cleaned up the furniture with a towel and sprayed some deodorant on it. The commercial had promised that the bottled scent was a chick magnet, and Agni wondered if the deodorant's purported aphrodisiacal effects would work on anyone if they knew he was responsible for the piss-soaked chair in front of him. Not for the first time, he wished the powers that be had come up with a better way to intimate him about the future he was called upon to prevent from materializing.

There was no time to dwell on his condition though. Agni had to hurry. His vision seemed well on its way to becoming a reality, given that he had read about the boy in a news article a couple of days ago. It had not been relegated to a tiny little portion of newsprint, as most suicides often are. The boy had belonged to the Harja community, and they had protested the findings in front of the police station in Maduram, demanding a murder investigation. Things had got out of hand and the cops had responded with an iron fist, which was why the newspapers had given the case a fair share of attention.

His mind made the connection immediately, and he hit the road. It would have been simpler to fly down to Maduram, but who had that kind of money? His job was not a high-paying one, though he was expected to work unreasonable hours. And if he was to stretch his inheritance to last a lifetime, luxuries had to be pared down.

Once in Maduram, he checked into the Queen Hotel, which was not too far from where the victim lived. The porter insisted on carrying his small suitcase to the room, which had been painted in shades of yellow and brown to make it appear cheerful. It had a single cot, a tiny television set, a small table, a chair, with a bathroom, where the commode was wedged a little too close to the shower. There was also a red plastic bucket and an orange mug.

Agni handed him a generous tip and the porter became quite voluble in his gratitude. 'Thanks, *saar*! My name is Pandi. Please call me, saar, if you want anything else—cigarettes, beer, newspapers; I can get anything for you, saar!' He winked at Agni, in case he had not made himself clear.

Agni smiled his thanks. 'I do need your help. My paper sent me here to cover the case of that dead boy who lived in these parts and the mystery surrounding it. The cops are saying it is suicide, but my editor is not buying that because we all know how corrupt they are. All they care about is money. I am here to find out the truth and make sure that the poor boy gets justice.'

The porter looked suspicious when he heard that Agni worked for a newspaper, but nodded vigorously in agreement when he made his stand clear. Looking over his shoulder to make sure the door was shut, he spoke in a whisper, 'You are a good man, saar! My people have always been treated unfairly by upper-class bastards who think we are only fit for cleaning up their shit. My father did not believe in sending me to school where people like me are looked down upon and ordered me to work as a cleaner for the truck drivers. That is why I am working like this in my old age instead of retiring in Dubai.'

Agni nodded sympathetically and that was all the encouragement the old man needed to continue. 'Nowadays, things are different. The government says that we have the right to study, and there's also the quota system. Our children work in big companies and make a lot of money, but the rich masters cannot bear to see us overtake them in every field. Some consider it a personal affront that the children of the men and women who scrubbed their toilets and swabbed their floors are now pillars of the community and wield the kind of power and prestige that they cannot hope to achieve. We have worked hard and sacrificed so much to get to where we are and yet they try to grind us down and leave us in the dirt. They rape our women and kill our boys. How long are we supposed to put up with this?

'That rich bitch distracted our boy from his studies, wearing her slutty churidars! Decent girls ought to wear half-saris before they are married and proper saris after. Girls nowadays are spoilt by their parents who don't teach them our traditions, letting them copy the immoral northerners who ape the white westerners blindly. It is disgraceful. They think their children are too good for the likes of us but I say they are not worth the ground we walk on.

'Having seduced our boy and having scratched her itch, that heartless harlot abandoned him when her parents found out. Now he is dead and she is sitting pretty in some foreign country. How can this be justice? It is time to teach them a lesson. We will not let his death go unavenged!'

'If only the police would do their jobs and track down the miscreants behind this atrocious crime . . .' said Agni.

'The police are corrupt through and through. You said it yourself, they care only about money. They would willingly sell their mothers, daughters and even granddaughters into prostitution if it meant they could get a few lousy bucks out of it. Why, they would bend over themselves if you pay them enough!'

Agni laughed and the curmudgeon was gratified. 'It is true enough. But if the tax-paying public aided by the media put enough pressure on them, they will have no choice but to turn over the case to the CBI, so that those responsible for this boy's death will spend the rest of their days behind bars if they are lucky or wind up with a richly deserved death penalty.'

The porter shook his head pityingly. 'You are not yet wise in the ways of the world like this old-timer. Enough money will exchange hands and those bastards will get away with murder. Nobody will remember this case. But sometimes we have to take the law into our own hands in order to get the vengeance we deserve. You are not too far from the action. Keep watching and, soon, it may even be tomorrow morning . . . you can shout our story from the rooftops and let those so-called forward-caste bastards and their bitches know that we will no longer allow ourselves to get screwed over and we will fight back with fire if that is what it takes.'

Agni deliberately kept his expression blank, as though he were not sure if he ought to take the old man seriously, before allowing a somewhat-condescending smile to spread across his face in a transparent effort to mollify. The porter looked worried that he had perhaps said too much but he was relieved to note that Agni was really as stupid as the rest of his tribe of scribes, who cared only about the affairs of glamorous film stars and chased after lurid rape cases. Extracting a promise from Agni that he would call him if he needed anything, the old man made his departure.

Sometimes it was as simple as that. In the beginning, the biggest challenge in missions like this was fighting the panic. How was it possible to find the proverbial needle in the haystack with the clock conspiring against him? The visions were blurry affairs on the best of days, and woefully short on details. But with time he learned to believe that the answers would come to him if he did not disrupt the tranquillity of his mind with endless questions that did nothing but kick up a dust and hinder his vision.

Upon further inquiry, Agni discovered the name, address and school of the deceased boy's lover who had flown the coop. Her school had five buses and one van which he could rule out. All he could do was be present at the bus stop closest to her house in the hope that it would be the one the mob would target, although there was the very real possibility of any of the other buses being targeted.

Agni usually discouraged himself from allowing his brain to get hyper-analytical about things, but he could not resist pondering over the insane pettiness and sheer stupidity of it all. What kind of satisfaction could the araksha get by killing a poor boy, who, despite suffering from a broken heart, had his whole life ahead of him?

Sure, it had manipulated the situation masterfully to spread discord and turn people against one another so that it could engineer a lot more innocent deaths and leave the city devastated by a tragedy that would cast a long shadow over its future. But he could not help thinking that if it had been him who had actually managed to escape from hell, he would have either devoted his life solely to the pursuit of pleasure, or made the attempt to atone for whatever evil he had been guilty of by taking a stab at saving the world and redeeming himself.

The arakshas, who had amassed great stores of power and occult magic thought differently, he supposed. Or else they had been subjected to so much pain and suffering that it had become a natural impulse to spread misery. In such a case, Yama's attempt to rehabilitate sinners did exactly as much as the reviled prison system and more stringent forms of punishment favoured by the civilized world. Thinking like that did him little good, and Agni quieted his suspicions by watching the idiot box till he dozed off.

On the very next day, Agni was keeping a watch on the bus stop when it all began. Almost all the seats were filled with students and a few teachers as it was the last stop en route to the school. He sensed the presence of the araksha, although he could not pinpoint its exact location. Taking the briefest of moments to scan the scene, he debated and discarded the option of looking for the araksha. Things would start unravelling soon and he had to act immediately.

Without pausing to think, he summoned Chandrama and Suryama to him. They were the legendary four-eyed hounds of Yama, and the sons of Sarama, Indra's faithful canine aide. Varu had referred to them as Chandu and Suri, and Agni did too. The ghost dogs emerged at his side, larger than the mind could conceive, and Agni always wondered whether a few, if any, were alerted to their formidable presence until it was too late.

Chandu's glossy coat was the colour of clotted cream and Suri's was honey interspersed with streaks of gold. Their noses alone were black. Both were massive, and even on all fours they loomed over the tallest of men. High-set ears rested on rectangular heads that sloped into strong foreheads before breaking off into straight planes. The sharp angles of their noble faces ended in a square jaw that could easily snap a large man in half. Well-arched necks, chests, forequarters and hindquarters were powerfully muscled. They were built for speed and strength. Deep-set eyes glistened with intelligence. When provoked, they would glitter like rubies, and it would be the last thing the offenders saw before their throats were ripped out.

It was a risk bringing them to a fraught situation like this with volatile passions running amok, which could prompt the two to leap into a killing frenzy. The scent of the araksha infuriated them, and Suri, the more hot-headed one, growled low in her throat. 'Let's do this, you two!' Agni murmured, and in that same tone he gave them their orders. The dogs bristled in anticipation before taking off like ejected missiles.

They tore through the crowd; later, many would wonder how they had been knocked off their feet and on to their bums. The araksha saw them coming but did not retreat. Just before Suri launched herself on to the araksha, the thing looked at Agni and smiled. It was the grin of a maniac, but Agni would dwell on that later and wonder why it smacked of satisfaction, replete with the knowledge that he had only temporarily staved off the inevitable and the fires of Yama's hells no longer held any terror for it.

Agni then called to his fingertips the red flames that were Yama's to command, and hurled them in a graceful arc into the bus, and it caught immediately. They could not harm the living, although Agni knew mortals who had sustained burn injuries, believing themselves to be on fire. However, he had to take the risk. Those armed with petrol bombs could only gawp at the spectacular conflagration as it held them mesmerized. Images of them being subjected to the very extremes of pain if they persisted down the dark path they had wandered into flashed among the flames. As they watched spellbound, decent folks fought like maniacs to get the children out, aided by the bus driver and the conductor who urged the kids out.

While the rescue was going on, Agni turned his attention to the araksha. Suri had it pinned to the ground, but she howled when her quarry opened its mouth and spat out a poisonous green mist into her face while simultaneously driving a long knife into an exposed flank. Suri drew back in pain, knocking down the bodies that thronged around them. Agni hurled Yama's noose around the araksha, and he was pulling it tight, when the second araksha moved to plunge its dagger into his side.

Agni heard Chandu's warning growl and moved just in time. The blade was coated with the same green poison and it managed to scratch his side before Chandu's jaws closed shut on the rotting arm that had held it and tore it from the socket. Agni had managed to hold on to the noose and he increased the pressure till it sliced through the ribcage, severing the creature neatly in half. Quickly, he bludgeoned the one who had surprised him on the head with Yama's danda. Agni shot out a final burst of flames to dispose of the remains of the pair and then he was fleeing back to his car.

He felt the effects of the poison and knew that it was a mortal wound. Surprised at the relief and ecstasy that beat back the regret over his own stupidity that had got him killed, he drew deep on his flagging resources to send the hounds back to whence they had come. Suri would need the services of either Danvantri, the divine physician, or Yama's step siblings, the Ashwini twins.

Chandu and Suri were not yet ready to leave. The latter was reeling from the injuries she had sustained and was berserk with rage. There were many in the crowd who already had one foot in hell, and the hounds would have liked to hasten the transition but they responded to the steel in Agni's eyes and returned to where he sent them. Agni heard the sirens and looked backwards only once before starting the ignition and driving away from the place.

It was about an hour later, when his life force was almost entirely spent, that the car careened into a tree. Agni was slouched over the wheel and did not stir, trapped as he was in the limbo world between life and death. He thought he saw Varu's face, eyes large with concern. Like in his dreams, she was in one of Yama's accursed hells. Agni wondered if he would see her soon, but before he could ask the question, her face vanished, leaving him alone with the pain.

4

Varu's Book

Why are people obsessed with stupid dates, anyway?
I can't be bothered!

Dearest Agni,

I know it has been ages since we have spent quality time together, and you believe it is mostly my fault. What can I say? Life sucks! It always has, always will, and there is nothing either of us can do about it! The truth is, I have been busy. Knowing how that twisted mind of yours works, I can practically see you turning up your nose at my marriage. Admittedly, it is far more work and trouble than I care for, but it is not to be blamed for the fact that I have lost touch with many of those who were once a big part of my life.

You know that it has long been a dream of mine to become an author. I figured it was time to kick-start my career. After all, the plan is to go the distance and create a body of work that is not only deserving of every prestigious award out there but which will also be mentioned in the same breath as the giants ruling the literary pantheon. Of course, you will not hear me complain if I make a buttload of money as well and become famous.

In the interest of easing my ambitions from the glossy world of imagination and daydreams to the harsher terrain of reality, I decided to get off my backside and actually write. Needless to say, it was rough going, especially in the beginning. You of all people know about my starting troubles and how gun-shy I can be about venturing into hitherto-unexplored territories. But thanks to the stubbornness, which Mom always insisted would be the death of me, and good old-fashioned persistence, my first book has been successfully completed.

It is absolutely awesome and I love it. Even if I do get around to having kids some day, this book will still have the right of the firstborn! The next step, of course, is to find a publisher for this baby. The hope is they will offer me the moon and stars for the chance to publish it!

Before that, though, I want you to take a look at it and tell me exactly what you think. Nobody knows what I have been doing with myself, holed up in the room with my laptop all these days. You are the first person with whom I am sharing my little secret. It has a little piece of me, and who better than my twin to provide an honest critique without breaking my heart and tearing my soul to shreds?

I know you hate emotional *atyachaar*, so it is time to wind up. But a little something about the book first . . . It is about Yama and Yami, the celestial twins. They have a few things in common with us (Duh! That's why I picked them, in case you were wondering, and not because mythology is selling like sex nowadays) and I am sure that you will learn to love them as much as I do! Plus, it is absolutely fascinating, with lots of love, sex, death, violence and magic!

This is the first hard copy, so allow me to stress on the importance of guarding it with your life. If anybody else gets their grimy hands on my baby (inclusive of the busty bimbos you insist on hooking up with!) without my express say-so, don't blame me if I kill you with my bare hands!

The original plan was to have a long chat with you during this rare weekend visit to Ma's place, when the two of us will actually be under the same roof, and tell you about it in person. But hubby dearest insisted on coming along by springing this whole 'surprise weekend getaway to a fancy beachside resort' on me! We have to leave after breakfast and I know you will be joining us only then, and that does not leave us sufficient time to talk.

I am too impatient for you to see this though, which is why I am leaving this note and my manuscript in your backpack. Call me as soon as you are done, okay? Or better yet, the two of us can take a holiday, leaving the rest behind! Take care! You are too stupid to realize it but I will always love you more than anybody or anything else in this whole wide world.

Your loving sister, best friend and favourite person,

Varu

5

The Double Funeral

Agni floated on a sea of pain. Every nerve ending and sensitive part of his body from his head to his toes was on fire. 'To the well-organized mind, death is but the next great adventure,' Albus Dumbledore had assured Harry Potter in *Sorcerer's Stone*. Agni tried to comfort himself with the words, confident that it was unlikely the great man was full of shit, wishing only that the whole thing was over and done with.

The effects of the poison stole over him in inexorable waves, vile green stuff mingling freely with his bloodstream, contaminating the entire system. Agni could visualize the toxin filling up his body, making its way to the heart, which was inadvertently hastening the process by pumping double time. Blood from an ugly gash on his forehead dripped on to the steering wheel while he tried to assess the rest of the damages he had sustained. This definitely included at least two broken fingers and a nice assortment of cuts and bruises.

He waited for his life to flash past him but, instead, dormant memories stirred, bringing up the last time he saw Varu. It was at her funeral. She had gone away and got herself killed like the insufferable jackass she was. The predominant emotion at that time had been rage. He had been angry with the greater forces that governed the universe, which had decreed that she die young. Mother and Father got an earful for marrying her off to a loser who had made her last three years on earth absolutely miserable before killing her off. He was mad at Varu for lacking the sense and gumption to refuse her deadbeat suitor.

The rat bastard—who had the temerity to believe that he held the franchise on Varu's entire heart, every second of her time and her whole attention—had been driving when the crash that claimed both their lives happened. Agni refused to even glance at his remains, galled no end that *he* lay by Varu's side, united in death. At least they had separate biers. Her remains had had to be put together tightly, bound from head to toe, and placed in a freezer with a glass case, for her last audience. She was dressed in a red silk sari with a garish gold border that clashed terribly with death.

Her face was covered in turmeric paste (she had hated the stuff, and when their mother told her about its antiseptic properties, its value in ridding the skin of acne and making the skin clearer, she hated it some more and declared that it made her look like she had been stricken by a particularly nasty strain of hepatitis) and her forehead messily smeared with sandalwood paste and kumkum (she had loathed this too).

A massive rose garland was placed over her shoulders. There were more flowers outside her coffin, and the entire setting was so vulgar that Varu, who had subtle taste and an understated sense of style, would have been appalled.

Every one of their female relatives and family friends crowded around her body, shrieking in distress, pounding on their chests, tugging at their hair, slapping their foreheads and lamenting the cruelty of fate for taking one so young. The unearthly ululating was harsh on the ears; it set one's teeth on edge and shredded the nerves, but they still kept at it, the infernal noise punctuated by the doleful long-drawn-out note of a conch shell that was being blown at regular intervals.

If Agni had been inclined to participate, he would have told them that she would have preferred her send-off to be accompanied by the soulful strains of classical music, perhaps even the raucous folk songs she so dearly loved, even though it would have been hugely inappropriate. Anything but the dread sounds of mourning.

Varu's friends from school and college had shown up in great numbers. They huddled together in a corner, sobbing softly. Nearly all of them had a favourite Varu story to share, and they talked of her thoughtfulness, generosity, cheeky sense of humour and helpful nature. Agni would have preferred this form of grieving, but at the time he was in no mood to decide what worked best during a funeral.

Mother draped her hands over the bier, as if she could hold Varu close to her that way, and refused to stop weeping. No food and very little water had passed her lips since she had heard the news. Father sat outside with the men, stone-faced and red-eyed, listening endlessly to commiserations and condolences.

'Stop thinking about my funeral, you idiot!' her voice shrieked in his head. 'You better get those wounds taken care of before it is time for yours! Don't you dare roll over and die!' Agni looked around wildly, hoping against hope that Varu had come at last. But all he could see was a shattered windshield with entire chunks missing, no doubt because they were embedded in his person, making their presence felt with sharp, jabbing pains.

Agni could not help thinking that he had been almost dead for what felt like the longest time, and he wondered why his boss was taking his own sweet time about it. Though he had worked for Yama during the course of what felt like forever, he had never seen or heard from him. The reason seemed painfully obvious now, and Agni awaited his coming with mixed feelings.

6

From Varu's Book: The Troubled Twins

Being a member of a dysfunctional family is a terrible thing. It is right up there with the evil that is *not* having a family. And it is particularly awful when you are a favoured denizen of paradise—supposedly a happy and blessed place with no room for mundane irritations like toil, strife and sorrow, which leave discontent or emptiness in their wake.

The celestials were a messed-up lot, and it was not unusual for them to be in a constant state of war with their enemies, both within and without. When not fighting the asuras, their demon half-brothers, who were always coming up with increasingly inspired ways to destroy their existence, they were embroiled in a never-ending conflict, either in their personal or political lives.

In fact, one of the oft-repeated jokes doing the rounds in heaven went something like this: 'The mortals have it easier than the immortals despite their propensity for violence and self-destruction, simply because they are stupid enough to believe in happy endings and the promise of immortality if they can make it to heaven. On the other hand, we are cursed with the knowledge that "forever" is a long time, and heaven is not all that it is cracked up to be!' Like too many jokes, it was funny mainly because it was an unpalatable nugget of truth that needed to be washed down with laughter.

Surya, the sun god, and his family were going through a particularly rough patch that was a microcosmic reflection of the foolish promise that was paradise. The hardest hit in the familial crisis were the twins—Yama and Yami, the issue of Surya and Sanjana. At least, that was what everybody thought, since it is a common belief that the children are the ones who suffer the most when a tragic family drama is playing out, despite the well-known fact that it is the very young and the very old alone who are better equipped to deal with catastrophes of epic proportions that have been known to wipe out the rest.

The twins had an older brother named Manu, who even at a young age treated happiness and sorrow, virtue and vice, and fortune and misfortune as one and the same thing, thereby sparing himself the aches and pains of emotional see-sawing that was the lot of most. He was so unflappable that he could watch his family implode without being hit by the disintegrating bits that seemed always to be flying around, anxious to do damage and infect their little corner of paradise with sorrow, which would spread like a stain over the rest of the time allotted to them. His siblings were less fortunate.

Yama and Yami made a charming picture when they played together in the palace grounds. Both were the colour of polished anthracite, with wavy jet-black hair and enormous eyes that changed colour with their moods—milky when calm, red when angered, grey in sorrow and a sparkling green that glistened when mirth caught up with them. They adorned the home of the sun god like rare black diamonds.

The pettier folk among the celestials liked to rue the fact that Yama and Yami did not have the golden complexion that made their parents the envy of so many. Yet, an unhealthy obsession with fairness notwithstanding, no passer-by could walk past without pausing to admire and coo over them, while acknowledging that they were truly special.

The currents of envy, admiration and sympathy that swirled around the twins would have been quite impactful if Yama and Yami had been inclined to pay attention but, mostly, their young ears would be ringing with the terrible altercations their parents always seemed to be in the middle of. They could only stare helplessly at each other, their toys and games forgotten, eyes wide with fright as the effluence from a rotten relationship washed over them; and they were merely bemused when well-meaning individuals pinched their cheeks and ruffled their hair without seeming to notice how battered they were inside, caught in the maelstrom of malice their parents' rocky relationship engendered.

'I hate you!' Sanjana would scream at Surya, tears of rage causing her kajal to run, making it seem as if a repellent insect was feeding on her face and swallowing it down with salty tears. 'I loathe every single thing about you. Just looking at you makes me want to pluck out my eyes and die. Your touch makes me feel more sullied than the most debauched of whores. Living with you is a nightmare from which there is no awaking. I will be content to live out the rest of my days in darkness rather than eke out an accursed existence with the likes of you for an eternity!'

'I, on the other hand, am overwhelmed with love for my foul-mouthed, nagging bitch of a wife,' Surya retaliated, stung by the venom in her words and responding in kind. 'You are a complete failure as a wife and mother. Lying with you is like bedding a vicious porcupine! Any conversation with you makes me want to rip out your tongue and use it to staunch my bleeding ears! Forget being a decent wife who is a bedrock of comfort and support, have you ever cared for our children? What kind of a mother is so caught up in being a bitch that she can't spare any time for them? You are so busy loving yourself that there is nothing left for your own family!

Surya continued, 'You wander around like a long-suffering martyr with that sickening woebegone expression on your miserable face that makes it so ugly, even though you have no cause for complaint and are wallowing in the lap of luxury and comfort, provided by dint of my labours. There is nothing in the three worlds that can make you content. I promise you, the next time that foul look dares to show up in front of my eyes, I'll tear it right off that blasted face of yours!'

Sanjana responded furiously, 'Since I am such a terrible wife and mother, you should just let me go and find someone more suitable to be the consort of the sun god, who is the epitome of all things bright and beautiful, though he is the lousiest lay—'

The sound of a ringing slap jolted the twins from the fugue of fright into which they had sunk while their parents clashed. They avoided looking at each other as they heard loud sobbing, the crash of furniture and cutlery being rudely dispatched from their rightful places, the shattering of glass and more swearing, punctuated with hysterical crying.

They knew what was coming. Mother would make a break for it, only to be dragged back by the hair and barricaded in her bedroom. She would remain imprisoned there till her will was temporarily broken and Surya deemed that she had been rendered sufficiently pliable. They doubted the chains, forged from their father's formidable will, would be enough to hold her forever. After all, even they were aware that Sanjana was always in flight, especially when forced by circumstances to remain shackled to immobility.

'What does "whore" mean?' Yami whispered to her brother, anxious to blot out the ensuing silence that clamoured with the noise of their terrible fear and uncertainty, clashing against each other like cymbals.

'Whore means "dirty woman",' her brother informed her. 'Mother always gets messy when she is upset. Her sari is in disarray, her hair looks tangled and her eyes become red. Father does not like it when she becomes like that, which is why I don't understand why he makes her upset in the first place! If only he would make her smile—'

'Don't blame Father! She gets vexed all by herself! And I just understood what "lousy lay" means . . . It is just like when I climb into your bed and you complain that you can't sleep because I kick you! Maybe Mother is just like you and won't share her bed.

Yami continued, 'Why do they have to fight like this all the time? It makes me want to cry. Let us not be like them. I don't want you fighting with me, even if I break your things, eat your share of the rice pudding or pummel you in my sleep. In return, I'll always love you. Promise me that you will never fight with me or ever say that you hate me, even when I have done something hateful!'

Yama promised her with the solemnity and truly noble intentions that only the very young can muster. Bolstered by their shared oath, the twins managed to find a way to live with their bickering parents. The younglings found it was not too hard to absorb into themselves the best of their parents and cut out the rest. It ought to have been enough, except it wasn't.

7

A Summoning

As he waited for death, wishing it would bloody hurry up, Agni's meandering mind took him back to the beginning of his own end. It had all started not long after his sister's funeral. For the longest time after Varu's death, he had drifted. Afterwards, for the life of him, he would not be able to remember much about this dark time, barring his desperate quest for answers and a driving need to understand the inexplicable.

The twins had been so close in life, so finely attuned to the other's needs and thought processes that it seemed incredible to Agni that the precious closeness he had shared with another human being had been jeopardized, and there was a very real possibility that it would be gone forever, only to be replaced with infinite space, crowded with emptiness. Surely something as paltry as death could not have the power to come between them, and so effortlessly at that?

While he drifted thus, his parents and friends could only worry, for he refused to allow anyone to get close enough to help. Formerly a tall, clean-cut, ridiculously good-looking boy with lustrous, thick black hair, Agni remained easy on the eyes but looked more like a drug addict with every passing day.

Always on the lean side, he now looked hollowed out, but his sunken, hooded eyes with their perpetually haunted air made even the most hardened pickpocket draw back in abject pity when he took to prowling the streets aimlessly. Prostitutes slinked out of dark alleyways calling out that they could get him off for the bargain rate of fifty to a hundred bucks, depending on whether he wanted them to use their digits or oral cavities. Some hissed that he could get it for free because he was so yummy, but Agni never slowed down, pausing only to think that Varu, with her morbid fascination for sexual trivia, would have been appalled and hugely intrigued by the going rate for cheap, disease-fraught sex.

During his reckless forays into the decrepit alleys, he chased after death, hoping to become a victim of senseless violence, hit by a stray bullet during a gang war, knifed in a street fight, or even run over by a truck or an inebriated celeb behind the wheel of his fancy imported car. But death eluded him with a persistence that outstripped even his relentless pursuit of it. So he refused to embrace life and the stalemate continued indefinitely.

Eventually, his wanderings led him to Kodakara. Agni felt expectancy stirring in his soul, where nothing thrived save desperation and despair. Varu had a soft spot for the charming little hill station. She had enjoyed the odd trips they had taken there over the years to get away from the summer heat that baked the plains and rendered them uninhabitable.

They had raced each other on hired cycles and gone horse riding and boating because Varu had insisted that not doing touristy things because one thought they were lame was actually lamer. They snacked on cardamom-flavoured tea and hot bhajis, allowing Mother to fuss over them, muttering that it was highly unlikely that the bhaji guy bothered changing the oil or washing his hands and that they were all risking food poisoning, or worse, because of this.

Agni loved Kodakara as well despite the fact that the place was as touristy as it got. Somehow it had retained its charm. Vast chunks of its natural terrain had been converted into plantations that grew cardamom, coffee, jackfruit and oranges, but the indigenous flora unique to the place continued to thrive in patches of ethereal beauty. A profusion of blossoms in myriad hues dazzled the eye and made you want to slow down just to look at them and breathe in the intoxicating scent, although if you were not careful, you could draw in a lungful of malodorous horse shit as well.

Nicest of all, Kodakara was beautifully maintained and well-deserving of its reputation as a princess among hill stations. Plastic had been banned, and its effects on the surrounding ecosystem had to be seen to be believed.

Agni dined in a Tibetan restaurant Varu was partial to. Over steamed momos and some seriously wicked thukpa, he let the memories wash over him till his noodle soup tasted like dead goldfish sliding down his throat. He considered calling it a night, but sleep had long ceased to be a buddy.

If his eyes ignored him and closed of their own volition, there were haunting visions of a terrible place where Varu was trapped in eternal torment. A host of dark creatures had her in their power and they took turns torturing her. She called out his name repeatedly with the inflection that had been peculiar to her, and her blood-curdling screams threatened to finish him off. He would always wake up with a serious case of the shakes.

Sleep was definitely not an option, so Agni decided that a moonlight stroll held far more appeal. Agni paid his bill and stepped out into the bracing night air. Lights from the valley twinkled merrily at him and Agni walked purposefully with the air of a man who knew exactly where he was headed.

The eateries, tea shops and bars that remained open for business late into the night sailed past him as he put some distance between himself and the areas of human habitation. Soon, even the twinkling lights that adorned the hill town vanished behind him, and he allowed himself to be swallowed up whole by the darkness that hid the goat track, which even in daylight was hard to spot unless one looked for it specifically.

It would take him deeper into the heart of the land, the parts that civilization had not yet managed to claim for its use. The jungle was still home to elephants, bison and sambar deer. Leopards and wild dogs were known to hunt the mountain goats, deer and the occasional poacher. Later, Agni would have no idea how his feet had known exactly how to take him towards the path that lay waiting for him.

It was not the brightest of nights, but Agni's vision was sharp and he could appreciate the beauty of the wattles, pines and assorted deciduous trees that hulked over him. Monkeys scrambled on the treetops, but they were strangely quiet and did not bother him with their incessant chatter. Agni sighted a mongoose that looked so well fed, it was disturbing.

A bison munched on a shrub a good way off from him and did not bother to look in his direction. Something scooted past him and Agni was sure it was a baby panther. The track he was following broke off into dozens of tertiary branches that would take him deeper into the wilderness, but his step never faltered, not even when there was no discernible pathway.

The anticipation that had taken root in his soul had sprouted wings and seemed ready to soar as he walked closer to the very core of that most exquisite of women that was Mother Nature. She was everything he wanted his woman to be—gorgeous, wild, an absolute savage, but pristine at the centre. A curious lightness had entered his heart after a long time, and it welled with heady emotion. He heard the sound of running water and almost ran, sensing that he was drawing close to something incredibly special. Every act of his, aimless or otherwise, had nudged him towards this.

Agni negotiated his way past a thicket of gnarly trees as the deep forest watched him impassively, free of movement or sound from the creatures it housed. He stepped into a ravine, past piles of rocks that stood stolidly, as though mesmerized by the beauty of the waterfalls that gushed forth from the heights of a sheer precipice in a silvery rush. It tumbled into the rocks below, eddying away into clear pools that shone like crystals under the moonlight. The spray from the force of its descent covered him with silken kisses, and its touch brought tears to his eyes.

For a long time, he stood there as one transfixed. Slowly, he walked along the ragged bank that caressed the curves of the stream, picking his way sure-footedly past the jagged rocks and the moss slick with moisture. Easing himself on to a stone shelf, he got down to his knees and looked into the water. A face distorted by mild ripples looked back at him, teasing him with its grotesque mien. Agni looked up in a hurry, and there she was.

Gasping in shock and awe, Agni could only stare as the apparition solidified before him. She was dark as the fabled blue lotus that was used to refer to the likes of Krishna and Draupadi in the old comics he and Varu had devoured as children.

Dressed in a silvery sari, she shimmered in front of him, the moonlight bouncing off jet-black hair that ended at the back of her knees. An ephemeral presence, she was nevertheless robust, with abundant curves and a chest that could only be described as buxom. Thick lashes framed the largest pair of eyes he had ever seen, gazing out at him from an exquisite face that was adorned with nothing but a large red bindi. For the briefest of moments, he looked into the opaque depths of her eyes and flinched as though he had just been goosed with a live wire.

With eyes looking down, Agni knew that though he had shut the gateway to his soul, he lay exposed to her scrutiny. And in the steadfast way she looked at him, he finally came face-to-face with himself. Every one of the emotions he had fought so hard to contain in the wake of Varu's death came surging to the surface—the debilitating sorrow that had leached away his sense of purpose, the apocalyptic rage that had sent him careening into self-destructiveness and, finally, the all-encompassing lethargy interspersed with bouts of nervous energy that had made an aimless drifter out of him.

The silver goddess—for surely she must be one—made no move, but he felt her compassion as surely as if she had drawn him into an embrace and worked her healing magic on him. The excesses of his misery were siphoned off along with the self-pity that had undone him. In her proximity, Agni was able to draw from the well of her considerable strength and replenish his own reserves. Restored to himself and feeling like a new man, he who had been faithless for the better part of his life touched her feet in the age-old gesture of deep reverence and affection.

The lady in silver smiled at him then, and Agni would have moved the three worlds to be at the receiving end of it for the rest of his natural life. When she began to address him, the smile slipped off her face with quicksilver suddenness, leaving solemnity in its wake. 'We need you, Agni Prakash! The suffering, fear and uncertainty that have roiled within may have left you feeling bereft, but it is also the fire in which your character has been tempered. Mercifully, it leaves you adequately equipped for the tasks that you must undertake on our behalf.

'The three worlds have always been at war and, in all likelihood, always will be. Some call it the fight between good and evil, but it is hardly that simple because the two are mostly interchangeable. Virtue and vice are both imposters, and the insufferable selfishness of the former is matched only by the arrogant wickedness of the latter. Mostly, though, gods and men alike are always in a state of conflict, either with themselves or with those around them because it is in their very composition. We are all made of contrasting elements that aren't meant to coexist and yet cannot exist without each other. It is the fundamental paradox that defines all of us.

'A rare few can, on occasion, find it in themselves to achieve that crucial balance, and they give cause to believe that it is a state not impossible to achieve and is probably the only thing worth fighting or dying for. Suffice to say that the battle without beginning or end is fought between those who seek to maintain the natural balance that everything has the potential to achieve and those who seek to upset it, mirroring the ascendancy of all that is deplorable within themselves.'

Agni hung on to her every word, listening harder than he ever had in his life, nodding involuntarily, perfectly in agreement with everything she said. The goddess took in his rapt expression and nodded her approval before picking up the threads of their one-sided conversation. 'It is a war that everybody has to fight at some level. But only a few are chosen to enlist in this struggle so that they may avail of the opportunity to make a tangible difference. It falls to the great majority to get embroiled in the petty struggles of life, never knowing the losses they have sustained or comprehend the very nature of their existence. Only the special ones are called upon to make the ultimate sacrifice and devote everything they have so that they may contribute something of real value.

'You have been chosen, and great power will be yours to wield. What you do with it rests entirely in your hand and, unless I am much mistaken, you will be a worthy champion. But perhaps seeing will help you understand better!'

The goddess held out her hand and Agni took it, wondering at the lack of hesitation on his part despite knowing that in doing so he was no longer flirting with death so much as consummating his union with it. He already loved and trusted her more than he had anybody else, and would have willingly gone with her no matter how perilous the journey and how great the sacrifices that would be demanded of him. The idyllic setting that had so soothed him vanished, and a void opened up, beckoning to him with tongues of fire.

8

Gateway to Hell

It was the kind of scene that even the most skilled of wordsmiths would be hard-pressed to describe with a semblance of coherence. Suffice it to say, it was beyond anything the human mind could conceive, despite its age-old fascination with every form of excessive evil. The deceased, who had been found wanting in the highest court of all, were stripped clean of clothes and artifice, their bodies and minds revealed to be in the final stages of decomposition before being taken to Yama's hells, where they would serve out their sentence.

Only then would they be returned to the cycle of birth, in the hope that all that was rotten in them had been scoured and, once cleansed, their souls could be safely released. But that was a long way off, and their struggles against the handlers sickened the senses.

The handlers were the soldiers of Yama—*Yamaduttas*. Personally hand-picked by the king of the damned, they were the chosen ones. There were mighty warriors and great monarchs among them, the veterans of many bloody battles. But there were also far too many ruffians and brawlers who had liked nothing better than a good fight. During their tenure on earth, they had stained their hands with so much blood and participated in so many endless orgies of killing that any chance for redemption had long passed them by.

They were damaged from having suckled too long at the swollen teats of the terrible goddess of destruction.

However, the bloodthirsty brutes had been judged with a touch of clemency on account of mitigating circumstances, indicating that they were villains—simply not of the worst kind. Accordingly, their sentencing had been moderated, and after doing time in varying hells as penance for a shorter duration, they were allowed to pay off their debts to the three worlds in service to Yama.

Yama's soldiers were apparitions of smoke and steel. None would think them insubstantial as they were powerfully built, armed to the teeth and bristling with menace. They descended upon the souls of those who had been barred from paradise for having succumbed to the worst in them. The evildoers would be quickly disabused of the fanciful notion that death brought in its wake release, rest and peace.

The ghastly enforcers were accompanied by the abhorrent things that derived their sustenance from death and decay—ghostly hyenas that cackled with macabre glee and giant crows that cawed raucously. The vultures that rounded out the group were mostly silent, busily and boldly engorging themselves on the dead, who stumbled or faltered in the dark passage they were being forced along, although the flapping of the wings and sounds of their feeding could be heard by those upon whom they feasted.

The dreadful racket raised by the wails of terror, screams of anguish and strident shouts of the unrepentant rent the air, mingling with the dissonant notes of the grunting and heckling tormentors as they herded the sinners towards the slaughterhouse.

The condemned would find themselves journeying past deserts that were booby trapped with sinking sands, steep mountains where the sharp rocks cut their feet to ribbons, and jungles with trees that attacked out of nowhere, branches wrapping themselves around the limbs or throats of the unwary, marshes that dragged them into their suffocating depths and predators that hunted them, while wasps and scorpions harried them endlessly.

Rain lashed at them, tearing into them with the ferocity of thrown spears or exploding shards of glass. The sun beat down on them, sucking out their hope and flagging vitality, leaving them bereft. Stones rained down on them and winds ripped into them, tossing them about like rag dolls. Hunger and thirst became persistent companions whose incessant demands could not be met. Their bodies punished them from within, leaving them grappling with phantom pains emanating from organs that were no longer able to fulfil their purposes.

Using their clubs and whips with gay abandon, the Yamaduttas prodded the wicked along, giving them a taste of what lay ahead. They dealt heavy blows to the skull and exposed limbs, whipped what was left of their pitifully exposed backs till it was a bloody mush, providing tender morsels for the birds and beasts of carrion to feast upon, and kicked them when they fell to the ground, ignoring their screams for mercy and the blood that had no business flowing out of a corpse but which did so anyway in copious streams.

Blood flowed merrily, a living organism that gathered momentum as it lapped up their despair and pain, making it all the way to the fabled River Vaiterani. The river originated from mysterious caverns high above Yama's kingdom. Trickles of blood oozing from the bodies of slain devas and asuras, the detritus and poisonous fluids of incessant warfare in heaven and on earth merged into streams of sickness that sought each other out, forming its body. Born of malevolence, Vaiterani stirred out of somnolence, its currents leaping to meet each other as it began the descent downhill to the bowels of Yama's abode, urged on by mighty slabs of rock, drawing towards them all the blood and everything putrid that had formerly drenched the three worlds.

Vaiterani burgeoned into a swelling mass of blood and pus. Hundreds of sister rivers filled to bursting with corpses, bones, severed limbs, viscera and the bodily fluids of the deceased, originating from the wickedest of places, where sanity had given ground to bloodlust, rushed headlong in their frenzied desire to throw themselves into the embrace of Vaiterani. Free of restraint, they negotiated their way past the gullies into the valleys and plains of death, meandering endlessly through the abode of the god of death, drumming up a dolorous beat that smacked of retribution for the damned.

The macabre sights in all their unvarnished glory were fatal to mortals. Agni could not have taken it all in without losing his mind if it had not been for the goddess who stood as a buffer between him and the chaos without, absorbing the worst of it and leaving him with just enough to make him begin to understand and make his way towards eventual comprehension. She allowed him just a glimpse of what lay ahead for those whom, according to Agni, had already been punished enough for the heinous sins of a billion lifetimes. But there was more. So much more that it seemed hardly possible that such monstrosities could come to pass.

Every conceivable form of torture or implement designed to inflict agony was present in the many hells that constituted Yama's domain. Agni was struck dumb by the magnitude of what he had been made witness to. He saw the hounded beings that had once been human consigned to an existence in which they were subjected to the extreme rigours of the torture of the flesh and mind alike. He saw the pitiful creatures writhe in unceasing pain, puke up blood in copious gouts and empty their bowels and bladders while their oppressors came up with increasingly ingenious ways to prolong their suffering.

Agni looked into their eyes, which were lolling about madly, crazed with the surfeit of ill usage, beseeching for forgiveness, or simply glassy from having endured too much. He knew that he would carry that image to his own grave. He sensed they were nearing their destination and were drawing awfully close to the farthest reach of this accursed place. The lady squeezed his hand gently for moral support, but even so, he was not prepared for what he saw next.

The worst offenders hung suspended from chains secured to the roof of their individual stone cells, which had been rendered impenetrable. It effectively isolated them from the others confined to the dank dungeon. Hot coals roasted their feet and provided the only illumination in the area that was opaquely black. Having traversed the terrors of every one of the hells that had led them there, they were nevertheless far from broken and certainly not repentant. None cried for mercy or raised their arms in supplication. The fires of hell had failed spectacularly to douse their wickedness, serving only to fan it so that it blazed hungrily, eager to devour.

They were monsters from before they had been subjected to a monstrous system. They had thrived in a thousand hells and a thousand more would prove inadequate to bring them to heel. Feeding on the horrors that had been perpetuated against them, they grew stronger and refused to break, knowing that no chain was strong enough to contain the evil in their souls forever. Agni caught a glimpse of the unspeakable things that lurked in their eyes and heard the poison in the curses they uttered, the string of threats and their cries for revenge. Even in eyes that were shuttered and tongues that remained silent, Agni saw the iron resolve that would never shatter.

Realization dawned and Agni knew why he was being shown these things and what was being asked of him. He drew back in rank terror, knowing that no amount of force, divine or otherwise, would be able to hold these creatures in check and that it was only a matter of time before they would break free to seek vengeance. Agni would have braved every one of the hells he had seen rather than do what the goddess was asking of him.

But the visions persisted, the settings shifting with jarring intensity, battering away at his senses, forcing him to open his eyes to the reality that he had made a habit of running away from ever since Varu's passing. Agni saw the ruins and scorched remains of a world he barely recognized as his own. Almost nothing remained of a civilization that had gone from strength to strength and reached the zenith of prosperity.

The excesses of humans had finally caught up with them, and a catastrophe of apocalyptic proportions had shattered everything they had built. Only the blackened shells of houses and commercial buildings remained, and the roads were ruined beyond repair. There was no electricity, everything was plunged into darkness.

Law and order had broken down completely. He saw creatures barely recognizable as humans led by the creatures he had seen in Yama's stronghold, hunting down the sorry remains of humanity: people who had nowhere to run but ran anyway. A pervasive madness seemed to have taken them all captive, and Agni instinctively knew that there was no hope for any of them. The part of him that had sufficiently withstood the assault on his reason recognized what it was he was seeing. It was the future and he knew it was closer than any of them could have imagined.

• • •

Agni shut his eyes tight, childlike in his hope that when he opened them again it would turn out that the whole thing was nothing more than a fevered dream and he was actually asleep in his bed at home and that none of this had ever happened. When he opened them again, the silver goddess stood before him in the sylvan spot where he had first decided his life was hers to do with as she pleased. When she looked at him, Agni felt her confidence in him and the surety of her belief that he would be her chosen warrior in a mighty cause. He felt his courage return, emerging from his own deep-rooted knowledge that he would never let her down.

Drawing in a quick breath, he addressed her, 'Are they out there in the world even as I say these words out loud? What do they want with us? They are responsible for all of that, aren't they?'

The lady nodded in affirmation. 'Yes, you saw it for yourself. No prison can hold them indefinitely. They are not welcome in heaven and on earth, which is why they seek to seize both for themselves. Their malice is directed at the gods who decreed that they be trapped in hell but that will not stop them from making Mother Earth their battleground. It is their desire to choke the life out of her by subverting the mortals and making them embrace the evil that resides within them so that all things good and pure, which are anathema to the arakshas, the accursed ones, can be effectively snuffed out. However, in all fairness, they are not entirely responsible, and some among the humans have always been willing accessories.

'It is an age-old battle that will never be resolved. In another age, the devas, asuras and the heroes among the mortals fought the arakshas together. They were truly the devouring demons, and they had once been human. All of creation stood on the brink of destruction when their numbers threatened to overrun the three worlds. Driven by madness, they were impervious to pain. The misery and suffering of others was milk and honey to them. It took the combined might of all the devas, asuras and men to defeat them in battle and return them to the deepest bowels of Yama's fiefdom from whence they had escaped. It should have ended there, except it never did.

She continued, 'The devas and asuras resumed fighting each other as did the humans who fought among themselves over land, gold and women, which resulted in nothing more than a steady waning of their powers. It is a brave new world and the old gods have little sway over it, having faded away. Sensing this, the arakshas grow stronger and the most dangerous of them have managed to get away from Yama's stranglehold over them, free to roam your world and get up to their old tricks. Soon, more and more of their brethren will join them and your species will be wiped out. The destruction of the three worlds will then be complete.'

Agni shook his head in disbelief. He could not help thinking that if he had read such a thing in the pages of a novel, he would have thought it ludicrous. Choosing his words carefully, he said, 'Can't the devas and asuras put their differences behind them and fight these things again?' His words dried up when Agni realized exactly how lame they sounded.

'It cannot work that way this time around. The arakshas were men and women once, and to them must fall the task of setting things right insofar as it is possible. Time slips away faster than we can afford to lose it. You have only to look around to see the extent of the damage they have already done. They are invisible to the humans, who outnumber them but fall far behind them in terms of cunning and capacity for evil. Mother Earth's bounteous gifts to her children are being poisoned. The water bodies are choked with refuse, trees are being felled faster than they can grow, toxins are being released into the air humans breathe and few, if any, bother replenishing the resources that are being used so carelessly.

'Values have become redundant, and people can no longer be bothered with virtue or little courtesies. They grow increasingly selfish and intolerant, looking for reasons to destroy one another while the great majority cannot be bothered with the lapses of their fellows, secure in the illusory comforts of a world that has shrunk to the extent of their shallow needs.'

Agni found his voice, 'It shall not come to pass. The end of the world has been predicted before and it has never happened. We will not allow ourselves to stoop to that level of depravity.'

She watched him quietly for a few moments, gauging him, a silvery presence floating on the surface of the water. 'Will you be one of the people who will stand against the inevitable? Will you fight the temptation to embrace the worst in you? Born of my will, you have been chosen. And now you must choose. Will you enter my service and embrace the cause, or will you be content to walk away, leaving the fight to somebody else?'

If he had been the hero she was making him out to be, Agni would have risen to the task, as if he had been born for it, but he was no hero and, as it turned out, he was little more than a kid who was grappling with a personal tragedy. She was asking of him things that he could not give. 'I cannot do this thing. It has never been my style to go around picking fights I can't hope to win. On most days, I am not even one of the good guys, and even my mother won't describe me as a warrior. It is nice of you to think so highly of me, but the truth is that I am not worthy and am hopelessly unqualified for whatever it is you have in mind.' There was more he wanted to say but his confusion was keeping pace with his mounting panic and suddenly the urge to scream became uncontrollable.

The goddess waited patiently, lending him her quiet strength till he could find his own. 'Do it anyway. There will always be more questions than answers, scepticism over faith and fear rather than courage. The three worlds need you, and it is time for you to step up. There is nobody else we can turn to. No matter how many times you back away from the path that is yours to take, you will be returned to it. For that is how it must be. Now rise and do what you must!'

Agni had not realized it, but he had sunk to his knees. He did as she asked and rose to his full height. She held out both her hands and he placed his own in them, casting aside his doubts and fears for the moment and finding a measure of the courage and resolve demanded of him, thereby making a commitment that was holy and entirely binding. It would be a union that would last till death did them part. Perhaps not even then.

9

A Time to Live

Agni was still in a dreamlike state but, mercifully, he was no longer in pain. Nor was he at the accident site. Since he wasn't being rushed away in an ambulance, sirens blaring for all they were worth, he assumed that it was all over. 'Death is not half bad,' he mused, as his body allowed the sparkling currents of what felt like a lonely and sublimely beautiful section of a river to take him wherever they wished. The river hugged a landscape of inexpressible beauty clothed in the verdant greenery of charming meadows before winding down in its even course towards dense forests that looked majestic and uncompromising.

For the briefest second he wondered what had become of the car and accident scene he had left behind, though it certainly wasn't of his own accord. The strain of thinking was unwelcome though, and Agni stemmed it, content to return to the embrace of the silver river that had rescued him from the despair that had become his constant companion, even before he had been fatally stabbed by a monstrous escapee from hell.

Having unreservedly given himself over to the silken caresses of the river, Agni felt the presence of the silver goddess, and he thrilled to her presence and exciting proximity. On particularly dark days, his need to see her had been an all-consuming one but she had never responded. Not long before his fatal encounter with the araksha, he had come dangerously close to hating her. But all that was forgotten now that the prospect of seeing her loomed ahead of him. If only it hadn't taken a poisoned dagger to bring about the desired meeting.

The job she had saddled him with had been a demanding mistress who had insisted that every infinitesimal speck of his life essence be devoted to her. Even his body had been enslaved to her will, honed as a weapon to be used in service. The visions he dreaded so much, with their piecemeal glimpses of the past, present and future in a farrago, left him wrestling with his own mix of doubt, fear, hope and resentment, more often than not at a heightened risk of biting his own tongue off.

Nobody had cared to inform him about how his work mattered in the larger scheme of things, and he may just as well have been a glorified goombah with blinkers, chasing after creatures that would not have looked out of place in B-grade horror movies. Varu was gone, followed closely by his parents, sick with grief over the loss of their daughter (to an accident) and son (to they-knew-not-what). He had no friends, and it had been far too long since he had held a woman in his arms.

Trapped in a void, he had fought off nightmarish apparitions in what felt like a constant stream that looped over itself repeatedly, trapping him under the alarming regularity of its occurrence. Worse was the knowledge that he was on borrowed time, that eventually his best efforts would come to nought and he would be torn apart by the maelstrom he had fended off in vain.

It was the futility of it all that had terrified him—all were the playthings of fate, governed by a predetermined blueprint of the soul that propelled the individual to the allocated destination. Everything done along the way, be it good or evil, and everything experienced, be it pleasure or pain, made not a lousy whit of difference in a world that was on the fast track to hell.

To his surprise, as the end of the road for him drew nearer, there was no anger or resentment, only the meandering river that cleansed him of all the toxins he had picked up over the course of a long journey as he stood poised on the brink of the great abyss—the threatening, incomprehensible chasm that stretched between the land of the living and that of the dead.

With a prophet's vision, he knew that his time had not come and that he was not going to die. Not yet, anyway. It was with tears of frustration in his eyes that he found himself deposited whole and healthy, with nary a scratch on his person, which had only recently been subjected to extremely rough use in a green meadow. There was a surfeit of blooms in riotous colour that throbbed with life as if to mock him who had welcomed death's clammy touch and been so thoroughly rebuffed. And on the water's edge, the silver goddess stood looking at him, her wondrous eyes as opaque as he remembered and far more beautiful.

'We need you . . .' she whispered. The gossamer tone was nevertheless tinged with steel, and Agni knew it was not a plea.

He bowed low as exhaustion stole over him, throwing his formidable will aside as though it were nothing, bending his spine nearly double. 'As you wish!' he replied, surprised to note that his voice was steady.

'Your service has been exemplary and we are grateful. But your journey has only just begun. The age draws to a close and these are dark times. Virtue has given ground to vice, and avarice rules in hearts that no longer have room for love or kindness. With their new-found devotion to the immediate gratification of selfish needs, men and women have given up moderation to pursue lustfully after dangerous desire and potent passion. Mother Earth suffers from all of this and she is no longer able to protect her charges from the destruction that draws close.

'The time has come for you to test your mettle against these unbeatable odds. There is none more suitable than you to undertake a mission of paramount importance. Yama's formidable strength is failing as the curse on him is slowly claiming his powers, and

Rodhana, the barrier erected to protect the portals of hell, begins to weaken and crumble at the edges. His enemies, both within and without, grow in numbers, their powers on the rise as they stand poised to move in for the kill. With him gone, there will be precious little to stop them from establishing a new world order, but for that to happen, everything else will have to be torn down.'

'I don't understand . . .' Agni interrupted, shocked to hear that Yama, the infallible scourge of the three worlds, was in trouble. 'What is wrong with him? What curse is this? Aren't you all immortal?'

Something flickered in the depths of her eyes for a split second, but when she replied, her gaze was as inscrutable as ever, 'Nothing lasts forever, not even the gods. As for Yama, in a bygone age he made a mistake that proved costly. By sparing the life of a young ascetic Satyavan, he set a dangerous precedent. He was moved by the pleas and sheer tenacity of his wife, Savitri, and was finally overwhelmed by her clever manipulation. People began to believe that the dead could be brought back to life if only Yama could be talked into letting the departed return.

'Shortly thereafter, a father begged him to spare his only daughter who was yet a child, but Yama could not do so, bound by the ironclad dharma of his vocation. Infuriated, the bereaved father cursed him, saying that it was clear that since only beguiling nymphs in widow's clothing were the sole recipients of his mercy, Yama was unworthy of the powers that he commanded and that some day his enemies would succeed in stripping away his immortality and he would only be able to watch impotently as his life essence slipped from his grasp, leaving him as helpless as the victims he has claimed over the aeons.'

'The powers that be cannot afford to let such a thing come to pass, can they? Surely there are certain contingency measures in place if the unthinkable were to happen?' Agni heard the desperation in his voice, brought on by his unwillingness to shoulder the enormous burden she seemed determined to place on his shoulders. He tried in vain to block a vision of the world ruled by arakshas—those accursed creatures who had been filled to bursting with hurt and pain, sustained solely by their thirst for retribution.

'Yama will be saved . . .' she replied. 'The love that the faithful have for him will prove stronger than anything his enemies come up with. And it is love that will save him.'

Agni groaned aloud, sudden fury replacing his frustration. 'Too much store has always been set by love, that most vapid and useless of emotions. Love is sufficient to make the sanest of men and women go bonkers, and I don't have to point out to you that the vilest of crimes are carried out in the name of love.

He continued, 'The truth is that love is never enough to throw back the forces of hate, grief, anger and rage. It never has been and it never will be. Tell me you have something better than this. Give me reason to believe that I am not just another fool tilting at windmills!' He never would have dreamed of raising his voice in the presence of the goddess, but now it reverberated in his skull with the might of repressed rage.

'You don't understand now, and I am not here to argue the merits of love. There are truths beyond the reach of wisdom, logic and rationale. Experience alone has the power to guide you to them. In the meantime, find the faith that remains concealed within and cleave to it.' She spoke gently with infinite tenderness, and Agni felt the rage retreating as quickly as it had appeared.

The goddess went on with barely a pause, 'It has been prophesized that when Yama succeeds in winning the heart of a mortal woman, she will voluntarily give up the pleasures of heaven and earth alike for his sake and it is she who will find a way to revive him and restore order to the three worlds. At the time of the prophecy, nobody thought that such a thing could ever be.

'But it has already happened. There is such a girl chosen by destiny, who will become the consort of the lord of Patala. But she is in grave danger. The Hatakas—the possessed ones spawned by the necromancer—have already got to her once and they will do everything possible to prevent her from being united with Yama. Only you can help her.'

'The Hatakas have already got to her . . .' Agni felt despair take root in the pit of his stomach, radiating upwards till it threatened to choke him with its acrid taste. He had tangled with the necromancer and his fiends only once before, and the encounter had resulted in his most bitter defeat to date.

Many innocent lives had been lost in that battle, and Agni had never forgiven himself for it. In fact, even now, in the presence of his goddess, with so much time and so many victories behind him, he could scarcely bear the memories that he had buried deep in his subconscious.

'Yes, they got to her and killed her.' Agni wondered why such a thing should lend a note of satisfaction to her overall bearing. The goddess smiled ever so slightly—later Agni would be sure he had imagined it—before continuing, 'They have been tricked into thinking that they have disrupted the natural flow of her allotted timeline and thereby altered her destiny. It is their belief that she no longer poses a threat, which will buy you some time and help you reach her first.

'The girl's mortal coil has been destroyed but her spirit is intact and has been taken into safekeeping by Goddess Ganga. It will be your task to secure her release from the goddess, who has taken a shine to her and will be unwilling to surrender her to a fate that will see her spend eternity in the netherworld, which even among the celestials many foolishly consider to be inauspicious.

'You will track the river to its very source and persuade Ganga to give up her charge. From that point, she will become your responsibility and you will guard her with your life while she fulfils her mission and proves herself worthy of joining the ranks of the immortals.

'It will be an arduous journey, and you will be dogged every step of the way by enemies who will come for you with their weapons bared or hidden behind false smiles and promises. But you must find a way to succeed or else all will be lost.

'Remember that you cannot lose the will to live when you still have so much to offer. And you cannot give in to defeat. You are all we have . . .'

The goddess had said all she wished to and began to fade. A thousand questions demanding answers rose like a tidal wave and crashed over him, leaving him floundering and gasping for breath. 'Wait!' he cried out. 'Don't go! Please! I cannot do this on my own.'

'I have faith in you, Agni Prakash. And you are not alone. You never were,' she murmured and smiled that sad little smile of hers again. And then she was gone, past recapture. .

10

The Necromancer

Lost somewhere deep within the Siwadri Range, far from the prying eyes of civilization and topographers, nestled within a jagged row of peaks, was a forested valley that was unlikely to find its way into tourist guides any time soon. Massive trees, grown gnarled and hoary with age, stood with their trunks bared in an eternal grimace as though from the effort of having clawed their way past the earth that had been reluctant to give them entry.

Almost crowding them out were the scrub brush and weeds growing with wild abandon and threatening to choke the very life of the ecosystem they had encroached on. Snake-like vines crawled over everything, twisting and writhing like a gorgon's mane. The foliage was dull of visage, yet glowed with a hidden animosity. The cloying scent of decay permeated everything. It was the lair of predators.

At the very heart of this inhospitable terrain stood an ashram built entirely of stone and timber, framed by sal trees. Inside, everything was in disarray. Piles of skulls and bones lay all over the place, and there were stains of blood, shit, urine and other bodily fluids everywhere. Animal skins had been hung haphazardly on the wall, and a few rolls were propped up in a corner to be used when needed.

This was the home of Naganara, the necromancer, foremost practitioner of that most forbidden of the occult arts. The great man did not seem to be in residence at the moment but a quick glimpse into the past would have revealed that he had lifted the ring on a trapdoor located at the furthest corner of the ashram and, at that very moment, was making his way down a winding flight of stairs, into a cavernous passage that burrowed deep into the earth with serpentine twists and turns.

Naganara was a tall and powerfully built man. Clad in ill-fitting garments, his body was hard and dark as polished oak. Would-be assassins had found to their dismay that the sharpest blade would break against his adamantine skin and venomous snakes would fall dead at his feet, the poison in his veins that much more potent than their own. Narrow eyes, green as a cat's, outlined distinctly against the sharp planes of his face, peered effortlessly into the blackness of the dark that unspooled ahead of him, for he considered it an intimate friend and ally. Long, wavy hair the colour of midnight, interspersed with a few strands of silver, bounced against his broad shoulders as he pushed on purposefully towards his destination.

The necromancer knew that something had gone wrong, and he paused mid-stride. *Agni Prakash*. The name rang out in the chambers of his mind and Naganara mulled over it as he resumed walking. Yama's lieutenant fascinated him. Like him, Agni was a wielder of powerful magic; but unlike him, he was so myopic that he would have trouble finding his own butthole with both hands behind his back.

'That is the trouble when something as precious as magic is freely bestowed on the undeserving,' he thought, not for the first time. 'He is but a mere slip of a boy, playing with a toy he has not even begun to comprehend. It is amazing that he has come this far without blowing himself up! And yet, if my assumption is correct, then this will be the second time he has managed to escape me . . .'

On and on he walked, negotiating the subterranean labyrinth with practised ease, past the criss-crossing corridors and winding pathways that led up, down or in dizzying circles to guarantee disorientation. But Naganara never hesitated and stopped only after ascending a flight of stairs that led to a final trapdoor that ultimately opened into a massive cave.

The roof arched high above, splitting into scores of stalactites, poised like thrown daggers. Shelves had been cut all along the circumference of the semicircular cave. It was surprisingly dry in there and bitterly cold. So cold, it could burn like a tongue of flame. At the very centre was an intricately drawn yantra with strange markings and ancient inscriptions. On it was laid the naked corpse of a beautiful woman, perfect and unmarked in every way. Naganara did not deign to look at her or the other smaller forms that had been placed in neat rows on the circular shelves.

Taking in a lungful of air, the necromancer sighed with satisfaction. It had all begun at this very spot, which had become the seat of his power. Naganara had been given the key to unlocking the mysteries of the dark powers that governed the universe, and he had not flinched. Instead, he had absorbed it all into the very core of his being, and it was still not enough. Magic was powerfully addictive and he was hooked. He would rest only when he had mastered all the magic there was, which would make him the undisputed sovereign of sorcery. All those who had obstructed his way had been torn apart, and Agni Prakash would meet exactly the same end.

Slowly, he walked towards a slightly raised shelf that stood at the very centre of the rock wall. Climbing up, he pushed a ring that was hardly discernible to the naked eye, and the stone ledge gave way, leading into a narrow passage. At its end, there was a cavern. Green water bubbled up at its epicentre from a mysterious groundwater source, deep within the rock, and spilled forth into a broad basin. Steam rose up in a sulphurous mist and the water was scalding hot to the touch.

Without hesitation, Naganara stripped down and, depositing his cotton kurta and loose pants on the edge of the spring, he waded out till he was waist-deep in the water, inhaling the vapours of the fabled Niryana Pushkara—the lake of the twisted spirits. Loosening the drawstrings of a small pouch he had been carrying, the necromancer took a pinch of a red powder and tossed it into the waters surrounding him, muttering incantations under his breath, his voice growing in power and intensity, building to a crescendo that would have caused the hearts of the living to burst had any been witness to his performance of the age-old ritual.

The response was instantaneous—the waters turned black and a rumbling from deep within sent tremors across the rock floor. Then the wailing began in earnest as the spirits howled in protest, disturbed from the restless slumber they had been condemned to, rising to the surface in a rush of sludge and grey ooze. Decaying faces bared their fangs at him, while slime-covered limbs tried to slither over his robust frame, begging for release from the limbo they were trapped in. But the moment they touched Naganara, they exploded and evaporated into the nothingness from whence they had come.

And still the onslaught continued, more and more of them rising in a dreadful pall of thick smoke. He ignored them all as they gathered around him in ever-increasing numbers, hissing, shrieking and clawing at themselves and each other, straining to escape the bonds that held them fast, desperate for a taste of life and fresh blood.

Suddenly, they all went silent and with howls of despair fled into the depths of the spring, leaving behind only the reek of decay. Naganara smiled in cold satisfaction. It meant that Himsa was close. She was the consort of Adharma (vice) and violence was the domain over which she presided. Her blood ran in his very veins and the privilege of communing with her was his birthright.

A sudden jet of water burst forth from the pool as the waters swirled around him, boiling and hissing, spraying him and scattering the remnants of the damned. When Niryana became placid again, Himsa raised herself from below and stood suspended over him, her skeletal frame bent and shrouded in robes that hung transparently on the dreadful spectre.

Naganara looked into the dead eyes of his ancestor and paid obeisance with joined palms. Raising his head, he watched while she solidified before his eyes, drawing sustenance from the offering he had prepared for her. Her eyes were dead and the lips never moved but her voice rang in his ear, low and hard, 'The time draws nigh . . . Yama's power wanes and soon he will be too weak to stand against his foes. Even so, there is a while to go before the deed is properly done. Do you have the girl?'

'No! The bumbling fools I dispatched to bring her to me could not have made a more thorough hash of the business had they tried! They were given instructions to bring her body to me after the deed was done. But there were some unforeseen events, and they fled, content to merely confirm that she was dead. Of course, they were made to pay many times over for their presumption.

'However, it is of no consequence because, for the moment, she is lost to herself and Yama both. I have sent the best of my Hatakas to be on the lookout for her. He will track her down eventually, and she will be mine to do with as I please.

'In the meantime, I have arranged for Yama's pet poodle to be taken care of as well. I summoned the arakshas and they were fed on the toxic blood of my best *veshas* before they took the hunt to him. If all goes to plan, the poison will finish him off, and his body will be brought here so that I can compose a fitting epitaph for him.'

'There is no body till there actually is a body to speak of . . .' she hissed at him, causing the water to explode in little geysers that scalded him. 'You are far too arrogant for one who is a long way off from accomplishing what he swore to do in memory of his ancestors, who have long suffered under the yoke of Yama. Agni Prakash is not dead as you sensed even before you showed up here!

She, whom I abhor above all else, got to him before your arakshas could complete the job.

'He cannot be allowed to find the girl and lead her to Yama. You must make certain of it. There is no need for me to spell out the consequences if failure is to be your lot. When the Yamaduttas get their vengeful hands—'

'There is no need for all that, is there?' he interrupted mildly, although his eyes burnt with sudden white-hot intensity. 'Yama's pet poodle will lead the way to the girl, and they will both be captured. When their cold remains are placed at my feet, I will personally ensure that they spend eternity as our willing slaves. You will have your vengeance, and my forebears will feast not on the flesh and blood of corpses but on the pure *tejas* of an immortal. As for me, I will have consolidated unlimited power for my use. The three worlds will be mine for the taking! It will be as I say!'

'I will believe it only when the deed is done. Save your crowing for then!' Himsa retorted.

'What about her whom you abhor above all else?' Naganara inquired tartly.

'Don't worry about her. Once Yama is finished and all hope for his resurrection is lost, she will be destroyed as well, condemned to spend all of eternity bereft of her powers and with only the memories of her abysmal defeat to sustain her!' Cackling with malicious glee, already envisioning the success of the mission Naganara had so carefully crafted, she left him, returning to the prison she had been forced into, without a backward glance.

Naganara climbed out of Niryana's torrid embrace and donned his apparel with surprisingly good humour for one who had just been informed that the setbacks he had foreseen had indeed been sustained. In fact, the news about Agni Prakash made him smile a little. He had almost regretted his decision to have him killed with so little ceremony and now he looked forward to meeting him again.

He returned to the cave and sat down at the head of the yantra. Himsa had done a thorough job. The corpse had been drained of every last drop of blood and bodily fluids. Only the rotted flesh and desiccated carcass remained. It was warm to the touch despite the freezing temperature in the cave. Naganara began to feed.

11

Doomed Love

She knew from the beginning that what had happened to her was a terrible thing and nothing good would come of it. There would be no pleading ignorance in the future if her worst fears turned out not to be unfounded. Yet, she welcomed it despite reservations, simply because it felt so unbelievably good to love and be loved in return. It was without a doubt the most beautiful thing that had ever happened to her, and she knew that death would be infinitely preferable to giving up her lover.

On what had started as just another day in her miserable existence, she had gone to gather flowers for the meditation hall before the prayer service began. Usually, they helped themselves to the blooms from the flower beds in any one of the lovingly tended gardens, but she had wandered deep into the woods. He had come to her then, appearing to materialize from nowhere like a rare and precious gift from the gods.

He was a beautiful man. Slight of frame and so lean that one would have been hard-pressed to find even an ounce of fat, he nevertheless exuded an aura of strength and raw power. She looked at those magnetic orange-gold eyes that were the most arresting feature in an otherwise plain nut-brown face and the careless manner in which he tossed back a thick fringe of hair that almost covered his forehead, and knew that she was in love.

It was love at first sight and there was no time or inclination on her part to deliberate over the wisdom of her choice. Needless to say, he was forbidden to her. There were many reasons for this, one of them being the vow she had taken; but the foremost was that he did not belong to the world of the living. Given that fact, it was madness to think they had a future, but she was stubborn and was all she could think of, whatever manner of creature he might be.

Her life had been entirely wretched and had stretched ahead of her like a monotonous wasteland with absolutely nothing in it for her save a slow death from an existence devoid of pleasure or meaning. She had been ready to welcome death if only to escape from her hopelessness. But then he had stepped into her life and changed everything. His simple presence made everything magical and worthwhile. He made her feel deliriously gleeful and deliciously alive.

Surely, it all meant something, since it was only fate's hand that could have brought the two of them together? Reasoning thus, she did everything possible to find a way to be with him even for a few stolen moments. There were eyes on her at all times and even an inordinately lengthy period spent in the privy would result in questions being asked. She had never thrived in the cloistered environment that had been her lot, and it had made her chafe at the chains that held her fast. But now that he was in her life, she felt suffocated when it was time to return to the confines of her existence. She could barely breathe if he was not by her side.

What she was doing was risky and dangerous in the extreme. If caught, torture and death would only be the beginning. The threat of discovery that loomed over them added a certain depth to their relationship, giving it a profoundness that sharpened and accentuated the overpowering intensity that characterized their forbidden passion.

Flinging caution to the wind, she escaped night after night to be with him. The darkness, the deep woods and the benevolent moon were the allies that conspired to bring them together. They would spend the nights huddled close together, talking about everything and sharing intimate details about each other.

He told her that he was a Hataka. In a former life, his mother had been murdered in a robbery attempt gone horribly wrong. He had vowed to avenge her and had tracked down her killer within a matter of days. It had been a boy not yet out of his teens, a hardened drug addict. He had been high at the time and laughed even as he confessed to the crime.

She wept when the sordid tale unravelled. He had smashed an empty liquor bottle on the killer's head and stuck the jagged edge into his throat and abdomen for good measure. Except he had made a mistake and killed the wrong guy. When the police came for him, he made a run for it and was shot down.

The gates of heaven were barred to him, but one of the greatest souls of the present age had taken pity on him and offered to save him from the fires of hell in exchange for his eternal service. He had been on a mission for his master when their paths had crossed. But on seeing her, his orders were forgotten and he had just wanted to be close to her. Her heart soared when she heard those words. Taking him in her arms, she drew his head to her breasts to soothe away the pain.

As he unbarred the secrets of his dark past, she felt achingly close to him and knew beyond a shadow of a doubt that he loved her every bit as much as she loved him. It was a hugely reassuring thought, and she clung to it, ignoring all that good sense had to say. Every second with him was a blessing and she had no wish to waste it by doubting his intentions or her ability to make rational choices.

She spent her days planning for the nights when she could be with him. Every second they were apart felt like an aeon and the torment could scarcely be borne. As time dragged on slower than a paralysed snail, her greatest fear would raise its head. What if he was not there in their secret glen? What if he had been persuaded to return to his master and his duty? She knew that it would be impossible to go on without him.

But every night he was there, waiting for her, ardent and impatient as she was. The love-struck girl considered seducing him to bind him more closely to her. But she was a virgin and did not know how, and he never made a move himself. It made her impatient with him but she loved him all the more for it. After all, wasn't it further proof, if any were needed, that he was not after the one thing that men supposedly always wanted?

Exactly thirty-four days after their first meeting, the unthinkable happened. He told her that he must go back to his master. When she heard the words, pain rippled through her entire being and there was none in all of creation as miserably wretched as she. She forgot her pride entirely and begged him not to leave her.

He hugged her and she pressed into him, trying to disappear into his flesh. Then he asked her to go with him. It was not possible for him to be a part of her world, but if she were willing, they could be together in the realms he occupied. He begged her to consider it. She never hesitated. Life meant nothing without him and it was a paltry price to pay if it meant she could be with him. He did not have to ask her twice. She would follow him wherever he chose to take her.

They left that very night. She felt not the slightest twinge of regret or remorse leaving the only home she had ever known. Even more surprisingly, there was no fear as she wandered off into the great unknown. Her lover was by her side. What more could she ask for? His mere presence imbued her with strength and she felt invincible.

She never looked back. A stray thought gave her pause. Her best friend would be worried sick about her. She did not have even an inkling about her spirit lover. There had been no time to explain. But she would not have understood. Now there was no time to bid farewell. The twinge vanished as quickly as it arose. There was no room for anything from her past in her future.

Their world was big enough only for the two of them. Recklessly, she plunged on, her heart brimming over with so much love and hope, it effectively drowned the warning signs that flared weakly, their implications ignored in the inexorable tide of fate.

12

Falling Star

When Agni woke up, he was shivering and soaked with perspiration. He was lying on an old *paai*—a sleeping mat made of korai grass. The last time he had seen one of those was in his early childhood, at his grandparents' ancestral home. It was surprisingly comfortable and cool. Through stuck-together eyelids that protested his insistence that they open and remain that way, Agni noticed that he was in a small hut that lacked almost all the amenities of civilization, though it was neat and clean. The place was illuminated by a lone hurricane lamp, the glass cracked in places and almost completely blackened by soot.

If his neck had not been so stiff, he would have liked to turn around and take a closer look at the foul-smelling concoction that was cooking away in the crude vessel that stood atop a carefully but crudely assembled wooden stove in a remote corner. Getting to his feet was a painful process but Agni somehow made his way to the entrance of the hut, which had a cloth curtain instead of a door. He noted that the hut was a short distance away from a small shrine that had almost completely been reclaimed by the forest.

Four-legged creatures that looked like foxes appeared quite at home among the dense bushes. However, Agni could not be absolutely certain in the dark; it was equally likely that they were jackals or weasels. He could hear the odd owl and crow from their perches atop the huge trees where they had gone to roost.

The shrine had been renovated in stone at some point but was now almost completely in ruins. Creepers grew over everything, and devotees had long stopped visiting the place, religious fervour having effectively been snuffed out by the fear of snakes and the inconvenience of making their way past such unfriendly turf. Agni wondered how it was that he had been brought here, and if there was some nefarious forces at play.

Thinking made his head throb, and on wobbly knees he crawled back to his paai. Memory stirred and he saw the goddess again just before she had faded away, having entrusted him with a mission—the success of which was wildly improbable at best—and forcing him to shoulder a burden that just might do him in. Worst of all, going by the infinite aches and pains that coursed throughout the length and breadth of his body, he could tell they had not even been fully cured the way he was led to believe in the dream or vision or whatever the hell it was he had seen. Perhaps none of it had been real and his mind was collapsing on account of his impending death, he thought hopefully.

'I wonder who brought me to this place in the middle of nowhere . . .' Agni muttered sourly as the odour of whatever was cooking assailed his nostrils again. The sound of his voice, hoarse and disembodied, was unsettling. So he decided to voice his thoughts in the privacy of his aching head, where the acoustics were marginally better. 'Even if I have been rescued by a cannibal who plans to have me for dinner, I would nevertheless hate to leave this place and chase after Yama's lady-love because I have to first find the haystack before searching for the needle in it! For all I know, there isn't even a bloody haystack!'

Agni tried to call out to his benefactor, but his throat refused to oblige, issuing instead a series of grunts that made him sound like a sow in heat. His arms flailed reflexively and suddenly they were pinned down in an iron grip, rendering him immobile, not a state he fancied in the least. Looking up at the face of his captor, Agni saw an ancient creature of indeterminate sex peering at him through eyes set in a face so lined and wrinkled it seemed on the verge of disintegration. 'Welcome!' the thing intoned. 'You are back in the land of the living at last!'

Pushing Agni back on the makeshift bed, the crone threw back the covers and dug a bony finger into the space between his ribs. The pain centres in his brain responded with agony, and he had to bite his lip to stop himself from crying out. His torturer trilled with satisfaction, 'The flesh is on the mend. That is a good sign. Now, be a good lad and don't try to move as yet. Weak as a day-old puppy, you are . . .'

Shoving him again for good measure, his captor, who seemed to be a female, bustled about the hut, talking all the while, 'Such a foolish boy! If it had not been for divine intervention, he would have left this world for good. This is what you get when you chase after death with such foolish abandon! That is the problem with the young and the restless! The endless resources of youth are wasted on them and they fritter it all away . . .'

'Who are you?' Agni asked, trying to get his bearings. 'How did I get here? Where are my things? Where is my car? What is this place?'

'You will have your answers as soon as you drink this up without fussing! And don't ask me what's in there.'

She thrust a coconut gourd at him and Agni stared miserably at the foul-smelling, sickly greenish potion he was expected to swallow. 'Toad stools and dog's vomit!' Varu's voice chirped in his ear. It was a game they had played as children when their mother placed 'healthy' grub on their plates and insisted that they would not be allowed to leave the table till they had consumed the whole thing. They would then proceed to gross each other out by trying to name the disgusting ingredients they were confident went into its preparation.

Suddenly, Agni was overcome by a wave of sorrow, and he brought the gourd to his lips, not looking up till he had swallowed every last mouthful. It tasted worse than it smelled, but as he had hoped, it had the effect of distracting him from the terrible grief that he had long accepted as his shadow companion.

'Who am *I*? That is a nice thing to ask one who has watched over you since birth and knows every little thing there is to know about Agni Prakash! Don't stare at me like that! Of course, I speak the truth . . . From the very moment your mother pushed your puny backside out and returned to her labour so that Varuna might see the light of day as well, I have stood guard over you. Poor Varuna! May the gods keep her safe and well wherever they have taken her.'

She drew in a raspy breath before continuing, 'It was I who watched over you when you thought it would be a good idea to jump off the roof with your baby blanket in lieu of Superman's cape and needed to have a twisted ankle taken care of. I could go on but the truth is that since the day you were born, Taravarsha has kept an eye on you, even if they were not always hers. Before you ask, the name means "falling star".'

'Then how is it that I know nothing of you?' Agni asked, perplexed, trying to make sense of her words.

'Don't worry, child. You are not to blame for not remembering . . .' was all she said by way of explanation, before lapsing into stubborn silence. That pissed him off. Royally.

'What about Varu? Why were you not there for her?' he snapped at the wizened old woman, who had paused in the middle of her bustling to look at him with eyes that were so full of kindness it made him want to stick a pillow over his head and bawl like a baby.

As for Taravarsha, if she was hurt that this was his idea of gratitude, she did not show it. 'It has been my fate to have more years in this world than those I care for and many were the charges entrusted in my care. I have done my best for all of them and continue to do so. Even so, many are lost to me. All that remain will also pass on, leaving me behind. It is how it is. No amount of crying will bring the ones who have crossed over back to the world of the living. It is only the foolish who refuse to recognize this simple truth.'

The ancient being ran her fingers over his hair, in a gesture that belied the harshness of her words, and she continued in a gentler tone, 'You and Varuna are both destiny's children. When your need is greatest, she will not fail you. Trust in her and find a way to move on, child. The road ahead is a challenging one for you, fraught with menace. Yet, the courage in your own heart and the goodwill of those who will freely lend a helping hand should see you past this. You are not as alone as you think. In fact, it was your personal choice that saw you isolated from those who would have offered their friendship and more.'

'What do you know of the mission I am to undertake? All this is so frustrating . . . Please don't take this the wrong way, but it is impossible to shake the feeling that there is something here that is being deliberately hidden from me. That I am but a pawn in a game, the rules of which remain incomprehensible to me. Tell me everything you know. Help me understand the things that are asked of me.'

'There are many secret truths in this world that fate guards jealously, entrusting them to that strictest of guardians—time. When the time is right, all will be revealed to you. If certain things have not been laid out for your scrutiny, it is probably because it is better that way, and to do otherwise would be to disrupt the natural balance that, of all things, is truly sacrosanct. That is all I can say to you. There is no need to look so angry! Have a care . . . You will reverse the healing process if you work yourself up into a lather over trivialities.

'So much rage simmering below the surface . . . I hope you realize that all that unhealthy fury has its roots in the depths of grief, which in turn is the result of an untimely loss. If you are not careful, that toxic emotion will consume all that is fine and noble within you, including all the love that great heart of yours has to spare. You will be left with little else but pain and anger. Go too far along this slippery slope and you will be lost, both to yourself and to those who love you best.'

Agni turned away from her without a word, wondering why people always felt that a long-winded lecture took the edge off suffering. Taravarsha seemed to have read his thoughts and, with a slow sigh, she placed a shabby backpack on his lap, noting with satisfaction that his eyes lit up at once. Urgently, he felt around till he found what he was looking for and a tiny little smile appeared on his face. The years dropped away when he did that, and he looked like an earnest schoolboy. It broke Taravarsha's heart.

'Don't worry too much about the things that are unknown to you. When they do come into your possession, you will think longingly of the days before knowledge stole away the bliss that is ignorance.

'As for your mission, all I know is that you won't make it without a little help, and I will personally ensure that you have it. That is all you need to know for now.'

'Um . . . thanks!' Agni sputtered, quite unable to find the words that would frame an adequate response. 'You still have not answered all my questions. Do you know what happened to my car? And how exactly did I get here?'

'You were brought here to me by a friend who is keen to meet you once your recovery is complete. As you can see, I am no longer a spring chicken. That, coupled with the fact that I have sustained one injury too many no longer makes it possible for me to move around. This friend serves as my eyes and ears and limbs. I am expecting her to visit soon. It should not be long now. As for the car, I don't think you are strong enough to handle the bad news yet.

So I am going to insist you get some rest. There will be plenty of time for talk later.'

Agni wanted to tell her that the one thing he did not have was plenty of time, and he ought to have begun his search for the girl who loved Yama a few months back, but he did not. Instead, he waited till he was alone before digging into his backpack and pulling out a worn manuscript. There, by the fading light of the hurricane lamp, he read till sleep claimed him.

13

From Varu's Book: In the Shadow

Surya was a doting father and the twins were the apple of his eye. The moment baby Yama was placed in his arms, Surya knew that he was destined for greatness. Dark as he was, the little bundle exuded a radiance that rivalled his own and a raw power that exceeded that of even Indra's, their king and the mighty wielder of the thunderbolt. Surya was proud of his son, and great were his expectations from Yama. Yami did not share the exalted status of her brother in Surya's heart, but she was nevertheless beloved.

As for Sanjana, Yama loved her dearly. Their mother was beautiful, enigmatic and gentle even at her most distant or restless. Yama loved her even more than he did his father and as much as he loved his twin. When he sensed her presence drawing close or felt her gentle fingers absent-mindedly stroking his hair, his heart would sing a rhapsody of untrammelled glee.

Only he understood that she was a sensitive soul who was not made to handle abrasion in speech or deed. All she wanted was someone who would love her and leave her in peace. He wished he could tell her this, but she had locked herself away in the haven her mind provided and there was no getting around that particular barrier.

Yami, who tended to take a sterner view of her mother's affectations, was perfectly content to ignore her mother as reciprocation for the way she seldom bothered with her. It was even worse when Sanjana's eyes lost the sheen of secret dreams that were her only solace and fastened on the twins as though she were seeing them for the first time. That piercing gaze would burn bright with a savage need and yearning so powerful that it would make Yami detest her mother and Yama desperate to find a way to give her whatever it was she sought so frantically.

Every one of his attempts was in vain. Things between Surya and Sanjana continued to deteriorate faster than they could be fixed and the corrosive acid that was the only possible result of the toxic equation the couple shared burnt away the fabric of their combined existence. The children could do nothing but watch in helpless frustration.

Just when things became truly unbearable, something happened and for the longest time neither Surya nor the children could begin to comprehend it. On the surface at least things seemed better but not one of them was deceived, for underneath the calm they knew for certain that someone they loved had torn away the net of their feelings and escaped their demands, leaving them behind with broken hearts, the victims of unrequited love, burnt so badly that the wound would never stop hurting.

Surya shook off the inexplicably persistent feeling of loss and betrayal by shielding himself from the unpalatable truth that his worst fears had been realized. Something nameless and indefinable had disturbed the unbalanced equation he had shared with his wife and it was evinced by the fact that she no longer struggled against his powerful feelings for her or his authority, nor did she make any attempt to run away from him. In fact, she seemed pitifully eager to please and serve him in every manner he desired. It was what he had always wanted and yet he had never been more unhappy. But as far as the three worlds were concerned, the sun blazed as merrily as it always had and everybody looked at it and was reassured by its unchanging brilliance.

The twins knew in their own ways that their lives had been turned upside down, even though an intense scrutiny spanning the landscape of their existence revealed nothing and gazed back at them with unchanging sameness. Yama's heart no longer sang when the consort of the sun god was in his vicinity. Instead, loathing filled his soul and he shrank back in revulsion when the alien scent of her filled his nostrils. He never said it out loud but the creature that looked like the goddess who had birthed him and behaved like her in every conceivable manner was no longer his mother but merely his father's wife.

Yami did not have anything like the peculiar bond shared by her twin and mother. Even when her mother was sitting with them and watching them play, she seemed to be completely unaware of the presence of her children and may just as well have been an inhabitant of another world. At all times, she was far away, tucked away in a world of her own making where nobody was allowed entrance. Only her busy thoughts and whimsical dreams that surpassed anything her reality had to offer were her constant companions. Yami was used to having a mother who was not there. She had been perfectly content to cleave to her father and Yama. But that was earlier.

In recent times, not only was her mother aware of her at all times but she also seemed to have grown increasingly antagonistic. Yami felt pinned by a pair of ice-cold eyes that were constantly watching her every move with palpable malice. Under that unbearable gaze, her confidence eroded and she quailed in the face of the implacable hostility that was directed at her. The fluid grace with which she had traipsed gaily all over the sprawling grounds of the sun god's castle was replaced by an awkward gait and a self-consciousness that was painful to watch.

Nothing she did was good enough for the lady of the castle, who seemed to be only a shadow of her former self but nevertheless found ways to make Yami's life intolerable. 'What are the odds that a daughter of the sun god would turn out to be black as sin? It is because there is evil in your heart, and destiny has decreed that you will darken the illustrious name of your father, court disgrace and come to a bad end. If you think you can get away with being a spoilt little brat forever, you are mistaken, my little strumpet. I'll burn the decay in your soul with Agni's fires if that is what it takes to straighten you out!' she snarled softly at her charge, making sure that neither Surya nor Yama were in the vicinity, glorying in the hurt that she had inflicted and saw reflected in those bewitching eyes.

With an assassin's razor-sharp accuracy, she zeroed in on Yami's biggest insecurities and went after them with every weapon her spite lent her. When she was not bewailing the fact that Yami was dark of countenance, her posture, her body, which was still not free of puppy fat, or her lack of morals and sound character came under censure. There was nothing Yami could do to escape the power of that gaze or the venom in the hateful words, and she wilted under the constant fusillade directed at her. Yet, she was Surya's daughter and Yama's twin, and though her spirit had retreated deep into her embattled person, it was still there and it defied the constant effort to destroy it forever.

Yama could not bear to see his twin so desperately unhappy, and he immediately went to great lengths to make her feel better. Surya abetted his son's efforts in his own way, making it a point to spend a little time with her even though his own house felt increasingly like a battlefield.

'The entire world worships me for the gift of radiance and light that I have bestowed on them but you are the precious spark that brightens my world. Without you, my darling daughter, and Yama my existence would have no meaning!' he whispered to his daughter, somehow knowing that to say it out loud would mean placing her in harm's way.

Between the two of them, father and son always succeeded in bringing the smile back on Yami's face. It made the mother who was not their mother livid, and she bided her time, knowing full well that the duo would not be around forever to look out for their precious Yami. Sooner or later, she would get the chance to do irreparable damage and was content to wait. In the meantime, three more children were born to round out the perpetually unhappy household—Sani, Manu Suvarni and a girl, Tapati.

Motherhood did nothing to soften Surya's consort, and the love she bore for the infants born to her only served to sharpen the hatred she nursed against the children that preceded them, particularly the twins. It seemed inexplicable to the few who saw past the surface to the core of her antagonism. Mothers can be indifferent, criminally negligent or have a marked proclivity for eating their young, but it is rare for one to want the children of her husband dead.

They all had entertained varying degrees of suspicion, but none would know for certain until it was far too late that Sanjana had indeed succeeded in leaving them. Under the cover of darkness, when the sun rested, she had walked out without meaning to ever look back at the travesty her family life had been.

The truth was that she hated her husband a lot more than she loved her children and she wanted no further truck with the lot of them. Her father had forced her into this hellish marriage, so she would not return to her childhood home. Instead, she channelized the power of her great need to be free from bondage and turned into a horse so that she may roam the three worlds, wild as the wind, without a care in the world.

Her transformation was almost complete when she felt a pang and a strange tugging at her heart that threatened to hold her back. Terrified of the implication and the unwelcome image of the dear boyish face with eyes that worshipped her, Sanjana tried to flee from it. But the final thread holding her to the past would not snap. Glancing around her with the desperation of a cornered animal, she caught sight of the shadow that was all that remained of her old self.

'Nothing in the three worlds can persuade me to remain here with my husband. But I cannot let my children grow up without a mother. You are my only hope. Stay here in my stead and be a mother to them. It is your destiny to be the consort of the sun god. I am sure of it and all is as it should be. Perhaps the two of you will make each other happy and things will be different.'

'I cannot refuse you . . .' her shadow answered, 'but your place is here with your husband and children. The peace you seek will continue to prove elusive if you destroy your family to go after it. Instead of journeying into the very heart of your unhappiness, you would do better to be content with what you have. Things may just work out eventually.'

'If something is rotten, it deserves to be torn down. You couldn't possibly understand . . . My husband—the lord of the thousand rays—has been given the responsibility of giving the three worlds the gift of light. But when he returns to me at dusk, he brings darkness in his wake. Nothing can escape his penetrating gaze, and he absorbs all the evil he sees, which causes his lustre to diminish. He returns to me so that he can rid himself of the sin he has absorbed and regain his former brilliance. Every single day, he steals away a little more of my essence, leaving me drained. Soon, he will have robbed me of everything. I cannot make the ultimate sacrifice and give up everything that makes me what I am to be divided between my husband and children.

She continued, 'Your magnanimity in not refusing me will ensure that you are rewarded. And I can leave in peace knowing that my family has not been destroyed. You are Chaya, the shadow and cool shade that will serve as a refuge for those of us who cannot withstand the heat and scorching intensity of the sun god! May the gods bless you!'

With those hastily uttered words, Sanjana fled, leaving Chaya to make what she could of her leavings. It was not a bad life for one whom nature had never intended to infuse with substance. In the early days of the great deception, Chaya could not have been more thrilled. She could hardly believe that fate's grand design had decreed that her husband be one of the most powerful and illustrious of the devas.

One look at the handsome profile of her spouse, a whiff of his masculine scent and the feel of the power he exuded made her go weak in the knees. She loved him fit to bursting and was a willing slave to every one of his needs. It was just too bad for her that the husband she had secured for herself did not love her in the least, for his heart belonged to the one who had left him in the lurch. The knowledge filled her with bitter resentment and she hated Sanjana for running away with Surya's heart.

Chaya did everything possible to help him recover from the loss he wasn't even aware he had sustained, but her efforts were for nought. Slowly but surely frustration and bitterness replaced the love in her heart, leaving it hollowed out and ice-cold from having been excluded from the warmth of the sun. Even the arrival of her own children would not bring her peace or fulfilment.

Surya's partiality to the twins did not help matters much and she envied them for their father's love. It would have been clear to a blind dog that was incapable of steering clear of its own excrement that he loved them a lot more than Chaya's children, though the latter were littler, fairer and adorable.

Chaya's rival was beyond her reach and she could not harm her; but the twins weren't and the shadow harnessed her hatred and directed it at them. 'Nasty little spoilt brats whelped by a filthy filly who would rather spend eternity being mounted endlessly by stallions rather than do her sacred duty towards her family!' she thought balefully. 'Why should I be stuck with the products of another's womb? Why should I care when their own mother didn't? If she did not want them she should have drowned them in the river, like the other lousy mothers who have no time for the by-blows of their whoring! By all rights, they ought to be dead . . .'

Having willed it, her secret animosity acquired a life of its own and Chaya knew that it would be the implacable weapon that would bring the twins down and deal the mortal blow that would destroy them forever.

Surya would not be able to stop her because, as she constantly reiterated to herself, 'He may not love me as much as he does the children of that bitch but that has not stopped him from crawling into my bed, and for as long as he seeks the comfort of my flesh, I'll have him where I need him to be in good time.'

While Chaya plotted thus, the twins grew wary but not too much because they genuinely believed that no harm would come upon them, provided they stuck together. If fate had not chosen to play them for fools, their belief alone would have made it true.

14

Feeding Frenzy

Naganara ate with gluttonous abandon and the relish of a true connoisseur, smacking his lips and sighing with pleasure as he gorged on flesh, tissue, muscle, bone and organ. A low keening sound emanated from the dead dish that made up his repast, and it was music to his ears. Black wisps of smoke rose up from the fast-disappearing corpse, hovering helplessly for a moment before dissolving quickly into nothingness.

When nothing remained, not even the bones, he seated himself at the centre of the yantra, in the *vajrasana* position, to speed up digestion and make his body hard like a diamond. Eyes closed, hands forming mudras of power, he began chanting. The words were undecipherable, their meaning obscure, but the voice that intoned them was so powerful that the walls of the cave shuddered and the air went deathly still. On and on, the syllables poured forth from his lips in a never-ending stream, growing charged with a current that electrified the senses.

Naganara's tongue hurled the words with a plangent roar. Plucked out from the core of his being with a booming intensity and charged with iron intent, the words gathered a life of their own, mining into the heart of the earth, extracting energy from deep within, siphoning it off and infusing him with it. Shock waves from this intrusion into the core of the planet were felt as nature fought against it.

Tremors were felt for hundreds of miles, fish died in waterbodies that became poisoned, birds dropped dead mid-flight as the air was befouled and animals fought their way out of natural habitats as they fled in terror. Entire swathes of arable land went barren, rendered accursed, doomed to remain fallow for many years to come.

Inhabitants closest to the necromancer felt their hearts thudding madly, their eardrums throbbing with sudden pain and violent spasms that weakened their limbs. Capillaries in their eyes burst and made them weep blood. Babes sickened and died while still in the womb. And still the necromancer wouldn't cease his infernal chanting. On and on it went for days, without an end in sight.

Fire coursed through Naganara's body and his blood boiled. His eyes glistened red and sparks flew from them. But he stopped only when he knew for certain that his tremendous effort had borne fruit and the Narakamayas were nearing release. The sudden silence that swallowed up his terrible voice was deafening and chilled the blood.

Getting to his feet slowly, the necromancer walked unsteadily, as though drunk, along a short, narrow passage that the cave opened into. Rolling aside a boulder, he emerged into a clearing. An irregularly shaped bit of parched earth, it was hemmed in by trees so massive that they formed a vast canopy that barred passage to light from the sun and moon alike. It was his personal breeding ground, and something was stirring beneath its uneven surface.

The Narakamayas were just emerging in response to the dark magic that had called them forth, and Naganara watched with satisfaction as they tore themselves free from the ooze that had been their cocoon, shrieking from the effort. They were shaped like men but twice as big, with predatory muzzles pulled back in a perpetual snarl to reveal irregular but sharp fangs. They were built like killing machines; corded muscles and sinews strained against the reddish skinless flesh that could barely hold them in check.

There were seven of them, and Naganara was pleased. They had been summoned from the confines of the Varudha, where Yama had imprisoned them in a bygone age, their prison reinforced by the force of his will. Spawned by hatred and madness, and driven by a killing fury, they were indestructible. They all looked alike but the necromancer knew the telltale signs that made them unique.

Bhaya was the one who inspired fear in those who happened to be in his vicinity. His victims would feel their blood turn to ice and paralysis set in when they saw their fates reflected in the twin pools of death that were his eyes. Their hearts would explode, blood drenching the earth, leaving behind the contagion of fear.

Sokka and Dukkha were twins. Pale as corpses, they brought the unwelcome gifts of grief and sorrow. Working more subtly than the rest of their brethren, they planted the seeds of their offerings, so that they may germinate into a rich harvest of despair, misery, envy, resentment and discontent, bringing to fruition the promise of apocalyptic destruction. Their victims would take their own lives, their paltry resistance stamped out by the twins.

Vyadhi spread pestilence in her wake, claiming lives in an indiscriminate haze of pain and suffering. It was Trsna's job to fan the flames of desire, undiluted by moderation or good judgement, till it became wild and insatiable. Krodha engendered anger, allowing the heat to build, blowing the victim apart in a cataclysmic explosion, taking many more along.

Naganara summoned these six to him. 'Go forth into the world, in whichever direction your feet choose to migrate, for they will be driven by my will which has brought you into being. Spread the gifts you bear in every direction, sparing no one. Show no mercy and consume everything in your path, till there is nothing left.

He continued, 'Go with my blessings! None will be able to withstand the Narakamayas, irrespective of whether they choose to travel together or alone. You will be invincible!'

With nods of acknowledgement, the six set off to do the necromancer's bidding. Only the seventh remained. He was Sudhana—a killer who killed because that was the sole reason for his existence. And he did it without any of the compunctions that humanity imposed. You could see it in his eyes, filled to bursting with acid hate that promised death.

Even his liberator feared him just a little. But there was no sign of it when he gave the creature his instructions. Without a word, he left to do the bidding of the one who had given him not only his freedom but the giddy prospect of endless bloodletting. Agni Prakash and all who accompanied him were the chosen targets, and Sudhana looked forward to hunting them down. There would be plenty of collateral damage before the deed, and the three worlds would become his personal killing ground after. He looked forward to that as well.

Watching him go, Naganara almost felt sorry for Agni. This time there would be no mistakes. The arakshas had been no match for Yama's lieutenant, even when bolstered by the necromancer's magic, but Sudhana was a different breed of evil altogether, and he would not stop till he had crushed the life out of Agni. The other six would set in motion the events that would culminate in the end of an age. Naganara would have not only the vengeance he sought on behalf of his forebears but also unlimited access to magic to feed his addiction.

Visions of the future danced before his red eyes. It was a brand-new world, one that had been stripped bare of the technological advancements that men and women had so painstakingly accumulated at the expense of all else in creation, just to make their superficial, supremely selfish lives easier. The former masters and mistresses of the universe were little more than the lowliest animal now, fit only to be enslaved and used as their betters saw fit.

The magic wielders would stake their claim as the rightful rulers, and Naganara would be at the head of the newly restored order of necromancers. He had waited a long time for the future that he himself had been the architect of and it was finally within reach. Counselling himself to be patient, Naganara waited for the inevitable.

15

Guardian Angel

While Agni slept off the grave injuries he had sustained, Taravarsha crouched next to him in silent vigil. Even in repose, a frown marred his features, indicative of the fact that he could not shrug off the angst that coated him like a second skin The trajectory of his life was such that violence would be a constant companion, and if he were to survive it, then he must learn to fortify his person within the armour of inner peace, his benefactor mused as she gently smoothed away the lines that creased his forehead.

Taravarsha was a magical being from an age so long ago that none in the present age even knew about it unless they kept their eyes and ears open to the clues left behind in obscure mythology. She was a creature closely affiliated with the earth and all its living things. For reasons she had chosen not to dwell on, death had never come for her. It could be because the world still had need of her and the services she alone could perform, and that made her feel young at heart.

Born with the gift of healing, honed over aeons of experience, she continued to do what she did best. Taravarsha set broken bones and whipped up miraculous cures for all ailments that beset the flesh. She could fix the diseases of the mind or a wounded spirit as well. But that was not all.

In the days of yore, she and others like her had specialized in caring for the needs of Mother Earth, who gave life, sustained her charges through the years allotted to them and received the remains into her embrace when death came calling. They had worked tirelessly to make sure that her bounty was evenly distributed among all living things, and what was taken from her was replenished in one form or the other. But that was before man rose to the top of the food chain with a savagery and ruthlessness that is yet to be matched in the long annals of endless time.

Nobody had anticipated that the viral excesses of humans would threaten the very nature of existence and lead them all to doom. There was less and less that she or anybody else could do to curtail the relentless damage. Soon, there would be nothing to do but stand by and watch the world disintegrate into wretched ruins, fit only for carrion birds. But it would never do to give up hope. While there was life left to her, she would do what she could.

A shadow detached itself from the encroaching darkness and approached her side. Its features were indistinct, heavily robed and hooded, but you could tell by a certain indefinable quality that it was female. It was a land spirit who was known to the aged healer as Dharami. While a mortal, her life had been tragically cut short. She did not merit a place in one of Yama's hells and neither could she warrant a seat in heaven because she had been too full of soul-crushing hatred and unspent anger.

Dharami's bitterness over the things that had happened to her spilled over into her afterlife, making it accursed. It was anybody's guess as to what would have become of her if the goddess had not seen fit to take the unfortunate soul into her service. And so she remained, her spirit entwined with the land that had been so cruel to her, but in the hope that some day she may be free.

Taravarsha stirred and nodded to the apparition. 'I am glad you kept your promise to watch over him, Dharami. This one here is in your debt. If it had not been for you, he would have been lost even to the silver goddess.'

'Don't tell him that! He likes me little enough as it is. Why you have adopted him as a special favourite and coddle him so, I'll never understand!' She had no features and no shape; her voice was heard only in the mind of the one to whom the words were addressed.

'You don't have to understand. It will suffice if you do as you are told. And it is your fault that he has come to harbour such strong feelings against your kind, given what you chose to reveal to him. It was rather foolish of you to hope that he would understand . . .'

'I chose no such thing, and the entire thing was a horrible accident. But the bastard tried to kill me! I saw it in his eyes; he had every intention of killing me where I stood and would have done it too if he had been able to. But let us not talk about that. It only makes me angrier than I can stand.

'Be that as it may, when I saw him by the side of the road, he was not long for this world. There was blood everywhere and the poison was doing its work with indecent haste. It is too bad that I am so soft of heart. Anybody else in my position would have left him there to die like a dog!'

'It was wonderfully humane of you,' Taravarsha interrupted before her companion started off on one of her harangues. 'Try not to be so hard on him. He has known too much pain and suffering. He has battled the arakshas for so long and seen more evil in this life than most do over several lifetimes, so his world has fallen into shadow, and he has almost lost the ability to see what is still good and beautiful in this world.

'But let us not dwell on such things. Tell me what you have learned of Naganara's movements so far.'

'The news is not good, I'm afraid. Naganara performed a summoning. I did not even have to get too close. He is so reckless when it comes to using his magic that he could not care less that it leaves distinct trails that even a blind man could follow. As his power grows, so does his arrogance. We can be certain that he has been informed about his plans going awry as far as this boy here is concerned.

'The necromancer's anger must have been a terrible thing to behold. Mercifully, I was not around to witness it. He called forth Himsa, and I cannot be certain, but it appears that he somehow tricked a *kanya* into helping him. As you know, the voluntary sacrifice of life constitutes the basis of some of the most powerful magic there is. On the strength of that, he was able to perform a conjuring as well. You know what that means, don't you?'

The old woman drew in her breath sharply. 'Either Naganara has added finesse and deviousness to his ever-expanding arsenal, or he has gone and found some like-minded allies. How bad was the damage this time?'

'It is the worst yet! Vast tracts of the countryside have been desecrated almost beyond repair, and the death toll continues to mount. You would think the humans would notice their brethren dropping dead like flies, but life is no longer as precious as it used to be. None of them care because they can always make new babies!

'As for the necromancer, I cannot say for certain what manner of creature he has brought forth from the hidden realms of darkness, but it cannot bode well for this world or its inhabitants, and certainly not for the sleepyhead yonder. These are ugly times we live in. As always, humans have no idea about what is happening under their very noses, and by the time they do, it will be too late.'

'Perhaps it is too late anyway . . .' Taravarsha shook her head with uncharacteristic sorrow. 'Humans started out with so much promise but now they have allowed things to deteriorate to such a point that there is little that can be done to salvage the situation. At best, they can only delay the destruction that has all but caught up with and overwhelmed them.'

'How was it that I came to be involved in such an unholy mess, I'll never know! It is the sheer hopelessness of it all that disturbs me to no end. You promised me that the great Agni Prakash holds in his hands our hope for salvation, and I must watch over him at all times, even though he made that cowardly attack on my life. But would you just take a look at him?

'Those arakshas sent by Naganara have injured his body and spirit so severely that he may never recover. The necromancer fed them with poisoned blood that he had harvested for this express purpose. The numbskull was completely unaware of what was in store for him and he blundered into the snare like the unsuspecting fool he is. And if this is his condition now, I can't even begin to imagine how the goddess expects him to survive whatever monsters the necromancer has dug up from the pit of evil and successfully complete his mission.'

'Even you cannot deny that he is a very brave man to do what he does, Dharami. He has repeatedly been tossed into the deep end of the pool and left to fend for himself, no questions asked. It is a miracle that he remains consistently good at what he does. I trust that your disillusionment with the champion of virtue notwithstanding, you will continue to make your formidable resources available to him and me as well.'

Dharami's quicksilver demeanour changed at once, becoming softer and more appealing, making her seem youthful and vivacious. 'You know that I will never refuse you, even if you demand that I aid the necromancer in whatever evil his black heart has managed to concoct! For your sake, I will even give the fierce puppy another chance to redeem himself in my eyes. You are the mother I have never had. All you have to do is issue the command and it will become my mission to honour it.'

A beatific smile lightened Taravarsha's sombre features. 'You are a blessing, child! I do have need of you. Now more than ever, it is important that you keep an eye on Agni and the necromancer from your vantage position. You must be alert to any threat to Yama's lieutenant and do whatever you possibly can to avert it.

She continued, 'While he is with me, he is safe. Find out as much as you possibly can about the kanya who was sacrificed. In the Vedic age, some held the belief that a virgin, also known as a kanya, or *kumari*, was the living embodiment of divinity, and as such a vessel of raw power. If delivered to the wrong hands, great evil may be perpetuated.

'The *kanyadana*, or the "gift of a virgin" is also potent. This means that the poor girl was somehow fooled and she voluntarily offered up her life for the express purpose of performing a conjuring. Look into all possibilities and report back to me.

'Take care of yourself as well and stay out of harm's way. The conjuring would have released creatures that can inflict harm on even someone like you. Go in peace and may all our endeavours succeed!

16

Divination

Dharami disappeared as silently as she had arrived, and Agni wondered if she had been nothing more than a fragment of his overheated imagination. He had no idea who or what she was, but for some reason the apparition had seemed furious with him and seemed to think that he had tried to kill her. A vague memory made a sluggish attempt to squeeze itself back into his consciousness but gave up all too soon, and Agni sat up, pleased to note that he no longer felt like death warmed up.

Even Taravarsha seemed pleased with the progress he had made. His appetite had been restored and he tucked hungrily into the steaming plate of food she handed him. It was boiled rice with a generous helping of stew made with chicken and potatoes, and there was a big glass of milk to wash the meal down with. Agni was reminded of his mother's cooking. 'Whom were you speaking with while I slept? Clearly, she did not have a high opinion of me . . .'

'That was Dharami, she is your guardian angel. It was she who brought you here to me and safety. You owe her your eternal gratitude. Fortunately, it is not the last we have seen of her. Before you start bombarding me with questions, I'll just say that your paths are destined to cross time and again in the future, so there will be plenty of time for the both of you to delve deeply into individual backstories and clear the backlog of questions either of you might have.

'Why don't you concentrate on finishing your food? You must have a second helping. That battered body you have been so negligent about needs all the nourishment it can get!' Spooning some more chicken and potatoes over the rice, Taravarsha proceeded to repeat the information Dharami had delivered.

'Given Naganara's close affiliation with Himsa and his resorting to increasingly more powerful forms of magic, if I were to hazard a guess, it would be my reckoning that he has released the Narakamayas.'

Agni screwed up his face in concentration, his spoon poised in mid-air, and said, remembering, 'I know a little about the Narakamayas. They are the progeny of Himsa, the goddess of violence, and Adharma, the god of immorality, are they not? Bhaya, Sokka, Dhukka, Vyadhi, Krodha, Trsna and Sudhana. There is an ancient prophecy that it will signal the beginning of the end when the seven are allowed to roam freely in this world. Rather like the four horsemen that precede the apocalypse. I thought they were creatures from the world of fables and mythology! Can it really be possible that they walk among the living now?'

'Full marks to Varuna, storyteller extraordinaire and researcher par excellence!' the healer said solemnly. 'Unfortunately, they are real. There is a lot of bad blood between Yama and Himsa's descendants. In another age, he vanquished them when they sought to snatch the reins of power from the celestials led by Indra. Like all things evil, they cannot be destroyed but merely contained. Yama was given responsibility over the seven and he made them his slaves, using them as judiciously as possible in order to carry out the designs of fate.

'Naganara appears to have gained control over the Narakamayas and unleashed them upon the world. One or more will come after you . . . The rest will no doubt be engaged in encouraging the humans to scale greater heights of folly than they have already managed. It is a two-pronged attack that Naganara has launched against you and mankind.'

Agni ruminated on what he had heard and found that it did not go down well with his excellent supper. Shoving the plate aside, he looked into the milky depths of Taravarsha's eyes, willing them to reveal all the secrets they carried within, before he spoke, 'Environmentalists have been saying for years that the damage done to the planet is already irreversible and, like Varu was fond of saying, they have been ignored much like Cassandra, the foreteller of unfortunate truths. Everything seems to indicate that we are hurtling towards an unthinkable end, and yet that is hardly any reason to roll over and play dead, is it? But tell me more about Naganara. I had a brief encounter with him once . . .'

Agni swallowed quickly. After all this time, he still could not bear to talk or even think about it. If Taravarsha noticed, she tactfully chose not to dwell on it. 'They say that he carries the blood of Himsa in his veins and is the greatest sorcerer that ever lived. An adept at the arcane art of necromancy, he has formidable powers.

'Modern men and women are children of science, whereas Naganara and I are from an earlier age when earth magic held sway. We shared a powerful bond with the forces of Mother Nature, and there were many among us who were capable of harnessing her power. With the passing of the ages, our numbers dwindled to the point of insignificance and the magic lost some of its potency, because few possessed the skills required to wield it and the source itself had undergone unforeseen changes.

'The climate and geography of the planet changed drastically as mankind discovered science and technology. Civilization has almost reached its zenith, and humanity has little use for the elementary forces of nature. It has even less use for sorcerers and their spells.

'Magic wielders needed many years of intensive training before they could bring their powers to bear. Even then, it was hardly enough, for they had to be prepared to sacrifice a little piece of their hearts, souls, minds and bodies in order to make the magic potent. The fact that it drew so deeply from their life essence gave them cause to pause and refrain from using it indiscriminately and wastefully.

'Science, on the other hand, does not waste its time with such niceties and is more suited to the greed, impatience and sick self-love that have come to characterize men and women today. Money is all one needs to enjoy all the benefits that science has to offer, which means everything one can possibly need and so much more, for which there is no discernible purpose, is at one's fingertips, to be used and discarded carelessly.

'Naganara, needless to say, is furious with this state of affairs. He lives for the magic he has been stealing from the core of Mother Earth like a parasite that sucks its host dry. The price he has paid for its use has blackened his soul and given him delusions of grandeur. He seeks to release the arakshas and unleash their fury on mankind to create widespread destruction and pandemonium across the world. The subsequent chaos will be manipulated to meet the ends of him and his kind.

'With the clock turned back, all the progress mankind has made will be lost. With humankind almost completely decimated, the magic wielders will become the masters of the universe. The Narakamayas, arakshas and humans enslaved by them will emerge triumphant,' Taravarsha concluded.

'I hear you, and I wish that the dark words you uttered would galvanize me into action. The trouble is that the whole thing seems to be a ludicrous fantasy, and the logical part of my brain refuses to accept such things as a possibility. Doomsayers have been predicting the end of the world forever and yet we endure.

'Sometimes I think it is best to let this planet and its inhabitants blunder on in their inimitable ways, rather like bickering lovers. They are forever thinking up inventive ways to hurt each other but then they kiss and make up. All is forgotten. Why should anybody be called upon to interfere? What if we only make things worse? History is full of tragic tales about the crimes committed against humanity by those who sought to make the world a better place. Why can't we just leave things to fix themselves? Don't bother to reply. I have been informed that there will always be more questions than answers and there is nothing anybody can do about it.

'In the meantime, I remain as uncertain as ever about how I must proceed. The goddess wished me to seek out Yama's consort by tracing the Ganga all the way to its source and, if mythology is to be believed, that is somewhere in Shiva's matted locks, though there is no map that reveals the best way to get there. Even if I can make it to the source, it is doubtful that Goddess Ganga will be sitting pretty with Yama's bride-to-be neatly wrapped in a package for me to whisk away and hand over to the lord of the underworld.' Agni threw up his hands and shrugged dispiritedly.

'For someone who has devoted the best part of his life to fighting the denizens of hell, your lack of faith is truly appalling.' Taravarsha wagged her finger at him. Gathering up the remnants of his dinner, she dumped them unceremoniously in a remote corner of the hut before returning with a flat-bottomed earthen vessel.

Agni watched her work, irritation and frustration coursing through his veins in a merry race. He had been hoping that she would shine a light on the path everybody seemed intent he take, though none had bothered with giving him directions. Instead, Taravarsha had merely commented on his lack of faith, almost as if she enjoyed annoying him.

A knife flashed suddenly, and Agni gasped. Grabbing her patient's finger, which she had slashed without so much as a by-your-leave, Taravarsha gathered several drops of blood in a vessel before daubing an ointment on the cut by way of an apology. Agni was asked to hawk and spit into it, and he obliged without question, glad that he had not been asked to squat over it to evacuate his bowels or masturbate into it in the interests of divination.

Taravarsha ignored the scepticism that radiated from him in waves. In fact, she seemed to forget he was there, staring deeply into his blood and spit, occasionally adding a few more ingredients from stoppered glass jars that she seemed to pluck out of thin air. Agni squinted but he could not make them out. Suddenly, her eyes rolled back into her sockets and she sat still as a stone.

Agni watched her for a long time but nothing else happened. Looking at her face, he saw that she had journeyed away to a place that was beyond his reach. Her skin was stretched tight across her features, and he could almost feel her energy draining away in great bursts. As she weakened before his very eyes, Agni hoped that the arduous journey through the mazes of time would not prove too much for her.

Sensing that there was little he could do, and feeling like a voyeur, he stepped outside the hut for the very first time. Taravarsha had informed him that the shrine was some distance from Thenurai, a village a few miles north-west of Maduram city. It was ironical that they were a stone's throw from River Vayana, on whose banks a mighty kingdom had thrived, because in these parts there had been no water for drinking or irrigation for many decades now. Most of the drought-ridden inhabitants had gravitated to the urban areas, and this bit of parched land lay mostly forgotten.

He relieved himself against a tree and imagined the look on Varu's face if she were to see him urinating in a public place, even if it was almost entirely deserted and there clearly was no toilet for miles around. There was only one entrance to the temple and it was immediately below a crooked tower that retained the slightest trace of its former ornate grandeur.

Vigilant faces carved into the stone glared balefully at Agni, brandishing their weapons menacingly at him as he wandered around the overgrown temple porch. Surprisingly, the idol of the resident god was still in the sanctum sanctorum, though it was completely unadorned. Even hardened thieves had thought better of carrying this fearsome-looking deity away, for it was none other than Sani, the chief of the planets and a beneficiary of Shiva's powers of destruction.

Superstitious folks were terrified of Sani, believing that his baleful influence brought misfortune into their lives. But thanks to Varu, he knew better. Sani was Yama's half-brother who had been entrusted with the task of making people answer for their misdeeds in this life itself so that they may reform and redeem themselves and be spared the agonies of his elder brother's hell.

Sani had no friend or foe but treated all alike, sifting through deeds, weighing meritorious acts against sinful ones, and collecting the debt owed. Ultimately, his purpose was to straighten up the mortals and steer them towards the path of liberation, even if it meant cursing them with a string of ill luck in the form of disease or fiscal loss, or inducing his brother to bring death into their homes. Understandably, many felt they were better off without his stellar services and tended to give him a wide berth.

Not Agni, though. He was curiously drawn to the deity and crossed over into the sanctum sanctorum for a closer look. The idol had four arms, two of which held a trident and a mace, while the other two made the gesture of benediction. The eyes were half-closed (or half-open if you were an optimist), and there was something strangely lustrous in that countenance that remained unworn by the ravages of time and nature both.

'It must suck to be you,' Agni said to the idol. 'I of all people ought to know what it is like to make people pay the price for their actions, both voluntary and involuntary. It is rather like cleaning shit, isn't it? The task is onerous enough when it's your own bum but it is so much worse when you are forced to clean up after others, wouldn't you say?

'I wonder if, unlike me, you get decent remuneration for such a thankless task . . . Vacations, bonuses, perks? I highly doubt it.

If virtue was rewarded as richly as vice, your brother's hell would probably be empty!'

When no reply was forthcoming despite the sparkling wit on display, Agni curled up at the foot of the idol. As usual, his thoughts drifted to Varu. She would have insisted that there was a reason he had escaped death and recovered at the shrine of Yama's half-brother. Agni would be damned if he knew what that was all about, and it was his last thought before he fell asleep.

Taravarsha found him there. She gently shook him awake. 'Wake up, child! We don't have any more time to lose.'

Agni was alert in an instant, feeling more energized than he had in a long time. Taravarsha spoke in a whisper, 'A shadow hangs over your future but much of it was veiled from me. All I know is that events of great import have been set in motion and you seem to be in the thick of things. Know that you will not be alone in this quest. The gods in their infinite wisdom have decreed that you will have the aid of a Kritya, blessed beings who are born to magic. I was shown where this one is being held captive. You must free her first and then she will take you where you must go!'

'But of course! I suppose you cannot tell me whether my quest will be a success or a failure, or provide me with anything useful to go on? All you can tell me is that I have to find one girl in order to find the other.' His tone was sarcastic, but Taravarsha forgave him because his smile was affectionate.

'That is correct. When you were born, an astrologer foretold that you would be surrounded by the forces of Shakti—the feminine divine. Your mother misunderstood and was worried sick that you would become a libertine, devoted to the passionate pursuit of pleasure, and squander your life away on drink and ceaseless carousing with loose women. If only she could see you now.

'But you must hurry! All is lost if Naganara finds out about the Kritya. I can sense his aura close to her although she is not yet enveloped by it and he is as yet unaware of her gift. That is a stroke of luck for us and we must take advantage of the situation. It is important that you get to her first.'

Quickly, the healer gave him instructions while they walked back to the hut. Agni gathered his belongings and gratefully accepted the packet of food she had pressed into his hand. He had had another of his dreams while he had dozed at Sani's shrine. Needless to say, it had not been pleasant. It was time for him to begin his journey, though he didn't know the way.

Taravarsha blessed him, 'Go with god and return safely on the successful completion of the quest you have been chosen to undertake. Remember that your life is a precious gift, and Varuna will be furious if you throw it away.'

17

Sivagami Math

A lot of care had gone into the selection of a suitable location for Sivagami Math. At the time the need for it was conceived, the founders in their wisdom decreed that for the purposes of the *math* to be fulfilled, the elements of secrecy, remoteness and inaccessibility were imperative. In order to get to the place, the first stop was Bodiyankara, at which point River Kotta had to be crossed. Once this barrier was overcome, the roads became increasingly narrower till they disappeared altogether and left one staring at the formidable forest known as Yakshavana, which lay beyond. Most of those who made it that far dared not go further, for it was said that it was home to monsters and evil spirits.

It would take extraordinary courage to brave the terrors of the forest and make it to the far side, after which the route was tortuous and nearly impossible to traverse without prior knowledge of the way. After this, a high mountain had to be scaled almost entirely by foot in order to reach the summit. And there, on a scooped-out hollow of uneven land, surrounded by crags and comfortably ensconced within hundreds of forested acres, stood Sivagami Math, home of the Kanyas.

Stone-lined pathways led to medium-sized buildings that were built entirely of sun-baked bricks with wooden rafters; they served as classrooms, a hall for prayer and meditation, dormitories, a refectory, a recreation room and an infirmary. Furnished solely with wood and organic fabrics, it was an ecologist's dream. Modern inventions were unknown in the math, and the inhabitants lived without almost all the things the rest of the world took for granted, like electricity and the host of conveniences it had showered down upon its partakers.

It was a place of great natural beauty affording breathtaking views of the surrounding mountain range. There were nature trails aplenty that would lead intrepid hikers to pretty-as-a-picture meadows, crystal-clear streams, glorious waterfalls and valleys carpeted with flowers sufficient to delight the heart of Wordsworth.

The math was an ancient one, caught in a time warp where the more things changed, the more they remained the same. It had been established at a time when the intermittent gender wars that had long been the bane of humanity took a sudden turn for the worse. The story went that a long, long time ago, before history had begun to be recorded, there had lived a great king named Satyavana who had done the impossible by uniting the entire known world under his rule. He had been a fine example of the Stoic notion that a good king was the best form of government. Under the just rule of Satyavana, his subjects were happy and prosperous.

The king had a hundred wives, but none of them had given him a robust male heir to secure the line, though daughters he had aplenty. Proving that he was cut from the finest cloth, Satyavana named his eldest daughter, Satyavati, his successor. Even the best of men are not without vice though and, for this ruler who was, in every other respect, a paragon of virtue had a weakness, it was women.

He had taken a hundred concubines for himself and one among them, Duruvi, bore him a son. Satyavana loved them both dearly. Tension mounted when the issue of succession came up again. The question of whether a bastard born on the wrong side of the marital bed would make a better sovereign than a royal princess was keenly debated.

Satyavana's consort, Aksha, worried endlessly that her daughter's life was at risk. Duruvi was also sick with anxiety, convinced that her son would become a casualty of petty politics. The king's wives and concubines circled each other warily, claws drawn and sharpened, jostling for power.

Things came to a head when Princess Satyavati and every one of her sisters died under mysterious as well as gruesome circumstances. Poison and witchcraft were suspected, for the royal brood had gone to their deaths vomiting up copious amounts of their own infected blood, which had turned a deadly shade of black. Their hair fell out in clumps, lesions erupted all over their bodies, oozing pus, and they died one after the other, writhing in agony, beyond the help of the best physicians in the known world.

Satyavana died shortly after. Some said it was of a broken heart, while others insisted that it was Duruvi, the sorceress, who had got rid of him to make room for her son. The hundred queens of Satyavana joined hands and declared war on his concubines. Duruvi was captured, publicly flayed and decapitated.

Then the killing began in earnest, and Queen Aksha, whose grief over the loss of her husband and only daughter had driven her to madness, swore that she would not rest till the world had been scoured off its whores. Initially, only those who made their living with their bodies were targeted but soon the dragnet sought out dancers, artistes, women who remained unmarried, widows, those branded as witches, and just about anybody who might be considered inauspicious, including little girls who were butchered because they bore the mark of a whore.

The killings went on for long years. Vengeance had been given its head and it went berserk, an indestructible killing machine that could not, and would not, stop. That was when the Kanya cult was established by those who had ascended to power and had not yet traded reason for madness.

As per tradition, the story began in a tiny thatched hut that stood just outside the math where the founders spirited away the little ones they managed to save. Young girls were taken in before the age of ten and remained there for the remainder of their natural lives, after taking the vow of the Kanya.

The commandments were simple—the girls were to remain virgins throughout their lives, dedicate their minds and bodies solely to God and devote themselves to a life of prayer, sacrifice and service. It was thought that, while they stayed true to their vows, no harm would befall them. In fact, the Kanyas would be greatly revered and many would seek their blessings. The punishment for men who sought congress with the Kanyas was death. The cult believed that they would reap their reward in the afterlife, when the pure Kanyas would be taken as wives by the celestials themselves.

To them, their virtue would be the fortress within which they would be kept safe while they lived in a cruel world that had never been kind to their sex. They turned to old-fashioned virtues inculcated in them and strove to be a shining example of the meritorious effect an 'auspicious' woman was conventionally thought to have on the community at large. Thus, this particular math endured as the years rolled on, nearly forgotten by the civilized world but continuing to offer a haven for girls who were not wanted elsewhere.

No man was allowed within the confines of the math, which was largely self-sufficient. Suppliers of comestible requirements and other necessities like tools, wood, leather goods and medicines would bring their goods to the trust established for the purpose, and the caretakers would have it delivered to the math with the aid of donkeys, although a fair number of the beasts had lost their footing and plummeted to their deaths on the way to the math. Discipline was strictly enforced and any infraction of the rules incurred swift and merciless punishment.

Gurvi Ananthamma, the reigning head of Sivagami Math, ran the place in a manner that an army drill master would have approved of. It was her firm belief that things ought to be done the way they always have been, and that it was only presumptuous bumpkins who thought they knew better than their ancestors. Her charges numbered just under fifty, and Gurvi Ananthamma took her responsibility of taming their minds and bodies very seriously indeed. Spiritual education was imparted under her personal supervision in the form of lengthy lectures, admonitions and more lectures. She was the chief educator, although some of the elder Kanyas were put in charge of the younglings and delivered the occasional sermons to their older charges as well, on how best they ought to conduct themselves in keeping with the dictates of their order, which were:

> The emphasis on preserving purity: 'By not allowing ourselves to become contaminated in mind, body and soul by the baser passions, we are the lone islands of virtue in a world that has become increasingly stained with sin.'
>
> The paramount importance of virginity: 'It is the strongest armour a woman can wear which will protect her from the advances and excesses of the male animal. Marriage and childbirth are both forms of slavery, and by keeping our virginity intact we are truly liberated from the pleasure and pain alike that can be derived from the flesh.'
>
> The practical advantages of virtue: 'The world is a jungle ruled by men. When animals posed a threat, the creatures were either domesticated or hunted down ruthlessly. Today, even the mighty lions and tigers are displayed in zoos, their habitats destroyed and their spirits mangled past recognition. Women also posed a threat and they were subjugated as well, forced into degrading roles of maid, mother or whore, determined by the whims of their overlords.

> 'Our virtue has saved us from the tyranny of men and it will continue to do so in the ages to come, for the wise have decreed that a man who visits harm on a Kanya will incur the wrath of Goddess Shakti, and her rage will chase him across thousands of lifetimes, condemning him for the rest of eternity!'

Thus the inmates of Sivagami Math lived a quiet life, having been taught that a woman of class should be seen, not heard. They had virtue forced on them, the decision to give up the vicissitudes of the material world that had been made for them by caregivers who had chosen to turn them over to the math.

A Kanya was expected to dress simply and modestly. In her infancy she was garbed in a loose-fitting cotton gown. During her teen years she wore a half-sari and as an adult she donned a sari. The girls wore no jewellery, save the single red bangle worn on each wrist that was presented to them when they came of age.

They lived simple and useful lives, performing the chores allotted to them by the gurvi. The Kanyas grew their own vegetables and fruits in the fertile lands of the math. They also had a few dozen cows, chickens and goats. Their labours went a long way in meeting their own nutritional requirements. The residents of the math would also send milk, eggs and simple packed meals to the Sivagami trust, which would then see that it was distributed among the needy. Those among the Kanyas skilled with a needle would stitch articles of clothing like dresses, skirts, blouses, sweaters, shawls, mufflers and hats for the less-privileged denizens of the outside world.

They took care of each other. There was a nursery for the babies and toddlers. The aged and infirm were tended to by those allotted to the task. Kanyas with the aptitude were put to work in the infirmary. Some of their home-made remedies for a host of bodily ailments were also sold periodically by the Sivagami trust.

The math was their entire world. They all lived and died within its premises, knowing nothing of the world outside.

For better or worse, the Kanyas were taught that by renouncing the world and upholding their vows they would remain safe in this life and the next. Most of them lived their entire lives bearing this in mind, and even went to their graves secure in this belief. Others had believed this notion for so long that they refused to entertain other possibilities—not even when some of the younger Kanyas died suddenly and/or disappeared altogether, as though they never had been.

18

Shrill Cries of Death

She was only four years old. The little girl loved her mother. But clearly nobody else did. They all went out of their way to make her life miserable. She knew why it was so. Everybody made sure she knew the story, and it was a tale of woe that she knew by heart.

Her mother had run away from home and married for love. But her grandfather was having none of it. He was a powerful man in their native town, and the slur on the family name was not one he could allow to go unpunished. The lovers had been tracked down, and her grandfather had had her father bludgeoned to death before dragging her mother home.

The patriarch did not know that her mother was pregnant. If he had found out, he would have been apoplectic with rage and killed them both. But a cardiac arrest got to him first. His surviving wife and new head of the family possessed a slightly less choleric temperament insofar as meting out actual physical violence was concerned, but her acid tongue made up for it.

Her mother and the child of shame became little more than menials in the palatial mansion her grandfather's father had built. Nobody wanted them, but nobody would let them go either. The girl's mother had two brothers. Both despised her for having brought shame on the family, or so they claimed; but they essentially resented the onerous chore of feeding two extra mouths, although both mother and daughter were on starvation rations.

Their wives were so ill-used by their husbands and mother-in-law that they felt it was nothing less than their sacred duty to share the misery and make her mother suffer the way they did. She seemed inured to acute pain though, and the only way to get to her was through her daughter. So with true diligence, most members of the household took to abusing the little girl.

She was slapped for being naughty or pinched for being loud. But most terrible of all there was the verbal abuse. From her grandmother she heard: 'I never thought a child of mine would turn out to be such a bitch. Your mother must have got the taint from her father's side. My family is of noble stock and we are virtuous people. There were quite a few rotten apples in my husband's—your grandfather's—line. His mother and sisters especially were beset with the vices of their whorish natures.

'Even so, it would have been possible to undo her infamy. Having got rid of the bastard who seduced her, I planned to get her married speedily to a poor relative of mine, who had a beautifully pliable personality. But then you came along—little bundle of misery—and ruined her future. Now the world knows our shame, and it will be the end of your mother and us both!

'No self-respecting man will have you for a wife, and you will remain an accursed creature for life. Mark my words: You will come to a bad end. It was an accursed day when that no-good father of yours violated my daughter and impregnated her with you!'

From her aunts, she was used to hearing, 'Isn't she an ugly shade of brown? It is too bad. If she had been fair like her mother, there might have been a slim chance of some deluded loser taking her as a wife. But now it seems like the little parasite will feel free to sponge off us for life. Worse, she could follow in her mother's footsteps and run away with a petty thief or procurer and bring further disgrace to our door.'

Her uncles also tended to look at her as though she was a particularly abhorrent specimen of humanity but mostly they ignored her. However, that wasn't the case with her cousins. Her mother's big brother had two sons and the other one had a daughter. She hated them all.

The two boys were bullies. They put sand in her food and twisted her arm behind her back, forcing her to eat it. At other times, they pissed into the water that her mother had carefully drawn in a bucket from the well. Her female cousin egged them on and so it went. Her mother tried to protect her as best as she could.

This unhappy state of affairs would have gone on in perpetuity had the boys not begun advanced mathematics in school and been presented with brand-new geometry boxes. The dividers, protractors, set squares and rulers had them tickled pink. But it was the compass that made them feel like mighty warriors.

One day, the future barroom brawlers and wife beaters pinned the little girl down while she tried to fight them off. One held her arms down while the other sat on her legs and tried to force her eyelids open long enough to try out a little experiment on penetration with the compass. The other sister, whose mother had not shamed herself, suggested using matches.

Her mother arrived on the scene. Things that had been simmering below the surface for a really long time came to a boil and exploded out of her in a scalding rush. Picking up a broomstick, she walloped the two boys and the girl till her arms threatened to fall off. Their loud shrieks brought out the entire household.

Her grandmother spat in her mother's face and began spewing obscenities for daring to manhandle the precious heirs. Her aunts were screaming shrilly. Her mother's big brother took one look at his sobbing children and slapped her mother across the face so hard that her neck snapped back with an alarming crack and she fell in a heap on the muddied ground. Her sari was askew and her petticoat bunched up behind her knees.

That was the moment the girl snapped. Something awakened in her blood and, like a somnambulant monster, came awake, fighting its way to the surface, throwing aside everything in its path. Even as a howl of primeval rage sounded, the magic tore itself free and sliced into her tormentors like shards of glass, shredding them to pieces.

They were defenceless against it. They stared in horror at each other as blood spurt forth from their noses and ears. An aunt tried to stanch her daughter's bleeding, but she was blinded by the blood oozing out of her own eyes. She tried to call for help, but the blood gurgled in her mouth.

It was a massacre, and it was over in seconds when their hearts gave out in their chests and they fell dead. Her grandmother was down, along with her precious sons, their wives and children. But the strange howling that sent a thrill of abject terror coursing through the veins of all who heard it would not stop.

Servants who rushed to the scene—drivers, watchmen, cooks and maids—suffered the same fate, with blood spurting out in copious bouts from every one of their orifices. Only her mother remained as the glass shattered windows across the family home and the doors were torn from the hinges. Light bulbs exploded in their sockets and heavy furniture of teak and rosewood was hurled into the walls. The dust rose like a shrieking banshee, shrouding everything in its vulgar and coarse embrace, whirling into mangled eyeballs and coating lungs.

Her mother watched the carnage, and for the first time in a very long time she was so glad it hurt. One way or the other, it was all over for her. But something had to be done about her poor baby. It was with fierce pride that she gathered up her little one into her arms to quiet the distraught child and stop her from uttering those shrill cries of death. She held her for a long time, till the rage had spent itself and the child fell silent, utterly spent.

Her mother stopped only to gather her paltry savings and pack a little bag with food and bare necessities. Then they were fleeing into the gathering gloom as the gibbous moon, ever the friend of lovers, thieves and the damned, glided into the sky.

The wild flight of the woman who had been especially chosen by capricious fate to duly exercise its taste for sadistic pleasures mirrored most of her adult life. Every single year of her life and each one of the things that had happened to her coalesced into the crushing weight of that one night when she finally found her long-dormant spirit and fought like never before to give her child the chance she never had.

The cops were hot on her trail and they had released the dogs. But try as they might they could not catch her that night. Her existence had taken such a bizarre turn that it no longer felt like her own and so her feet moved of their own accord, while her arms clutched their precious burden, propelled by a force she was only too glad to submit to.

She held her daughter close, feeling her soft body pressed trustingly against her, memorizing every single detail—the feel of her hair brushing against her chin, her little feet wound tightly against her spine, that delicious baby smell—taking it all in, lingering over it and savouring it in the time she had left.

The dying woman ran for three days and three nights, stopping only to allow her little girl to rest and eat. The feat she performed was impossible even for men in their prime, let alone a frail woman like her, but she managed to do it. Nobody ever knew how. Mother and daughter found themselves at a thatched hut that stood outside the place they had been guided to. A small sign informed them that they stood outside Sivagami Math. The woman who was wearied past all endurance peeked in and saw a stone-lined pathway. The place looked nice and tidy. In that light it wasn't clear but there appeared to be a sort of vegetable patch, or maybe a herb garden. The sight of it made her glad.

The child had woken up but she was strangely silent. She had been that way throughout their incredible flight. Quietly, they entered the hut. Together, they shared a small packet of biscuits that had been hoarded away as a special treat and took sips of water from a plastic bottle. They lay down on the straw mat, arms wrapped around each other.

The mother's breath was ragged, and it came out in rasping gasps. Her limp and tired hair was matted with sweat and blood. She kept dabbing at her mouth, nose and ears with the edge of her pallu. The feet that had led her to safety would never walk again, torn and bleeding as they were. But her heart was glad. The little girl who had long been her life was special and had been singled out by the higher powers for great glory. A mother could not ask for more.

Sleep was a long time coming for both of them. 'Mother loves you so, so much! You must always remember that . . .' She would have liked to say more but the tears had snuck into her eyes and it took a lot of effort from her rapidly dwindling reserves to keep them in check. It would never do to distress the little one who had been blessed by the gods.

In the morning, Gurvi Sampoorna found the four-year-old fast asleep next to her dead mother. The old mother had learned to deal with everything she encountered with calm acceptance, but on that day her heart broke a little when she beheld that blessed miracle and the price that had been paid. She gathered the poor mite into her arms, accepting her as a Kanya.

Gurvi Sampoorna would name her Minothi. The name was from a beloved fairy tale told by an elderly Kanya when she herself had been a child. Minothi was a princess who had saved her kingdom from an invading army led by its bloodthirsty commander-in-chief. Gurvi Sampoorna gave the child the name of that remarkable princess, hoping that some day the little girl would be even more storied than her namesake.

19

By the Deathbed

Gurvi Sampoorna enjoyed the love and respect of nearly everybody at Sivagami Math. Like practically all of them, she had been left in the thatched hut outside their abode while still a babe, along with an assorted group of young girls sent there by the trustees from an unknown location. From a young age, her talent and potential was apparent. She was an expert in everything she took up, even if it was only for a day.

The young Sampoorna's IQ was formidable, and her memory was prodigious. After taking up the mantle of *gurvi*, she did everything in her power to make Sivagami Math not only the safe refuge it was meant to be but also a haven of learning, where the power of the mind was harnessed and turned inwards to unlock the happiness and tranquillity within. She taught her charges the power of positive thinking in order to help them create a reality they could live with. Gathering together the sparks within herself and her Kanyas, she lit a blazing fire that warmed the heavens and lit up the world.

It was Sampoorna who persuaded the Sivagami trust to allow them to have books other than religious and spiritual tomes so that they might educate themselves. She encouraged the Kanyas to sing and dance. It was she who suggested that the age-old healing techniques still used in the math be made available to those outside as well.

The great woman now lay on her deathbed. She was ninety-one years old. Age had caught up with her great spirit and her body was shutting down slowly and painfully, but Sampoorna was far from rattled and her will was indomitable. She had asked for Minothi to be assigned to her care, and the young Kanya, who was twenty-one at the time, gladly acceded.

The Kanyas were dedicated to service, but most were not enthusiastic about work duties in the infirmary and dreaded being assigned the ward designated for the elderly. The nursery with its screaming babies who would wail shrilly, the endless shit-laden cloth diapers that needed to be washed, the malodorous little bums that needed scrubbing and the snot-filled noses that had to be cleaned were hardly the most pleasurable of activities. Cleaning out the stables that housed the livestock, which entailed shovelling muck and hosing down the cows, was yet another dreaded chore. But both were still preferable to the elders ward.

Even so, Minothi would not have traded her duties for anything. She considered every second spent with Gurvi Sampoorna a gift from God, and would have been content to launder her soiled linen for the rest of her life if Yama saw fit to spare her.

The gurvi was asleep when Minothi entered her cubicle on cat's feet with the matriarch's supper, which consisted solely of rice gruel. Soundlessly, she emptied the bedpans. That task accomplished, she hovered by her bedside, waiting patiently for the gurvi to awake so that she could ensure that she partook of the nourishment provided for her.

Her eyes took in the wasted form of the matriarch and she stood still, assailed by a nameless fear. The flesh had melted off the bones, leaving only a brittle skeleton covered with loose folds of wrinkled skin. Eyes that had once been alive and piercing had sunken so deeply into their sockets that they seemed to have disappeared altogether, leaving a gaping hollow that signified decay. Her breathing sounded heavily laboured to even Minothi's inexperienced ears, and she knew it was a bad sign.

Tears stung her eyes and Minothi was fighting for composure when a claw fastened itself to her wrist. She jumped but the sound of the gurvi's voice calmed her. She helped the gurvi into a comfortable position to feed her. Having consumed a few mouthfuls, she started to speak.

'Listen carefully, child, for I haven't much time. It is awkward to have one leg in this world and the other in the next. But I am excited about it, I truly am! If what we have been led to believe is true and not entirely garbage, then my husband awaits me on the other side!'

The gurvi chuckled, but it was too much for her, and racking coughs set her body violently atremble. Minothi made her drink a few sips of a herb infusion laced with honey and a touch of pepper. The coughing fit subsided at once. The old lady was anxious to resume. 'But let us not talk of the adventures that await me on the other side. I have done my best by you, but there was no way of knowing that our time together would be so brief! But perhaps it is all for the best and my passing will be of some worth to you. We may yet succeed in doing the needful to get you out the cage into which you and circumstances both conspired to entrap your essence, which I know is struggling to free itself!'

Overcome with emotion, Minothi replied, 'I owe my life to you! And you have given me so much more than what I deserve. I have been practising hard like you told me to. Forgive me for having failed you! I haven't been able to control my mind, like you wished for me, and urge it towards a state of tranquillity in order to manage the thing.

'My efforts have come to nought. My mind remains the wild beast it always was. I have tried to chain it to my will but it only becomes worse.' This time, Minothi could not stop the tears and her voice cracked with the effort of holding it in check.

The bony fingers squeezed her own. 'You are too hard on yourself, child! If only you loved yourself as much as you love me, you wouldn't be in this situation. Hurting yourself for imagined transgressions has not done you any favours. It would have broken your mother's heart if she knew you felt this way.'

It was with great effort that Minothi composed herself. The gurvi began talking again, her calm voice working its magic on the young woman she had taken under her wing so long ago. 'Listen to me! As you know, it is our custom to accept into our fold little girls under the age of ten who are entrusted to us by their caregivers. The younglings are taken in following an examination to ascertain they are pure in spirit and flesh. Other than that, we do not delve into their pasts, since as far as we are concerned, their lives begin from the moment they are chosen to walk the path of the Kanyas.

'Your case was special though. My yogic vision made it apparent that you had been chosen to be the bearer of something rare and precious that would some day see you employed in a truly noble cause. It was an honour to be given the opportunity to mould your talent.

'We both made some mistakes along the way, but I have no regrets. I know that it has been difficult for you. It was this that prompted me to undertake a certain voyage on your behalf.'

Minothi drew in her breath sharply. The gurvi was considered to be one of the self-enlightened spiritual masters of this world. Her knowledge of universal secrets was second to none. They said that her mastery over the senses allowed her to travel through the catacombs of time at will. In her time on earth she had always endeavoured to alleviate the injuries wrought by ignorance and share her knowledge with as many lives as she could touch within the cloistered existence that had been chosen for them. Minothi waited with bated breath to hear what she had to say.

'Shortly before my body failed me, I undertook a journey into your past. Thanks to our sessions together, I already knew of the circumstances that had conspired to bring you to our doorstep, but I was able to go back even further in time and encountered a *pitrani*, one of the female ancestors of your lineage. Her name is Kashika.

'The pitrani informed me that she was a Kritya, a superior being who is born to magic. A long time ago, in another age, the gender wars were in full sway and the odds were hopelessly skewed in favour of the male of the species. The brain was proving to be no match for the savage brawn, and it looked like the end of the world was imminent as the female population dwindled to dangerously low levels.

'Mother Earth herself rose in defence of her daughters. She decreed that henceforth the worthiest among her daughters would be endowed with her own powers, and the forces of nature would be theirs to wield in her service. The chosen ones were called the Krityas. By wielding their newly bestowed powers, they were able to turn the tide of battle. Not only that, they found a way for both sexes to coexist in harmony, just like Shiva, when they stand united as Ardhanarishwara.

'The pitrani told me that her blood ran in your veins. Your powers will be needed once again to stand with Mother Earth as she stands poised to take on a dangerous threat, which, if allowed to advance unimpeded, may destroy everything of value in this sinful world and plunge us all into prolonged darkness.'

Minothi tried to take it all in and suddenly she felt almost as bad as the gurvi looked. 'You have seen what happened. The abominable things that I did at the tender age of four. As you know, I survived the horror of my past by doing my utmost to bury the memory but it still plagues my thoughts, dreams and practically every other waking moment.'

Minothi shuddered as a painful memory inundated her being. She saw her mother running in the gloom and felt the great love that had given her the strength of purpose to withstand her mortal injuries. Every step had been agony and yet she had run steadfastly to her death, to give her child a chance to live. Through a haze of pain so palpable that it cut into her like a knife, Minothi saw her mother lift her pallu and dab at her eyes, ears and nose to wipe away the leaking blood from the grievous injuries sustained while her daughter went on a killing rampage.

Minothi had been a quiet and reserved child, introverted to a fault, and so meek that nearly everybody in the math had walked all over her. She never resisted and seemed to welcome the punishment. The gurvi had tried to help her, and during one of their sessions, they had unlocked the memory, revealing an old injury that had made a suppurated cesspool of her subconscious.

It had been too much for Minothi to handle and she began to see-saw violently between bouts of depression and simmering rage that would explode out of her at the oddest moments. There had been times when she had resented the gurvi for forcing her to confront the thing that was proving too much to bear. But when the old woman's health had failed, she was sorrier than she could say.

Minothi had convinced herself that the events leading up to her mother's death were a freak occurrence that would never happen again. Now the gurvi was telling her that this magic was in her blood and that she must harness its power. But she was terrified of it. The thing was a monster that fed on blood, and she had long suspected that it was inevitable that she would lose control over it. And then . . . She refused to go down that road and promised herself that she would never let the monster out of its cage and she would die with it rather than let it roam free.

'Don't blame yourself for your mother's death, Minothi. Do not presume that your flawed interpretation of events, clearly beyond the limited comprehension of mortals, is close to accurate! To me, it seemed that your mother saw you as her deliverer from the suffering that was her lot in this life, and she was truly grateful for the blessed release you gave her. Why, thanks to her services to the three worlds for bearing and delivering a Kritya, the higher powers may have seen fit to release her from the endless cycle of birth and rebirth!

'Isn't my interpretation of the exact same events more heartening? I could be wrong, but it is my belief that the wiser head within these confines rests on my neck, and you will do well to pay heed!'

Minothi listened to the gurvi's words and willed herself to accept them as the truth. But when that failed, she filed them away carefully, aware that they would comfort her the next time her personal demons overwhelmed her. Silently, she begged the gurvi to stop saying things she had no wish to hear.

'The magic is a gift, child, and in your hands, it will never be anything but a blessing.' The gurvi's voice throbbed with the force of her faith and her body protested. A violent fit of coughing took hold of her, and this time it took longer to die down. Minothi was almost glad. Still, the gurvi continued the moment she was able to.

'Do not be frightened by it. There is no greater enemy than fear. Always remember that the magic will reflect the heart and soul of the wielder. It can be anything you want it to be. You have made the choice to refrain from using it, and I did not want to rush you. Magic that powerful can be detected by those on the lookout for it, and can serve as a powerful beacon for the worst sort of predators. By not using it, you took yourself out of harm's way and I could not grudge you the safety it afforded.

'Yet, by pretending that it is not a part of you, you cannot actually make it so. The magic was given to you for a reason, and when the time is right, it will emerge from you, and when the moment arrives, you must be ready to gather it in your palms and guide it in the right direction. Believe in your ability to do the right thing, Minothi. I know this to be a fact, and you have to take my word for it.'

'I will never forget these words, Mother, and will hold on to them while there is life left in me.'

'Thank you, child. I cannot ask you for more. And don't look so sad about our imminent parting. Who is to say our paths won't converge again in good time? Be happy for me. Personally, I am excited about whatever lies on the other side.

'In the meantime, I want you to promise me something . . . You shall spend the night at my side and take a little trip with me. There is a little something in it for you which will help guide you along the path that is yours to take. Can you do that for me?'

'Of course! I will do as you say.'

The gurvi settled back into her bed, clearly worn out, and shut her eyes at once, entering the domain of deep sleep from which she would never emerge. Minothi kept vigil by her side. Exhausted as she was, sleep proved elusive while her thoughts stampeded through her head, throwing up so much debris it actually hurt.

In the darkest hour, before dawn, the gurvi breathed her last. Minothi had finally fallen into a fitful slumber and so did not awake during her mentor's death throes. She sensed her loss though in the nightmarish lands where the tides of slumber had unceremoniously dumped her.

She was free-falling into an abyss where something terrible lurked at the very bottom. Kicking wildly and clutching at everything with hands that were utterly ineffectual, she sought to find something to break her fall. But there was nothing to hold, and her descent proceeded unhindered.

The fall should have killed her; pain ratcheted through her entire being. The pitch-black darkness that enveloped her was so complete that she was blinded. Foul terror coated her throat and its sour taste made her gag. Alerted by her discomfort, the fiendish creatures detached themselves from the darkness and closed in on her, serrated teeth and claws gleaming white.

Trying to get to her feet, Minothi felt their slimy and scaly bodies rub against her back and legs. Swallowing back the screams that fought to escape her throat, she made herself believe that it was nothing more than a bad dream. It worked, and the foul creatures left her alone briefly.

She found herself standing in a long passageway illuminated by a single flickering candle that was almost completely spent. The gurvi was standing at the other end and seemed to be trying to tell her something of the utmost importance. Minothi tried to bridge the distance between them but the passage was blocked by the fiends and other creatures.

Wolfish dogs bared their teeth and boldly nipped at her heels. Wraiths swooped down, screaming shrilly, their feminine features distorted and their fanged mouths and forked tongues darting snake-like to puncture her flesh. Powerfully built demons brandished clubs at her and growled menacingly, advancing as though they meant to crush the life out of her.

Minothi's bowels threatened to turn liquid with fear, but she gathered herself and resolved that nothing could stop her from getting to the gurvi and finding out what it was that she was trying so hard to tell her.

She drew on her magic and it enveloped her like a safety blanket as she walked purposefully to the gurvi, who was smiling at her. The foul apparitions melted away, driven back to where they had come from. The darkness dissipated and the strange world she had found herself in was bathed in light.

Hugging her tightly, the gurvi drew back to look at her, seeming proud and pleased with what she saw. The matriarch appeared to have recovered fully, and Minothi allowed hope to take root. But the gurvi shook her head and began to disintegrate before her eyes. She kissed her gently on the forehead one last time, and removing something from her own neck, she fastened it around Minothi's.

She recognized it at once. It was the pretty pendant the gurvi always wore around her neck though wearing jewellery was strictly forbidden at the math. Minothi had always wanted to ask about it. She could feel its comforting weight on her chest, and her lips parted, urged open by the weight of the queries. But the gurvi was gone. And the questions remained unasked and unanswered.

When Minothi woke up, she was in the infirmary. Trishana, her best friend, had been waiting by her bedside and looked relieved to see that she had regained consciousness. 'Whatever was the matter with you? We found you lying senseless on the floor next to the gurvi who had died peacefully in her sleep. That sour-faced old sow Ananthamma said that you were from inferior stock and did not have the guts to take the death of our revered matriarch on the chin. Others were more understanding though. Naturally, we were sorry about the passing of the gurvi.

Trishana continued, 'You missed the funeral rites. We sang all her favourite songs and a special feast was prepared in her honour. I couldn't enjoy any of it, thanks to you! You were dead to the world in the infirmary, and the healers said that you had fainted from exhaustion and shock. Apparently, you were weak from not having eaten properly during the gurvi's illness. I knew that you had a weird crush on her, but this is ridiculous! Aren't you going to say something?'

'There isn't much to say except that I am sorry she is gone. Things will not be the same without her here.' Even Trishana fell silent at that. Minothi felt something heavy on her chest, pulsing as though alive. A huge smile broke across her face, and her friend looked relieved and puzzled at the same time. She did not say anything, but Minothi knew that she thought her quite mad.

20

From Varu's Book: Growing-up Pains

Yama and Yami stood poised on the threshold of adulthood. They had just about had it up to here with childhood, and were in a tearing hurry to grow up and leave it behind. Clearly, those who suppose it to be a halcyon period of innocence, fresh beginnings, fun and games, undiluted by the burden of responsibility, are the ones for whom it is nothing more than a distant memory to be looked back at through the filter of nostalgia.

The elder of the duo had definite plans for the future. Yama wanted to be the greatest warrior the celestials had seen and a bona fide hero, whose name would be whispered in hushed awe in every corner of the universe. Plus, he was tired of facing the backlash from the foolish decisions made by his elders and was definitely not inclined to sit on his backside, waiting in vain for the change he wanted to see. He figured that by making his bid for power he would be able to reshape everything in creation to suit his principles and ideologies.

As the star student of the preceptor of the devas, Brihaspati, he had already distinguished himself as a master of letters, adept at dharma, and was an unbeatable fighter as well. Almost all the celestials agreed that the son of Surya was one of those extremely annoying creatures who excelled in every field there was, in addition to being good-looking and likeable. The consensus was that he would surpass the remarkable achievements of even the sun god. Such talk made his father proud.

As for Yami, she was not sure what she wanted for herself, although she did know for certain that she certainly did not want to become anybody's wife. 'Yama, I know how father feels about this kind of thing, but I refuse to get married. I am perfectly content to be Surya's daughter and Yama's incredibly talented sister! If anybody turns up here with marriage proposals, I want you to send them packing with a swift kick to their pompous and presumptuous little backsides!' she would tell her brother.

'I agree that there is no one among the celestials who is good enough for you but I am nevertheless surprised at how strongly you feel about this. It was my belief that you would want to leave this place as quickly as possible if only to rid yourself of a certain someone who shall not be named! Why would you want to languish here and let your "incredible talents" go to waste any longer than you have to? Marriage could be your way out of this place.'

'Because I have been dreaming of escaping this iron cage for as long as I can remember and I will not allow myself to be coerced into trading one prison for another! Besides, this is my home, and I will be damned if I let some interloper drive me away from it before I deem myself ready to leave. The thing is . . .' Yami hesitated a little, wondering if she should broach an extremely painful topic.

The truth was that she had long nursed a secret desire to join the ranks of the fabled apsaras and become proficient in the sixty-four art forms, particularly dance. It was the innermost desire of her heart to perform in Indra's famed *sabha* and hear the thunderous applause of an enraptured audience hopelessly enamoured by her beauty as well as the sheer mastery with which she exercised her craft. In the pursuit of realizing her dream, she hoped to be fully rid of her insecurities and break free from the prison of her fear and soar across the heavens, having blossomed from being the ugly duckling to the graceful swan. It would have been the perfect panacea for her restless spirit, which had been imprisoned for too long within a rigidly regimented regime.

Surya would not hear of it, though, when she raised the subject, and acted as though she had suggested that her dream was to leave heaven and serve mankind as a prostitute! 'It pains me deeply that a daughter of mine should entertain a sinful desire to join the ranks of the immoral apsaras. Such a thing is unheard of and I would rather see your tongue cut off than hear you utter such words again!' His consort had trouble hiding her gleeful smile but even that did not cut to the quick the way her father's disappointment in her had.

Thinking of that incident made her morose. Yama seamlessly broke into her depressing thoughts. 'You don't actually have to become a dancer, paint yourself prettily and adorn yourself with diaphanous garments and ornaments to feel beautiful and admired, you know. The apsaras have their merits, but as far as I am concerned, they have nothing on you. Why do you always feel the need to do something dramatic or stack up achievements by the dozen to feel good about yourself? Why is it so hard for you to see what everybody else sees when they look at you—that you are remarkable and absolutely perfect? It is not necessary for you to prove anything to yourself or anybody else for that matter.'

Yami smiled gratefully at her twin, who with a few well-chosen words had made her depression vanish. She had no idea what she would do without him. Every time she looked at herself in the mirror, the overpowering urge to kill herself over her inadequacies had to be fought and subdued, but in her brother's eyes she saw herself reflected as the embodiment of perfection and it made her feel as special as he always insisted she was. This was another reason she knew she would never marry. It was impossible that she would see the same projection of herself in another's eyes.

Wordlessly, she threw her arms around his shoulders, loving how reassuring it was to be with him. 'How are things at the *gurukula*? It is too bad that females have been excluded for so long. Who decides these things anyway? Perhaps I could teach your revered guru a thing or two!'

'You probably could!' Yama agreed with her, sighing a little. Things with his guru had always been complicated. In the early days, when the venerable sage had inducted him into the passageways of learning, Yama had been struck with wonder. The Brahman was erudite, well-spoken and thoroughly masterful, and his young pupil had always looked at him with awe and respect. He had promptly placed his guru on a pedestal and Brihaspati had been flattered. But Yama's precociousness, rapid mastery of the mysteries of the Vedas and insatiable appetite for the secret stores of knowledge that the sage had hoarded made his guru wary.

Brihaspati parted with some useful secrets he had accumulated over the aeons, but parsimoniously, of course, setting an age-old trend for mystics from the east who, barring a few notable exceptions, believed in harnessing a wealth of information before shrouding it in secrecy, to not be imparted at all or grudgingly. They would always choose to part with only a teeny portion to a few chosen ones, before taking the rest with them to the grave, leaving the three worlds poorer for their patented selfishness. Yama's clamouring for more unsettled Brihaspati. As if that was not bad enough, all his pupils treated Yama with the kind of awe that, by right, belonged only to him, their teacher.

Consequently, Brihaspati could not stop himself from undermining his star pupil or setting up roadblocks in his academic career, although he was careful to conceal his true intentions. On the surface, he always came across as a model guru who sought to bring out the best in every one of his pupils and, in the case of exceptionally brilliant students like Yama, push them towards greater heights of excellence. But it did not take long for his student to see past the subterfuge and deduce that his idol had feet of clay. Brihaspati would have preferred outright rudeness to the silent contempt and disapproval that emanated from his charge, which contaminated his entire gurukula, infecting the rest of his students and making them all question his worth.

'My time with Brihaspati has not been entirely wasted, and there is so much I have learned but, nevertheless, it has been very frustrating. It feels like waiting, begging bowl in hand before our dear guru, while he chooses to occasionally flick a coin at us. The only thing I know for certain is that one cannot unearth the mysteries of the universe while poring endlessly over the scriptures or reciting them by rote. Experience is a far better teacher, and I can hardly wait to leave that place!'

'Don't let him get to you!' Yami remonstrated. 'That fellow is cantankerous because his wife, the redoubtable Tara, is having an affair with Soma, the moon god. It is quite the scandal, don't you know? I heard *your* mother say as much to her cronies. They referred to her as the "adulterous whore" but were not entirely successful in masking their envy because she seems to be the only one who is enjoying an amorous adventure to the fullest!'

'Clearly, your marked preference for scurrilous gossip comes from *your* mother,' Yama teased her affectionately. 'Honestly, though, I never really understood the preoccupation most have with the sexual shenanigans of others. There are so many issues that if examined closely would unlock the gates to the mysteries of the universe, but it would take one in a million not to be bored into a stupor by that sort of thing, whereas even the wise have a gluttonous appetite for useless things.'

'I only brought it up because it is obvious to me that the venerable Brihaspati feels threatened by your vitality, not to mention your virility. You are even better looking than that Kama everybody keeps gushing about and, unlike him, with his toy bow and flower-tipped arrows, you can handle yourself in a fight.

'Naturally, the poor cuckolded bugger will be jealous and try to slow you down. You should take it as a compliment that even the high and mighty feel threatened by you, even though there is a way to go before you fully realize your full potential. The way I see it, you will be well advised to stay put and put up with all the muck he shovels your way because it is only for a little while longer. Besides, if you leave the gurukula before he authorizes it, Brihaspati will curse you so quick, you will be reborn on earth as a worm faster than he can prematurely ejaculate!'

'For a silly little twit, you give decent advice!' Yama tugged on her hair, knowing that she hated getting it mussed up. 'But I promise you that the day is not far off when all will bow before my power and pay heed to my judgement!'

'It is a good thing you are not an egoistic brat or a mass-murdering megalomaniac then,' Yami said tartly, patting her hair back into place while her brother promptly messed it up again. There was no option left but for her to bring out the heavy artillery and fling a cushion at his face.

The twins had been fully engrossed in their conversation and too busy giggling like children to notice that they were being watched. Chaya stood some distance away, camouflaged by the shadows. She could not hear what was being said but she saw plenty. The casual intimacy they shared so effortlessly never failed to make her hackles rise and the bitter bile of envy flooded her mouth with its acrid taste.

Chaya had been deeply hurt by a recent event involving the detestable duo, and seeing them chat and laugh as though it did not affect them in the least made her furious. Cautioning herself not to allow herself to go down a certain dark path she had traversed in the past only to be badly burnt, Chaya nevertheless found herself barrelling down that very road. Yet again, she experienced anew the raw pain that induced her to give in to taboo longings that had only grown in intensity, in defiance of her attempts to bury them.

Chaya emerged from her reverie just in time to note that Yama and Yami were continuing to pummel each other with pillows, and Yami was giggling, albeit in a muted tone, in the vain hope that none would catch them red-handed during their shenanigans. Grimly, she fantasized about Yama dying in a godforsaken war, leaving Yami as bereft as she herself was. In an alternate scenario, Yama went on to marry a strumpet and spent all his time lost in her company, having no further need for his twin. A favourite ending saw Yami come to a bad end by becoming as immoral as the nymphs she idolized, tarnishing her reputation and earning the contempt of both her father and brother, who would want nothing more to do with her.

Smiling to herself, Chaya turned and walked away from them. She wished them the joy of each other, knowing that the tragedy she had long orchestrated for them was close at hand. Then it would be her turn to laugh. But in the meantime, it was time to revisit the hallways of memory to get reacquainted with humiliation and anger so that they would sustain her on the long road to revenge.

21

Waiting

Minothi thoughtfully fingered the heavy circular pendant she wore around her neck on a thick, black ribbon. It was inscribed with the image of a goddess she could not identify, but it didn't matter. The Mother Goddess was worshipped in so many forms, both benevolent and blood-curdling, across the world that it was a fool's errand to try to keep track.

She had worn it for ten years now, since Gurvi Sampoorna had passed away. It was said that those you loved truly were never entirely lost to those who made room in their hearts for the memories, but Minothi felt that was rubbish. The gurvi was gone beyond recall, and Ananthamma had taken her place after Sampoorna's two immediate successors had died one after the other, from a strange ailment that came and claimed their lives before anyone was the wiser.

'It was all very convenient for that witch Ananthamma!' Minothi mused privately to herself. A lot had changed at Sivagami Math under her brand of leadership. The new gurvi said that her predecessor had been alarmingly progressive, and in steering them away from the centuries of tradition that had guided them thus far had exposed them to danger once again.

'It was thanks to her heretical ideas that bad fortune made its way into our Sivagami Math, heralding its entry with inauspicious omens. We lost two cows when they were birthing their calves and the remaining cows have continually given us sour milk. The weather has been unseasonable and in our entire history we have not been buffeted so often with such terrible storms. You all remember that fell night when the banyan tree was struck by lightning and caught fire. Over four hundred years old, and it was destroyed just like that!

'Shortly after that, the gurvi's health took a turn for the worse and she succumbed. If that were not bad enough, Kamakshi *atti* and Thilagam atti followed her to the grave, though both were women in their prime.

'In this time of great tribulations, I shall once again restore the ancient traditions that have kept us safe for so long.'

The Kanyas resigned themselves to what felt like a life sentence, behind the iron bars of a cage that had shrunken in size and made their despair achingly acute. Life in Sivagami Math went on as usual but with a certain oppression that slowly stripped the inhabitants of their spirits and left them feeling bereft and utterly miserable. They still occupied themselves with chores and charity, but there was no shaking the feeling that life had passed them by a long time ago and was not coming back. Most swallowed their resentment over their fate and gave themselves over to unchanging routine, till all the fight slowly went out of them.

Minothi had not yet reached that stage, but it was only a matter of time. At thirty-one, she felt closer to a hundred and fifty. Her body had lost the suppleness of youth and she had gained weight. What had once been a fine head of thick, wavy hair was sparser now, and every time she plaited it as loosely as possible, it looked increasingly like a scraggy rat's tail. She was too self-critical to have noticed it, but her eyes were and always had been her best feature. Almond-shaped and black, they were wonderfully expressive and drew you in immediately.

She was not the only one struggling with her weight. As adherents of spirituality, excess of any kind was not encouraged, and yet the rules had been relaxed when it came to food. Alcohol consumption was strictly forbidden, but there was every kind of foodstuff to be had. Seafood was hard to get in these parts, but since they raised their own livestock, there was an abundance of chicken, egg, quail, partridge, pigeon, mutton and lamb as well as milk and milk products. Fruits and vegetables were plentiful, as were curds, butter and ghee.

The kitchen regularly churned out deep-fried delicacies like vadas, pillowy crisp puris, seedai, cheval and murukkus. An assortment of sweets saturated with sugar such as laddoos, halwa, adhirasam, bholi and kadalai mittai were served up every other day in addition to payasams. The trust often sent them chocolates, creamy cakes, biscuits and other goodies. During festivals, they even got ice cream.

The Kanyas ate well and, barring a few, it showed on their waistlines and rendered them positively steatopygous. Trishana had of course eaten like a ravenous sailor but retained her impossibly slim figure while Minothi had a harder time of it. Thinking about the rampant gluttony and her own ample curves depressed her, and she returned to her gloomy thoughts instead.

Gurvi Sampoorna's talk of Krityas and magic had made her dread the possibility that she would be forced to unchain the beast in her. But she had worried needlessly. It had all been very anticlimactic indeed. Nothing had happened. There was no room for anything but hopelessness in her life. Now with Trishana also gone, things were at an all-time low.

•••

'This is bullshit!' Trishana had complained fiercely as they sat trailing their toes in their secret spring nearly six years ago. They had stumbled on it entirely by accident while still children. Gurvi Sampoorna had encouraged them to go for long walks in the surrounding woodlands and sometimes she would accompany them herself. 'Communing with nature is a wonderful spiritual experience!' she would say often. They used to have picnics in the great outdoors, sing songs during their rambles and even camp out under the stars when the weather was amenable.

Minothi and Trishana liked to take off by themselves whenever possible, and they preferred to give the well-trodden paths a miss and take, instead, the narrower trails favoured by the creatures of the woods.

It was one such narrow path that was practically hidden by the brush that led to the spring. The girls had negotiated their way past a thorny thicket that served to deter all but the most intrepid of intruders, and had found the dear little spring, with its water crystal clear and cool. Honey flowers and bluebells grew in wild profusion on hedges that abutted the grassy bank of the stream.

Minothi and Trishana loved few things better than playing in the stream during the hot summer days and had whiled away the happiest parts of their childhood there. Gurvi Ananthamma had banned unsupervised excursions into the woods, but on that day, Trishana had dragged Minothi along after aeons, insisting that since that demon spawn Ananthamma was having a hush-hush meeting with her hand-picked coven of witches, they wouldn't be missed if they sneaked out while the others took their afternoon siesta.

'It is unnatural to keep us locked up like this in the interest of preserving the hymen. All they have accomplished by forcing abstinence on us is that they have made us susceptible to the advances of the first one-eyed beggar to cross our paths!' Trishana opined.

Looking at her, Minothi was a little envious as always, because she was a vision of natural beauty. Trishana had porcelain skin, shiny, black hair that fell past her shoulders in a sensuous sweep and a slender yet voluptuous body that most women would have happily killed for. In the world outside, she would have probably been wooed and wined and dined by movie stars, accomplished athletes and business magnates. Hers was the story of the desert rose whose fragrance was wasted on the uncaring sands of time. Next to her, Minothi felt shorter, fatter and browner than she actually was. Even her curls felt frizzed up worse than usual when they were together.

'If you are going to risk life and limb, I suggest that you hold out for a handsome prince, or at least a halfway-decent specimen of manhood with all his sense organs intact! Just the other day, the demon spawn told us about the ingenious ways in which runaway Kanyas were tortured and killed. There hasn't been a successful escape since the math was founded because everyone joins hands to hunt them down, or so she said.

'Most of the escapees did not make it far as they either fell off the slippery slopes or were devoured by wild animals. Those who managed to get past these natural barriers were quickly apprehended. If a Kanya is caught with her virginity intact, they are merciful, and she is quickly stoned to death. In other cases, the Kanya's hair is shorn, she is branded on the chest with a hot iron to mark her disgrace, paraded around like a captured animal and either buried or burnt alive. Sometimes, they were stretched, spreadeagled, on the ground, bound to stakes and their privates smeared with chilli powder, or mutilated.'

'Shut up already! I came here to have fun, not listen to such morbid talk!' Trishana shuddered delicately as Minothi had known she would. For all her sharp talk, she was a gentle soul who abhorred violence. 'I can't help but loathe this accursed place! Between Gurvi Sampoorna who showed us a world of possibility and the demon spawn with her obsession for those sordid stories in the newspapers where everyone seems to be getting laid or trying their utmost to get laid, I am well on the way to becoming stark raving mad!'

'It could be worse . . .' Minothi began cautiously, a sudden vision of herself after she had burnt down the math and every one of its inhabitants flashing in her mind's eye. With Gurvi Sampoorna gone, she certainly had no fond feelings for the math, but she did not want to give voice to her innermost thoughts for fear of where they might lead her. Trish had no such qualms though.

'How can you stand it? Have you noticed the very air we breathe within the confines of the math? It is closed and befouled by the nastiness of suppressed desires, crushed dreams, ever-present despair and a crushing resentment. If we persist in breathing the stuff for too long, it will kill us. Maybe not today, nor tomorrow, even the day after, but eventually it will get us all and we will become a version of the demon spawn ourselves. We will have that mean glint in our eyes and become petty, spiteful and resentful of the younger ones because they still have hope.

'The worst part is that life has so much to offer. There are girls out there like us who are globetrotting and flying off to space to explore the vast unknown, running their own companies and even countries, playing sports or forging their own paths. It is a world of infinite possibilities. But here at the math, we might as well be living in the Palaeolithic period, excepting the fact that the Neanderthal men have moved on to greener pastures.

'I am sick of getting up at the crack of dawn, singing nothing but devotional songs, meditating endlessly to the point where it makes me want to hurl and performing the same old chores.'

Minothi looked at her reflection in the water and tried in vain to smooth her hair. Her looks, as always, depressed her, and Trishana's uncharacteristic despondence was affecting her as well. 'Cheer up, Trish! We will never ever become anything like that demon spawn and you know it. Not all of them are bad apples. Gurvi Sampoorna thrived in this math, and some of the older Kanyas are so inspiring. They are living proof that a lifetime of happiness, contentment and fulfilment is well within our grasp, if only we pause to look within and embrace the spirituality residing there.

'As for the utopian picture you painted of the choices available to girls nowadays, let me remind you that the more things change, the more they stay the same. It has always been a man's world, and men don't share power. Remember that case we read about in those newspaper clippings? A girl was imprisoned by her father in a windowless cellar for twenty-four years. She was raped and forced to bear seven of his children! Things are hardly better for girls closer home. Female infanticide is still rampant, even in these liberated times. Females of all ages just might get gang-raped and murdered for daring to dress "inappropriately" by forgetting a dupatta, or draping a sari provocatively! And if they want to drink alcohol or work late, they are branded as women of loose morals and considered fair game for all manner of abuse.

'You forget the horror stories that include acid-throwing and trafficking and talk only about the girls who have all the things you want—the freedom to just be whatever they wish to be—or maybe the girls who are married to Mr Perfect and raising his children. Are you seriously going to tell me that they are perfectly happy with their lives and want nothing else? I bet they look at us and envy us the peacefulness of our existence. It is the way the cookie crumbles . . . The grass is always greener on the other side.

'The mind is sometimes a treacherous creature and instigates us to chase after things that may not necessarily be good for us. It is what the gurvi always told us. Have you forgotten?'

Trishana splashed her in the face then, and Minothi was annoyed because her hair looked worse than ever, with the gluey strands plastered over her scalp. She was considering a sharp rebuke when the sadness in her dear friend's eyes silenced her. Sensing her concern, Trish grinned wanly. 'You have all the makings of a future old-fart gurvi of Sivagami Math. I suggest you save the lectures for your clueless charges if there are people out there still cruel enough to abandon their baby girls in this shithole. That said, I'll admit your words were not entirely devoid of sense. Whenever I feel like crap, which is often nowadays, I tell myself to be content because I am not somebody's sex slave, or a decrepit beggar living on the platform, but it is so hard.

'There are days when I am filled with so much yearning that it actually feels like dying. All I want is to know what it feels like to be loved. Sometimes I imagine it so vividly that it is almost real. It would be absolutely amazing to be held close, or to be kissed by somebody who makes me feel safe and so complete that I couldn't possibly not be happy and perfectly content. It is all I want for myself, and if that is not to be, I would settle for the perfect kiss and ask for nothing more.'

Alarm bells went off in Minothi's head, and her heart hammered away in her chest. Hastily, she forced herself to speak with all the flippancy that she could muster, 'One lousy kiss will never be enough, especially if it is perfect. Have you known anyone to be content with a single bite of chocolate if it were as sinfully delicious as you wish it to be? I bet there are thousands of knocked-up girls out there, puking their guts out and wishing they had settled for chocolates instead of kisses.'

'The point is that the heart wants what it wants. Even if one of its desires were fulfilled for the briefest of moments, I'll be grateful for all of eternity. A cherished memory is better than the empty regret which will be all we have if we are forced thus to remain virtuous.'

'The point is, the heart is stupid and you should crush it with the weight of your brain! As for the acrid taste of empty regret, may I suggest you fill it up with chocolate or ras malai?'

'May I remind you that the only thing worse than absolute wretchedness is to be fat and wretched at the same time? Whoever heard of Prince Charming rescuing a fatty from the dragon?'

Trish would have gone on, but her best friend had splashed water and drenched her nearly from head to foot. They had laughed then, glad for the friendship they shared. There was no way for either to know that that would be the last time they would be together in their secret place. A few short months later, Trishana disappeared. Minothi would never know what became of her.

•••

She had thought about her friend often. She hoped and prayed that Trish had got what she wanted before she died. Then she would weep, appalled that her treacherous thoughts kept reiterating her deepest fear that the beautiful and gentle Trish, who had asked the world for nothing but a perfect kiss, was no more.

That had been a long time ago. She was thirty-one years old now, and her days stretched endlessly ahead of her. The depression had sneaked up on her, and there were cold and empty nights when she went to bed with unshed tears, screaming soundlessly for help, though none could possibly hear those mute cries of distress. Her final thought before reluctant sleep took her in its arms was that it wouldn't be the worst thing if she did not wake up in the morning.

Without fail, death always gave her a wide berth, and she always woke up, consoling herself that the new day would bring with it something to live for, though it never did. And so she fiddled with her pendant and waited. Because there wasn't anything else she could do. So she waited and waited—for what, she did not know—even if that meant there was a distinct possibility that she was waiting in vain.

22

Stolen Souls

Agni rose slowly from the bedbug-infested spring mattress in the crappy hotel he had checked into at Bodiyankara. The clock told him it was 9 p.m. His knees buckled as the wooziness hit him, and he sat down heavily on the bed, scratching at the red bumps that had cropped up on his neck. The nightmares and visions were back, vying with each other to rob him of the respite sleep ought to have offered.

• • •

Varu and he were sitting together on a park bench, talking and laughing. It had been too long, and Agni was enjoying every bit of it. Suddenly, Chandu and Suri appeared in front of them, unsummoned. His sister clutched at his arm in terror. She was scared of dogs. They closed in on Varu, snarling at her menacingly. Agni was furious and he shouted at them to back off but neither budged.

The next moment, Chandu leaped at Varu and she screamed in agony. A powerful square jaw snapped shut on her heel. Agni pounced on the great dog, determined to prise open those jaws of death, using Yama's danda as a club, bringing it down repeatedly on the massive cream-coloured forehead.

Suri was having none of it and she tore into him, the streaks of gold in her coat glinting angrily. Agni fought her desperately, trying to get to Varu, whose cries for help were bouncing shrilly off the walls deep inside his skull. Try as he might, he could not make his way to her.

Chandu dragged Varu away to a fiery chasm in hell where the accursed awaited her with arms outstretched. Berserk with grief, Agni summoned up the red flames and burnt Suri to ash—except she wouldn't burn.

•••

Wearily, he stumbled into the bathroom and splashed some tepid water on his face. His bloodshot eyes stung when the water hit them. Agni leaned over the sink, trying to get his bearings. He had been hard at work the past few days, trying to track down the Kritya and the near-mythical Sivagami Math, which Taravarsha had told him was the place she had lived in.

Hardly had he begun digging, when the dirt turned up in spades. He had bumped into one of his classmates from what felt like another life at a local coffee shop. It was the kind of coincidence that was common enough in his line of work, and yet he had difficulty accepting it, let alone taking it for granted. Vinay was currently working as a private investigator who had been hired by an influential family to look into the disappearance of their maid's five-year-old daughter. He had made little progress, although the few clues he had managed to unearth had led him to look closely at Sivagami Math. Agni told him that he was doing a little investigative reporting himself on the missing girls.

'We are barking up the right tree all right!' Vinay said between bites of a piping hot samosa. He was a short, stocky man who proudly displayed the few hairs remaining on his pate by anointing them delicately with a heavily perfumed hair gel. 'Something is seriously wrong in virgin land all right. But good luck getting anyone to spill. The freak show is run by a trust and they are fanatical about secrecy. There is no proper road leading to the math, and it takes forever to hitch-hike across extremely inhospitable terrain to get there. The damn place is in the middle of nowhere, and faces absolutely no infringement from a rampaging tourism initiative.'

Agni nodded in agreement and took a sip of his coffee, which was surprisingly good. 'I also find the whole thing bloody bizarre. In fact, not a single person I talked to had gone to the math themselves or even knew anybody who had.'

'That is not the worst of it . . .' Vinay did not bother with swallowing his food before butting in. 'The trust runs a counselling centre for women who have been raped, slapped silly or otherwise traumatized by the "worthless" men in their lives. If anybody wants to know the true meaning of cruelty, they should try living with my migraine-inducing wife. But who cares about the agonies endured by men? Anyway, as I was saying, the trust has an orphanage as well, and on paper at least they are the original bleeding-heart society. But it gets murkier . . .

'A lot of the druggies and hookers who turn up at the counselling centre coolly leave their little ones at the orphanage. Most never return, but the few who do and demand their brats back are sent back empty-handed. If they prove to be annoyingly persistent or seem inclined to raise a melodramatic ruckus aimed at the newshounds, they simply disappear.

'As for the orphanage, it is straight out of a horror show. It has been tarred with the brush of scandal on more than one occasion, and there were murmurs of the ill and harsh treatment of the kids, unhygienic conditions, improper care, swindled funds and the whole kit and caboodle. But all these unsavoury stories have been hastily squelched, though the place still stinks of an unwashed latrine, with the result that even the most callous or desperate mothers have begun to think twice about leaving their children there.

'The next unsavoury twist in this sordid saga is that a great number of kids have begun to disappear off the street or from cribs while in the nursing homes in the seedier parts hereabouts. Some babies have been snatched from their impoverished homes. Witnesses have reported seeing them at the infamous orphanage.

'The lovely folks who run the place claim that, occasionally, lost or missing children are turned over to them on account of the fact that the locals have no great love for the cops, and they make sure the kid is safe and warm before calling in the authorities. It is true that in a few cases children have been reunited with their parents, but here's the kicker, these kids have almost always been those who were violated or badly hurt in some manner. Babies are never recovered.

'Now, the trust always sends the girl babies to Sivagami Math and, naturally, this makes the whole thing suspicious. The trustees insist that they only send the babies after a mandatory waiting period, though they are vague about how long that is. In one case, the distraught parents were told that the baby had been sent to the math, but had died there.'

Vinay paused for breath and to call out for more mint chutney. 'If there are so many questions being asked, surely the cops would have looked into the place by now?' Agni prodded gently.

'Local authorities are unwilling or unable to intervene or ask too many questions because the thing is unlikely to brighten their career prospects. Clearly, there are some political bigwigs involved, though I'll be damned if I know who they are. Many folks around here have no idea about the Kanyas, and the few who do, treat them with superstitious awe and are content to give them a wide berth.

'As far as I can tell, their existence is practically nun-like, except that nuns aren't cooped up like chickens and are active in the fields of education and philanthropy. All they do is sit inside and pray for sinners like us or have lesbian orgies from dusk to dawn. Some of the people I spoke to warned me that great evil will befall anyone who thinks or speaks ill of the Kanyas. Since I haven't been struck by lightning or impaled as I eat, we can safely assume that is superstitious nonsense, but even so, there is something about the place that gives me the creeps.'

'It is hard to believe that such a place exists in this day and age. What is more, they seem to exist beneath the radar of mainstream consciousness. I am surprised that there aren't newshounds and paparazzi camping outside the stone walls to find out what goes on in there. Even the feminists and human rights activists who ought to have been howling for blood are suspiciously quiet. Isn't it odd?'

Vinay shrugged his fleshy shoulders indifferently. 'Initially, I thought there was sex, drugs and trafficking involved, given the abundance of feminine pulchritude. You are probably salivating at the prospect of a sexploitation story but it's all squeaky clean. No men have set foot on the grounds of the math since its inception. They are ridiculously strict about it.

'I talked to a lot of the older folks in these parts, and they swear that there have been no runaways in living memory, or any suspicious activities. A few Kanyas die, having contracted some disease or the other, plus there are bound to be a fair share of old farts who croak without anyone giving two hoots about it. But when day-old babies and very small children die or disappear, it becomes a tad suspicious. But even that may be ascribed to the fact that these freaks have allowed science and technology to pass them by, still relying on potions, mantras and the rest of that gobbledygook.

'I'll tell you one thing though. I dug up a report about a five-year-old who was hit by a car. It was a hit-and-run. No one came forward to identify the victim. So I am going to submit that in my findings and get the hell out of here. I simply don't care enough about these luckless bitches to risk my health over them. Take my advice and hasten to the red-light districts, or track down the devotees of Yellamma who are supposedly still following the devadasi tradition, if you want the nasty stuff.

'There is a reason nobody talks about this place. You know how the dead don't tell stories, right? Take my word for it, get your arse in gear and run from this place as fast as you can!'

And that had been that. Agni mechanically splashed some more water on his face. Not feeling any better, he returned dispiritedly to the bedroom, banging his knee against the square edge of the table that had been inconveniently located en route to the bed. Swearing foully, he looked up and saw Dharami seated on the hideous faux-velvet orange sofa, watching him warily.

Like the last time he had seen her, she was attired in a heavy robe and hood in the darkest shade of grey that made all her features indistinct. Now, as then, her voice was a murmur in his head. 'Taravarsha required me to gather information about the missing Kanya, and I was required to deliver my findings to you.' That was one way to cut to the chase, Agni thought bemusedly, plonking himself on to the ugly sofa's twin, which was identical, barring a few stains of dubious origin.

'You look terrible!' she said, watery-grey eyes squinting at him. 'Why do you always have to look like you are at death's door?'

'It is good to see you too, Dharami,' Agni responded, keeping his voice level. 'Now that we have put the pleasantries aside, what do you have to say to me?' Stifling a yawn, he worried at his offending neck till he drew blood. His bête noire looked at him with ill-concealed disgust.

'I have quite a bit to tell you, actually, and none of it is good!' her voice trilled in his head with malicious glee. 'But before I proceed, tell me, what do you know about people who eat the dead?'

'Do you mean cannibalism? I don't take as harsh a view of the subject as does the rest of civilized society. If non-vegetarianism is perfectly acceptable and folks can relish a chicken wing, raw fish, bull's balls, frog legs, cockroaches, lizards and snails, then human flesh need not be off the table.

'Why waste a perfectly good body by simply incinerating or cremating the damn thing when somebody or something can derive nourishment from it, especially when cleaned and cooked to taste? "Waste not, want not" used to be my grandmother's motto!'

To his surprise, Agni heard a sound that was suspiciously close to laughter. Unable to believe it, he continued hastily, 'Varu, my sister, found the subject fascinating. Apparently, there are sects, monastic and others, in various parts of the world, where members typically feed on the dead and use them for esoteric purposes. It is just one among a host of kinky practices, including fornicating with menstruating prostitutes, partaking liberally of urine and excrement, quaffing booze out of skulls and the like.

'I was informed that these individuals, by embracing death and all things putrid, seek to transcend the same. They believe that these practices will help master the senses and make them better equipped to deal with the challenges posed by a world given to excess. They believe that, to the well-ordered mind, faecal matter is no different from other forms of matter since it is all derived from the same divine source.'

Dharami nodded, her attitude towards him considerably improved. 'I am no expert on the subject, but your sister's understanding of it makes a good deal of sense. However, after what I have seen and heard in recent times, it is obvious that Naganara has employed methodology gleaned from arcane lore perfected by the enlightened masters, who have transcended life and death to accrue vast stores of knowledge, and perverted it for his own purposes.

'The necromancer has been choosing his victims carefully. They are usually very young, babies even. He chooses the ones he wants, has them suffocated so that the bodies remain unmarked, and then abducts the remains. I am not sure about the sorcery involved, but by interfering with the manner of their passing and then consuming them, he appropriates for himself the essence of their being and traps their very souls within himself.

'Those unfortunate creatures remain bound to him, unable to escape and, thwarted from the natural course that follows death, where their mortal remains are returned to the earth and their souls continue on the path preordained by samsara which they must take, till they have run the course and are released from its inexorable diktats.

'The power he has over them is complete, and he keeps them to be used and discarded as he sees fit. Some of the lost souls he uses to take possession of living bodies, usually those who might be of service to him. For the dead who are trapped in limbo, the living are anathema, and they feed on them, consuming them from within like a cancer, little by little, till there is nothing left.' Here she paused meaningfully, waiting for Agni to put the pieces together.

'Then we can assume that at least a few higher-ups in the trust and math are possessed? That would explain the babies and children who have been declared deceased or missing from these parts. And the Kanya he used in the conjuring—' Agni stopped abruptly.

A bad memory struggled to the surface, and Agni had to force it down with every ounce of energy he could gather. His teeth were clenched and the veins stood out on his forehead and neck.

•••

In response to a vision, he had gone to a small nursing home in a forgotten town in Karnaka, far from the nearest metropolitan city, Belogu. Even going by the poor quality of the intelligence fed to him, this particular one had been vexing. Normally, he was called upon to hunt down escaped arakshas and dispatch them post-haste to Yama's abode.

This time, though, he was merely shown a baby. It was a beautiful baby girl. The mother had delivered it after what was clearly a difficult labour. A bored-looking doctor scribbled something on a pad and departed, handing the baby over to a sleepy nurse. The nurse checked the patient's blood pressure, fiddled with the intravenous tubing, inadvertently tugged at the catheter, which made her patient cry out in pain, injected something into the IV solution and left the room. A little girl watched with worried eyes, huddled up in a corner of the room.

Sometime in the darkest hour of the night, a man opened the door quietly and strode into the room. He was a compact and wiry man. Orange-gold eyes took on an eerie cast in the dark when he brushed aside the thick fringe that fell over his forehead, looking like a tawny tiger on the prowl. Taking in the measure of the inhabitants, he went straight to the bed where the mother lay too fatigued to notice the approach of death.

Almost tenderly, he placed the webbing between his thumb and forefinger on her throat, spreading the remaining four fingers on the back of her neck. Pressing hard with the thumb, he gripped the windpipe in a chokehold, crushing it hard, cutting off the oxygen supply to her brain. He held fast till her heart and lungs quit and the weak hand that had struggled in vain to prise herself free from that deathly grip dropped limply to the side. Pausing to inject something into the baby and her sister, he packed their unconscious forms into a capacious holdall and left as stealthily as he had come.

There was no time to ponder over why Yama's lieutenant had been summarily asked to intervene in this particular instance of trafficking. Agni had located the nursing home easily enough, as he had seen the name and logo sewed on the nurse's uniform. He had stood in a state of constant vigilance for days on end, as there had been no indication of the time frame, worried sick that he might have missed the window.

Finally, a heavily pregnant woman and her weeping daughter arrived. The mother was on her last limb and collapsed on to the stretcher that was wheeled out to her. To Agni's relief, a kindly support-staff member took the girl under her wing and even gave her some food from the tiffin box she had brought along. It was always the random act of kindness that got to him.

The baby was safely delivered and, midway through the graveyard shift, the trio were in the exact position that Agni had seen in his vision. He waited for the nurse to leave, and when all seemed quiet for the night, he sprang into action. Quickly, he placed the baby next to the mother, although handling the impossibly tiny and fragile newborn was without doubt the most difficult task he had ever attempted.

Mission-impossible accomplished, he wheeled the cot to an empty room further down the hall. He returned for the little girl, who did not stir as he carried her and left her with the rest of her family. Then he arranged three decoys beneath the sheets and hid in readiness for the killer.

Adrenaline coursed through his veins, keeping him wide awake. Even so, he had almost dozed off when Creepy Eyes arrived on cat's feet. To his surprise, instead of going to the bed and presenting his back to Agni, he lunged at his hidden assailant with the uncanny instincts of a hardened killer.

A wicked-looking knife flashed in his hand. Agni dodged just in time as it struck a glancing blow on his shoulder, drawing blood instantly. They grappled in the dark, and it took Agni every ounce of his strength to wrap the *pasha*—Yama's noose—around his neck, till those terrible eyes bulged out of their sockets.

But with superhuman strength, Creepy Eyes freed himself from the noose and, before Agni could bring it to bear again, headbutted him right in the face with all his might. Agni heard the cartilage break well before he felt the pain. Before he could recover, Creepy Eyes had landed a solid double blow to his throat and liver before landing a knee into his groin, which Agni just managed to dodge. Even so, he collapsed. Blackness closed in on him and the room spun like a top.

Agni knew that he would pass out soon. His assailant was closing in for the kill. Without pausing to think, Agni raised his fingers. The red flames hammered into Creepy Eyes and he screamed. To Agni's surprise, he smelled singed flesh. The creature who had almost killed him was not an araksha, but clearly he was not entirely human either.

Creepy Eyes was enveloped in the red flames and was screaming for all the world to hear. He fled through the open door in the time it took Agni to rise painfully to his feet, determined to chase him down and finish him off.

But even as he gave chase, Agni knew that something was wrong. He felt it in his bones and urged himself to greater speed, ignoring the sticky blood that was trickling down his side and the fact that the injured parts of his body, most notably the shattered nose, were sending frantic signals to his brain, begging for pain relief. The creature was standing in front of the neonatal unit. Only a pane of glass separated it from the impossibly tiny and fragile beings that were still warm from the womb. A chill crawled up his spine as naked fear took hold of him.

The red flames had dissipated. Burnt skin peeled off the creature's body, only to be replaced with something almost metallic. He was being pulled apart and reassembled in front of Agni. Only the eyes were no longer golden; they were a piercing shade of green, and they held him transfixed in place.

'You may have the powers of Yama, but you are too much of a weakling and a fool to use it as he would! Even before I crushed your testicles, you had no balls! You will die screaming like the eunuch you are, and be sure to tell Yama that it was Naganara who sent you to him. Be kind enough to inform him that I am coming for him and his twin both!'

Almost lazily, he waved his hand at the glass and it shattered into a thousand pieces. With a flicking motion of the wrist, he directed the shards at Agni in a deadly hailstorm. Simultaneously, green flames shot out of his fingertips and the incubators with their precious burdens caught immediately, triggering the fire alarms. With a last look of satisfaction at Agni, who was screaming louder than the alarms, the necromancer vanished into thin air along with the physical remains of Creepy Eyes. He did not notice the silvery-white presence that had cast a protective net over the fallen lieutenant.

• • •

Tears stung his eyes at the memory of the fire and his worst failure. Dharami did not notice. 'You are right, of course. Naganara's creatures are all over the place, and there are some among them who are more dangerous than the others. These would be the tainted souls who have become attuned to the needs of their captor and learned to enjoy the killing. Between the lot of them, they have been preying on little girls and babies all over the southern belt and turning them over to the orphanage from where they are sent to Sivagami Math, where it is convenient for them to simply disappear.

'As for the missing Kanya, my guess is that she was somehow tricked by the Hatakas. If life at the math is what it sounds like, then the poor deluded girl would have seized the opportunity to get away only to wind up in Naganara's paws and help him conjure up the Narakamayas. She traded one hell for a worse one! Poor thing!

'I have been there, you know, and it is every bit as bad as it sounds. It won't be difficult to show you the way. The problem is, despite my best efforts, I could not pinpoint the Kritya.'

'Thanks for everything, Dharami.' Grim purpose was once more written on his face. 'I am glad that you are here. Let us leave for the math at once. If you couldn't find her, then Naganara hasn't as well. Will you go with me?'

'Taravarsha asked me to help you and so it is my job. There is no need to ask.' Her voice was curt, but Dharami seemed pleased as well. 'Meet me at midnight by the woods. From there you will have to walk, and it is better you travel at night.' She rose to leave. The excitement of the hunt was upon her and, without warning, the remains of her damaged body and spirit revealed itself in ungainly bits and pieces as her robe parted. Agni averted his eyes, but not before she caught the look of horror in them. With a hiss of fury that scalded his insides, she gathered her robes in a huff and rushed past him, faster than the eye could follow.

Chiding himself for his lack of sensitivity, Agni packed his things quickly and checked out of the hotel. He was hungry but did not dare risk room service. If the friendly parasites that had shared his bed were any indication, the kitchen was highly unlikely to pass muster in a health inspection.

Agni stopped for a quick bite at a tiny eatery that looked relatively clean. There was a good bit of distance to cover and he was anxious to leave. The second-hand bike he had bought to replace his beloved car awaited him, and it cheered him up immediately. It was a gorgeous 'pearl stardust white' Kawasaki Ninja that he had managed to purchase at a throwaway price.

The previous owner had treated the lightweight superbike with the love and respect it deserved, leaving the parallel twin engine, the FCC clutch, with its advanced assist function, multifunction digital display and seventeen-inch ten-spoke wheels in mint condition. It filled the hole in his heart that the loss of his dear departed Innova had left. Varu would have called him fickle, and the thought made him chuckle.

As he rode into the night, he wondered if he really had tried to kill Dharami. Another memory beckoned to him, but he brushed it aside. He had had enough for one night. Besides, he needed all his wits about him to track down the Kritya and make his escape with her.

The bike ride revived him somewhat. It was a beautiful night, and the nearly full moon looked radiant. On reaching the woods a couple of hours later, Agni found a place to pitch his tent. The great outdoors had to be better than what passed for hotels in these parts. Mercifully, it was a cool night and Agni managed a short nap before it was time to quit dithering and begin his quest.

23

Veshas

It was an unusually hot and sultry night, given that the altitude at which they were located ensured that the climate ranged from pleasantly chilly to near-freezing. Minothi found herself tossing and turning for the better part of the night. Her discomfort was so acute that sleep proved to be increasingly elusive. She kicked off the blankets, drank some water and threw a wet cloth over her eyes in an effort to cool off and get some rest.

At the point where the fine line between wakefulness and slumber was blurred, the pendant turned white hot, summoning her to a state of high alert, pulsing with a kind of desperate urgency. Minothi had not felt it since that one time after the gurvi's passing, and she sprang to her feet in answer to her beloved mentor's call, her blood hearkening to the call of possible adventure.

She snatched the pendant from her neck and turned it around in her hand, willing it to show her a way out of the morass of tedium that she was entrapped in. For a long few seconds, nothing happened.

Scarcely able to breathe, Minothi prayed that this time the waiting would not prove to be anticlimactic. She swore to herself that if that were the case, she would raze the math to the ground and disappear screaming into the darkness of the night. When she held it in the palm of her hand, willing it to help her, white light flared, and she felt it drawing her within, to the secrets that were about to be revealed to her.

Still in her nightgown, with the pendant clutched tightly in the palm of her hand, she was floating, past her sleeping sisters, through the walls of her dormitory and over the stone-lined pathway she knew so well. Suspended high in the air, Minothi took in the contours of the math as she soared past the meditation hall, the refectory and the kitchen, guided by the light of a waning sickle-shaped moon. Bundled up in a remote corner of the math, amidst a thick copse of silver oak trees, were the infirmary and the nursery. Only the oldest, youngest and sickest of them all were housed there.

Everything was happening too fast, and Minothi could scarce take it in as she sailed through the air, exhilaration coursing through her veins and effectively subduing the instincts that were screaming a warning. She soared past the locked door and found herself in the corridor leading to the nursery.

Her heart almost stopped beating when Nirmala atti, the demon spawn's right hand, walked right through her in an almighty hurry. She felt like cobwebs and smelled of rotten fruit. Minothi gagged, and the woman paused and looked over her shoulder in sudden alarm, before shaking her head and walking on.

There was a row of empty cots in the nursery. A few abandoned cribs lay in a corner. It was hardly surprising. Over the last few years, the number of babies left in the hut outside the math had dwindled to almost nothing. Their way of life had few takers in the modern world, and Trishana had insisted it was a good thing. In recent times, most of the younglings were so weak and malnourished from the arduous journey to the math that they did not survive long. Their caregivers had been devastated, reduced to hysterical fits and bouts of intense weeping.

Angered over the emotional derailment on display, the demon spawn declared that henceforth nursery duties would be handled only by the more experienced Kanyas who rounded off her coterie and were almost as cruel and callous as she was. Nirmala atti was one of them, despite being the healer in charge. At the time, the youngest Kanya was twelve years old, and the nursery lay empty and unused.

The mellifluous sounds of children laughing, singing rhymes, and the pitter-patter of their little feet, which had delighted them in Gurvi Sampoorna's time, were no longer heard in the math as it took on an increasingly spectral and sombre ambience. Minothi wondered why she had been brought under such remarkable circumstances to an empty nursery. But within moments she had her answer.

Her incorporeal form sank without warning through the wooden floorboards, and she almost cried out in fright as she descended into a massive subterranean chamber that stretched as far as the eye could see. Lit torches were stuck in brackets in the wall, and they cast a smoky pall over the place, illuminating almost as much as they concealed within their shadows.

The initial rush she had experienced in the wake of her nocturnal adventure plummeted during the course of her descent, leaving her feeling drained, mentally and emotionally. That was when abject terror stole up her spine, radiating through her nervous system with a throbbing intensity, and she was unable to breathe or even fully process what she was seeing.

There were about thirty cots arranged in neat rows, and only five were empty. Children between the ages of two and ten lay on—or rather, were tied down to—the little beds. They looked wan and listless, almost corpse-like on the hard mattresses where they had been imprisoned for almost all their young lives. The entire place reeked. Minothi noticed the stained sheets and overflowing chamber pots, which made her gag.

Bony chests heaving, rising and falling with rhythmic precision, were the only indicator that life had not yet been extinguished. Puffy lips that were cracked and peeling lay half-open as tiny tongues flicked out in steady nervous tics, trying desperately to moisten them. Some thrashed about, their limbs violently akimbo as the pieces of knotted cloth held them firmly in place. Many slept the sleep of the drugged, and Minothi suspected they had been sedated.

At the far end of the underground cellar, there were shelves cut into the wall, with wooden worktables and benches below. The shelves were lined with bowls, bottles and jars, liberally stocked with powdered herbs, spices, medicines, plant products and animal fat. Mortars and pestles of varying shapes and sizes, weighing scales, bronze vessels, earthen plates, measuring vats, blankets and cooking utensils were arranged neatly on the remaining shelves and tables.

Pitchers of milk, honey and ghee had been covered and placed in the cool corners of the cellar, away from the wood furnace, which was blazing away to provide a degree of warmth in the icy underground chamber. A huge pile of split logs had been assembled and placed nearby for immediate use.

Blunt and sharp instruments, animal bladders and horns, metal rods, cotton swabs, hollow gourds, suturing threads, binding ropes and cylindrical stones were some of the scarier implements on display. Several breeds of poisonous leeches had been placed in huge mud jars filled with water. They used these creatures for bloodletting in the infirmary, and Minothi could identify at least three poisonous breeds—samudrika, karvura and indrayuda—thanks to Trishana, who had an unholy terror of the bloodsuckers and had made it her business to know her enemy.

But what got to her the most were the huge, furry rats locked in wooden crates. She could feel her flesh crawl and feel the revulsion mirrored in those malevolent eyes as they stared up at her silently, tails whipping across the bottom. Her mind refused to consider what probable purpose the vermin were to serve.

Horror settled in the pit of her stomach and her head throbbed painfully as her brain overheated, trying to take in the unspeakable evil she was witnessing. How could she have been so criminally blind and negligent? A long time ago, back when Gurvi Sampoorna had been with them, she had read about the underground cellar in an old journal that had been unearthed, thanks to her efforts to know more about the history of the math.

The records were kept in the gurvi's private study and went back as far as the seventh century CE. But they had been woefully neglected and were in dismal shape. The palm-leaf sheaves, which had been threaded together, had almost completely disintegrated. The inscriptions had crumpled in places and were impossible to decipher.

Minothi had been given the task of salvaging what information she could and record it on paper. It was a laborious task but one she had enjoyed immensely. Gurvi Sampoorna's predecessors had clearly not had her vision and foresight, judging by the haphazard records they had kept, but there was one exception to the rule. Gurvi Meghalai, who had been in charge sometime in the seventeenth century, had assigned a similar chore to a young Kanya, who had acted as the resident scribe and historian.

The meticulous notes she had made were fascinating to read. The history of the math as well as the events of their time had been noted. While perusing her chronicles, Minothi had found something supremely interesting but had been disappointed with the brevity as well as the incomplete nature of the notes. The sordid saga had taken place a few hundred years ago, and the dates were imprecise.

The scribe had written of a secret passage that had been tunnelled under the math a long time ago, connecting it to the summer residence of the king, by order of the *rajamatha*, or queen mother, one Akhilandeshwari. Apparently, the dowager had used it to visit the math regularly in the company of her handmaidens.

She had been a terrifying personage. On her orders, a few Kanyas who had been hand-picked would be raised as veshas. The chosen ones would be fed on the root of the karavira plant, which had poisonous properties, although it was used to treat scorpion stings and snakebites. The trick lay in the dosage, and the children were given increasingly strong doses till it mingled with the blood and made it venomous, while strengthening their heart and eyes, making them stronger and keener.

Their diet included toxins extracted from various roots, fruits, tubers and stems, as well as other substances with known poisonous properties, such as the infamous svetapushpah and rakthapushpah, the white and red flowers of the oleander plant. In addition to this, they were also fed the venom culled from snakes, scorpions and a few breeds of poisonous fish.

All this resulted in rendering their very touch nocuous. The veshas were then sent on covert operations to take down the enemies of the king before being put to the sword themselves. These activities were brought to an abrupt halt when the king's enemies, spearheaded by a rival ruler named Nedumaran, finally formed an alliance and defeated him in battle.

The rajamatha sent for the veshas in the dead of the night and they were escorted from the math by her heavily armed handmaidens. Nobody knew what became of them after that. The scribe made no further reference to the terrible evil perpetrated at the math. It made Minothi want to pull out her hair in abject frustration as her morbid curiosity had been left unsatisfied.

At the time, she had driven herself into a frenzy trying to find more information on the subject until finally the gurvi herself had bade her to stop. 'It may or may not have happened, child, but when confronted with evil of this magnitude it is best to step aside rather than stare too deeply into its depths. Vice has certain addictive qualities that tend to exert an unholy attraction on the viewer, mesmerizing with its macabre allure while seducing the unwary into its forbidden and sticky clutches till there is no going back!'

Minothi had been reluctant initially, but she had obeyed. Slowly, it had retreated into the forgotten hallways of her memory where she had banished it, dismissing it as the concoction of a diseased mind. On the gurvi's instructions, she had spoken about it to no one, not even Trishana.

A tidal wave of guilt crashed into her, and she felt dizzy as her eyes once again took in the nightmarish scene. So many children had been killed or, worse, restructured as monstrous weapons of destruction, while their sisters remained oblivious to their plight. The Kanyas had been obsessed with the trivial minutiae of their own pathetic lives, to the detriment of all else, and the blood of innocents now stained their hands.

Her head felt like it was going to explode, and she shook it, trying to clear it. Hearing a sound, she looked up. It was the demon spawn and her boon companion Nirmala atti, their faces revealed by the light of the torches they carried. They were descending down a steep flight of steps made with well-seasoned wooden beams.

'Don't tell me that more are dying on us!' the demon spawn barked in a voice that could make ears bleed. 'I emphasized the importance of getting the dosages right. How hard can it be for you lot to follow a few simple instructions?' She was a tall, heavyset and robust woman of about forty-eight. One of those women whose face was a dead giveaway of the fact that she was the very depository of vice. Her countenance was toad-like, with beady eyes that seemed always to glare and flabby lips set in a perpetual snarl.

Her companion registered varying degrees of surliness on her visage and glowered at the kids as if it were their fault that they were not thriving on a steady diet of poisons. Nirmala atti was a short, squat woman who had become obscenely fat. She was fifty-six, and wore her thinning hair in a tight, well-oiled plait that accentuated her badly receding hair and impossibly rugose skin. Her sari was usually loosely draped to proudly display the fact that she cared not a whit about the fact that her fleshy, oversized boobs were sagging and resting on a protuberant belly that had at least three tyres too many.

The duo inspected the beds and Nirmala atti pointed out the ones that would not make it past that night. There were twelve of them. 'We have been following your instructions down to the last letter. In the beginning, they are given extracts from powdered roots, tubers, barks, pith and then minerals in tiny portions. There were mild symptoms on display like an aching head, parched mouth, increased body temperature and fainting spells, which subsided within a day or two, after cold compresses were steadily applied over their faces, necks and chests, coupled with plenty of hydration.

'Others showed more severe symptoms—vomiting, phlegmy secretions from their orifices, delirium and dysentery. They also complained of chest pain, a burning sensation in the stomach and severe headaches. The worst cases suffered from convulsions and seizures.'

The demon spawn Ananthamma responded angrily, 'They ought to have been given vinegar and lemon juice every half hour while the things they had ingested were still being digested, to counter the effects while allowing it to be assimilated by the body. The limbs should have been rubbed down with cold flannels, and sesame oil massaged on to the belly to soothe the body, to bring down the temperature and allay the irritants the system has been exposed to.

'The problem is that you are all a bunch of lazy cows who would rather plant their fat backsides on cushy chairs and eat themselves silly than work hard to discharge the duties given them! Have you forgotten what is at stake? We have sworn our undying allegiance to the one whose name we are not worthy enough to utter. We must do as he asks. Do I have to remind you that he hates being disappointed?'

The demon spawn was breathing hard, and Nirmala atti was looking increasingly sour. 'It is not our fault that these accursed brats come from poor stock and are the products of bad blood! They are all weak little runts and not worth the effort we are expending on them. We did follow the prescribed measures. And when they failed to work, we gave them mouthfuls of pure water of ammonia. In extreme cases, we bled them carefully from the arm. The leeches were also used to let out the bad humours but, as I said, their bodies are not strong enough to turn things around.

'The good news is that five of them are adapting well to the rigours of the regime, and another three will join them soon. They will soon be ready for the venom we have gathered from the snakes, scorpions, centipedes, as well as rat semen.'

'Good! I want them monitored throughout. Watch out for swellings, lesions, respiratory disturbances, irregular palpitations, impaired vision and poor hearing. Bleeding from the ears and nose is also a bad sign. Make sure there are sufficient quantities of pure water of ammonia, honey and coconut milk. Bleed them carefully from the jugular vein if things get out of hand. Be on constant vigil. I will not have them dying on me!

'As for the hopeless cases, remember what I have stressed on countless times in the past. Be sure to toss them into the garbage pits and burn the remains immediately. I want somebody stationed there till nothing remains.'

'It will be as you wish, gurvi! I will personally oversee things here and make sure that reports are made to you by the hour.' The gurvi nodded curtly, and this emboldened Nirmala to speak up: 'When can we expect that remarkable man, gurvi? Will it be soon?' Her eagerness was a palpable thing and her mammoth mammaries heaved in pleasurable anticipation.

The gurvi's response was sharp, 'Why don't you rein it in, like the chaste Kanya you are supposed to be? The last thing I want is an encore of that disgusting episode with that sex-starved vixen Trishana and the vulgar shenanigans she got up to with Veera! We are here to serve the master's wishes and make his vision for the future a reality. But that does not mean we have to forget our vows and uncross our legs for the master's minions.

'It is not what the master would wish either, which is why he never sends the same one twice. Veera is an exception, I'll accept, and it is not my place to question the master's decisions, for wild and unruly though he may be, the Hataka clearly gets results. It is a source of great shame to me that the same cannot be said about you lot despite the discipline and exacting methodology I have strived to inculcate in you!'

When Minothi heard her friend's name, the blood rushed to her head, boiling over with the heat of the rage that had lain dormant and impotent for so long, drowning all else in the course of its chaotic ascent. The fanatical gleam in the gurvi's eyes, the sight of Nirmala atti adjusting her sari to show off her belly fat to better advantage, the mean-looking rodents in their wooden cages, those leeches lying in the water and the surgical instruments arrayed with such precision drove her to an uncontrollable rage.

Something buried deep within her surged to life, snapping the iron restraints she had placed on it as if they were made of paper, revelling in the fresh lease of life given to it after aeons of imprisonment, which had only sharpened its potency, making it that much more savage. Her pendant pulsated urgently in warning, but she was no longer under its power, and her own magic flung it aside.

The magic broke free and she gathered it to herself with fierce joy before releasing it in a deadly strike. Black smoke issued from her chest, spreading over everything in an oily stain, destroying everything it touched with its grasping tendrils.

A strange keening spilled out from her lips, a deadly siren call of destruction. It sprang forth from her pain and guilt, gained momentum from her despair and grew strong feeding on her latent rage. The glass jars and bottles shattered at once, flinging deadly shards at everything. Nirmala atti was covering her ears and trying to shield herself from that terrible smoke that wrapped itself about her exposed body, swirling in mad spirals and peeling the skin off. On and on it went till Nirmala atti was lifted off her feet, the grotesque form suspended in mid-air, and her chest exploded in a hot geyser of blood.

Bronze vessels, plates, surgical implements and metal rods were dislodged from their secure spaces on the shelves and careened into the beds bearing the children. The little ones shrieked, struggling against their restraints, convulsing as the whites of their eyes alone showed, biting on their tongues and going absolutely berserk with terror.

The sound of running footsteps could be heard as four of the demon spawn's minions came tearing down the stairs to see what the ruckus was all about. They did not make it all the way down. The magic stopped them in their tracks, and the black smoke consumed them. They went to their deaths fighting its embrace and feeling the pressure of the infernal wailing build before it ripped their hearts out.

Ananthamma advanced on her, tearing off the tendrils that grabbed at her, wielding a cauldron and flinging the boiling contents in all directions. Then she flung the empty vessel at the monster who stood poised to undo all the hard work she had put in to make her master's hopes for a better future come true. But the magic cast it aside and swallowed the dreadful epithets she was hurling at Minothi before slamming into her. A black cloud lifted her bodily off her feet, consuming her whole before it spat out hundreds of little pieces of her mortal remains.

The ancient buildings of Sivagami Math quaked as their foundations rumbled. Minothi rose up into the air, a typhoon of unstoppable destruction. Her magic building on itself till it was relentless as a tidal wave. Entire chunks of the buildings collapsed on the sleeping residents, who woke up screaming in terror before death closed in on them. The others shut their ears to the other-worldly vocal emissions that soared to the stratosphere, enveloping them in a shroud of unbearable pain. Unable to stand it, many banged their heads on the stone wall till their bashed and bloodied brains allowed them to hear no more.

Minothi saw the destruction through the thinning haze of her formerly unstoppable fury. Heaps of rubble were all that remained of the math. The light of life had been extinguished from it, and the souls it had contained had departed on the dark journey to Yama's court. The paroxysmal shrieking that had bespoken so much anguish subsided into a plaintive moaning, a dying whimper as its owner was left crumpled and utterly broken.

She collapsed on the smoking ruins and rocky remains, welcoming the pain as the sharp edges sliced her shoulder and cut into her back. Unable to take in the sight of the destruction she had single-handedly wrought, she fled from the monster she now knew she was. There was nowhere to run, but she ran from herself till the blackness mercifully closed in on her.

He found her like that, catatonic, bleeding and curled up on the remnants of her rage gone rogue. His non-committal gaze scanned the field of debris. Boulders, smashed rocks, splintered wood, pieces of cutlery and metal rods, the fractured bones of the ancient math were all that remained. It was hard to believe that the chubby, diminutive child-woman, who looked every bit the drooling imbecile, had been the architect of such complete and irrevocable gloom.

She did not resist when he bound her wrists and ankles after gagging her. When he had emerged from the secret passage, long hours after the annihilation of the math, it had taken him a while to clear a pathway through the rubble. He threw her over his shoulder like a rag doll before retracing his footsteps. Without a backward glance, he descended into the inky blackness below, taking her with him. Within moments, the darkness had taken them both into its hidden depths.

24

Journeyers

Dharami was still mad at him and was being stubbornly reticent despite his many attempts to get her to engage in conversation. She was probably still smarting from his response to her appearance, or because she claimed he had once tried to kill her. As for the former, he would have liked to tell her that it did not bother him in the least. About the alleged attempt on her life, knowing her as he did, she had in all likelihood pushed him to it and more than earned it.

It had been a long time since he had cared or even thought about his own looks. Doing what he did, it was hard not to know that the outside of things mattered not at all. It was all the odds, ends and unmentionables within, with their capacity to light the path for others or warm them with kindness when the going got rough, that mattered. He owed her so much, not only for saving his life but also for being at his side on the dangerous quest he had been asked to undertake.

But he said nothing. There were other far more important things to focus on, like how not to get killed while on an extremely dangerous journey through a tortuous terrain.

Agni had to leave his bike behind once they made their way deep into the woods known as Bandavana that fronted the hills they had to scale. He did so with exceedingly ill grace.

With a doleful air, which made Dharami impatient, he concealed it as best as he could in an abandoned warehouse on the fringes of the woods, hoping against hope that it would escape the notice of petty larcenists. The land spirit accompanied him for a short while in terse silence before he heard her voice in his head: 'I am going to go ahead and study the lay of the land some more. Ever since Taravarsha asked me to keep an eye on the math, and the Hataka who calls himself Veera, I have done my best to do so. He is a canny one, and I am yet to figure out what he does at the math, though I have spotted him there often enough.'

'There is something I wished to ask you about. It has been a while since it fell to me to hunt down the arakshas but I am familiar with their ways. But the last time they laid out a trap for me, I wound up poisoned and at death's door. What was that all about? Is it connected to the missing girls and the math?'

Dharami nodded. 'My guess is that the arakshas were released by the necromancer and fed on the poisonous blood of veshas. They probably coated their weapons with the stuff as well. Clearly, he considers you a threat if he is going to such lengths to have you killed. In fact, it is the very thing that reinforces my own confidence in Yama's lieutenant, especially at times when he sobs like a baby over a beat-up two-wheeler or needs me to bail him out of the ugly messes he is always getting into.'

She waited for him to rise to the bait, but when he didn't, she pressed on, 'As you have correctly surmised, the missing girls, lost babies and veshas are all linked to the math. The necromancer's lapdog Veera is behind it. I am sure of it.

'Since he can operate only through the mortal coil he has taken for himself, the Hataka would have to make his way through Bandavana, except I have never ever seen him in these parts. There must be another way concealed from us, and I am going to try and see if I can find it.'

'You do that,' Agni said distractedly. Bandavana loomed ahead of him, a solid wall of trees that invited him to step into its domain and out of the world he had always known. He did not fancy venturing in there and spoke quickly to take his mind off it. 'What puzzles me is the role of the Kritya in all this. If her fellow Kanyas are running a trafficking ring in the math, poisoning little girls and selling off babies to a cannibalistic sorcerer, surely she ought to have put a stop to it? Since she hasn't done anything of the sort, it makes me wonder.'

'I am aware of your propensity to assume the worst about the members of the fairer sex who have been thrust into your life,' she said, her voice hard, 'but the Kritya has not used her magic and that means she is almost as clueless as you are about both her powers and the shadowy happenings in the math. We will find out soon enough.

'In the meantime, follow a north-easterly course till you stumble upon Yatupava—a wicked stretch of marshland, which is about three days of hard travelling away. Be wary of Bandavana; it means "forest of monsters" in the parlance of a bygone age, and it is not advisable for the living to venture into it. There are creatures slumbering there that must not be tangled with. Yatupava is even worse, and under no circumstances are you to risk your way through it even though it will cut the travel time in half. You need to make your way around it and on cat's feet at that, till you arrive at an almost non-existent trail, which is hard to find if one is not looking precisely for it. It winds upwards through the hills, leading into Maroli. I'll be waiting for you there.'

'I'll see you then! Good luck to you, Dharami!' he said breezily. 'Hope you are able to manage without a strong man to watch over you.' To his satisfaction, she sputtered at his dig, and he walked into no man's land with a faint smile on his lips.

As she watched him walk forwards, backpack slung over his shoulder, with that loose saunter that was somehow elegant, indignation gave way to apprehension. Dharami wondered if she should have warned him about the *raktavarttas* and *suchayalas*. The problem was that he had such a cynical and fatalistic bent of mind that it was risky to tell him about the blood fiends or the monsters that were unmatched in terms of sheer ferocity.

His mind would have dwelt on them constantly and, brave though he may be, the apprehension he was sure to feel at some point would act like the whiff of blood that predatory creatures like them would be irresistibly drawn to. It was better this way. If he followed the directions she had given him, he would be able to escape the *varttas* altogether. As for the *yalas*, she had not yet sighted one and, hopefully, they were extinct.

There was no use in brooding over a decision already made. Agni had his magic to protect him and, mercifully, some of her sharp intellect had rubbed off on him. The best thing she could do for him was to hurry over to the math and find a way to unlock its mysteries and unmask the Kritya before Veera zeroed in on her.

A host of vyada birds descended on Bandavana, some way off in the distance. They were raptorial creatures, and their cries sounded like shrieks of demonic laughter. It was not the best of omens for Agni, who had already disappeared into forbidden territory where he was unwelcome, and Dharami murmured a quick prayer to the gods to keep him safe. She had already cast a protective spell over him. It had to be enough.

Agni was already missing Dharami, crotchety though she was on the best of days. The woods were dank and dismal. Dense brush and trees of towering mahogany, teak and rosewood clustered so thickly it was practically impossible to see the sky or even draw a measure of comfort from the familiar sight of the sun, moon or stars.

Thick bark-like roots growing in gnarly clusters on the uneven surface attempted to trip him up. Impossibly tall trees with massively girthed trunks barred his passage. Low-hanging branches stooped grotesquely and spiny leaves struck him across the shoulders or slapped him on the face. Brambles, prickly shrubs and thorny plants grew with wild abandon and made it rough going. Large, virulent spiders scurried across the branches; Agni suspected they were poisonous. He tried to ignore the inescapable feeling that they were crawling all over him, feeling him up, and worse, with their furry legs.

Soon it began to drizzle and kept up for nearly two days. Agni forgot what it was like to be dry and comfortable. He had no appetite, and the biscuits, energy bars and cheese he had brought along remained unopened. When he stopped infrequently to rest, nightmares plagued him, and he woke up just when the evil things that had circled him in sleep had closed in for the kill.

The rain kept up but Agni forced himself to carry on. He wrinkled his nose at the smell of the moist, rotting vegetation and the dead scrub that choked the muddy streams. The ground became uneven, soft and yielding under his feet, a clear indicator that the marshes Dharami had advised him to skirt were close. Shadows danced about everywhere, teasing and taunting him with veiled hints of the things they concealed. He heard the incessant rustling of the vegetation, the occasional snarl of a predator, calls of birds and the chittering of insects.

He could see Yatupava stretched out ahead of him, a slovenly, snoozing organism with patches of weeds that thrived on the slimy water that lay spread thinly on the menacing mud that belched and farted, slowly feeding on the trees that stood bent almost double and dying, as their waterlogged roots eroded steadily. Large insectivorous plants waited, their leaves spread invitingly in the manner of diseased whores, wafting their sickly sweet odours and displaying their brightly coloured flowers to lure unwary insects.

Carefully, he walked around it, placing his feet only when the shifting surface beneath him felt firm enough to walk on. The rain stopped as suddenly as it had begun. Steam rose in a sulphurous cloud and Agni could barely breathe. Leeches somehow found a way past the denim and socks he wore. He became aware of them only when they had drunk their fill and fell off, only to be trod underfoot as he exacted a bloody revenge.

The insects ignored the industrial-strength repellent he had slathered over every visible bit of skin and worried him endlessly, some tiny as gnats and others as large as a fist. He cussed silently and wished he could gather them together and personally feed them to the hungry plants that dotted the marsh. Lashing together thick but pliant pieces of bark, he fashioned protective gear to wear beneath his knees and arms to ward off the insects and protect himself from the unusually colourful snakes that slithered past. They did serve the purpose, but underneath Agni was uncomfortably hot.

Every so often he heard the hissing of bigger snakes or saw evidence of ecdysis. Catlike creatures scampered up the trees faster than the eye could follow, furtive and ever so quick. The spoor he found indicated that there were other more massive creatures concealed in the gloom. He heard their feral grunts but not once did he actually see any of them, though he was on high alert and his eyes were sharper than most. Bats winged past, making for the canopy afforded by the giant trees.

There was something about this place. Like its name suggested, it seemed to have materialized from the realms of myth and fantasy, where monsters roamed at will. For a long time now, Agni had felt isolated and cut off from the world he inhabited, but here, far away from the familiar trappings of civilization, the transition was complete, and Agni felt more alone than he ever had.

Visibility was poor, and the light was always pale and diffused. During the day, the volcanic heat was so oppressive that his light T-shirt became soaked with sweat. At night, the temperature plummeted without warning, leaving him shivering and uncomfortable.

Anxious to be clear of this stretch and make it to the pass Dharami had told him about in order to make the ascent, Agni trudged on, stopping only to eat the sorry fare he had thrown together and rest his eyes briefly. The days rolled on, indistinguishable from each other, and he started to feel trapped, with no way out. Dharami was nowhere to be seen and, try as he might, he could not get rid of the feeling of doom that enveloped him.

One morning, trudging on, he wondered if he had misheard the directions Dharami had given him and had got hopelessly lost. It was a very real possibility since it was impossible to get his bearings without any help from the sun or stars. The air was so muggy that he may as well have been in a fuggy sauna. Agni could not see beyond fifty feet, nor chart the progress he was making despite being a seasoned trekker. There was no clear course to follow, and everything in that accursed place seemed to grow in a confused mess with scarcely any rhyme or reason.

Agni stopped. The air around him had gone still. The incessant buzzing of his irksome winged companions, interspersed with the odd rustle, hissing or growling from the denizens of Bandavana, had ceased abruptly. There was something lurking out there but he could not pinpoint its location. With his back against a massive oak, he waited.

The thoughts that had been whirling moments ago retreated, leaving a purposeful calm in their wake. Gently, he summoned the magic and the danda materialized in his hand, an old friend and a fellow veteran of shared battles. The creature appeared on his left side, a massive and bristling thing.

It looked like a grey pincushion with long quills about three to five feet protruding from its back and sides, perched on stout limbs that were muscular and clawed. The thing was much too big to be a regular porcupine, and the rest of its body was protected by armour-plate hide. Its leathery muzzle was drawn back to reveal rows of sharp teeth.

Bending low and stamping angrily as if it meant to charge, the thing unloosed its impossibly large and curved quills. They flew through the air, a deadly hailstorm of arrows slicing through the leaves and grass with the ripping sound of a pair of rough shears. The danda pulsed with a reddish glow and Agni moved like lightning, cutting and parrying the deadly quills, slicing or turning them away so they fell harmlessly to the forest floor or got embedded in the thick barks. His drawn face was imperturbable, but the eyes were curiously animated and they flashed with cold intensity.

His movements were effortless as he performed the dance of the warrior, his steps liquid and graceful. A single misstep meant death, but he never faltered, and the danda was an extension of his arm as they worked in perfect harmony.

But the danger was not past and Quills, maddened by his dance of precision, charged at him, snorting with fury. It moved swiftly for a creature of its bulk and closed the distance between them well before Agni had fended off the quills. Rather than make the futile attempt to step aside, he dropped to his knees and slid under its armoured belly. The danda once again flared to life and red fire burst forth, hammering into its underbelly, tossing up the creature mid-air and flinging it aside.

Agni held the danda steady, the red fire tearing into the monster in a relentless attack, but Quills got to its feet in one smooth motion, its muscled limbs rippling. It came at him again, deftly dodging the flames, and in the time it took him to bring the danda to bear, it dealt him a powerful blow with a clawed foreleg before the red fire tossed it aside, and Agni felt his flesh rip at the flank.

Gritting his teeth against the stabbing pain as his head snapped back in agony, he prepared for the next charge, balancing on the balls of his feet and ignoring the pain that raked his side. Quills circled him in anticipation, sensing him weakening. Agni knew it was a supernatural monster that hunted merely for the thrill, not sustenance.

Launching a savage offensive, Agni moved first and took the attack to the creature. He hurled the pasha around its thick neck in a single fluid motion, at the vulnerable spot between the bristly head and the armoured hide. Tightening it steadily as Quills reared back with a furious whipping motion, he might have been dragged off his feet, but he went with its momentum, allowing his heels to slide towards it, never releasing his hold, though his arms were nearly ripped out of the sockets.

Then, when he was so close he could see the thick, grey hairs that stood out from its heaving nostrils and smell the rank odour of its foul maw, he stuck his danda in the creature's eye, and the red flames lasered in and its head exploded. Nimbly, Agni stepped aside as Quills rocked on those massive limbs, as though preparing for a fresh charge, before it dropped down with a heavy thud.

Agni stood still for a moment, feeling light-headed and drained. The magic always did it to him. He tried to remain clinically detached and pretend that it was just another weapon. But it was intoxicating and he felt invincible. Every time he brought the magic successfully to bear, he was a god on earth and more. It was the elixir of immortality, and he wanted to get drunk on it and stay that way forever.

When he wielded the magic, there were absolutely no doubts to plague his every waking thought. More importantly, the terrible wound he had sustained with Varu's passing no longer throbbed with intolerable pain. When he wielded the magic, life was good.

The feeling passed quickly, leaving him feeling hollowed out, empty and ridiculously close to tears. Reeling like a drunk man, he stumbled away from the spot. Where was Dharami? And would he ever be clear of the accursed marshes?

Thinking of the devil made him pause. He wondered if she had told him nothing about the supernatural creature that had attacked him simply because she was aware that a part of him would have welcomed the chance to use the magic? The thought depressed him and he dropped to his knees against a large tree, praying that sleep would claim him before his fears did.

25

From Varu's Book: Between the Sheets

There were a lot of females who were enamoured by Yama's burgeoning masculine beauty. His classically sculpted features, impressive physique and magnetic persona made him irresistible to the opposite sex as well as his own. Chaya had found the twins to be obnoxious brats as youngsters, but though she still detested Yami, her feelings for Yama had altered. She was not impervious to his physical charms, but what drew her to him was his innate kindness.

Yama was the quintessential nice guy who treated everybody well. He adored his stepsister Tapati, and she responded in kind, declaring on more occasions than anybody cared to count that he was her favourite person in all of heaven. The baby was quite the chatterbox, and he listened patiently to her endless yammering when he was not playing silly games with her and her brother, Manu Suvarni.

But that was not all, Yama was the only person in the entire celestial kingdom who could not only withstand the baleful influence of her firstborn, Sani, but seemed to have a strange affinity with him as well. Yami, in contrast, was nice enough to the three younger children but she was too self-involved to take them under her wing the way Yama did.

'Yami is a snooty little bitch for not giving my children the time of day, and Yama is a master of manipulation,' Chaya would think to herself whenever anybody complimented her on the friendly rapport all the siblings seemed to share. 'The only reason he puts up such an elaborate charade of cloying affection is to make me look petty and mean-spirited by comparison. Then he and his father along with the rest of the judgemental busybodies around here will feel perfectly justified in looking down at me as if I were the typical nightmarish mother who favours one child over another!'

Despite her thoughts on the matter and her cold hauteur towards him, Chaya found herself taking umbrage at the fact that he continued being nice to all the inhabitants of heaven to the sole exception of herself. She grew increasingly resentful of the fact that he could love everybody unconditionally but treated her as though she were a piece of dog turd that had befouled the convivial atmosphere of the palace.

'I may not have been the best mother to Sanjana's children,' Chaya thought defensively to herself, although she wanted nothing more than to pour her heart out to anyone who would listen, knowing that there was nobody, 'but that self-righteous bastard ought to give me the benefit of the doubt, because there are certain mitigating circumstances in this case that he knows nothing about. His mother is the devil, not me! She abandoned them while I stayed behind to do my best for them.

'And it is not like his twin is the most perfect specimen of flawless femininity in Indralokha. She is moody, bad-tempered, foul-mouthed and a drama queen if there ever was one. But you wouldn't know it from the way Yama and his father moon over her, embracing her flaws as ardently as they do her virtues!

'If that is not enough to make me want to kill myself or, better yet, their precious Yami, both father and son are perfect beasts to me! Yama gives me a wide berth as if afraid of catching something potentially fatal by breathing the same air as me. Surya, my dear lord, is even worse. To him I am part maid and part whore, to be used and discarded as he sees fit.

'Even when we make love, I am supposed to lie still like a corpse while he pumps away at me, avoiding my eyes and my lips, calling out another's name while he spills his seed into me. When he is done, he leaves my bedside in an indecent hurry, leaving me feeling soiled and used.'

Chaya's eyes were wet with tears, and she had to bite her knuckles to stop herself from keening and wailing like a wounded animal. Before this life had been thrust on her, she had been neither happy nor unhappy. It was only belatedly that she had realized that such a state was a lot more bearable than her current mindset, in which rage, frustration and misery were her constant and only companions.

She hated the weak, pathetic and snivelling thing she had been reduced to, but even painful awareness was not enough to snap her out of it. All she wanted was for Yama to look at her the way he did his beloved sister and make her feel equally cherished. The need grew to such unbearable heights that she could scarcely bear it. Since such a thing seemed unattainable, she wished Yama were dead so that Yami would be deprived of him too.

When Yama was at the gurukula, Yami missed him so much, it left her with a palpable aura of misery, which delighted Chaya, although it did little to alleviate her own emptiness. Perhaps it was the reason why she awaited his infrequent visits with an ardour that rivalled his twin's. It was on one such occasion that she made an incalculable error in judgement that proved very nearly to be her undoing. She had been surprised at how happy seeing him in the palace again had made her. That night, on her instructions, a feast had been prepared to welcome him back. At its conclusion, Yama had thanked her politely, eschewing his usual practice of keeping his interaction with her to a bare minimum to look into her eyes for a fraction of a second.

Chaya had been so happy, it was ridiculous. That night, driven by the inner madness he had unwittingly awakened, she took a perfumed bath and dressed herself in her most alluring garments before taking herself to his private chambers. He was fast asleep and looked so handsome in repose that she could barely stand it. Gently, so as not to disturb his slumber, she crawled under the sheets to snuggle up next to him, almost like a child who had missed her mother. For a few blissful moments, with her breasts pressed against his muscular back, Chaya was perfectly content, and she could almost believe that elusive happiness was hers at last.

The sound of tiptoeing woke her from the light sleep she had slipped into. Panic flooded through her being, and she almost leaped off the bed and out of the window like a robber who would rather leap to death than answer for the crime. The mad impulse was stillborn when she saw who it was that had robbed her of the near-perfect bliss that had been hers short moments ago. It was Yami.

'Yama! Wake up!' his twin whispered, shaking him, not yet aware than anything was amiss. 'You are hardly ever home, and I cannot allow you to waste the little time we have sleeping like a lazy lump!'

Chaya struggled to free herself from the restricting sheets that held her fast like coils of rope. Yama woke up in a hurry and, sensing the alien presence in his bed, he kicked away blindly, and Chaya found herself in a heap on the floor, her clothes in disarray and her pride in tatters. The twins looked at her with identical shock on their faces, which turned quickly to horror and disgust.

Dormant rage surged to the surface, and Chaya sprang to her feet and pushed into Yami, her eyes flashing with fury. 'I did not believe the rumours but tonight you have proved that you are a stinking harlot who was born to bring infamy to the family name! What business could you possibly have in the male quarters at this hour of the night, when the virtuous ought to be asleep in their own beds?

'It is bad enough that you have gone astray, thanks to your raging libido, sharing your body with everything in possession of a phallus, from the bulls in their pens to the lowly stable hands, but now you seek to corrupt your brother as well, dragging him down to the depths of evil with you! You filthy whore . . .'

The twins were still in the throes of extreme shock, but when Yama heard the vile epithet hurled at his beloved sister, especially by one who had the gall to talk ill of his sister despite being the one caught in a compromising position, he lost control and kicked Chaya so hard in the gut that she went sprawling for the second time that night. Doubled over in pain and gasping for breath, she was still not done.

'Today, you have gone too far, Yama, in your misguided attempt to defend the slut who is eventually going to come to a bad end, make no mistake about that. For the grave sin of kicking your mother and one who has sacrificed so much for your sake, there is no escaping punishment. Everything that you hold dear, from the rays of the sun to this despicable trollop, will be lost forever to you. Darkness, death, decay and the dread sounds of damnation will be your only companions. When my words have come to pass, look back on this day and rue the actions you so thoughtlessly committed, that too for the sake of such a one as your sister! Repent for the rest of eternity, for there will be no undoing what you have done today.'

Spittle flew from her mouth from whence the acid sprayed forth, burning them all. Her chest heaved with the force of her passion, and her hair billowed madly in the wind that seemed to have been conjured from the blackness of her hate. Yami dropped to her knees and buried her face in her hands, unable to contemplate such a terrible thing coming to pass, praying fervently that Chaya's words would never come true.

Yama looked at the mother-who-wasn't with an even gaze, never flinching in the face of her fury. 'Do your worst, you evil bitch!' His words were a whiplash, but Chaya was too far gone to retreat and already hurting too badly for his words to get past the armour of hate and fury she had donned to protect herself. Her wrath not yet spent, she spat at him before stalking out of the room, pausing only to favour them with one last look of such malevolence that Yami began crying afresh and there was nothing Yama could say or do that offered her the slightest measure of comfort.

Not many knew exactly what had happened that night, but it was no secret that Surya summoned Chaya to his private chambers the very next day, grim of visage and bristling with suppressed rage. Once the door was firmly locked behind them, he struck her hard across the face without further ado and, grabbing her by the throat, lifted her bodily till she started to choke. Lowering her to the ground, he tightened his stranglehold on her throat, which had already turned an ugly shade of purple. 'Yama told me everything! No mother would accuse her own daughter of being a whore or curse her son in such a harsh manner, even if he had been guilty of a grave crime. You are lucky that I wasn't there, for nothing could have stopped me from choking the life out of you! Tell me who you are and what happened to my wife!'

Chaya prised off his hand and flung it disdainfully against him. 'I will tell you the truth! It was not I who fled from it all this time! There is no need for you to threaten me. Your wife ran away a long time and three children ago. Needless to say, it must not have been a very difficult choice given the fact that you are a cad and a brute! Nobody in their right mind would be able to spend a lifetime with you, without wishing themselves dead or being driven mad! There, I have said it, and you can beat me to death if you wish, but it cannot be unsaid.

'You don't have to look so shocked either! It is no secret that you continued to love her, though she played you for a fool and walked out on you as well as the children in the guise of a mare so that she could sport to her heart's content with the stallions. You did not mind wearing the cuckold's horns, just so long as you could pretend to have the perfect wife. It was enough to have someone who looked exactly like her to warm your sheets and bear your children, allowing you to escape the fact that the one you loved so dearly never felt the same way about you and escaped your clutches at the first opportunity that presented itself!'

'Keep talking! Give me a good reason to kill you where you stand.' There was no mistaking the menace or intent in his tone, and the fight went out of Chaya when she realized that if she kept pushing him, he would follow through on his threat to kill her.

When she finally spoke, she sounded as defeated as Surya looked. 'I have done my best by you and the children, but the situation always demanded more than I had to offer. As for Yami, she is her mother's daughter, with the same proclivity for licentiousness and disregard for decorum.

'The only reason I was there in that room was because it had come to my attention that she may just try to get her brother to sin. It is not the first time they have been seen in each other's private quarters at indecent hours. Despite your disapproval, she continues to spend time with the apsaras. The tales I could tell you about some of the other vices she has embraced! You can choose to ignore the facts about your darling daughter that are staring you in the face, or you can nip this evil in the bud before our family name is defiled!'

'Save your breath! I am well aware of how much you care about the well-being of this family.' Surya snapped at her, but tiredly, and Chaya heaved an inward sigh of relief. 'The next time you slander my daughter, I'll rip out your tongue. Even if she were the tramp you claim her to be, she'd still be twice the lady you are. I am going to look for my wife. You may leave or stay as you prefer.' And without a backward glance, Surya was gone.

Chaya crumpled to the floor, nearly dissolving in a fit of intense sobbing. She would never be able to forgive the lot of them for what they had done to her, or herself for swallowing her pride and staying despite having been cast aside. But there would be no more tears, she resolved fiercely to herself, wiping them away with the edge of her sari. There would be a day of reckoning, when Surya, Yama and Yami would pay for what they had done to her, and she sensed that it was not too far in the future.

• • •

Yama knew his sister very well. It would be just like her to dwell on the events of an unhappy night and worry herself into knots over a certain unfortunate affair, which he believed was best forgotten. He had contented himself with telling his father the gist of it, although he did not think it was his place to let him know that Chaya had been in his bed. Yama had no idea what to make of it and wondered if her plan had been to sink her fangs into him while he slept.

Worse was the slightest pang of guilt he was experiencing, although for the life of him he could not see how any of it could have been his fault. After all, to the best of his knowledge he had never sent her any signals intimating that she was welcome in his private chambers. It disturbed him to think about it, and Yama was content to leave the whole messy incident behind.

Yami was different, though, and she could not stop thinking or talking about it. It was well on the way to becoming an unhealthy obsession. 'Nothing lasts forever. Isn't that right, Yama? There are no exceptions to the rule. Those who believe in forever and ever are pathetic fools.

'What if the day comes when we become estranged? You will go on to become one of the protectors of the universe and a wielder of tremendous powers, busy with the cumbersome task of maintaining order in the three worlds. Father will marry me off, and I may be under the thumb of someone who is jealous of my affections and will frown upon the two of us being as close as we are now. Having been forced along entirely different paths, sooner or later we will not have the will to make the long commute back into each other's hearts, and we will feel lucky if we bump into each other during weddings or grand yajnas. It is inconceivable now, but what if we grow to hate each other? Such a thing is not without precedent.'

Yama held up his hand to stop the flow of her bruising words and shook his head disapprovingly at her. 'You should really watch that mouth of yours, Yami. Sometimes, you say these unspeakable things, as though by saying it out loud you can somehow prevent it from happening. Your attendants have told you that the wishes you make will never come true if you give voice to them and, being possessed of the most twisted mind there ever was, you have assumed that, by the same principle, you can make bad things go away by uttering them. That is not how it works though. When you speak evil, it will take that as an invitation into your life.

'I agree that even the strongest bonds of love are not unbreakable but that is neither here nor there. Just because there are siblings out there somewhere who have grown apart, been torn apart, or in enmity departed, it does not mean that we will join their ranks, although if you keep yammering about our impending separation, I can't promise that I'll be able to stop myself from throttling you!'

Yama stopped when he saw the troubled expression on her face and cursed Chaya for what she was putting them through. The ugly family secret was out, and their nebulous suspicions had been confirmed. Surya had belatedly made the effort to chase his runaway wife down, and by untold effort, managed to find her in the guise of a horse. But for Sanjana, returning to the suffocating existence she had fled from was not an option, so Surya transformed himself to seek his beloved's acceptance on her own terms. From their sporting, the Ashwini twins were born, and Surya divided his time between his duties and his old and new families as best as he could.

Yama had mixed feelings about it. Knowing that Sanjana had left him broke his heart but he hoped that she was happy wherever she was and, out of respect for her, would never mount a horse again. Yami was disgusted with her mother, and ashamed of her father, for sacrificing his dignity on the altar of foolish love. 'Don't you see that Chaya is the victim and the biggest casualty in mother and father's toxic love affair? And you had to compound her misery and humiliation by kicking her out of bed! It is a small wonder that she wants us all dead. They say that children have to pay the price for the sins of their parents the same way they have always felt entitled to the largesse of their labours. If that is true, then we deserve all the terrible things she wished for us!'

'Shut up, Yami! We don't deserve to be punished. My sharing a bed with her would have hardly made things better for any of us. Be careful about the things you believe in, Yami. Your beliefs will have power over you on account of the strength of your conviction. Believe in us, not the foul words of a bitter, disillusioned woman who seeks to drag others into the cesspool of her misery. Trust me when I say that her words will not come to pass. After all, she is not a muni who has spent an entire lifetime stockpiling ascetic merit to curse at will!'

'You're right, of course, although knowing that you are right is not going to make my reservations on this issue disappear like magic!' Yami told her brother. 'Aren't we the charming family, though? Mother runs away to be a horse, no less, to avoid a fate where she and father end up killing themselves, and leaves her shadow to look after us. A demon that feeds on the hearts and souls of the young would have been a better choice!

'But let us not talk of such things. It is too depressing. Let us just focus on the fact that your future is looking good, especially since you have been released from Brihaspati's gurukula without anything untoward happening, and you will be joining the army! It is only a matter of time before you are covered in glory, and every nubile female out there will cast her net, hoping to catch you. It is all very exciting! This is what we should have been discussing instead of all that talk of gloom and doom. With time, we'll forget all about our sordid family life and be as happy as we can possibly be.'

26

A Bridge of Flesh and Blood

Kashika was not the sort to feel sorry for herself and looked upon self-pity as the predominant character trait of unmitigated fools. But that said, her unusually long time on earth had put her through more than her fair share of hardships. She had lived long enough to see her dream come true, and lived even longer to see it all crumble into dust. But she was strong and regretted nothing. No matter what happened, she would always say, 'What will be will be and there's no point in crying over these things.'

Having earned the right to rest in peace for eternity, she had promptly shunned it. The great energy and the tremendous willpower that had helped her pull off seemingly miraculous things were not to be wasted on rest and relaxation, irrespective of whether she was alive and kicking, or not. 'Everything that is has already been. All things that grow and thrive will soon decay before their ultimate destruction. And that which has been destroyed will rise in order to flourish again before it dies again.' So she had instructed while alive, and she believed in the veracity of her words in the afterlife as well.

The dead, whether they are mourned, feared or forgotten, exercise a degree of power over the affairs of the living. Some bonds are unbreakable and even death can never hope to sunder them. Love and duty, hate and ill will, pain and rage have always had the capacity to transcend the end of a mortal life. But blood ties are the strongest of them all. For is there anything greater in the worlds of God and man to match the raw power of a mother's love?

Kashika was a pitrani. As an ancestral spirit she had watched over every one of her brood and their offspring as well. She cared for them all, but she had waited a long time for the one who carried in her blood the terrible gift only a few among them had been chosen to bear. Her patience had been rewarded, and the child of her spirit came into being, one of destiny's chosen ones, who would resurrect Kashika's dream all over again.

Unlike Kashika, her offspring, young Minothi, the bearer of earth magic, did not have many advantages going in. From the very beginning, she had been tossed into the deep end of the pool and left to sink or swim. These trials of strength were necessary. Unlike in Kashika's time, when the magic wielders had been many and had pooled their resources, this time around there would be just the one. Circumstances dictated that the combined strength of her heart, soul and mind had to be sufficient to fulfil the purposes for which she had been singled out.

Her travails and tribulations were the trials of strength and endurance that were meant to pare off the weaknesses in her character and prepare her for the price the magic always exacted, irrespective of the cause in which it was employed. But the girl was almost broken.

Horrified by the magic in her blood, Minothi had treated it like a disease-bearing organism and herself like the carrier, and tried to bury it deep within her. Needless to say, it had torn free in a cataclysmic explosion of the sort she had tried so desperately and foolishly to prevent. Unable to deal with the implications, Minothi had locked herself away from a reality she could not face and thrown away the key.

It was not possible to follow her down the dark path she had taken but her ancestor vowed to try. Gurvi Sampoorna had made contact with Kashika shortly before passing away and, on her instructions, kept Minothi close and built a bridge with her flesh, bones and eternal spirit to allow the pitrani a means to help her hopelessly lost descendant when the time came.

While Kashika waited, the Hataka Veera hefted Minothi across his shoulders with scant respect and carried her away into the tunnel below. Lost to everybody and everything, herself included, she was not in a position to process the indignity of her situation and allowed herself to be abducted.

Her kidnapper was repelled by her. All through the long journey through the tunnels that wound their way underneath Mount Maroli, twisting and turning like the entrails of a living organism, she lay passive, slack-jawed and drooling. Fed up of lugging her around, he plonked her on the floor and, untying the rope that had bound her feet, tied it around her neck. Using it like a leash, he dragged her along and she tarried behind him, a complaisant cur.

The shell that had once been Minothi still wore her thin, handwoven nightgown, which was so torn and tattered it no longer clothed her in the manner intended. She wore no shoes, and remained indifferent when her bare feet were shredded to pieces on the rocky terrain, causing her to slip repeatedly on the blood. When Veera made her rest her feet, she assumed whichever position he placed her in, like a hideous wooden puppet. She never spoke or slept, but stared with unseeing eyes into empty space.

If Naganara had not wanted her unharmed and alive, Veera would have given in to the urge to bash her head against a rock. Instead, he force-fed her a few roots and berries that had been begrudgingly foraged by him to keep her alive and made her swallow a few mouthfuls of water.

On more than one occasion, Veera was tempted to slap her silly. She was like a giant baby and had to be cared for like one. Feeding the blob was one thing, but he drew the line at taking care of her personal needs. The first time she soiled herself, he hurled her to the floor and kicked her hard. She did not cry out in pain or clutch the afflicted calf.

Veera grabbed her chin and tilted her face upwards. Very slowly, he pulled back a delicate eyelid with the point of his curved dagger and held it tantalizingly close to a fixed and staring pupil. She did not even blink. Clearly in the place she had disappeared into, physical pain had no meaning for her. Suddenly bored, he tugged on the rope and they resumed their journey. The cow would get hers when he turned her over to the necromancer. By the time he was through with her, she would be praying for the fate of her dear departed friend Trishana.

He did not notice the pendant that pulsed urgently from the hollow space between her breasts. Minothi treated it with the same indifference she had the pointy end of the dagger. And so they journeyed, the Hataka and the Kritya, till they arrived beneath the ruins of the summer residence that had been built for a king, who had turned it over for Rajamatha Akhilandeshwari's personal use.

The edifice had been constructed at the far end of what had once been an elaborately constructed artificial lake, complete with reeds, water lilies and lotuses, planted with such consummate skill that these easily passed for a bona fide creation of Mother Nature at her finest. Now, it was almost empty, and reeds grew as high as the knees, providing a secure habitat for snakes and scorpions both.

What had formerly been a well-laid garden had long ago been reclaimed by the elements that had stripped it bare of its beauty, leaving only harrowing ruins in their wake. Man-made miniature mountains and artificial pools that had formerly stood pretty now gave it a decrepit look.

A stone lion stood at the head of one such pool, its starved jaws gaping open waiting in vain for the water to gush out of its mouth and trickled down to the depths below. In its present condition, it could have easily passed for a particularly ugly gargoyle that had been originally installed to ward off the evil eye of the envious.

The crumbling three-storeyed palace had a brick foundation, with mostly wood-frame constructions that had held up very poorly against the moisture and encroaching rot, with the result that entire sections had collapsed. The central inner-courtyard with its adjoining rooms had survived somewhat amidst the ruins, thanks to the varying combinations of stone and mortar that had been used.

The mother-of-pearl that had once inlaid the luxuriously appointed rooms had long been stripped away along with the paintings, sculptures and ivory carvings. Time had marched on, leaving the former bastion of power behind. But something malevolent lingered on in the ancient ruins, and it remained safe and secure in its remote location, far from the eyes of civilization. It suited the purposes of the necromancer and his chief minion.

The tunnel ended at a rusty cast-iron door. It opened into a dungeon beneath the forgotten palace. Veera led his charge, who was neither willing nor unwilling, within. There was a staircase winding up the bedrock to a discreet room in the palace. It could be reached by pushing up a slab of stone. On the outside, there was a single iron ring.

The secret location that had borne witness to unspeakable atrocities was made entirely of stone and had weathered time very well. Its makers had ensured that not a ray of sunlight or moonlight, nor even a drop of water, could penetrate its depths. The place remained cool, dry and almost fully intact.

Veera led his charge and fastened a chain round her neck and secured it to one of the iron rings that were embedded in the wall. She might be little more than a potato that walked but that would not stop her from being the ideal bait to lure in a certain sucker who had been in his sights a long time. With a little help, he looked forward to presenting Yama's lieutenant and the Kritya to Naganara.

Of course, Naganara would not be expecting a foul-smelling, raggedy wretch of a woman who seemed to be in a coma. Veera shrugged. It was not his job to be concerned about such things though. He pulled out the clothes Trishana had last worn and left them in a little cloth-bag by her side along with a bottle of water and some berries.

The trap had been laid but there was time to spare. It was highly unlikely that Agni Prakash, who needed help finding the nose on his ugly mug, and who was at present blundering about in Bandavana, may actually track the Kritya down any time soon. By the time he tracked down the powerful magic that had been released to its source and in the improbable event he found the concealed entrance to the hidden passage that would lead him to the one he sought, Veera would be able to arrange a nasty surprise for him.

In the meantime, he needed to hunt and replenish the mortal coil he had chosen for himself. Since they were a long way from human habitation, he would have no choice but to settle for the blood of a deer or an ox.

Minothi was all alone. She sat there unmoved, even when the chill of the night goose-pimpled her flesh and the light of the torch wrapped her within its warm embrace in a wasted gesture of sympathy.

Willingly had she disappeared into the void, and the abounding nothingness was what she needed more than anything else. Most people, even the kindlier among them, would have become annoyed with this brand of self-destructive obduracy, but Kashika was not most people. Finally, her descendant was alone and she would help her, even if the aid offered was unsolicited.

27

The Pitrani's Story

The pitrani did not grow angry with Minothi for locking herself up in such an impossible state nor did she pity her. Instead, she merely drew closer to her, a soothing presence filled with love and compassion, which was never intrusive or invasive. Kashika allowed the currents of their preternatural connection to move back and forth like the ebb and flow of a tide. Blood recognized its own even if Minothi couldn't, and it would not turn on the alien yet entirely familiar presence that had gently integrated itself into the very fabric of her being.

'I am going to tell you a story, precious child of mine!' The tone was mellifluous and as soothing as a mother's lullaby. Minothi did not respond but something pricked her eye and she blinked. Once, a long time ago, as a four-year-old, she had pestered her mother for stories.

'You will like it, I think . . .' the voice continued. 'It is one of those stories that will make you cry a little and laugh a lot. More importantly, it will make you feel better about yourself. Those are the best kind, as you know. I'll show you some pretty pictures as well. Would you like that?'

Not intending to wait for a response that would not be forthcoming, the storyteller plunged on. 'A long time ago, there was a special little girl. She lived in a charming little cottage in a beautiful valley. Everybody loved her because she was good and kind. But that was not what made her so special. There was something else, something important! Mother Earth, who gives life and sustains all, had given her a wonderful gift.'

Minothi inhaled and held her breath for a split second before exhaling. In that space, she could see the little girl, as the voice slowly filled her mind. She had Minothi's own eyes—almond-shaped, black and piercing, but filled with laughter. She wore her hair in two long plaits and they bounced jauntily on her shoulders as she raced down a steep slope.

Suddenly, she lost her footing and tumbled all the way to the bottom. When she rose, the child was muddied but had miraculously escaped without a scratch and was laughing so hard that the entire place came to life.

'There never was a child who fell so hard or so often. But she never once hurt herself, and the people in her village insisted that she would be safe even if the little rascal had been inclined to fling herself off a cliff, for she was a special favourite of Mother Earth's, and no matter how hard she fell, the ground itself rose up to catch her and lessen the impact. But that was not all.

'As she grew older, the girl discovered so much more about herself. Wondrous things that set her apart from everybody else. But even then she knew, with all the wisdom of a subtle and complicated mind that was peculiar to her, that her talents were not to be revealed to all and sundry. It would make the others, especially the adults, jealous and they just might make the foolhardy attempt to steal it away or force her to use it for their own twisted purposes.

'Her parents knew about it though. And they did everything possible to shield her from the attentions of a world with a long track record for treating the special and different among them with its inimitable brand of cruelty. So while they looked out for her, she spread her wings and tested her abilities.'

Minothi saw a child of seven at play. Her dress was torn and muddied after a bit of fun and frolic. Her dark hair, plaited neatly by her mother, was almost completely undone, and she brushed it impatiently from her eyes as she blew on a dandelion, watching the fluff fly. Soon, nothing was left of the globe and she held the stalk impatiently in her hand.

With a mischievous glint in her eyes, she kneeled over the scattered seeds, gathering as many as she could in the palm of her hand. The seeds that the wind had carried farther away flew into her hand, as though in answer to her summons.

Like a magician about to perform a trick before an audience, she pressed her cupped palms into her chest and twirled about, kicked her legs sideways, almost lost her balance, but managed to land with a flourish, holding a pretty bouquet of dandelions in her hands. Grinning in delight to the sound of imaginary applause, she ran home to make a present of it to her mother.

'Isn't that a nice gift to have?' The voice picked up where the picture had grown blurry. 'I did tell you that Mother Earth loved her, didn't I?' Their bond was special. Her garden was the prettiest in the valley and bloomed all year around. She would spend hours at a time over there, sometimes talking to the plants, singing to the flowers or merely sitting in silence almost as if she could see life take form from a bountiful earth. Her parents were amazed at her gift, for she could even nurse a dying tree back to life!

It was the same with all living things. There were a number of stray dogs that roamed the valley and hunted in packs. Some among them were so gaunt, starved and fierce that they could actually grab the little ones by the shoulder and drag them away. But Minothi could calm them with just a look or an impish smack on the nose. They even took biscuits from her hand, gentle as lambs!

The little girl continued to make like a magician. Twirling her hands about, pretending to hold a wand, chanting magic words with elaborate enunciation, making deep bows, she demonstrated how she could heal all living things with just a touch, a word, unlimited flair and a pinch of showmanship.

Seeking out injured birds, wounded squirrels and colic-stricken horses, she would fix them so they were better than new. Once, she abandoned her bed for a nocturnal adventure when she sensed the presence of a bison stricken with a severe ear infection waiting politely behind their cottage without uttering a single sound. Her parents could only watch in stupefaction as she tugged at its ear before planting a kiss on an extremely unclean nose. Nuzzling her hand tenderly in profound gratitude, the bovine had then departed quietly.

'People soon started to talk about her strange powers. Her parents had tried to keep her remarkable abilities under wraps but she was a light that shone far too brightly and it was impossible to hide its effulgence. Those in need of her services started trickling in. They brought in sick children, loved ones and pets. Many simply came to seek her blessings or ogle at her, but her father turned them away. Mostly, though, it seemed selfish not to share her unique powers.

'Though still a child, she helped them all. Unfortunately, there are always a few rotten ones who can't resist biting the hand extended in friendship; they make the attempt to hoard something precious, keeping it all to themselves. As a result, when she was nine, something happened and it forced her to grow up all at once.'

Minothi could feel the child's apprehension in the days leading up to when 'something happened'. Her existence had been a joyous one and she genuinely liked to help those who needed her. But the sharp tang of dark forces could be felt in the air, and its metallic taste reminded her of blood. The clean air of the hills was marred by the occasional rank odour. There was something in the shadows but they always melted away into the blackness from which they had come before she could identify the threat.

In her sheltered little corner of the world there had never been any reason to be afraid and she saw no need to let the fear in to roost. Instead, she became increasingly watchful, her senses on high alert. So when they came for her, though they chose the darkest hour of the night, she awoke immediately.

The wind howled and dogs bayed at the moon. The child's first concern was for her parents. Their safety was paramount to her, but they were having none of it.

'When the bad men came, her mother pushed her into the storeroom. Urging her to keep quiet, she locked the door and shoved the key into the sugar bowl. Her father was trying to buy them both time. He was a gentle and kind man who had never been violent in his life. The only soul in the whole wide world gentler than him was her mother.

'Young as she was, the little girl knew that her parents would not be a match for the monsters that had come for her. They had sealed all routes of escape and were closing in on their quarry. She heard the sounds of things breaking, stuff crashing to the floor, glass being shattered and the sound of splintering wood. Her mother screamed and she heard her father's calm voice telling her not to be afraid. But before he could finish what he was saying, something cut him off, and the child heard the meaty thump of his body as it struck the floor hard.

'She was struggling to get the door open but it refused to budge and her panic mounted. There were more sounds from above. Slashing sounds and muted grunts of pain. That was when the girl let go of the fear and acted. The door flew off the hinges and she was running faster than she ever had to the front of the house. Not once did she stumble.

'The men with the covered faces had already wounded her father badly. There were too many of them. There was blood all over her father. He was urging her mother to run but she would not leave him. Slowly, one of the assailants walked towards her as if he had all the time in the world.

'As it turned out, he didn't. Because he was the first to die. Heat built up inside him till his entire body caught fire and he was incinerated where he stood. The others quickly met the same fate, even the ones who were prowling inside. Nothing remained of them but little piles of ashes that were swept away by the wind.

'The Kritya, for that was what the child had always been, stood like one possessed. Even her mother was terrified. Her eyes burnt red like coals, the long hair billowed out behind her and her arms were raised as she called down the wrath of the divine mother to punish the wicked.

'Seeing that her baby was slipping away from her, the mother ran to her and fell at her feet in supplication. Raising her hand to bless the one who crouched at her feet, the Kritya turned her attention to the dying man. This time she did not bother with showmanship. She called upon every ounce of her skill to save him.

'Then she blessed them both one last time before she walked out of the front door. Her mother was too distraught to speak. Her father was calm and seemed to understand. "Go with God, dear child of mine. May our lives, love and prayers keep you safe from harm, now and forevermore. Always remember to use your powers in service to your fellow humans and Mother Earth who has claimed you for her own. And if the need arises, don't ever hesitate to destroy those who seek to do evil unto others."

'The Kritya, for that was what she was, stored his words in her head and her heart so that they may always resonate with her. She ventured into the world to do her father's bidding and make it a better place. Sometimes her efforts were a spectacular success and at other times they were a resounding failure. But she always did her best and hoped to God that it was enough. Sometimes it was and sometimes it wasn't.

'She did not live happily ever after but that was not necessarily a bad thing. And sometimes it is enough to simply live the life charted out for you instead of chasing after non-existent fairy tales.'

Minothi waited for the final images to unspool in her head. The Kritya was quite the impressive figure—teacher, warrior, healer and overall do-gooder par excellence. It was all very awe-inspiring. Finally the images died away save one.

A formidable lady cloaked in grey stood before a miserable, half-naked creature who looked like a scabrous, overripe beggar. Her hair was iron-grey and the eyes flickered like lit candles. Even though she was as insubstantial as the air around them, she exuded power and filled the dungeon with her presence. With a start, Minothi realized that *she* was the grotesque apparition that looked like it had escaped from a sewer after a bout of wrestling with its furry denizens.

Shaking her head, Minothi spoke in a voice that was creaky with lack of use, 'How much of that story is true? I am guessing that a lot of it was made up to protect my fragile psyche and galvanize me out of the comatose state in which you found me.'

'I'll admit it . . . According to the story, the little girl was beloved because she was good and kind but in reality it was because she was pretty and vivacious,' replied the pitrani, twinkling a little

Minothi grinned back, but it quickly changed into a grimace as her dry and cracked lips protested the use they were being put to. With concentrated effort, she spoke again, 'The little girl's father did not make it. She could not have saved him.'

The pitrani nodded but her expression was neutral. 'Neither of her parents survived that day because the little girl could not open the door. When their killers finally tore down the door, she did turn them all to ash. But by then it was too late and though she went on trying for days on end, her mother and father could never be healed.

'Fortunately for her, one of the foremost Krityas of the age found her there, alerted by the magic that had been expended, and everything changed after that. But that is a story for another day. All you need to know is that the pain, guilt and regret never goes away, not even when death cuts short this existence. The only thing to do is to wait for time to dull the anguish and keep yourself busy doing something that does not make you feel like a waste of space.'

'Your case is different! I have the blood of innocent people on my hands . . .' she began.

'That is tragic! All I can say to you is that no matter how hard we work to have it otherwise, there will always be things beyond our control. Krishna was a participant in the mass slaughter that decimated his entire clan, but as I recall, he didn't spend the rest of eternity hating and punishing himself. It may not seem possible now, but eventually you will learn to live with everything you have done and maybe even forgive yourself.

'One thing is certain though, your big tragedy is certainly not sufficient reason for you to throw away the precious life and gifts given to you and willingly offer yourself up to the first murdering blackguard who turns up to subvert the power you wield to his use. Then, whether you like it or not, there will be even more blood on your hands, and soon all the opportunities for redemption and atonement will be gone forever. Make no mistake, this will be your fate if you insist on disappearing into the doldrums of despair while playing the unfeeling vegetable.'

The words were harsh and felt like a resounding slap across the face to Minothi. Nevertheless, she felt better than she had in what felt like forever. She took in the state of her tattered garment, bloodied feet with their criss-cross cuts and broken nails, and her scratched arms, felt her tangled hair and became aware that she smelled worse than the contents of a chamber pot. Despair quickly gave way to disgust. Slowly and painfully, she got to her feet.

Only then did she realize that she had been chained like an animal. Furious, she tugged at the chain around her neck, but it would not give.

'I suppose the thing cannot be used to heal my body and procure some decent clothes? Perhaps rustle up a decent meal and about a gallon of ice cream?' Minothi inquired, only half-joking.

'Fortunately, you still have the use of your hands and, hopefully, a functioning brain as well, and those ought to see you past the present crisis,' came the dry reply. 'Listen to me carefully, child. Our time together is almost up and there is more I need to tell you. Yama's lieutenant is searching for you and when he comes, you need to go with him. The silver goddess has entrusted him with a mission and it falls to him to track down the bride of the ruler of the damned and unite her with him. He will not be able to do it without you.

'You must use your powers to help him. Perhaps if you stop fearing the magic and learn to believe in "the thing", it will serve you in good stead.

'Yama's lieutenant does not know it yet, but the quest does not end with the discovery of the one you seek. Before she can begin the journey to the netherworld, it falls to her to round up the Itvaras, the condemned ones, and the two of you will have to protect her till her mission is accomplished.'

Minothi could scarcely keep up with what Kashika was trying so urgently to say to her. Who on earth was Yama's lieutenant? Did they actually have to go on a wild goose chase to find a bride for the lord of the underworld and a legion of the damned? That was madness! And it was so unfair. She had only just recovered from a traumatic experience and surely she had earned the right to take some time to heal? Not only that, she genuinely wanted to make amends for everything she had done and help others, only without the thing, as far as it was possible.

But no, the universe in its infinite wisdom not only saw fit to have her imprisoned in a dungeon of horrors but had also sent an emissary to inform her that she was to accompany someone she had never met to traipse off into unknown territory on an impossible quest from which she might never return and, yes, find a way to use the damn thing without destroying everything in creation.

Minothi cheered up at the thought that death was a part of her future, but sobered down when the pitrani, who had been looking at her intently, began to fade before her very eyes. 'I am glad you are feeling better and thinking of making a future for yourself that does not involve death and destruction. But remember, the silver goddess needs you. Serve her well and you may be given the chance to start life afresh. In the meantime, you owe her, and a few others as well, a debt, which it behoves you to pay back with interest.'

Minothi shook her hand frantically. 'Wait! You can't go now! There is so much more I need to know! Please!'

But her frantic need was not enough and she knew Kashika was not going to stay.

'There is no need to look so sorrowful, child. I know you are resourceful enough to extricate yourself from this mess and find the road destiny has directed you take. Believe me, the worst is behind you. And help is on the way!

'It will not be easy for you to trust the magic but don't forget the talisman of power given to you by a wise and beautiful soul who loved you more than she would have her own daughter. As for the answers to your questions, you will find them as you go along.'

And just like that, she was gone, leaving Minothi alone in her prison. She shook her head and wondered if she had imagined the whole thing as she took in her surroundings. She was in a chamber that had to be at least twenty feet across, and long, with a high ceiling of stone and thick walls. There were no windows but the place seemed decently ventilated through a system of iron pipes. There was a lone torch burning in a bracket provided for the purpose. Iron rings and chains hung from the walls. It was not a pretty sight.

Minothi was grateful to her ancestor for helping her in this time of need, but it would have been convenient if the pitrani had helped her out of the chains and spirited her away from the medieval torture chamber before dumping a cumbersome mission on her lap. What she wouldn't give to have a bath!

Wrapping her fingers around the chain, she tried to prise it loose, but it didn't budge. With mounting fear, she worried if her kidnapper was around. What if he came back? What were his plans for her? She tried not to think of rape, murder or torture, but her brain refused to oblige and insisted on inundating her with a number of images that showed unspeakable things happening to her.

She tried to remember Gurvi Sampoorna's words from when she had tried to teach her to subdue her mind. But the harder she tried, the more her thoughts went into a tizzy. She screamed aloud in frustration and then it happened. The thing came alive in her blood, a silent gathering spawned from her need. Hardly daring to breathe or dwell on it, she allowed it to the surface, feeling it pool at her fingertips.

No sooner had she placed them on the chains than they snapped like rotten twigs. Joy flooded Minothi's body and she laughed aloud in giddy relief before she slowed it down. But her happiness became more pronounced when she spied a cistern in a corner of the dungeon, half-filled with rain water.

The water was ice-cold but it felt heavenly and she cleaned up as best as she could. There was nothing she could do about the fact that she looked like she had been in a fight with a wild animal but she felt much better. Her abductor had thoughtfully left her some clothes, which she donned in the dim light of the torch. She tried to ignore his offerings of berries and water, but the latter was too much to resist, and she gulped it all down, choking and spilling some of it on her outfit. Something was troubling her, but she pushed the thought aside. Her first priority was to find a way out of there.

She tried the door from which they had entered, but it would not budge. He must have fastened the bars outside. Her only hope was the staircase with the stone slab on top. She stumbled up the stairs, ignoring the pain her wounded feet had to endure and pushed against the trapdoor. Try as she might, she could not get it to budge even an inch in her weakened state. 'Could it be that I've lost some weight?' she wondered exultantly, before chiding herself and trying to focus on the fact that she was in mortal danger. Minothi was debating whether she ought to call forth the damn thing when her senses began tingling and she felt as though she had been goosed by a dozen live wires.

There was something on the other side. She strained her ears for the sound of footsteps, anything, but there was only a deep silence tinged with menace. Her heart hammered against her chest, a mad staccato sound, and she could feel the magic gathering in a concentrated rush as it slipped free to probe the source of her terror. And for the briefest of moments, Minothi saw it clear as day.

Fear slammed into her gut with the force of a sucker punch and she gasped aloud. Crippling cold crept up her spine, making her hair stand on end. The stench of it assaulted her nostrils, and her empty stomach churned as the bile rose thickly in her throat, scalding it with its acidic punch. With exquisite enjoyment, whatever it was turned in her direction with sightless eyes and, faster than she could withdraw the antennae of her magic, latched on to the remnants and licked it up.

Minothi felt its touch through the layers of stone separating them and shrank back from the forced intimacy; she felt as though a thousand maggots were crawling over her flesh, burrowing into the softness, and she nearly lost her balance. And just like that, the thing withdrew. She knew that it was toying with her, knowing as well as she did that she could not escape.

Quietly, she retreated down the stairs, fleeing to the dark ends of the dungeon, which felt marginally safer, trying to fight off the encroaching despair and calm the bestial thing within her that struggled to be let loose. Suddenly, a mental image of a pair of unmoving naked legs thrust itself into her mind's eye. The rest of the body was buried under a pile of rubble, and only the tiniest portion of a garment that had been hitched up to expose the limbs was visible. One of the victims of the massacre at Sivagami Math.

Minothi shut her eyes and prayed for calm. And she waited for the evil that stood poised to devour her.

28

A Crossing of Paths

Dharami was relieved to find Agni safe and sound at the base of Mount Maroli, at the start of the trail that wound upwards through the range. 'It is good to see you!' her distinctive voice resounded in his head. 'And not a moment too soon. Something terrible has happened! Sivagami Math is no more . . .' Dharami paused mid-sentence when she caught sight of the blood-soaked bandage. For a few moments she said nothing, and Agni thought she looked stricken.

'Taravarsha left a few things in your backpack in case . . .' she murmured hesitantly. 'You will find a salve to apply on it and a potion to drink.' Agni was surprised, but he rooted around and found the things she had mentioned. He quickly stripped off the bandage, trying not to yelp like a puppy while she was watching so closely. Dharami gasped when she saw the awful gash on the side of his abdomen but said nothing while he attended to it. The salve felt heavenly and the throbbing subsided almost immediately. Like most of the aged healer's concoctions, the potion tasted worse than it looked. Varu would have called it frog shit but he knew it would help him heal faster.

'Thanks for the warning about the friendly little creature,' he said jovially but regretted it when he saw the look on the land spirit's ravaged face. But she instantly disappeared behind her cowl all at once and merely looked sullen.

'I did not tell you about the suchayalas for your own good. It may have been a mistake and not very fair to you—' she said, her voice choking.

Agni grinned, knowing that this was the closest she would come to an apology. 'I don't blame you at all and you don't have to apologize. Taravarsha said you are my guardian angel, and needless to say, you were acting in my best interests,' he intoned with mock solemnity.

'Fortunately, it was a yala you ran into. It would have been so much worse if the varttas had got a hold of you. They are blood fiends and just about the nastiest piece of goods you are ever likely to run into. Nobody knows what they actually look like because they are invisible creatures who can latch on to your thoughts and take whatever beguiling form they think will lure you to them while they feed on your blood and turn your brains to mush!

'They are particularly partial to children and trick them into thinking they are rushing to their mother's arms. But that was before they were banished to Yatupava. The varttas would have given anything for the chance to feed on someone like you! There are other things there as well, not quite as dangerous as these two, but nevertheless, it is best to give them a wide berth like you did.'

Before he could reply, she changed the subject abruptly. 'We must hurry! I fear the Hataka has got his hands on the Kritya but, if I am right, we may just have the slimmest chance of rescuing her before she is delivered to the necromancer. Quickly! I will tell you everything on the way.'

Agni shrugged tiredly. Time was hardly ever on their side and all the impossible things he was expected to do were almost always supposed to have been done on the previous day. His wound protested vigorously but he followed Dharami as she led him up the trail. Dusk was approaching but there was enough light to see, and after the insupportably muggy atmosphere of Bandavana, the cool, dry mountain air was a relief.

Rocks loomed over them on all sides, and Agni was pleased to note that they cut him off completely from the forest, Quills, bloodsucking fiends and whatever else lived there. It was a narrow trail that angled upwards so sharply that it was hard to find a foothold on the loose stones and sharp incline. After what felt like a whole lot of climbing, the path levelled out and led to a pass.

They made better time as they traversed the marginally wider corridor that led right through the rocks, having left the slopes behind, and Dharami let Agni know all the things she had discovered. 'Sivagami Math and most of its inhabitants are no more. I sensed a massive expenditure of magic in that place. It had to have been the Kritya. Clearly, she has no control over her powers, but they are practically unmatched. It is a scary thought because even I have seldom seen destruction on this scale!'

'What about the missing children? Did you find out what happened to them?' Agni took a deep breath and geared himself for bad news.

'Not much remains of them, I am afraid. It was easy enough to locate the place where the magic had originated. Since Veera does not take the only known route to the math, to the best of my knowledge, I had already surmised that there was a secret passage. Sure enough, I found a dungeon beneath the rubble and a man-made tunnel leading out of it.'

Agni nodded. 'The missing children were kept there to be experimented on with poisons, I suppose, and Veera must have spirited them away to Naganara. As we suspected, at least a few of the Kanyas had to be involved.'

'The gurvi was definitely a part of it. As usual, it is the people who are outwardly obsessed with purity who have the filthiest souls. Thankfully, the high priestess got her comeuppance. I found the mangled remains of her body in the dungeon along with a few others. The rest of the foundation had been razed to the ground.

'My guess is that the Kritya found out about the veshas, and they must have attacked her. Her magic would have boiled over from where it had been hiding and must have taken her by surprise, causing her to lose control. I don't think it was her intention to kill the children.'

'Except they are dead just the same. Let me see if I have this straight . . . This person finds out that a gaggle of her fellow celibates are kidnapping girl babies, imprisoning them in a dungeon and feeding them toxins to make them over as deadly weapons. She is so appalled that she promptly kills them all indiscriminately—the good little girls as well as the bad apples—before destroying the only home she has ever known. And then she disappears into a secret tunnel with the guy who was running this entire shebang on behalf of an evil necromancer. Did I miss anything?'

'You haven't even met her and already you have her pegged as an evil mass-murdering lunatic! Just so you know, it is unlikely that she went willingly with Veera. He seems to have carried her a long way and then she was dragged along like a dog on a leash! Where is your compassion?'

Agni did not reply, although he thought it was interesting that she was so concerned about his lack of compassion for one who clearly had not shown much of it to her victims. Still, he had been told that the Kritya was needed for their quest to succeed and it would never do to go into this harbouring ill will towards her.

Varu would have called him out on his attitude as well. She had long harboured a policy whereby she would dismiss all the women he found passably attractive as bad news and rush to the defence of the members of the opposite sex he tended to be critical about, most notably her giggly girlfriends.

'You have the natural arrogance of your sex, Agni!' He could practically hear the voice he loved so dearly. 'Most men have no idea what it is like to be boxed into a stifling enclosure, reinforced with stupid rules and regulations designed to control every single thing from how you wipe your arse to how you wipe the arse of the child you just have to push out your "delicate parts". It is the sort of thing that can drive you apeshit crazy!'

Dead or alive, his twin usually made sense. Agni smiled at the thought and missed the look of extreme irritation Dharami shot him. Since the Kritya had literally been locked in a box all her life, it would hardly be a surprise that her brains were slightly addled. Besides, the magic always did things to you. At the very least, he ought to reserve his judgement till he actually got to know her and heard her version of events.

'So where are we headed?' he asked Dharami conversationally.

'I did not follow their tracks all the way, because as a self-respecting land spirit, I have a deep abhorrence of all things that involve burrowing deep below the surface, a space fit only for worms and worm food. But if I were to hazard a guess, it seems apparent that the passage leads to the ruins of an ancient palace that lies at the rim of the valley over the pass.

'As I mentioned earlier, there is a slim chance that we can get to the Kritya unnoticed. Veera needs to feed if he is to keep his mortal coil strong and intact. If I am right, he would have concealed her carefully in the ruins and gone hunting. With a little bit of luck, we can make off with her before he is the wiser.'

Agni thought she was being overly optimistic, but he held his tongue. They did not speak much after that and focused on the trail that had begun the descent into the valley. He could already see its outline. Silhouetted sharply against the magnificent canvas of the night sky were the rolling meadows, grassy knolls and lumpy hillocks painted in shades of velvety grey, black and silver, the peculiar pigments unique to night-time. The lakes and ponds mirrored the pearlescent glow of the moon and captured the brightness of the stars in their placid waters.

It was a breathtaking view and yet Agni had a premonition that something sinister lurked in that forgotten valley. Dharami did not appear inclined to speak to him and seemed impatient, though they were covering ground at a good pace.

'What are you so worried about?' Agni asked her gently.

'You know perfectly well what is bothering me!' she snapped at him. 'The Kritya used the magic, for better or worse, to end the madness that had gripped that infernal math. In doing so, she alerted Naganara's hound dog to her presence, but for some strange reason, she did not kill him along with the rest but instead allowed him to capture her. What if the magic has turned inwards and destroyed her? What good will she be in helping us find Yama's bride?'

'As you know, I have my own concerns about all this. In fact, it is almost an absolute certainty that we are walking into a trap. If the two of you were able to sense the Kritya's magic, then Veera would have got wind of my presence when Quills took a pass at me. He will know we are on their track, and soon when I run up against whatever he has managed to scrounge up from the sewers of his raging depravity, I'll no doubt be thinking fondly of Quills!'

'Why do you keep doing that?' she asked. To his surprise, she seemed more concerned about him than the Kritya and their mission combined.

Ignoring the look on his face, Dharami went on in the manner of a schoolmarm, 'It is unspeakably tragic that you lost that twin of yours but that does not mean you have to go through life acting as though there is nothing in it worth loving. The goddess commands your respect and she has entrusted you with a certain duty that you perform with mechanical precision, and without ever taking off those blinkers. But you don't believe in anything or anyone, not even yourself. This is the reason the suchayala made a beeline for you.'

'Quills attacked me because I lack faith? Wow! And here I thought—'

'The yala came after you because you are so convinced that no matter what anybody does or doesn't do, bad things are going to keep happening. Your entire belief system is steeped in this hideous premise and since you are convinced that your surmise is right, it has become the very nature of your reality.'

'I had no idea you were a card-carrying member of the "a positive attitude is all that we need to shrink the hole in the ozone layer, end poverty, wars and disease and make shit smell sweeter" brigade!

'I hate to burst your pretty pink bubble, but the truth is that people can get killed in a freak accident while laughing at a joke. Babies can die in their cribs while gurgling away—and Quills, sorry, the yala, would have savaged me irrespective of whether you had warned me or not, regardless of whether I had anticipated it or not. It was always going to be a part of my reality. The magic makes it so, and for the others, reality is always going to stink worse than their shit because life makes it so. That is the sad truth.'

'The sad truth is that there are times when I want to knock some sense into your empty head with a cudgel despite knowing that it would be an endeavour in futility. And there is absolutely no reason for me to hang around listening to your depressing prattle!'

The land spirit flounced away just as they stepped clear of the track, leaving the pass behind. Agni let her go. She was not as angry as she pretended to be at him, and he knew she would want to reconnoitre the place. Despite the power of Dharami's positive thinking, it was unlikely that Veera would leave the Kritya alone for them to find and rescue. By the time the sun rose on the morrow, the valley would have been torn apart by violence.

Agni remembered something and quickened his pace. Taravarsha had warned the land spirit that some of the creatures summoned by Naganara could hurt even ones like her. 'Why is she so damn proud? The stubborn creature should have stayed with me.'

A slight breeze had sprung up, ruffling his hair, whispering soft warnings into his ear and stroking his face with the grit it carried. Agni had already caught a glimpse of the ruins. They lay behind a copse of trees. The wind whooshed past, rustling the leaves. Twigs snapped under his feet. Agni felt he was being watched, that something was following him. But nothing showed itself. It was eerie. He hoped he was merely being paranoid.

There was something about the valley. It defied belief that civilization could have passed it by so completely and left it to its own devices. It was slightly perverse that countless places of natural splendour had been despoiled by mankind in the mad dash towards advancement while this little slice of hell had been passed over and left to thrive.

Not a single village, hamlet, or even the ubiquitous eatery, could be seen in the vast desolation that stretched out on the other side. Agni actually missed the concrete jungle he had left behind, including the traffic snarls, flashing lights and, above all, the jostling, surging crowds that gave an illusory feeling of security even as it afforded the same feeling of safety to the predators who lurked in the thick of things waiting to rob you blind or slit your throat.

Those were his thoughts as he skirted a rise and found himself confronted with the sprawling detritus of a massive edifice. The brick wall that had once encircled it had been torn down by unknown forces, and the stumpy remains were a forlorn reminder that it had been nearly six feet thick at the base. A moat must have surrounded it at one time, though nothing remained of the drawbridge or the crocodiles that likely circled it. But the partial remains of a monolithic gateway beckoned him inside.

Dharami uncoiled herself from where she had been concealed and landed next to him with her graceful, quicksilver movements and stood silently by his side as he surveyed the place under the cover of a massive oak. Together they went in silently. Agni wondered how the danda would hold up against the spirits of dead crocodiles in case they still lingered, thriving on the miasma of maleficence that hung over the place like a shroud.

Time had caused the structure to implode. The formerly sturdy walls, high terraces and massive pillars were no more. Only the fragments of stone columns, intricately carved cornices and slabs remained, providing an abundance of nooks and crannies for scorpions, lizards and snakes to frolic in.

The aqueducts constructed to fill the artificial lakes stood exposed, while the dilapidated, shapeless stone monsters stood with their maws thrust open with feral intent. Within the palace walls, squarish rooms with interconnecting narrow passages were discernible, leading to the courtyard. Dharami led him to a room at the very back and motioned to the iron ring on the floor.

Agni pulled with all his might but it would not yield. 'Veera is clever,' Dharami's hushed voice sounded in his ear. 'He has placed an enchantment on it.'

'So that I would have to use magic and he will be alerted, right?' he whispered back. 'But there is more. Something does not feel right about this.'

'No, it doesn't . . .' Agni looked up with a start. The land spirit had eased herself into the dungeon below. Slowly, he retreated into the shadows, his back to the wall, his senses tingling, sharply alive with anticipation. Long moments elapsed with excruciating slowness. Dharami was such a moron for taking such risks with an unhinged, murderous and unknown entity.

•••

While he fretted thus, Minothi was staring at the slender, heavily robed apparition in front of her, flickering like a candle about to go out. For the briefest of moments, she tensed, wondering if it was the monstrous creature that had come back for her. But something told her it wasn't. Besides, if it was the awful thing she had sensed, 'the thing' would have gone berserk.

'My name is Dharami!' a pleasant voice whispered in her head. 'We have come to rescue you from the Hataka Veera. Listen to me carefully. The sooner we get out of here, the better it is for all of us. You need to trust me!'

'A short while before you came, I was trying to lift that stone slab,' she replied urgently. 'It just wouldn't give, even though I tried everything possible. And then I realized that there was something on the other side. It waited out there for a long time. Whatever it was, it seemed to be able to see through the stone. And I could feel it . . . I can't explain it. And it has to be out there. Is Yama's lieutenant with you? You have to go and warn him!'

'There are not many who can outfight Agni Prakash. He will be just fine. In the meantime, you need to get away from here. It would be lovely if you could do that without disturbing the enchantment Veera has placed above.'

'But I already told you that it cannot be done. And it is not for want of trying.'

She stopped speaking. Dharami was staring at the pendant that hung at her throat with a strange expression on her face. Parts of Dharami's face were completely transparent and Minothi could see right through. Other parts had patches of decomposing flesh and there was the occasional spot of fresh, dewy skin. It was the same with the eyes; one was bright and sparkling, while the other appeared to have been scooped out.

'That is a *tayaka*. Who died and gave it to you?' Her voice in Minothi's head throbbed with barely contained excitement.

'Gurvi Sampoorna gave it to me. The pitrani told me it was important. But I know next to nothing about it. Why was—?'

'There is no time to explain but your pitrani was right. Never ever let it go. Now we need to get you out of here immediately! Don't think about the Narakamayas. Close your eyes and listen only to my voice.'

Dharami's voice was divinely soothing, and Minothi did as she was told. The land spirit slipped her incorporeal fingers into the Kritya's and held fast. 'You can feel it, can't you?'

Minothi nodded in assent and wonder suffused her being. It was like slipping into a fluffy cloud, velvety soft, as gentle winds swirled restlessly. She smelled of rich soil and dry leaves, and there was the touch of the maternal in her. Minothi caught the scent of death but, unlike the monster, there was none of the black putrefaction, only a state of having been returned to the earth. It was strangely comforting.

'Yours is the power of the five elements that are the primary constituents of all things in existence—flora and fauna, the living and the undead, even the thrice-damned layers of stone that has you trapped underneath. No dungeon or chain can hold you captive against your will any more than it can me. It is your mind's doing that you did not succeed when you made the attempt to escape.

'But now you are a part of me and can come away with me.'

Minothi's eyes were still shut and she did not fight the odd feeling that suffused her, or the gentle rocking that signalled a slight alteration in her being and a slow shifting from below to above. There was nothing dramatic about any of it. One moment she was in the tomb of stone, while the next she was being lifted clear off her feet and floating through layers of rock, breaking free to the surface, where she could breathe and be free. At least till the hideous creature that lurked above came for them all, she thought with a giddy laugh.

Agni had been waiting, his senses on high alert, for what felt like an entire age and a half. He had almost made up his mind to blast his way past the enchantment and kick Dharami's imprudent behind, when she emerged from the solid stone as though from a still pool of water. She was not alone.

The Kritya stood, or, rather, cowered slightly behind her, as though she expected a big bad wolf to leap for her throat. Agni had been told she possessed powerful earth magic, although how that translated into flying through walls, he could not understand. He heard Dharami's voice, smug and self-satisfied. 'Yama's lieutenant or not, you wouldn't be able to do squat without me,' she trilled into his ear. 'And don't forget to thank me after you have dealt with the Narakamaya.'

As far as explanations went, it was unsatisfactory, but it would have to wait. Agni found himself staring at the Kritya. She was clad in Patiala pants and a loose, flowing kurta. Short and unprepossessing, her hair pulled back in a messy, unflattering plait, she would have been unattractive had it not been for a pair of bright eyes that were looking bashfully at the two strangers who stood before her. It was hard to believe this child-woman had actually torn down a centuries-old institution without the help of a nuclear bomb.

'You must be the Kritya,' he began, and stuck out his hand awkwardly. It was ignored. She seemed to have trouble making eye contact with the first man she had seen in too long a time.

'There will be plenty of time once we are clear of this valley.' Dharami's voice cut short the introductions. 'Let us get out of here.'

'My name is Minothi,' the Kritya said timidly. She was still standing huddled behind Dharami, when the land spirit soared upwards and outwards, pausing only to whisper in Agni's ear, 'The Kritya has a tayaka infused with great power. It will take you to Ganga! You are blessed with an abundance of dumb luck!' And she was gone, making Agni wish he could drag her around on a leash.

If the Kritya was right and there actually was a Narakamaya in the vicinity, things would get bad very fast, according to Dharami. Agni would not be happy that she had not taken the time to explain, but they could not afford to waste another second. Uneasily she circled the ruins, hoping that the poor thing had been wrong. And then she saw Agni collapse to his knees, his face pulled in a hideous rictus of unbearable pain.

Dharami had to find a way to help him. She had lied to the Kritya; the Narakamayas were invincible and even Agni Prakash could not hope to prevail over them. There was the faintest glimmer of hope though; she just had to get to them.

The land spirit was soaring towards them when the snare closed on her. She could see Agni locked in combat with Sudhana, the most implacable of the Narakamayas, but she could not call out a warning. And then she saw the Hataka leering at her through the gaps in the net that had enmeshed her—except it was not a net.

'No!' she prayed. 'Not like this!' Dharami struggled like a maddened beast determined not to cry out and distract Agni, but there was no way out.

29

Harbingers of Doom

Nobody ever saw them coming. They preyed on the fringe dwellers of society at first. Remote villages and towns that had been left behind by a world that worshipped on the altar of science and technology, isolated from civilization by geographical barriers and a stubborn insistence on clinging to an existence where life went on the way it always had, in an unchanging pattern, until an iniquitous infantry unleashed by the necromancer, whom they hadn't even heard of, charged into their midst.

None could make the connection between the sudden onset of madness that ravaged entire communities, driving them to extreme frenzies of orgiastic violence fuelled by the utter corruption of the spirit, before wiping them out in their entirety to the invisible spectres that took possession of their lives, concealed within the dark folds of night.

Bhaya was usually the first to slip unnoticed into a chosen place where the inhabitants slumbered. Lean and cadaverous, the lines of the face were pulled back so sharply it looked like a leering skull. Reddish flesh glistened as he moved among his victims, taking his time, knowing full well they did not know enough to flee, and even if they did, there was no escaping him and his brethren.

Foolish and pathetically hapless though the mortals were, they could nevertheless feel his presence. Nameless dread entered their bloodstreams and flooded their entire being with a senseless terror. They all had nightmares about their loved ones dying—hearts imploding within the ribcage, leaving them screaming and drowning in blood. The little ones howled through the nights, wetting their beds and refusing to calm down till their mothers slapped them senseless, infected as they were by a creeping horror that would not subside.

The twins would saunter into the settlement, their feet dragging. Sokka and Dukkha were both misshapen lumps of flesh, with shaven heads and blind eyes that leaked a watery substance, the former's a milky-white and the latter's an inky-black. Ever so gently, they would slip into the lush bodies of the living, gorging themselves on every happy or hopeful thought that lingered there, sucking them dry, till all that was left was a bottomless misery that would consume them alive.

Vyadhi followed. It had an emaciated frame, and its jaundiced eyes seemed dead and unseeing. There was nothing weak about it though, for within its form was the worst sort of vermin that spread death like a contagion, a cloying, invisible presence. But those cursed with an acuity greater than their fellows could hear its impending approach even in sleep, heralded by a sound like the buzzing of bees and the sickening odour of spoilt meat.

Close on its heels was Trsna. Like the others, she was skinless but glowed pinkly. Her eyes, red as blood, held the promise of pleasure, provided you were willing to embrace the pain. Those with a peculiar bent of mind welcomed her presence and were intoxicated by the thick, musky odour that wafted from her in dense waves, a curious amalgam of seminal fluid and bittersweet intoxicants.

Proximity to Vyadhi meant people toppling over on their sides, retching uncontrollably and reeling from incessant bouts of nausea.

Those under the sway of Trsna would begin to indulge in their dark passion-stoked fantasies with bacchanalian fervour, giving in to sensuous pleasures till they were fit to burst. Under the influence of her drug and enslaved by insatiable lust, they preyed on those nearest to them, oblivious to the fact that sometimes it was their own children or blood relatives they violated.

Krodha would then storm into their midst. He was bulkier than the others, his body thickly corded with muscle and his fists bunched up into cudgels that dealt indiscriminate blows. The undercurrent of violence fermented by his brethren would see its flowering then, and the lot of them would feast on the remains of the mortals and get drunk on their blood.

There were no survivors to tell tales but there were the rare few who managed to escape. And they wandered around, decrepit beggars who huddled miserably in slums, outside temples or just wandered the streets—eyes dull and rheumy, their broken bodies unwashed and scabrous, clothes torn to pieces, an abomination even among others who had sunk almost as low as them.

The Narakamayas stuck to the remote outposts of civilization because prudence dictated they do so. It seemed that the bright lights of the cities beckoned to them and they salivated in anticipation of the bounty they would find there. When the summons came for them, issued by the one who had brought them into being, it would be time, and the entire world would become their personal killing field.

30

A Lost Warning

Nobody paid any attention to him. He was vermin, a bottom-dwelling retarded loser, and nobody had any use for him. He had no use for himself either, come to think of it. Nobody would have believed that a few short months ago, before it was all shot to shit, he had an actual life. Truth be told, it was miserable and pathetic in the extreme, but it had been *his* crappy life, and had he a shred of sanity left, he would have done anything to have it back.

When first he had been forced to leave home, hearth, his wife and two young children behind to the mercies of the ghastly creatures that had overrun his village, he had taken to his heels in abject terror, not daring to look back.

He ran when the sun baked the ground and cooked his feet, he ran when the rain pelted him with big, fat water drops that felt like sharp stones, and he ran through the darkness that caused him to stumble and fall. He ran, though his lungs were about to burst. He ran until he collapsed, and when he came to, the young man in his prime was an old beggar, who did not even recognize himself when he slaked his thirst at a stagnant pool of water that had formed in a crater. Then he started to walk.

The decrepit beggar wandered wherever his feet led him, never stopping too long in any one place. The wretched creature had no will to live, but he did not die either, and it certainly wasn't for want of trying. He hardly knew what he was doing when he fought with stray dogs over scraps of food. They were mean, starved creatures and yet they did not bite him, sensing the encroaching darkness in his eyes that was coming for them as well.

Tall and raw-boned, he wandered around naked as the day he was born. His body was ravaged by myriad injuries. He pissed and shat wherever he happened to be standing, exuding an odour so rank it could floor a bystander a mile away. Pus-filled boils had erupted all over his sun-cooked face and limbs, and he scratched at them in violent fits with rotting, broken nails. He used the same to worry at his balls, which were being devoured by erysipelas, hoisting a single leg over whichever railing or upraised platform that presented itself.

There was something so abhorrent about him that people fled from him, cursing and pressing their hankies to their noses with expressions of supreme revulsion. Street urchins pelted him with stones and rats bit him as he slept. But he was oblivious to it all, trapped as he was in a nightmare, with only the necrophagous fiends and the memories of the terrible carnage he had been an impotent witness to for company. A haunting presence that wouldn't leave him be and which he couldn't, wouldn't let go of.

'I am sorry for leaving you alone,' he spoke into the shadows, the incoherent words tumbling and tripping over each other, speech as broken as the one who uttered them. 'It was foolish of me to take the goats to the market on that particular day. You see, I was a fool then and all that mattered to me was getting a good price for them. I thought we could fix all our problems if only there was a little more money. So I ignored the signs that there are worse things than debt and poverty.'

'I begged you not to go,' a phantasm only he could see and hear replied to him, turning the screw with great deliberation. 'Something terrible lived among us and they were going to toy with us, torture us to within an inch of madness, torment us till we begged for death and only then put an end to our misery.

'I remember how our skin would crawl and the fear would build to a fever pitch, making our hearts pound and bowels loosen. Oh, the sudden bouts of intense weeping! What about that time we made ungodly love right in front of our children! Eleven years of marriage, and you were the gentlest man I knew! Yet, you beat me so badly, and I responded by stabbing you in the thigh with my kitchen knife. All because the children would not stop crying. But even the crying was better than the nausea and the retching!

'You should have known and taken us to safety, away from those evil things.'

'I admit it, but please try to understand. I had not the faintest notion what was happening. In fact, even now nothing makes sense. I thought if we went on pretending that everything was normal, things would eventually return to normal. Please, I'll do anything to make it up to you.'

'There is nothing you can do! Our daughter told us about those creatures dredged up from the bowels of hell . . . She said that they were red monsters who came when the hour was late and slipped into our bodies! She said there was one inside her little brother and that was why he cried endlessly.

'I paid no attention and struck my poor child and her brother both. You did nothing to stop me from hurting them! You did *nothing*!'

'Forgive me! It was entirely my fault. I thought the child was stark raving mad. If anybody else had found out about her condition, they would have insisted that we take her to a doctor, and you know how medical bills can pile up. I was so busy scrimping and scrounging for every lousy coin, I thought this was an unnecessary expense we could not afford.

'My poor little girl . . . She was right. I saw them with my own eyes. They were leaving our village, shortly before dawn, after they had taken their foul pleasures with it, gliding away, floating on clouds of miasmic vapour and sepulchral gases. I could smell burning and their charnel stench. Like a coward, I hid behind the big gorse bush, unmindful of the thorns, lest they came for me as well.'

'But they did not, did they? You managed to escape, leaving us to suffer a fate I would not wish on my worst enemy. The things that happened that accursed night, while you were frolicking with whichever pox-ridden whore that had taken your precious money! How I wish you had been present to see the demoniacal fever that gripped us all, even the children, and the horrifying things we did to each other. Gross libertinage, senseless violence, sickness of the body and soul, more terror than could be borne . . . And in the midst of the carnage, those abominations feasted on the dead and the dying till there was nothing left.'

The beggar shut his ears to the accusations and his eyes to the vile images the fell voice conjured up in his head. But there was no getting away from it and he had been replaying it over and over again in his tortured mind. Vaguely, he thought to warn the living against the hordes of hell, but his mind was gone and who would listen? So his voice died away into nothingness while he waited for merciful death, blessed oblivion and a surcease of suffering.

He was the first of many. They turned up everywhere like a plague of unknown origin, in all shapes, sizes and various stages of decay, with eyes that were dull and rheumy. The numbers of the wretched, woebegone people swelled to epidemic proportions. Some were mute, the things they had seen having deprived them of speech. Others had lost hope and the will to live.

A few sang their tales of horror, and sympathetic onlookers who had stepped forward to part with a coin heard the raw pain and dire warning in their voices, even if they did not understand the garbled words, and walked away, anxious to forget. Mostly, they were ignored as they gibbered like drunken monkeys, drowning slowly in the depths of their unending agony. The portent they posed and the truth of unfathomable evil they heralded could not be stomached by human brains, corrupted with the taint of science and logic, until it caught up with them.

31
Manipulating the Elements

Agni had not been a fan of Baden-Powell and his boy scouts troop as a child, mostly because they forced him into itchy khaki uniforms and insisted he tie a scarf around his neck that made him feel he was being choked to death, while killer ants took his body hostage. Even so, he did like to be prepared and prided himself on being able to anticipate, if not every single curveball life threw his way, then at least a fair number of them.

Nothing could have prepared him for what happened that night in the ghost valley where the Kritya was being held captive. By a singular stroke of luck and with Dharami's help, he had managed to free the victim with next to no resistance from either her or the one who had kidnapped her. Then luck turned and spit in their faces.

Dharami had left them to search for whatever it was Veera had set on them. Minothi had looked positively alarmed at the thought of being left alone with him. He found that amusing. If anybody should have been apprehensive about getting stuck with a proven killer, it was him, given her blood-spattered track record. There was no time to dwell on that though, and he quickly led them to the way out. She followed him hesitantly.

Minothi wished Dharami had not left her behind. Yama's lieutenant did not look like the sort who could acquit himself decently in a fight. He was reed-thin and walked favouring one side, as though the effort cost him. But he was easy on the eyes. She gave him that.

They had almost reached the walls, when Agni stopped. The slow burn of a worrisome premonition of disaster was always harder to take than its actual fruition. His nerves had been stretched tight and plucked raw by the sharp edge of wariness, and now he sensed that the source of his unease was in the vicinity.

Minothi felt it too, in a familiar rush of blood charging through her veins and arteries, as her heart amped up the pace to dizzying speeds. For a moment, she was scared senseless and felt every hair on her body rise. It was the monster from earlier. Even if she had been inclined to allow the rage to build so that it may be incinerated in its flames, which she had promised herself would never happen again, instinct warned her that she was no match for this creature.

It took every ounce of self-control not to run and hide behind the man who stood a little ahead of her, tranquil as you please, with clearly no clue that the thing would wipe the floor many times over with him, even though he brandished what looked like a black rod that pulsed with a reddish light with almighty assurance. It took even more self-control not to push him towards the monster that confronted them, allowing it to make a meal of him while she ran like the wind till she became one with it and could take off into the remote wilderness.

The creature stood silhouetted against the inky blackness of the moat that stretched out behind. It had clearly been lying in wait and emerged rather lazily from behind the fragmented monolith. Man-sized and absolutely skinless, the soft flesh, layers of tissue and brittle bones gleamed red under the wan moonlight. Almost gently, it glided towards them with hypnotic fluidity and serpentine grace. It looked like a floating corpse, the rot having set in, leaving everything putrid and decomposing.

The Narakamaya Sudhana, Agni reckoned. It was death itself, unloosed by the necromancer, using the blood sacrifice of a willing

Kanya. It had no eyes that they could see, no ears, nor a nose. A gaping hole marked the spot that could have been a mouth. Yet, the indiscriminate mass of putrefying flesh never faltered as it came towards them, covering the distance faster than their eyes could follow. Minothi shuddered beside him, seeing the maggots that were crawling over every inch of the terrifying spectre that was coming for them, at exactly the same time he did.

Gently but firmly, Agni shoved her away from him. 'Run! Dharami will find you! Get away as fast as you can.' Minothi hesitated briefly, her skin tingling where he had touched her, but obliged. In a few short seconds, the monster would be on him, and she did not want to distract him by arguing. Her injured feet throbbed in protest as she moved away from Yama's lieutenant, but not too far. He was a fool if he thought he could play the big, tough guy and take on the chthonic monster all by himself.

Sudhana was just about to launch itself on Agni, when the red fire slammed into it, catching it and flipping it backwards. Yama's lieutenant kept up the barrage, an unrelenting wall of fire that pummelled the Narakamaya every which way, pinning it to the ground. Still he pressed his advantage, the exhilaration building as he rode the wave of battle lust, his eyes alight with savage determination, his shoulders set in the stance of a seasoned warrior, as he charged the creature.

Minothi watched, mesmerized, from behind the comforting bulk of a grotesquely disfigured stone lion. She wished she was as brave, resolute and skinny as him. Not that she was an expert on the subject, but he was such a typical male, exulting in the savage pleasures afforded by excessive violence. It was a heady sensation watching him burn the hideous apparition to a pulpy mush, and the thing grew excited inside her, straining against the leash that held it back. It was almost over, and her disappointment was palpable.

Yama's lieutenant was visibly weakening from the tremendous effort he had called forth. The flames died down and then the unthinkable happened. The mushy remains of the Narakamaya gathered itself from the ooze, reassembling the decomposing parts of its body with alarming ease. Except it was bigger now and more solid, grown fat on the flames that should have consumed it. Its menacing form towered over Agni, its mouth stretched open in a hideous simulacrum of a smile.

Quick as a cat, Agni shifted and prepared for the counter-attack. Sudhana was all over him in seconds, and withered arms reached for his throat as Agni struck him with the danda. He felt it slash through the festering flesh, which squelched in protest, and clash with the bone beneath. The white-hot magic exploded into the Narakamaya. Chunks of flesh splattered on the ground and on to Agni, who recoiled involuntarily. But it barely slowed. It was upon him before he could recover. Slime-covered fingers closed around his throat.

The breath caught in his windpipe, lodged there like a piece of food gone down the wrong way, and his body turned to ice. He shivered violently and the fingers tightened its vice-like grip. In a haze he released the pasha and it yanked Sudhana backwards, the noose tightening around its neck in a garrotting action, slicing through cleanly and severing the head. Agni spun away, weak and dizzy. The ground seemed to be shaking, and he fell to his knees.

The possibility of death loomed large over him, and he forced himself to fight, if not for himself, then at least for the sake of the one who had demanded the impossible from him. He needed help. Chandu and Suri had to be summoned, but he was slipping away fast.

He heard rather than saw the head fasten itself to the trunk. With an effort, he stood, his thoughts spinning incoherently. The tender skin of his throat burnt and it was as if the maggots had burrowed into his body and were feeding on his innards. Of course, Yama's weapons would prove ineffectual against death itself. Varu had written something about it, he was sure of it. He was sorry he could not remember more. Even the hounds would not be able to stop the necromancer's assassin. But he would not give up while there was life left in him.

Unsteady and struggling to stay on his feet, he gave ground before Sudhana, utterly outmatched in height and strength, as it advanced. Trying to buy himself some time, he threw the flames of hell at the creature again, but this time Sudhana absorbed it all into itself. Agni could see the maggots wriggling all over its face, feasting on the rotting remains of that ruined visage, and he felt the numbness take root deep within him as the aching cold spread all over him, paralysing him with it.

Sudhana's bony claws were reaching for his throat again, and he could feel its fetid breath on his exposed face, smell the rank odour of the dead that exuded from it in overpowering waves, and he thought of Varu. He heard the sound of shrieking in his head. It was drowning out whatever it was that his twin's voice was saying so desperately to him.

Suddenly, the Narakamaya faltered and drew back in confusion. Minothi reminded herself to keep breathing as she concentrated every fibre of her being on channelling the earth magic that had gathered in her fingertips and had been released in narrow strands, which wrapped themselves around the Narakamaya, twirling themselves around the softened skeleton and pulling it, seemingly of its own volition, away from Agni.

She could feel the reeking, foul fiend in her mouth, her nostrils and her very bones—the fetid stench of rotting meat and worse. Nausea racked her weakened frame and she fought to stay in control, the exhilaration of the magic overpowering her distaste as she insinuated her power into the creature, fusing it with the elements that swirled through it in infinitesimal specks.

Intuitively, Agni kept still, watching in disbelief as Sudhana wrapped its fingers around a smooth rock and, pressing its stinking maw to the stony surface, began to suck on it. He felt his gorge rise and was fighting the urge to throw up, when a soft hand pressed into his. And then he was soaring away, Minothi by his side.

'Just a little trick of illusion,' Minothi whispered. They watched from a great distance as the spell broke, and the Narakamaya looked directly at them. It was too far away from them to be certain but Agni heard a bestial scream tear through the silence that enshrouded the valley. It promised retribution.

The valley was disappearing fast beneath them and they could see the stark outlines of the mountains and forests that rose up to meet the night sky. Waterbodies shimmered in the distance and, to Agni's relief, they could see a million lights twinkling and the silhouettes of tall buildings that towered over the hills, bearing testament to the colossal achievements of the humans.

But all too soon, they were leaving it all behind and everything shrunk to dots before slipping into a swirling vortex of darkness. 'Where the hell are we going?' he asked his companion urgently. Her voice sounded small and scared when she replied, 'I have absolutely no idea.'

32

From Varu's Book: Guardians of the Universe

Yama was Twastha's favourite grandson, and it galled Yami no end that he seldom bothered to even register her presence while constantly exalting her brother's achievements. The revered architect of the devas had sent for him, and was pleased when Yama arrived post-haste at his resplendent palace. 'You have done the family proud!' the venerable patriarch said as he hugged him.

'As far as I am concerned, you are my daughter's only notable achievement. She was a colossal disappointment, but at least she gave birth to a worthy son, even if she abandoned him to pursue harlotry.' Yama's polite smile curved fully into a grimace almost of its own accord, which Twastha noted with amusement. 'Another peculiar quality of that shameful daughter of mine is her ability to inspire unconditional love in the breasts of the worthy males in her life, despite proving herself unworthy of them! But I have no wish to discuss the follies of one whom I'd rather forget. My sources tell me that the pretender who managed to crawl into the sun god's bed has dared to pronounce a curse over my grandson. What do you propose to do about it?'

Unlike Yami, he was not overawed in the presence of his grandfather. 'She can do her worst! I refuse to negotiate with the likes of her.'

Twastha nodded approvingly. He clapped his hands and his attendants brought forth an object wrapped in a silvery cloth. Twastha flung aside the cloth to reveal a beautiful black staff that came up to his shoulder and was thicker than his wrist. There were esoteric markings on it that gleamed ruby-red with the force of the power contained within.

'This danda will be your right hand. Invoking the blessings of the destroyer, I have charged it with his power. You will achieve great things with it. But most importantly, it will remind you that the escharotic power of those who hate and seek to destroy us can always be countered by the love borne by those united to us by the bond of blood!'

Even Yami was gratified at the grand old man's charming gesture, which served to allay even her worst fears regarding the curse. Time swept them all away on its tides. To no one's surprise, Yama established himself as one of the finest warriors the devas had seen and achieved the status of a legend. Even Indra, their king, was suitably impressed with his prowess and elevated him to the status of a *lokapala*, with the blessing of the creator, Brahma.

The lokapalas were the guardians of the universe, led by Indra himself, who had taken charge of the east. Yama, Varuna and Kubera guarded the south, west and north, respectively. The quartet would be regarded as the mightiest of the celestials and would enjoy the utmost respect of their peers. Surya was beside himself with pride.

Yama was escorted to Indra's palace by his personal guard, as a mark of his king's favour. It was a familiar path he had taken many times with his father but, nevertheless, it was a momentous undertaking, and his eyes took in the fabled beauty of his beloved Amaravathi as though for the first time. Every inch of it was perfection, crafted with loving attention to detail by his grandfather. The city was the fairest in the three worlds but its aesthetic value was secondary to what it symbolized.

Amaravathi had long represented the core values of virtue, hard work and sacrifice for the greater good, defying the belief that it paid to be unrighteous. Yama smiled to himself at the overly sentimental and idealistic assessment of his birthplace, when few knew better that the rot had set in at its core.

Even so, the city and its inhabitants had not stopped believing in the power of goodness, even if they were not always noble to a fault. That certainly counted for something, and eventually they would throw off the yoke of moral ambivalence and return to the pure state that had made them worthy of being the fortunate few chosen to live in the city of the gods. Yama had never realized it before, but he loved the place with an awe and passion that left him feeling humbled and grateful that he had been summoned to its service.

It was a momentous day, and Yama's ascent was celebrated with great pomp and ceremony. The turnout was impressive. Shiva, Vishnu and Brahma were present, and it seemed that every one of the thirty-three crore devas were attending the event with their families, as were the *saptarishi*s, and the semi-celestials, like the *gandharva*s and apsaras. They had all gathered in Indra's sabha for the ceremony, and once that was concluded, the king of heaven and his wife, Sachi, saw to it that they all feasted in style.

Even Brihaspati was all smiles and hugged Yama warmly. Surya had been responsible for this uncharacteristic outpouring of goodwill from his guru. Yama had never discussed the stormy nature of his and Brihaspati's relationship with anybody, save Yami. But the sun saw all. Without a word to him, he had arranged a matrimonial alliance between the twins and two of the preceptor's children by Chandramasi—Svana and Svaha. A date for the betrothal had been fixed, and the wedding would happen shortly after.

Brihaspati had been highly gratified, and Surya had patted himself on the back for his adroit manipulation of events, which would see his family reap dual benefits. The road ahead had been smoothed for his favourite son, and a highly fortuitous match for his daughter had also been made. Indra had also blessed the match, and the grand alliance would herald the beginning of peace and prosperity for his family.

At the end of a long day of festivities, Yama retired to his room, tired but happy, and at peace. He was thinking dreamily of all the things he intended to do with the opportunities given to him. Slowly, his thoughts veered towards his guru's daughter, who had been the cynosure of all eyes during the time he had spent under the venerable sage's tutelage. Back then, he had given her a wide berth since he had no intention of antagonizing Brihaspati more than he had to, but that wasn't to say her beauty had been lost on him.

While he dwelt on the lovely maid he was to marry, Yami's shrill voice broke into his thoughts, 'You are a swine, and a filthy, despicable one at that! What is wrong with you? How could you allow something so monstrous to happen?' Yanking his sheets away, she flung them to the floor and aimed a kick at his shins.

'What have I done?' he asked innocently, though he did have an inkling as to what had triggered this full-blown tantrum.

'You have agreed to marry a girl you know absolutely nothing about! If your concupiscent needs have got out of hand and you are that desperate to indulge them, you are better off availing the services of the apsaras. Since you are Indra's golden boy now, I am sure he'll be happy to send you his favourites. That is hardly any reason for you to agree to marry the first female that father has pointed you towards!

'Thanks to you, I am also expected to surrender to marriage, like the sacrificial lamb to the axe. Don't you dare play the innocent and ask what you have done! You know very well that marriage and its attendant horrors are not for me. Father knows me so well, and he still saw fit to promise my hand to the first moronic male who was ready, willing and able, without bothering to ask me how I felt! It is abominable, and I will not stand for it!'

Yami was practically in tears, her clothes in disarray and her chest heaving with the force of her tumultuous passions. Yama put his arm around her shoulder, but she flung it away in a temper. 'Calm down, Yami!' he said soothingly. 'Get a hold of yourself. Father did not tell me anything about this either, and you know it!'

'I know that, which is why I cannot understand your maddening equanimity about this whole situation. Are you in love with this Svaha?'

'Of course not,' Yama replied, hesitating briefly. Yami pounced on him. 'But you have seen her, haven't you? And you think she is pretty! That is so typical of your species. I have seen her myself. She is one of those annoyingly-good-looking creatures who seem to always have a reason to paste a stupid smile across their insipid features. Have you heard her speak? She chirps like a stupid bird fully inebriated on soma, or something equally mind-altering. Just the sort of thing bloody males want to scoop up in their hands and cherish.

'I find her sunny disposition suspicious and am positive it's a cover for the fact that she is as fake as they come. I abhor her already and find it hard to believe that you are all set to marry a lousy bitch whom I cannot stand!'

Unfortunately, Yama winced before he could stop himself, and his twin stared at him, stunned, looking as though she had been struck across the face. She was shaking her head in disbelief, when he managed to get a few words in before she could go on. 'Typical! You have given your runaway emotions their head and trampled reason and good sense underneath. Father only did what he thought was best. As you said yourself, he knows his daughter and has chosen a groom he feels is suitable for her. From what I have heard, Svana is a really nice boy.'

'I couldn't care less. For all I know, he could be a proper little piece of smelly turd with a teeny, tiny penis that is inadequate to satisfy a flea! He is not as good-looking as you or father, nor does he seem to be as sturdily built. This fellow is short and stocky, and his hair hangs listlessly on his narrow shoulders. And when he is not looking dour, he looks sour, as if he resents having been plucked off his mother's teat. How can Father decide that he is the right match for me?'

'You are being childish, Yami! And given the state you are in, it is small wonder that you cannot think straight. Give the poor schmuck a chance! He just might win your heart. Not only is he a lord of the flames and one of the six Agnis, but he rules over the realm of disease as well. If my sources are correct, Svana has been in love with you for a long time and had been pestering Brihaspati to ask for your hand in marriage. You should at least get to know him a little before rejecting him outright. Perhaps he can truly make you happy!'

'Is that supposed to make me feel better? To be honest, I have fallen for a good number of the celestials, and I dare say a good number feels the same about me. You know I have a soft spot for that gorgeous Kama, but that doesn't mean that I wish to be wed! If this Svana truly loved me, he should have approached me directly and had the gumption to propose to me and get turned down. Instead, he goes behind my back to my father, no less, and snaps me up! I hate him for doing that. Besides, there are other things to be considered.'

'Tell me about them, but breathe first!' Yama coaxed her gently, waiting for her to open a familiar can of worms.

'There are so many things. You know Mother and Father were desperately unhappy when they were together. They were so mean to each other and all they did was fight. Do you remember how they both always seemed happier when the other wasn't around? I swore to myself that I would never allow myself to be wed. Marriage is a ridiculous institution, and I don't see why we have to condone it. If the birds and bees can get by without it, why do we need it?'

'Don't make this about all the things that went wrong between Mother and Father. Our lives are our own and we can make what we will of them!'

'Shut up, Yama! I am not in the mood for meaningless platitudes. My life cannot be my own if I am not even allowed to have a say in my own marriage. Besides, I refuse to have sex with a rank stranger just because Father has promised me to him! The very idea is sickening and makes me want to have my privates boarded up for good. In order for me to give myself to a man, I need to be in love with him and trust him completely. Or he has to arouse me to such an extent that all else takes a back seat. And to be honest, I just don't see that happening. If Kama were to ditch his wife and propose marriage to me, I would run for the hills as though Indra's bitch were at my heels, and not even the fierce gales would be able to catch me.

'How many times have I said that it is enough for me to be Surya's daughter and Yama's sister? Because there is nobody I trust in the three worlds, save the pair of you! Not that it has ever done me any good.'

Mercifully Yami stopped talking then, but it was only because she was overcome by tears. Yama held her close and eased her into bed beside him. He picked up the discarded sheet and wrapped it around them both. They huddled together the way they used to when they were children, staying that way for a long time.

Yama waited for her sobs to die down before he spoke. 'I promise that you won't have to do anything you don't want to. All I ask is that you be patient for a bit. There is no need to make a decision immediately. There is some way to go before the betrothal. On the morrow, I take up my duties as a lokapala, and I was given to understand that we may have to leave Amaravathi for a while to make sure that the boundaries are secure.

'Use that time to ascertain what you want to do with the future. As you know, Father will be furious if we make him retract his word.

Take all this into consideration before you make up your mind, and if you still cannot go through with this marriage, then you have my support! But promise me that you will not do anything foolhardy while I am away!'

Yami managed a small nod, though she was feeling more hopeless than ever. There was nothing more to be said. Surya would not be merely furious but apoplectic with rage. Yama was being foolishly optimistic because, his support notwithstanding, Surya would never go back on his word and was likely to force her into this marriage, even if it meant making her circumambulate the sacred flames in chains. She could already feel the iron cage she had always feared closing in on her, and senseless panic gripped her. There was no escape for her and she was going to be wedded to Svana, of the potentially limp prick.

Yama held her tightly, sensing her distress, and suddenly she was exhausted. All she wanted was to go to sleep in her twin's arms and never wake up.

Chaya detached herself from the shadows. It had all gone much better than she had dared to hope. Yami was such a fool! Not only did she make it a point to spout mounds of garbage every time she opened that stinking mouth of hers, but she did so in a voice that was louder than that of a trumpeting elephant. This time, her imprudent words would be the death of her, she assumed gleefully.

While she had to strain to catch the gist of the conversation, the unfortunate individual she had sent to the private garden below Yama's room in the expectation of a romantic rendezvous would have got an earful by now. Smothering her laughter, she realized he had just been vilified for being short, stocky, sour and dour and having an allegedly small penis. She had nearly laughed out loud at that.

Slowly she walked over to him, her presence aimed to compound the misery and humiliation of the former lover who had only wanted to pour sweet nothings into the ear of his beloved.

She could almost feel his hurt being swallowed up by all the rage a spurned and embittered ego could muster.

Grabbing Svana by the arm, she led him away. 'This is so unfortunate! Ever since their father forbade them to visit each other at indecent hours, we all thought they had stopped their inappropriate behaviour! Alas! It is too bad you had to see and hear all those terrible things.'

Satisfied with the look of murderous rage on his face, she continued, 'Please try to understand! She is only a foolish child with all the insecurities and abject stupidity of one, and her father has spoilt her so. Once she is married into a respectable family, I am sure she will be cured of her immaturity.

'Please don't be angry at her for spending the night in her brother's chambers or read too much into their shocking conduct. They are as innocent as a pair of newborn lambs.'

Chaya wondered if she should tell Svana about how Yami had lost her virginity following an accident when she was playful roughhousing with her brother when they were children, but prudently decided that it might amount to overkill. The green-eyed monster had been awakened from its slumber, and it would do the needful without further prompting on her part.

Without another word, Svana stormed off into the night.

33

Lost in Utopia

They were still holding hands. Neither could be certain about anything else. There was a vague memory of having battled an indestructible fiend. Agni would not have made it if Minothi had not intervened. They had both been lifted away from the old ruins and were hurtling through time and space to they-knew-not-where.

The darkness that had closed in on them was complete and nothing could penetrate it, not even thought. Both had forgotten what it was like to have something firm underfoot to walk on, borne on a wind away from all things remotely familiar till everything they had known receded into the musty catacombs of memory, to be forgotten. The crushing blindness and debilitating deafness and dumbness did not seem to matter as much as the curious weightlessness and the feel of fingers laced tightly together.

Both tried to talk but their words were torn out from their throats before they could reach the lips and sucked into the vacuum they couldn't see, hear or smell. The silence was deafening, broken only by the occasional whooshing that threatened to rupture eardrums.

The blackness bore down on them, and they could feel it pressing against the surface of their sanity, smothering it to death so that the madness could break free from its dam and flood them with it. But they could still feel each other's hands. It was absurd how much joy and comfort they derived from the simple act, even as they seemed to disappear into the great beyond or a bottomless abyss. Her hands were soft and plump, inclined towards moistness, especially when she was under duress, like she was then. His were cool and dry, calloused from the battles he had fought. It was their only link to the fragile existence from which they had been snatched away, and they held on to the tenuous thread, their slender hope for reaching the shore and whatever lay in wait.

Entire aeons could have passed, or maybe it was a few seconds. Without warning, their stomachs dropped as they plummeted into the blackness below, twin stones discharged from a sling, following an invisible trajectory towards a crash-landing.

One after another, they landed in a heap on the floor of a garden, their fall broken by a cushion of soft grass. The sickle moon cut its way past a cloud to take a look at them, and even its watery glow nearly blinded them as they struggled to get their bearings, panting and gasping for breath in this unfamiliar place. Their senses were under assault, it seemed, and they were steadily bombarded with endless stimuli that spoke of quiet opulence, high walls and jagged spikes.

Gentle hands that felt like heaven lifted them tenderly, carrying them into an immense castle that towered over them, its doors thrown open in warm hospitality. Too weak to protest, Agni and Minothi struggled only when their clasped hands were pried free. But their captors—translucent organisms made of moonbeams and broken fragments of stars, resembling diaphanous garments of the purest silver tossed about by the wind—soothed them. Their velvet touch was gentle and firm as a mother's, filling them with the need to be taken care of. And they surrendered with a scary lack of resistance.

Neither Agni nor Minothi had had the luxury of hot water and a bar of soap in a really long time. Grazed elbows, knees and feet that were torn and grubby, speckled purplish bruises and blackened nails caked with filth bore testament to the fact. Both could smell the rank odour of the other and were suitably appalled.

They were lowered into deep tubs filled with soapy water to soak and remove the dust and grime. Once they were towelled down, the silver sprites took care of the injuries Agni and Minothi had sustained in what felt like another lifetime. Sweet-smelling ointments were applied on deep cuts and lacerations, which magically closed, the broken skin mended and bruises faded completely, leaving their bodies good as new. All the hurts of the mind and flesh had vanished as though they had never been.

Once they were wearing fresh clothes that were available in just the right sizes, the mysterious attendants fed the intrepid duo bowls of life-giving broth that warmed their insides and left them tingling with contentment. Then they were taken away to their respective chambers and tucked into warm beds, comfortably swaddled in the gossamer softness of well-being till they slept the sleep of the dead.

Those irresistible beings of the translucent, formless form met with resistance only when they tried to get Agni to part with his backpack and Minothi her pendant. Both struggled so violently that there was nothing to be done, and so they were allowed to hold on to their paltry possessions while they slumbered.

When Agni awoke, the sun was beaming at him through his window. He sprang to his feet, his head cloudy with sleep and his bed beckoning to him invitingly. Resisting the urge to sleep on, he relieved himself in a chamber pot under his bed and hoped there was a decent loo available. Minothi was still asleep in a room down the corridor, and he left her to it.

The castle was located in the centre of what seemed to be a grid, marked by wide tree-lined avenues that stood like silent sentinels watching over everything with unblinking eyes. The grid opened into intricate pathways that branched even further, leading to a confusing complex of marble pools, gardens, pavilions, ornamental topiaries and an array of smaller constructions for indiscriminate purposes. Over it all, there extended a massive stone wall, twelve feet high, topped with wicked-looking spikes. Beyond that lay a sea of sand baking under a hot sun.

The short walk, the sight of those spikes and the desert beyond left him feeling drained, as if every one of his resources had been thoroughly depleted. He was so exhausted he could barely move and, almost on cue, the sprites arrived to usher him into the castle, where a table had been laid out for him, groaning under the weight of food. There were eggs cooked every which way, fresh-baked bread with butter and jam, fresh fruits, juices, salads and delicious pastries.

Minothi was already tucking in and smiled weakly at him. Agni was not very hungry, but when he sampled the food he could not stop and ate till his insides were fit to burst. Between mouthfuls, they conversed about the strangeness of the place they were in. The sprites were unobtrusive but they might as well have tut-tutted, for they somehow managed to convey their displeasure over their charges using words to season food that was already balanced to perfection rather than relishing their repast in silence.

'I thought you lifted us out of there with whatever it is you do. And that you might have an inkling about where we were intended to go,' Agni began.

'I know you thought I did,' Minothi replied with a mouth full of creamy egg. She swallowed quickly and took a sip of her juice before continuing. 'But the thing is, I really have no idea about what exactly happened. Besides, the question is: Why have we been brought here, and by whom?'

Agni was chewing his way past a plate of Bombay toast, exactly like the ones his mother used to make, and he had trouble concentrating on the conversation. With concentrated effort, he swallowed and spoke again, 'You are the key. Just before we lost her, Dharami was trying to say something important to me. It had something to do with you.'

Minothi suddenly wished he would let her eat in peace. 'I cannot remember but there was a she, and I do believe she told me to remember something important. Everything feels so fuzzy in my head and, to tell the truth, it hurts when I push too hard to try and remember.'

Agni would have liked to continue talking, but the effort had exhausted him. Besides, as Minothi had said, it hurt too hard to think, and he gave up.

He tried to look up to see if she was faring any better but his eyes were closing. The beings shaped from the softest clouds billowed around him protectively and helped him into bed.

The days rolled by, and Yama's lieutenant and the Kritya did nothing but catch up on the sleep they had snatched only in small doses over the years, kept awake by a restlessness that threw open the doors to the clawed reach of nightmares. When they were not sleeping, they ate like they never had before in their entire lives, gorging themselves silly on superbly spiced meat dishes cooked on the spit or grilled to perfection—delicious cuts of venison, fillets of chicken and succulent fish, prawns, lobsters and crabs cooked in their shells, mussels, oysters—vegetables poached in butter, fresh fruits, soups, and just about every delectable sweetmeat the mind could and couldn't conceive.

On the days they managed to escape the seductive embrace of those silken sheets and the gluttonous delights of the dining table, Agni and Minothi wandered around the enchanted palace and its grounds while it threw open wonderful vistas for them to explore. There were pools of marble to frolic in, gardens that soothed the eye and senses, streams of the clearest water that could be followed to the source, hot springs that felt so therapeutic that neither wished to get up and leave, even when the hypnotic vapours turned their brains to pulp.

The air was sweet. The cool breezes were a constant presence, fanning away the anxiety and dread that had been their constant companions. When they happened to look over the walls, the desert glowered at them as far as the eye could see in all directions, without a blade of grass or drop of water to offer respite from the killing heat. The sight filled them with dread, which when juxtaposed against their days, which passed in perfect and pure bliss, made it that much harder to stomach.

They turned away from those monstrous dunes of death and fled into the cool and comforting insides of the castle that was catering so generously to their every need. Only a lunatic would venture into the world outside when it offered everything the mind and body could want and more.

Inside, there was a huge library filled with more books than they could count. They were magnificent books in covers inlaid with mother-of-pearl and spines of pure gold. Their pages told of tales more wondrous than any that had been recounted in the entire history of human civilization, running into thousands and thousands of pages, filled with magic, history, art, science and rare knowledge that was invaluable, entertaining and addictive. The happy reader could spend entire lifetimes doing nothing but read a single one of those books without ever reaching the last page.

And then there was the music. It came wafting out of nowhere, transporting away Agni and Minothi, making them willing captives to its seductive power. Held in a hypnotic trance, they could listen to it endlessly, allowing nothing to interrupt their unvarnished enjoyment of it. And how they danced! The sprites joined them in a fervent orgy of terpsichorean grace, twirling and whirling like mad dervishes. Happy as one could be.

It was the perfect existence filled with nothing but the good things in life. The convivial atmosphere was a panacea for wounded spirits such as theirs. And yet it wasn't. The surfeit of pleasurable indulgence ought to have palled but it never did. Every day when the sun woke them with its usual smile of brilliance, they felt a little weaker than the day before, less well-rested. Rather, it felt like being ill, having overdosed on chocolate and ice cream till their teeth were riddled with cavities, stomach overrun with germs and the entrails chewed up by worms.

Minothi became a tad more brittle and Agni tighter, like a clenched sphincter. Loving hands that nourished and nurtured, wiped off another smidgen of their inner essence so imperceptibly that it may never have been there in the first place. In that cocoon of light and softness, reflexes became fractionally slower, responses more sluggish and thought processes ground to an indefinite standstill.

Her reason for living dulled ever so slightly. His iron sense of purpose, which had driven him for so long, was chipped away speck by infinitesimal speck. It was only the beginning of a sweet and slow decline on a steep and slippery slope, slick with treacle.

Out of nowhere the dreams began, signalling a slight shift in the currents swirling around, and something within Agni retracted in response, a gentle realignment of the senses that had atrophied with disuse. He saw Minothi in his dreams and the phantasmagorical images prodded his deadened memory, hearkening back to a time when a dear face came to him only in the inhospitable realm of nightmares and drove him to live with demoniacal need.

•••

Minothi was walking away from him and their little slice of heaven, ignoring his desperate entreaties. She ran into the vast desert beyond and to her doom, driven there by voices that had taken reason captive. Agni was crying, begging her to remove the pendant from her neck and fling it far away, but she would not listen. She ran on without a backward glance, wilfully ignoring the sand demons that were closing in on her, smirking at Agni, whose warning cries were lost in the wind and swirl of fine sand.

She ran like a child who had been promised candy. And then the treacherous sands parted and demon hands reached out, dragging her into the quagmire, sucking her into it as she fought in vain to find purchase in the slippery tomb of sand. Agni could feel the grit that coated her eyes and nose and had been inhaled into her lungs and swallowed into a protesting stomach, where it sank into the bile that flooded her insides, secreted in response to her terror.

Little by little, the sand and the clawing hands fought to see who could drag her down quicker into the mire. She put up an almighty struggle, screaming all the while, aiding and abetting their efforts. All the while Minothi called out to him for help, but he could not move. By then the sand had filled her mouth and lungs. She flailed about in silence, playing out her death in mime till her fingertips were consumed along with the rest of her. Then, with an almighty belch, the sand demons who had taken her spat out the pendant. It travelled across the distance and whacked him on the nose.

•••

Agni woke up suddenly in the middle of the night. He could see the moon outside the window, but even farther, the sun blazed across the desert where summer was forever. An old instinct called out in warning. His heart rate picked up and he felt an all-too-familiar surge of adrenaline. Clinging to it like one trapped in a quicksand, Yama's lieutenant scrambled to his feet. A bulky form stood frozen and huddled in a corner, clutching something, no doubt assuming that the darkness concealed it. To his surprise, he was still able to move like greased lightning, though his muscles had grown rusty from lack of exercise.

Silent and deadly, he grabbed his would-be assailant around the throat in a fit of alien rage, tightening his hold, determined to squeeze the life out of the intruder. Minothi tried to scream but she only managed a subdued squeak and tried to use her fleshy buttocks like a battering ram. Agni let her go at once. Both were breathing heavily. He remembered telling someone he thought she was mentally challenged. *Dharami*. A name. He heard it like the whisper of silk. Something to hold on to while he dealt with the murderous woman who had whisked him away to nowhere and held his hand with infinite tenderness.

'What the hell do you think you are doing?' Agni demanded in a whisper.

'I don't know! But you have to believe me, the plan was never to hurt you! For many days now the pretty silver sprites have been asking me to relieve you of that accursed backpack you insist on toting around, though it is filthy. We have no need of it here. It is a thing of evil and will be the death of you. I saw it in a vision. You have to throw it out, far away from these hallowed grounds.

'And then we can live without the baggage from the past, without the horrors that await in the future, suspended in time, where every moment is perfectly blissful forever. It is what I want for both of us.'

Beseechingly, and looking more like a child trapped in a strapping woman's body than ever, she took his hand in hers. Agni stared at her and, for just a moment, he was tempted to acquiesce. He would have too, but then he remembered another little girl who had liked to hold hands and clamber on to his bed when she felt scared or after burying her dead pet. She too had made unreasonable demands of him.

Varuna. Varu. The pain hit him like a sledgehammer, fresh as the day when that particular wound had been inflicted. His dearly beloved sister who had joined the ranks of the departed and who came to him in his nightmares, where she implored him to save her from the torments of hell. *Arakshas*. He was Yama's lieutenant; he hated the job but loved the power that was his to wield.

Agni smiled and it filled the room with effervescence. It was good to be alive again. Minothi flinched when she saw the spark that lit up his eyes. Almost reflexively, her body responded, and she fought the long-buried things that came surging to the perimeter of conscious thought. In her mind's eye, she saw her mother's face, ravaged by suffering as she entrusted her to fate. Bodies leaking copious amounts of blood, lying dead. An unmoving foot. A body crushed under a pile of rubble. Small children lying chained to beds.

Sensing the panic that had come to boil and was bubbling over, Agni spoke soothing words. 'Don't worry. It will be as you wish. I have been warned about that pendant you wear as well. Let us do it together then. We will go to the main entrance and then I will throw my backpack as far as I can. You must also take off that pendant and fling it away. Good riddance to both. Let us do it immediately.' *Tayaka*. They both remembered it at the same time. A talisman that will help them achieve something important.

The silver sprites had gathered around them en masse, but they were no longer comforting, merely menacing. Red light flashed in their blind eyes, and they gathered round the duo as if to cut off their escape. Agni ignored them but he had the danda in his hand. An old friend that kept the enemy at bay. He started to walk and, to his relief, Minothi followed him, albeit hesitantly.

They proceeded along the tree-lined avenues towards the gatehouse, the sprites hounding them, their voices shrill in their ears, urging them to return, calling out dire warnings. Agni saw the walls rising up to the sky, illuminated by a rind of moon, the spikes glowering at him and the castle they were leaving behind. It was like an ugly toad that had eaten a hundred flies too many. How did they ever find it beautiful?

'Even if your captors pamper you to within an inch of your life, a prison is still a prison,' he murmured the words to Minothi over the hissing and spitting of the wispy creatures that chased them with increasing desperation. She nodded, but her eyes were wet with tears. She had been happy, even if it was all make-believe.

'When my debts are repaid, I hope to be as happy as I was here, but for real.' Her voice was thick with choked sobs.

On an impulse, Agni took her hand and squeezed it reassuringly and her resistance melted as she cleaved to him. The desert loomed ahead of them, its horizon smudged by the heat of a vicious sun that blazed on without respite, promising nothing but death by thirst, exposure, the bite of a poisonous reptile, or a slow, painful descent into its sandy depths. The invisible sand demons were everywhere. Minothi trembled and tightened her grip on his fingers. The pendant at her throat throbbed encouragingly.

Without pausing to think, lest it shatter their resolve, Agni led her past the gate, away from the cool night of their enchanted castle, past any chance for succour, into the terrible sea of sand that spread out ahead of them in endless, undulating waves.

34

The Scorching Sands of Time

The dunes they had to traverse were a virulent shade of orange, shimmering under the heat. A sea of sand rippled and seemed to stretch all the way to infinity. Not a single cloud broke the uniform blue of that sky, which belonged solely to a possessive, malevolent sun.

Agni and Minothi walked hand in hand into the jaws of that bleak landscape, while the enchanted castle with its strange denizens dwindled in size before disappearing altogether, like a fragment from a forgotten dream. It was only then that their breathing resumed its normal pattern.

Minothi had been watching her companion. He seemed jaunty, upbeat even, not in the least like one who had just stepped out from the lap of luxury to the depths of a fiery hell. It was very annoying. They did not have the provisions for an undertaking such as this. She wondered if the thing in her blood would come out of hibernation and conjure up a string of camels, barrels of water and food to keep body and soul together, even a manservant or two. Heck, she would have even settled for a pair of shoes, a big floppy hat and sunglasses.

Soon, they were not perspiring as both expected. The sun had sucked out every bit of moisture from their bodies. There was no saliva left in their mouths or piss in their bladders. It seemed like they had only just set out but already Minothi's lips and tongue were dry, swollen and cracked, and her throat parched and constricted. Her skull had become an oven inside which her brain was being slowly cooked.

They no longer had any sense of time. In the enchanted castle, every moment had been pure bliss; here in the burning wasteland it was an exercise in agony. The sun never seemed to set and Minothi had no idea how long they had been walking. It felt like entire lifetimes had elapsed. Even the landscape remained unchanged. Every few leagues they would stumble on a single blasted and ruined tree from which hung withered melons. She would pluck one with trembling fingers, tear it apart with her teeth and offer half of it to Agni, who would inexplicably shake his head, his bloodshot eyes trying to communicate something that was entirely lost on her. Deliriously happy, she would wolf down the entire thing, rind and all.

There would be relief for an achingly brief period and then the hunger and thirst would emerge from hiding to torment her afresh. She was too fatigued to wonder why it felt like she was literally going in circles. Perhaps it was a spiral that was winding down towards the wretched madness that would precede a painful death.

Minothi tried to unleash the magic. Perhaps she could drain every single waterbody on earth to slake the dry void that throbbed so miserably within her and drown the accursed desert beneath it. But it seemed even deader than she was.

The thirst was unspeakable, and Minothi wondered if she had the strength to wrestle Agni to the ground and suck the blood out of him, crack his bones and feast on the marrow to quench her need for something liquid to moisten her insides, if only for an ephemeral moment.

The object of her murderous thoughts remained cool and unflappable. He looked almost as bad as she felt and nowhere as handsome as he had been. Sun-darkened and harsh of countenance, his body had been stripped of every ounce of fat, not that there had been any to start with, leaving him with nothing but rubbery muscles. His effeminate eyelashes, thick eyebrows and hair were dusted with white sand, so he looked like an old man who might be better off if death hastened to claim him. But he did not seem disturbed by any of it and kept walking, placing one foot in front of the other. Occasionally, he looked off into the desert, looking like an ornithologist on the lookout for a rare bird.

Minothi's thoughts wandered. She giggled, thinking how nice it would be if Agni caught the bird. She would snatch it out of his hand, snap the feathered little one's puny neck in two and drink its blood before eating it raw, feathers and all. Still giggling, she addressed him.

'Are you not in the least bit concerned about our fate? By now, you must have divined that it is only a matter of time before this godawful place chews us up and spits out our remains for the sand lizards and ants to feed on. Is it your intention to go without an almighty struggle? If so, it would have been nice of you to leave me to my fate in that castle. At least that would have been a good and comfortable way to die.' Minothi heard her voice through a haze of acute discomfort, and it sounded a lot better than it had any right to.'

'If that was not real, then this isn't either. If I am not mistaken, we are in another realm altogether, where nothing is as we know it to be. As I said earlier, you are the key that is needed to unlock this puzzle.' He looked at her meaningfully, with the air of a smug and annoying know-it-all. To her consternation, he was looking better by the second, as if he had been given a refreshing draught of water.

Surreptitiously, she ran her eyes over herself from chest to toe. Unfortunately, the desert had not melted the fat off her. And three of her toenails were an alarming shade of purple. But the good news was that her tongue was no longer like a burr sticking to a parched throat. The talking must have helped. In fact, she had enough spit to launch a projectile in the direction of his eye. If she wished.

Instead, she said, 'You keep saying that. But the truth is I have absolutely no idea what the pendant can do, or what a tayaka means. Gurvi Sampoorna gave it to me shortly after she died. It sounds bizarre when put that way but it is the honest truth. I fell asleep by her bed and had this weird dream. In it, for the first time, the magic was under my control and I fought my way to her. Once she had reassured herself that I had mastered the earth magic, she handed over the pendant and disappeared. The following day, I woke up in the infirmary with her gift around my neck. It all happened a long time ago.'

Minothi remembered that awful night when she had responded to the gurvi's summons and found herself in the dungeon. If Agni was right and it was the pendant/tayaka that had brought them here, then they were in for a world of pain. And yet, the pitrani Kashika had asked her to trust it and the magic both. The good news was that thus far there were no dead bodies, although if she gave it a little more time, she and Yama's lieutenant would be nothing more than maggot chow.

Agni was watching her thoughtfully. 'I think I've figured it out. It was in Varu's notes. She is my twin and no—' he choked on the last word and proceeded hurriedly, 'as I was saying, she wrote a book on Yama and left her manuscript and notes with me. The thing about tayakas was among her handwritten notes, which are not always easy to decipher, though they gave her umpteen prizes for her handwriting while we were at school.'

He paused. Minothi's heart melted over his grief for his lost sister, and she even forgot her gnawing thirst. She remembered Trishana and tears filled her eyes. Wiping them off with her fingers, she sucked them slowly for the moisture before prodding him gently. 'What did it say about the tayaka?'

'Apparently, great sages performed penance to reap manifold blessings, subjecting their bodies to a lot of extreme austerities and, having attained nirvana, or whatever it was those folks were after, they repaired post-haste to Elysium, or its equivalent, leaving their mortal remains on earth. Since their bones and blood are charged with the potency of their ascetic merit, they are powerful talismans.'

'I take it that they don't simply turn to dust or ashes, or even provide a hearty repast for maggots and vultures?'

'Their remains cannot be destroyed easily,' he told her solemnly as though quoting from the sacred scriptures. 'Mostly, they make a gift of their corpses to disciples or rich patrons who build shrines or samadhis in their honour, and pilgrims throng to the place, hoping to receive blessings or relief from the ailments of the body or spirit. It would explain the odd miracle that supposedly occurs in our wicked world.'

Agni paused for a minute to make sure she was keeping up, and then with the air of a teacher who was pleased with the progress a recalcitrant student was making, he resumed his lecture. 'Some, however, are remiss about it and leave their bodies intestate. Varu had written that since their mortal coil is highly sought after by those who dabble in the evil arts, it is possible that they fall into the wrong hands. Tombs have been plundered for remains, and followers and worshippers have been tortured and killed to make them spill the beans on the location of the body.'

'That is all very well and good, not to mention droll, but what does it have to do with me? The gurvi was one of the enlightened souls and I loved her, but she certainly did not bequeath her body to me. While alive, she tried to help me control the magic, but that was a resounding failure. It did not matter to her though. She kept insisting that I had been singled out for a unique purpose.'

'She was right. I was told that my task to retrieve Yama's bride by tracking Ganga to the source would not be possible without you. Perhaps at the time of her death the gurvi used her ascetic merit to fashion a bridge that would allow you free passage across the realms. It is the most plausible explanation I can come up with.'

They both mulled the notion over in companionable silence. Minothi wondered if in reality she were actually shackled up in a padded cell and Yama's lieutenant was a by-product of her fried brain. That was the most plausible explanation *she* could come up with but she didn't say it out loud. Besides, hadn't the pitrani mentioned this mission as well? But there had been more. She racked her brains, trying to remember.

'The pitrani, my ancestor Kashika, told me about uniting the ruler of the damned with his bride. But she told me that it would not be over till the one you seek rounds up the Itvaras, or the condemned ones. We have to protect her till this is done. Is there anything in Varu's book about them?'

'There could be . . .' Agni replied with forced nonchalance and Minothi understood that he had no wish to pursue the matter. He did not want to read the book too quickly for fear that it would end and his strange communion with his sister would be over, leaving only intangible memories behind.

He was speaking again, 'For the moment, it is enough that we have figured out why we are here.'

Minothi was exasperated. She wished he would stop making her feel so dense. 'Why exactly are we here? If the tayaka is a bridge between realms forged to help me help you, surely it would have taken us to Goddess Ganga instead of to a desert where the blasted sun never sets.'

'The silver goddess told me that Yama's bride had taken birth on earth and that the Hatakas had got to her. They are the souls who have been taken hostage by the necromancer Naganara and they do his bidding. It was one of his minions who abducted you. Ganga has rescued the one we seek and has no wish to pack her off to the domain of the damned, so perhaps she does not wish to be found.

'The tayaka did lead us to her, but she thwarted us. I doubt she intends to hurt us but it would suit her purposes to keep us distracted for as long as it is possible. Besides, as far as hiding places go, this is as good as it gets, for who would think to look for Goddess Ganga in the middle of a desert?'

No sooner had the words been uttered than a billion sparks of light materialized in front of them, arranging themselves with glorious precision. Agni was watching it with typical detachment and Minothi felt a thrill of excitement.

An oasis had materialized in front of them, shards of light were aligning themselves with lightning speed and a snake-like rhythm less than a couple of steps away, a miracle under a cloudless blue sky that boiled over as the sun blazed on. Impossibly huge trees with curving trunks and leafy boughs formed a massive canopy that kept out the oppressive heat. As they stepped into the cool of its shadows, Minothi wondered if she had died and gone to heaven. But there was more.

They had hoped to see a well at the centre but instead there was a pool, its water a brilliant emerald. A waterfall of silver cascaded down the artfully arranged rocks at its far end. There was a massive multicoloured tent with a matching awning that dominated the scene. A smaller one appeared to have been erected for their use. A low table had been placed inside, and there were cushions for them to recline on. A big bowl of sumptuous fruit and a crystal decanter of something that looked impossibly delicious also awaited their pleasure.

The silver sprites sprang from the treetops and glided around them, fussing in typical fashion. They bathed and refreshed themselves in the pool. The soft and springy soil was so reviving that Minothi's decaying toenails became as pretty as they had been when she was a wee child. They stood under the waterfalls, allowing the force of the glorious water to pound on their heads, necks and scalps, rejuvenating them completely. Agni even set aside his prepossessing air to try and dunk her playfully.

Reluctantly, they stepped out and allowed the familiar silver sprites to dress them in fresh raiment, remembering a time when they had been committed to becoming bums who did absolutely nothing but eat, sleep and poop, occasionally diverting themselves with sinfully indolent self-indulgence while wallowing in the lap of luxury. Minothi, especially, remembered it all with fondness. They feasted on the fruit and the heavenly nectar of changing colours that was poured out for them in goblets of crystal.

Only then were they led into the massive tent for an audience with the one they sought. Minothi was excited and, for the first time since the destruction of Sivagami Math and her abduction, she was truly happy to be alive. Her worst fear next to the terrifying notion of becoming a cold-blooded killer had been that she would grow old and die in the math, trapped in a cage that grew smaller and smaller till her spirit stopped struggling for good, an entire existence leached away by insignificance.

It felt good to be free and traipsing around the various realms on a mission of earth-shattering gravity with a cute boy, even if he was troubled and often distant. And she had been given a second chance to make up for past mistakes. If that were not enough, now they were actually going to see Goddess Ganga!

Agni sensed her euphoria and, for the umpteenth time, wondered about her psychological well-being, not that he had his foot firmly on the right side of sanity. Even now he couldn't be certain if he hadn't ditched an awareness of what was truly happening in favour of a psychedelic alternate reality where anything was possible. For all he knew, he was nothing more than a beggar so far disappeared into madness that he sat in an anthill composed of his own excrement, while believing himself to be in a magical oasis brought into being by the will of a goddess.

Depressing scenarios aside, it was heartening to think that they just might have managed to find the famously temperamental goddess in such an unlikely place, but he had been warned that the tricky part was convincing her to release Yama's bride, whom she had adopted. He had the feeling it was going to be one of those bruising encounters that would be the emotional equivalent of wrestling with Quills, or the yala, as Dharami had called it. He wished the land spirit was by his side. Taking a deep breath, he lowered his head and entered the tent.

35

Ganga

She was seated on an exquisite divan, wrought in the purest gold and silver. At the divan's head stood a basin carved out of stone, placed on a raised pedestal. It was filled with sparkling water that rippled with the hues of a rainbow. Lamps hung from the roof of a tent of the purest gold, lit by smokeless flames that bathed her in a soft glow of heavenly radiance. Her fragrance hung over everything, teasing their nostrils with the scent of all things lovely in Mother Nature.

It went without saying that she was beautiful. Even her naked feet were so perfectly formed and adorned with delicate anklets of precious stones that anyone would have been content to gaze at those perfectly sculpted ankles for all of eternity. A sari of blue and grey draped over a resplendently naked shoulder clung to the splendour of her form with the intimacy of a passionate lover, hinting at what lay beneath.

A girdle of gold snaked around her narrow waist, accentuating the swell and curves of her upper torso. Her face was sublimely beautiful and none who looked upon it would cease to be haunted by it. The eyes were shining orbs that possessed a regal majesty and a wild passion that would never be fully tamed. Her hair was blue-black and flowed from her scalp all the way to her toes in a sweep of exquisite glory.

Agni drew in his breath sharply and voluntarily knelt at her feet, unable to prise his gaze away from that divine face and form.

Minothi followed suit, no less impressed. Their response elicited a charmingly dimpled smile from Goddess Ganga, enhancing her beauty a thousandfold.

'Welcome, Agni Prakash, and Minothi, the Kritya! Although, if I had been inclined to follow through on my original design, you would have been strangulated by flowers, suffocated by sweetness or swallowed up by the scorching sands of time. And yet you seek to repay my kindness and compassion by stealing away something dearer to me than all else. What do you have to say for yourself?' Her voice was mellifluous but beneath it there lurked an undercurrent of barely repressed rage.

Agni refused to flinch. 'Yama's strength is eroding, and the Rodhana has been breached. If it is not restored, the arakshas will overrun the world, and their numbers are more than anybody can handle. For aeons, they have been banished from the light and tortured to the point where nothing but pain has any meaning for them. If they are let loose, they will spread like a pestilence and destroy everything in creation. They have to be stopped, and for that, the prophecy has to be fulfilled and Yama has to be reunited with the one who was born to be his. Only she has the power to seal the breach.'

Agni stood tall before her, his conviction lending him strength. Passion set his chiselled features aglow, and he looked magnificent. The effect would have been enthralling had the goddess's mocking laughter not rained down like a hailstorm, pelting them both with rock-sized chunks of ice.

'That false goddess has trained you well, Agni Prakash. That speech was worthy of a parrot but twice as irritating. It is all very well and magnanimous of you to take up this noble undertaking on behalf of the three worlds. But I do believe you have seen what the realm of the damned is like. Will you condemn an innocent girl to eternity in that accursed place?

'Seeking recourse in cold logic, you have convinced yourself that sacrificing one innocent is justified because it would mean the safety of everyone else. But the question is: Would you sacrifice someone you love to such a fate? And if your answer is in the affirmative, which I doubt, then you are unworthy and deserve the torments of hell more than anybody else.'

Agni held her gaze. 'If the evil that has thus far been contained by hell is allowed to run rampant, you and your adopted daughter will perish as surely as the rest of us. It has been foretold, and it is inevitable. Death is coming for us all, regardless of whether we choose to see it or pretend not to.'

The goddess glared at him, and her anger made her words painfully poignant as she pressed on, refusing to give in. 'The death of that twin sister drove you demented with grief, and you were wandering around, aimless as a mongrel, with no loftier ambition besides filling its gut, voiding its bowels, mounting a bitch and licking its balls. Then you became enamoured of a mightily heaving bosom and devoted your existence to fulfilling the foolhardy whims of their owner. Surely you realize that if I were to merely hold out the promise of sharing my bed with you, it would drive every one of your so-called lofty ambitions out of that big head, even if I were to tell you that my beauty is like lightning and capable of destroying the very thing that worships it in good faith?'

Agni did not think it wise to say that having seen the deadly serrated edge of that terrible beauty, sexual union with her, implied or otherwise, held little charm for him, so he held his tongue. Varu would have approved. The goddess then turned her attention to Minothi. 'And what of you, Kritya? What is your fine excuse for this damnable expedition?'

'I am to assist Yama's lieutenant in his quest. The magic which was a gift from Mother Earth is to be employed in this cause. I could explain my motivations but you would only laugh at me and say that it is nothing more than a fool's errand. And if I may be so bold as to speak my mind, neither Agni nor I, or even the one chosen to be Yama's consort, have much choice in this matter. The die has been cast. One way or the other, we have to see this through to the very end. I daresay you know it all despite being reluctant to accept its inevitability.'

Minothi could feel Agni's admiration, and it emboldened her to look Goddess Ganga in the eye. For the briefest of seconds, what she saw was not hostility, but a sorrow so profound it broke her heart. It was quickly replaced with cold fury. 'Stirred as I am by those pithy little speeches, the decision remains mine to make. And it will not be made lightly, unlike Yama's lieutenant who is in thrall to a false goddess, and the misguided Kritya who seeks redemption by joining hands with one who seeks to send an innocent soul to hell.'

She beckoned to Agni. 'Not even I can ignore the truths contained in the waters, for it is where the past is buried. It is through the sifting of these oft-forgotten lessons that we can divine the future. All that is has already been, and will be again. That is the unbreakable law that governs the cycle of time.

'The living are blind to this truth, or simply choose not to acknowledge it, but I shall allow you both a glimpse into lost time in the hope that you will understand your role in helping its vicious wheel grind more and more into dust.' Agni walked towards her slowly, as if in a trance, and looked into the waters of the basin.

•••

He found himself staring into the visage of the one in whose service he had consecrated his life. Yama sat erect on a throne of skulls, but it was painfully obvious that he was failing. He fought the weakness that was eating away his life essence but that made him all the more tragic. There was courage in the ruined planes of that harsh countenance, indomitable goodness and compassion. Which was why it was so heartbreaking that it was not enough to keep the darkness that hounded him from inching closer.

Agni saw a beautiful lady trapped within a circle of arakshas who were closing in on her. A quick, clean death was not what they had in mind for her. She stood dignified and unafraid of what lay ahead. The purest of souls, she had accepted her fate, but it was more than what Agni could bear. Because by the time the arakshas were done with her, nothing remained but a pulpy bleeding mess for the carrion animals to feed on. He was crying then, and it was through the blinding tears that he saw her lips form a single word: 'Yama'.

He saw Varu too, condemned to the thousand torture chambers of Yama's hells, awash in her own red blood. She was barely recognizable but she seemed to know him. 'Don't you worry about me, Agni! My life is my own and I will never allow it to become ruined beyond the point of no return!'

And then he saw a man in the throes of primeval grief. His howls of agony made the skin crawl and the heart despair. He was a broken man with nothing left to his name, not even hope to heal his wounds. His danda lay uselessly at his side and his eyes stared back at him, as if from a mirror.

•••

He stumbled away from the basin lest he give in to his rage and smashed it over the perfectly formed skull of the terrible goddess who was watching him with a mix of pity and satisfaction. It was Minothi's turn now and she shot him a reassuring look before she went forward boldly to ascertain her fate in the unforgiving depths of Ganga's waters.

•••

The pitrani lay dying on the battlements of a great fortress. Corpses lay around her for miles and miles in every direction. Everything burnt. The flames rose towards the heavens, cackling with savage glee as they devoured everything with an insatiably ferocious appetite. Smoke shrouded everything in a thick haze, making the eyes water and the lungs burn. The smell of roasting flesh made the gorge rise. But worst of all was the pain in the pitrani's eyes and the tears that framed her lashes like dewdrops, glistening like a pearl just before they were sucked dry by the flames that consumed her.

Then Minothi saw herself. She had become death itself, the implacable destroyer. People fled from her in droves, stricken senseless by terror. No matter where she went or what she did, a cloud of darkness followed in her wake, its cottony softness serving as the shroud in which the countless corpses were wrapped like macabre presents.

She saw Trishana's spectral from. The flawless beauty she had so admired in her dear friend was gone. Instead, she was reduced to a thing of horror, an animated corpse in the final stages of decomposition and disintegration, that preyed on the living for sustenance. Trishana crawled into the body of a beautiful girl who lay in her lover's arms. Her eyes were alight with malice. Once she had possessed her victim, she used her body to throttle to death the innocent man who lay by her side. She looked up at Minothi, her eyes filled with a hate so potent it could consume you even in a dream.

•••

She could look no more and stepped away, unsteady. Agni came to her side, and together they faced Ganga, their steady resolution writ large on their features. It was Agni who spoke, 'What will be will be, and we have to do what we have to do. Give us the girl, and I swear to you on my sister's memory, that with every breath left in me, I will do the best I can for her. She will not know a moment's pain if I can help it. Willingly will I give my life to keep her safe from the danger that surrounds her. Everything that is mine to offer, I shall give to her.'

'I too swear that while there is life left to me, it will be my pleasure to serve the girl in whose hands lies the salvation of the three worlds.'

Ganga did not look particularly impressed. Agni tried again. 'For the longest time, I thought Yama was an almighty arse who sucked at his job, but I was wrong. He will be a good husband and a worthy protector for your daughter. She will be a good influence on him as well, and it is to be hoped that between the two of them, even hell will be a better place.'

Ganga looked exasperated but she seemed to have thawed, though her voice remained icy. 'So be it! On the morrow, my child will be given over to your care and you will begin the perilous journey to Yama's abode. You will begin at Vishnupada, traverse the heavens, descend to earth and then make your way to Patala.

'Every step of the way you will be hounded by the enemies of Yama, who are legion. Their numbers grow steadily even as we speak. More and more arakshas sense the weakening of the Rodhana and are breaking free. The Yamaduttas will not be able to stop them. The world has never before seen the like of the army of Hatakas that Naganara has created. They will be led by the Narakamayas.

'Their arsenal is formidable, and it will be interesting to see how you fare against them with your paltry defences, now that you have expended the power of the tayaka. I don't care for your chances, but I believe in my daughter.

'Now be gone from my sight! May we never meet again!'

36

Ganga's Daughter

The goddess lifted the child, who looked about four, into her arms and held her close, drawing in her warmth, hoping for relief from the aching chill within. Her little moppet did so love being cuddled and petted, so she submitted for a few precious moments but Ganga knew that she did not enjoy being held too tightly. Sure enough, she wriggled away like a worm and ran from her mother.

All tykes are adorable, but this remarkable child was a beauty. In fact, even Ganga's exquisite good looks paled in comparison. She was small and delicately made, a lovely sculpture of marble—chiselled, smoothed and polished to perfection. Her eyes were so large they filled her entire face and peered out at the world with childlike wonder and mischief. But sometimes they were so solemn and knowing that they appeared to be the keepers of the wisdom of the ages. Her hair was the colour of dark honey, interspersed with strands of burnished copper that glinted when they caught the sunlight.

Ganga drank her full of that dear face she had grown to love with an intensity that transcended all else, and her heart broke at the thought of their imminent parting. Those immense eyes looked back at her for a moment with a strange sagacity. The goddess rose to her feet and led her to the edge of their world, high on a mountain peak. Snow swirled about them, little flakes landing on their hair and eyelashes.

Both stared in silence at the ruins below. It was a sight that made them want to weep. Mother Earth was a mess. Her rich lands had been ravaged and left to die. They lay in massive diseased patches, no longer bringing forth an abundance of life-giving produce. The great trees had been cut down and entire forests had disappeared, leaving gouged-out chunks of empty space that oozed rot.

The waterbodies were in no better shape. As Mother Earth lay racked with a fever that saw her temperature soar, the lakes and rivers boiled over, killing the vegetation and the fish that they had long nurtured and which had sustained them in turn. Elsewhere, there were stagnant, fetid pools of contamination.

The mortals appeared to be the worst afflicted. They were ruled by the dark passions. Hate and fear made them mean-spirited, which in turn made them turn on each other, inflicting wounds on the body and the psyche. When the pain rebounded on them and made it too much to bear, they wallowed in the pleasures of the flesh till they grew obese on morbid self-indulgence while their insides remained hollow and empty.

Nitara, for that was the name of Ganga's daughter, looked long and hard at the scene of utter ruin and devastation. 'It looks like they can use all the help they can get. Something tells me that I am needed down there. Isn't it nice when the clouds of confusion are dispersed and everything becomes obvious? The coming of those two must be the reason behind it. You shouldn't have bullied them so.'

Ganga lifted a delicate shoulder and let it drop disdainfully. 'I could have made things a hundred times harder! Yama's lieutenant and the Kritya had to be tested. It was important for me to ascertain their worth before entrusting you to them. Even now, I do so only because it is your will. If it were up to me, I'd be content to let the mortals as well as immortals muddle through on their own.'

Nitara looked at her with those ancient eyes, set in an impossibly fragile child's face. 'You don't mean that! I know you too well to be fooled by that deceptively prickly exterior. It was you who rescued me when I was trapped in that void without any comprehension of what I was or what would become of me. I still don't know any of those things, yet there is no more panic, merely a blessed sense of clarity thanks to the security you gave me.

'I watched Agni and Minothi all through the trials you set for them and it made me realize something. The snare of flowers and honey you wrought for them was the same one which held me as well, though in my case your intention was altruistic, typical of a mother. But like them, I too have to leave all this behind in search of the reality I am meant to embrace.

'The three of us are meant to make this journey into the wilderness below. They are the answers to my prayers, though they have always been uttered without an inkling of the words or the urgent need that prompted them. This certain knowledge has made me feel so much better about all the things I have not been able to understand.'

Ganga could scarcely bear to listen to her speak thus. The ache within swelled and flooded her insides, filling her with pain so profound she could not stand it. Nitara trusted her implicitly, as well as she might, because there was none in her past, present and future who could love her as much. And yet there was so much that had deliberately been hidden from her by forces the child could not begin to comprehend, and the goddess felt she was no better than the others who had marked her for such a fate.

Nitara sensed her despair and drew closer to her, providing a measure of warmth and comfort. The goddess saw past the barriers of the mortals and what lay below. She could smell the burning stench of sulphur, metallic blood, and feel the miasma of agony that clung to the place her daughter had chosen to traverse through. She shuddered.

'I want you to be happy for me,' Nitara's gentle voice sounded in her ear. 'Ever since those two came in search of me, I have been feeling so relieved. The waiting is over, and the end is near. There is a certain finality to it that fills me with peace.'

Ganga did not trust herself to speak and worked instead to prevent the tears that rose in her eyes from spilling over. Matters were beyond her control now. Despite all her efforts to prevent it, Nitara was going to leave, and she was not meant to follow. But that did not mean she could not do all in her power to make the journey easier for her daughter.

'Promise me that no matter where the road ahead leads, you will make sure never to stray too far from the river, which contains my life-restoring power. Every one of the inhabitants of the waters will act on my behalf to keep you safe! It is my gift to you in addition to all my love and blessings! May it keep you safe from harm.'

37

Inside the Dead Body

Dharami kept telling herself that she would accept her fate with dignity. But it was hard to do so when trapped within the stinking, maggot-riddled corpse Veera had imprisoned her in. She cursed him and Naganara with every expletive she could come up with, but it was hard to come up with anything that would do justice to the intensity of her hatred.

It was the corpse of a pig. The Hataka had killed it and replenished his mortal coil with its blood. Dharami had been careless and so preoccupied with trying to warn Agni and Minothi about the Narakamaya that she had completely overlooked the possibility of a second threat. Veera had butchered the carcass, removed its innards and flung the stinking bristly hide over her, infused as it was with the terrible power of the necromancer's dark arts. In less than the blink of an eye, the trap sealed itself, leaving her to stew in her porcine prison.

For a land spirit free to roam the three worlds, closed confinement was anathema. Locked away in her hideous enclosure, her spirit would be leached away as the skin shrunk slowly, absorbing her essence till there was nothing left, reduced to dried blood and forgotten by all.

Dharami had longed to be released from her ties to the physical world and the half-existence she had been consigned to. With one leg on either side of the grave, belonging neither with the living nor the dead, she had felt torn in two. She still felt like the human she had been hundreds of years ago but also as physically insubstantial as the ghost she had become. With the ugly reminders on her body of the form that had once been hers, she still yearned to taste and smell, but mostly to touch or be touched.

Her need had been so great that she was occasionally driven to drink the fresh blood from a small animal, usually a little kid. Mostly, she had done it if her services for Taravarsha had required it; but if she were completely honest, she had done it for herself too—just to feel human again and, if possible, to have a few hours of transient sensual pleasure with a friendly face.

Agni had been badly injured after his encounter with Veera at the hospital. Dharami had shielded him as best as she could, using a silver net made by Taravarsha, but it had not been enough. He had stumbled outside and fallen unconscious in a lonely street, bleeding so heavily that it was terrifying. She had been desperate to save him and take him to Taravarsha. She had needed to feed.

The kid had bleated most piteously, and its cries so like a human child's had restored Agni to momentary consciousness. He had looked at her with revulsion and attacked her. The intention was not merely to wound but to kill. He had been too weak to finish her off and had fallen unconscious instead.

Sick with self-disgust, she had done what was needed and, with her form restored, had carried him away to Taravarsha. She wished that there had been time to explain it all to him. He clearly had no memory of the incident, but for that one moment when he had been lucid, he had seen a monster that needed to be killed. It was more than she had been able to bear.

Dharami did not want to leave the world without seeing Agni again. All she wanted was just a little more of her miserable half-existence. The Hataka had stuffed the remains into a sack and he was lugging her around. She didn't struggle and it was not only because she no longer had the strength to do so. She didn't want to give him the satisfaction.

Instead, while she waited for the slow release, Dharami kept saying Agni's name over and over again, like a mantra. It gave her strength and courage. Her every thought was focused on him. She prayed to the gods to keep him safe. Sorry that it was no longer possible to look out for him, Dharami hoped that he would find good companions on his voyage who would lend him their strength and support. Her goodwill was all she had to give him, and she gave it unstintingly.

The days rolled by but her condition remained unchanged. In tortuous degrees she weakened and her thoughts scattered, sucked up by the festering hide. Every second she lost a little more of herself, never to be recovered. Soon, Dharami would have no recollection of who or what she was. Even her name eluded her.

But she continued to say one name, like a mantra on a talisman, over and over again. *Agni. Agni. Agni.* She went on repeating it to herself long after she forgot what it stood for. But it was all she had to hold on to till the blessed end, which wouldn't come. The name and the endless suffering.

38

From Varu's Book: Spurned and Spiteful

Yami had had enough of feeling endlessly dejected. Yama had been gone for a few days now and she had become increasingly morose. She missed him a lot but she envied him even more. He had already travelled across the length and breadth of the three worlds, whereas she had barely been out of her father's palace. He had already covered himself with glory, and stood on the cusp of further achievement.

More importantly, he already gave off the heady aroma of success and possessed the air of one who knew what his purpose in existence was. He took pleasure and pride in doing his job well. Everybody looked up to him, and it seemed to augment his already formidable air of self-assurance.

She, on the other hand, still felt inadequate, unworthy, and genuinely believed herself to be a waste of space. If that were not bad enough, her father had arranged for her to be Brihaspati's daughter-in-law. The curmudgeonly old sage had a reputation for being stern, demanding and orthodox to a fault.

Ever since his wife, Tara, had cuckolded him, he was more irascible than ever before, and insisted that the women in his family remain barricaded within the *anthapuram*, like chickens in a coop. Women were seldom seen outside his palace walls, and most were forgotten, as if they had never existed in the first place. How could Surya sentence her to such a fate and Yama condone it?

Yami was so angry she wanted to knock their heads together. But thinking so made her feel petty and small. One day, she decided to pay a visit to the temple of the Mother Goddess, which was some distance from the palace grounds. She loved the long ramble to the temple, and it would be just the thing to make her feel better. Feeling defiant, she decided to slip out without informing anyone.

She quickly got dressed, without any help from her attendants. Grabbing a basket to pick flowers en route to the temple, she slipped away from the shroud of stifling oppressiveness. What she needed was a miracle that would stop the unwanted wedding in its tracks.

There were many ways into the palace and, as children, she and Yama used to count them. Of course, there was the main entrance with the gatehouse, facing east, a southern and western entrance, and a few posterns they had been delighted to stumble upon, but these were usually heavily guarded or barred.

Yami made her way towards the sprawling grounds to the rear of the palace and felt the same childlike glee she always did on spotting the forgotten little gate hidden behind the fronds of vines and creepers that had overgrown it. She let herself out, feeling like she had stepped into another world, where she could just be and do as she pleased without being stopped mid-stride by censuring eyes and stentorian tones that prattled on endlessly about good conduct that was expected of a classy lady.

The overgrown trail outside led to the woods, which were forbidden to the inhabitants of Surya's house. Needless to say, this had increased their appeal a hundredfold, as far as she and Yama were concerned, and they had spent many happy hours trying to get lost in there.

Yami had longed to see forbidden rituals that involved plenty of blood and gore or, at the very least, a full-blown orgy but she had been disappointed in her expectations. Her twin was always on the lookout for monsters to slay and become a hero, but he did not have much luck either. After Yama left for the gurukula and beyond, his twin made it a practice to visit the temple whenever possible.

It was a small circular hypaethral structure, without the traditional sanctum sanctorum but with an open mandap that had an exquisitely carved sculpture of Moha Bhairava. In the niches, there were circular enclosures reserved for statues of the sixty-four yoginis. The largest central enclosure housed Mahamaya.

Yami loved it. The power in that small place was palpable, and she needed it to suffuse her being and strengthen her resolve. Yami was walking along the lonely stretch, veering away to pick wild flowers when she was accosted by her fiancé, Svana.

Startled and more than a little shocked that he had turned up at a place no one knew about save Yama, she ignored the spark of fear before lowering her eyes and starting to walk faster. She realized too late that she had turned in the opposite direction of the palace and safety. By then he had caught up with her and, grabbing her arm, turned her around.

'What are you doing?' Yami snapped, the timbre of her voice belying the uneasiness she felt.

'I merely wanted a few words with my future bride!' he replied. There was a strange look in his eyes that made her decidedly nervous.

'My father would not approve of us meeting like this. Why don't you come visit us in the palace?' Yami tried to keep walking but he barred her path.

'Don't play the coy maiden with me, you little whore! I know all about your dirty secret even if your father doesn't. Staring at me like a wide-eyed doe is not going to change anything.'

'I have no idea what you are talking about, and I don't *want* to know. Clearly, you are a madman, and I refuse to converse with you any further. And have a care, if my brother found out about the filthy words you uttered, he would tear out your tongue and feed it to the crows.' Yet again, Yami tried to walk away but Svana grabbed her by the arm so hard that she cried out in pain. He forced her up against a tree and held her imprisoned, pinioning her arms behind her back and pressing his superior bulk against her.

'To think that in only a few short days my happiness would have been complete! I was to wed the girl of my dreams, but there was no way of knowing the height of your infamy. You are nothing but the most damnable of fallen women, for you have sinned with your own brother. For shame! To think that I gave my heart into the safekeeping of one such as you!'

'If you think I am a fallen woman then all you need to do is leave me alone and call off the wedding. Ask your parents to find a nice, virtuous girl and marry her instead. But you don't have the right to hound me like this and spew your filth into my ears. Let go of me at once!'

But Svana wouldn't let go of her. Instead, he rubbed his crotch against hers and she shrunk further back into the unyielding bark of the tree, utterly revolted. Her expression infuriated him further and he licked her ear before whispering into it, 'Do you still think I have a teeny-weeny—aargh!'

He did not finish his sentence; Yami had kneed him in the groin with all the force she could muster, pushed him away and was fleeing. She ran helter-skelter into the woods, hoping to lose him. A strange exhilaration coursed through her and, feeling more alive than she had in a long time, she ran, her feet flying over the familiar terrain, ignoring the branches that yanked her clothes and hair.

Svana was surprisingly fast and was quickly closing the gap. Weaving and dodging through the trees, she was hampered by the elegant garments and footwear she was wearing. Kicking them off only made it worse. Everything passed by her in a blur, and suddenly she knew with a blinding clarity that she was not going to make it to safety.

The shrine loomed ahead of her and, with a final burst of power, she picked up speed and launched herself through the portals and fell before the goddess. Her palms were joined in supplication, eyes shut and lips moving, when her assailant caught up with her. He dragged her to the stone steps leading into the temple and bashed her head repeatedly against the sharp edge of a niche till the blood ran down in a steady stream, splashing upon the stone idol that watched unresponsively. Bits of flesh festooned the place, and he himself was covered with little flecks of her.

Yami could not believe that it was going to end like this for her, but soon, even her regret was drowned in the tidal wave of pain and humiliation that engulfed her. Those twin evils receded when death approached and for brief moments lucidity was restored, Yami's thoughts turned to Yama. She did not even register her killer's presence, though he was swearing and shouting imprecations at her, all the while endeavouring to achieve higher levels of unmitigated savagery.

A little silvery cloud burst out of her dying form, and she smiled, urging it on towards Yama. It would find him, Yami knew. And then her eyes closed forever.

Svana stood looking at her remains for a long time. He was weeping. 'It had to be done,' he explained to the corpse. 'Some crimes are so terrible that only blood can wash them clean. Incest is one of them, and I needed to sever you from the sinner who thought he could lie with you just because you already had while still in the womb. Your fate and mine were always linked, whether in life or in death. When we meet again, I hope we can both forgive each other.'

Crouching over her, Svana pulled out the dagger he had brought for the purpose and plunged it into his heart, adding his blood to hers.

39

Ice Caves

Agni and Minothi woke up within minutes of each other, but they were reluctant to crawl out of the supremely comfortable beds into which they had been tucked, by the silver sprites no doubt, snug as the proverbial bugs in a rug. Reminding himself that Ganga had promised to relinquish her charge on that particular day, Agni willed himself out from under the covers, which seemed to have been made from the fur of a polar bear, incongruous quilts in an oasis. Reluctantly he threw them off and regretted his decision instantly.

The chill made the hair on his arms stand up. Snot oozed out of his sensitive mucous membrane and would have leaked out of one nostril, had it not frozen solid, effectively blocking its own passage. Agni stumbled along in the dim light, making his way past the narrow passage from the wider rock chamber where they had been bedded, trying to get his bearings.

If Ganga had gone back on her word and tricked them into yet another confounded pseudo-existence, he swore he would kill her, ignoring her beauty. But a man could not be expected to think straight with a full bladder; he needed to find a place to relieve himself.

He seemed to be in a cave. He stepped out to take a leak, when he found the large opening. The warm liquid rose up in steam as it hit an exposed rock. Agni took in his surroundings. They were high up in the most elevated range of a mountain. The air was thin and it was difficult to breathe, particularly after the impossible heat of the desert.

Further below, he could see the top of a glacier, pearly white under the rays of the sun, carrying on a shameless flirtation with the fluffy clouds that swirled around it and the rock of the mountain, which seemed pressed up against it. Agni could see the massive boulders, hunkered down like sleeping mammoths, breaking the monotony of the white snow that dusted their tops like frosting on a cupcake, all the way across a field of ice that seemed to descend downwards from where he stood at an impossibly steep angle.

There were no handholds or footholds as far as he could see. How they had been brought here was beyond him, and Agni wondered if they had been imprisoned. Since the heat of the desert had failed to melt them, Ganga perhaps hoped that they would freeze to death in this desolate land of ice and snow.

The black cavity of the cave entrance yawned open behind him, and frozen splinters of ice hung from the roof, looking like fangs, waiting for something succulent to sink into. Agni stared at it and then looked back at the sprawling icy wilderness in which he found himself. Its sheer vastness made him feel tiny and vulnerable, a gnat struggling in vain to avoid the giant boot that stood poised to crush it.

'If Ganga keeps her word, then the girl spoken about in the prophecy would be returned to the land of the living,' he whispered, praying that the silver goddess would hear him and reply. 'All the things that hunt her will converge en masse on us. Do you think we'll make it? We are all doing the best we can, stumbling through unknown territory on blind faith. What if it is not good enough and we fail anyway? What happens next?'

His queries were met with expected silence. Even the wind had nothing to say. He took in several deep breaths, trying to calm himself before he returned. His efforts were rewarded with a lungful of stinging ice and another blocked nostril. With fresh misgivings, he stepped back inside.

Minothi heard the sound of his footsteps and hastily wiped the tears from her eyes. It would never do for him to catch her in the middle of an anxiety attack. He already tended to look at her as though she were someone who might be better off in an asylum for the mentally impaired.

She had spoken very boldly indeed to the goddess about what needed to be done to save the three worlds, but in the cold light of dawn or in the dim interior of a badly illuminated cave, as was the case, Minothi felt thoroughly lost and more than a little clueless. She wished all the things that were happening to her in this bizarre dreamlike existence were happening to someone else. There was nothing she liked less than the magic and the things she was expected to do with it.

Minothi wished, not for the first time, that she had belonged to a boring family with a husband and two children, that they had a little house with a small puppy that would not stop piddling on the mat. She and her man would go to their jobs, which involved sitting at a desk all day, with nothing but an aching bum to worry about.

They would argue about mundane things like expenses and whose turn it was to do the dishes. She would be the mother with the prematurely grey hair and worry lines etched across a permanently fatigued face, who ran around like a headless chicken, looking after the demands of her husband and children. They would go through the motions, and the highlight of her life would be a particularly satisfying dessert.

By then she had dissolved in tears of self-pity, feeling cold and miserable. She even missed her pathetic past at Sivagami Math and the blessed comfort of unchanging routine it had offered. If only she felt less lonely and hopeless about every damn aspect of her life.

Agni and Minothi noticed the little child watching them with frank curiosity at exactly the same time. Her pretty curls seemed to have a life of their own as they bounced and glinted when she nodded warmly to him, enormous eyes brimming with cheerfulness. They looked at her in silence, wondering what exactly her presence meant.

'My name is Nitara! And I am the daughter of Ganga,' the moppet addressed them brightly. 'Please accept my apologies if you felt Mother was cruel to you. But hopefully, she will make it up to you eventually, as is her wont. Won't you come and sit with me? We can share some food and get to know each other better before we proceed.'

Wordlessly, they sat down, and Nitara placed a beautifully engraved plate of gold and a matching cup in front of her. A plain-looking hunk of bread appeared on the plate, but it smelled delicious. The child broke off pieces and handed them over to them. It tasted of meat and soup, warming their insides and chasing the chill away from their bones. They passed around the cup and drank the honey-sweet beverage, allowing it to fill them with a sense of well-being.

As they ate, Agni and Minothi exchanged subtle glances. What manner of creature was the elfin little one who sat in front of them, wolfing down the food with a hearty appetite? There had to be more to her than met the eye. She looked like a child and behaved like one. In fact, there was a certain quality about her that made one want to scoop her up and put her in their pockets, where they could keep the precious little thing close to them always.

How could they possibly hand her over to Yama and leave her to rot in hell? It was a nauseating idea, making them feel like pimps who had robbed a cradle to satisfy the forbidden urges of sexual deviants and dirty old men. They stopped eating at once and tried to understand what was going on.

Yet, there was no denying the fact that she was a powerful force of nature. Her eyes seemed to penetrate their hearts and souls.

There was no hiding from her. Like the river that had taken her before giving her back, she seemed to flow like a powerful current that swept away all in its path and took them where it would.

Nitara spoke again in her childish treble, 'If it were possible, I would have loved to have answers for you, but the truth is that they elude me as well, at least where I am concerned. But I do know that we will discover things for ourselves as we go along. You will think it strange, but there is much that is visible to me which is hidden from the eyes of mortals and immortals alike. Yet, when I try to look within, there is nothing but blankness, an endlessly empty place.'

Minothi remembered the time she had fled from herself and hoped never to return. 'Does it not scare you?'

'It used to, and I daresay it will again, sooner rather than later,' she replied with candour. 'Mother made sure I was happy and comfortable but there were these dreams. They were so clear and real, filled with images and characters who made me feel with an intensity that was so welcome! As I slept, they made me wallow in them, filling my soul with emotions so deliciously tender, there could never be enough of them. But then I would wake up and everything would be lost to me.'

She handed more food to them with a maternal air before taking more for herself. Only then did she talk again. 'The dreams stopped when the two of you came for me. I reckon it is because both of you had been a part of it. As I already said, some things are readily apparent to me and, even as Mother toyed with you, it was obvious that the two of you would lead me to where I need to go, despite her best efforts to thwart you. That is my destiny.'

Agni and Minothi could think of nothing to say but they could empathize. Both knew all too well what it was like to be a part of something they could barely understand, to be dragged, unresisting, as the currents bore them along relentlessly, little pieces of driftwood, tossed this way and that.

Agni remembered the questions and doubts that plagued him. If he could stop them from mucking up the still waters of his consciousness, the rhythms that governed the universe would take him where he was meant to go, even if a beating or two could not be evaded along the way.

Minothi was thinking along similar lines. If the fear that came from the things that were not clear to her was allowed to gain ascendancy, terrible things happened, but if she could find a way to allow it to dissipate, terrible things still happened, but it was possible to ride the wave of horror without drowning in it.

They had finished eating and waited for Nitara to say something. 'Do you know where we are?' she asked them. And even before Agni and Minothi could shake their heads, she was speaking again. 'We are close to Vishnupada, the place where my mother emerged from the divine protector's foot. Legend has it that Ganga offers her bounty to the three worlds. That she sustains life itself.'

'And she cleanses the soul of sin,' Minothi intoned reverentially.

'And in the process she has allowed herself to become covered in grime!' Agni added irreverently. 'The river is choked with sewage and industrial effluents. It seems nobody can resist taking a dump directly in its hallowed depths or washing their bums with the holy water. It also provides a great service to those who can't afford washing machines for their dirty laundry or have no water to bathe their pet buffaloes in!

'I believe custom dictates that the cremated ashes of those who have departed this world should be dissolved in the waters of the Ganga. The belief is that even hardened criminals are given a get-out-of-hell free pass if this tradition is observed. However, those who do not feel like paying for the cremation rites, or simply cannot afford to, dump the bodies into the river. Stray dogs and crows then battle it out for the best morsels before leaving the decomposing corpse behind as a specially engraved invitation for disease! How this can improve the hygiene of the soul has always been beyond me!'

Minothi was looking reproachfully at him, but Nitara laughed. It was the prettiest sound. 'It serves as a very literal reminder that the sacred and the profound walk hand in hand, I suppose. As for the belief about souls being purified and released from the cycle of birth and death, thanks to the munificence of Mother Ganga, it could be that faith itself gives the belief its potency,' Nitara spoke softly, tossing back her hair and tucking in her toes. 'Before Mother let me go with you, she made me look into the waters that house the secrets of the past. What I learned was not the lesson she wanted me to but nevertheless it was very illuminating. The three of us will make this journey together. We have been chosen, and the reasons for that remain obscure, but it is not important. We must pick up the skein unspooled for us by fate, circumstance and choice, and follow it till it runs out. Nothing must be allowed to stop us, not even fear, doubt or the personal demons dredged up from the past that follow in pursuit.'

Agni and Minothi remembered the grim visions they had seen in the water. Nitara replied before they could assemble their chaotic thoughts into coherent words, 'Don't let the visions bother you. Remember that they are only potential indicators of what could be and not the future. Therefore, the events that are yet to come to pass will be determined by your actions alone. Besides, there are other things from your past and possible future that the waters deceitfully concealed from you.'

Gently, she took the hands of Agni and Minothi in her own. She shut her eyes and, obediently, they did the same. The three of them sat that way for the longest time, awash in the warm glow of happy memories gleaned from various points in their lives. Agni and Minothi were surprised at the sheer volume of them all as they fell around them in a gentle shower. Little crystalline drops of perfect moments filled with luminous joy that eclipsed sin, grief and guilt, suspended in time.

How could they have forgotten that happiness was not an impossible ideal but something tangible, that had been and could be again? Agni remembered his childhood with Varu by his side, the good times he had with his friends and even the laughter snatched here and there between battles with arakshas.

Minothi remembered the sweets her mother had prepared for her, handmade dolls and the stories told at bedtime, long conversations with Gurvi Sampoorna and the moments of joy with Trishana. Holding hands with Yama's lieutenant.

Nitara's eyes were shining. The two who were to accompany her realized that she had given them back something of themselves that they had thought was lost forever. None of them would forget that moment in the ice caves, when the highly improbable actually happened—dead dreams were resurrected and hope was released from where it had been buried.

It was the reason the living went on living, even when there was no reason to. Little moments of perfect happiness always outweighed the many moments of profound sorrow. Always.

40

Himsa's Rage

The black waters of Niryana seethed and churned, like a pregnant creature carrying in its waters a billion wriggling snakes of all shapes and sizes and colours. Boiling spray hit Naganara with the force of a blow and it scalded him, but he did not flinch and held himself erect, standing in the midst of the chaos, calm as an enlightened being.

The long-dead creatures trapped at the bottom of Niryana felt the change. The chains that had long held them captive fell away. Emboldened, they drew closer to him, spitting like enraged cats. Almost imperceptibly, he made a warding motion with his hands and the foremost of the accursed turned to ash. The others fled, rising out of the lake and disappearing like little puffs of smoke, off to explore the bold new world that had been thrown open to them.

At the very centre of Niryana, Himsa hovered lightly. Her fury was palpable. The spectral form hung suspended over the roiling surface, a grotesque, misshapen skeleton, revealed by her see-through robes. The whites of those dead eyes seemed to be spilling out of their sockets, ooze from an insufficiently boiled egg, as she solidified on the strength of her anger.

The necromancer was unconcerned by the storm that had been released upon his head and held himself aloof against the barrage of invective and insults that were being shrieked into the hollow spaces of his head.

'Yama's whore moves freely in the three worlds!' was the constant refrain. 'If only the bitch who had whelped that miserable little bitch had poisoned her engorged, polluted teats and left her to die! She is with Yama's lieutenant and a Kritya, the same one your imbecile of a sidekick allowed to slip through his fingers. How dare you allow this to happen against my express orders?'

Naganara only grew colder as he watched her blow off steam. 'Nothing unexpected has happened,' he told the raging apparition with supreme nonchalance.

'It is stupid to plan everything down to the last detail,' he continued serenely, 'because even if you spend entire lifetimes trying to anticipate every eventuality, you will not succeed. I prefer to stir up chaos and manipulate it to suit my purposes.'

The place was eerily quiet. With the same casual air, he went on, 'Capturing Yama's lieutenant and the Kritya was never going to be easy. It is the same with the girl. Which is why I am not too concerned that they have survived as long as they have despite being hunted. But it will not be for much longer.'

Himsa stared at him belligerently for long moments, and Naganara held her gaze. She broke the stalemate. 'The good news is that the Rodhana is almost completely destroyed. Yama is ravaged by illness and cannot last long. Fool that he is, he does not conserve his energy but persists in fighting a battle that he cannot win. Because of his careless expenditure of energy, the powers that sealed the Varudha are weakening and there is nobody left to replenish it. My husband and I will finally be free after having been condemned to spend aeon after aeon in that adamantine cage! Once the erosion is complete, I will track down the bitch responsible for our fate, and she will feel our wrath, make no mistake!'

'That is good to know,' Naganara said agreeably. 'There is other good news as well. We now have an army of Hatakas the like of which the three worlds have never seen. Their numbers swell even as we speak.

'Millions of souls have been successfully siphoned away before their allotted time and been entrapped. They are everywhere now, indestructible and consumed by their endless hunger and anathema for all things living. It prompts them to take possession of warm bodies, subverting the individual to my will, before consuming the body and soul, making me their host organism. This way my arsenal will continue to grow.'

Naganara allowed himself a moment to savour his many triumphs. 'As you know, I successfully freed the Narakamayas, and they have been running wild and uncontrolled, spreading their special gifts everywhere. The Hatakas supplement their efforts very well.'

Himsa was looking grudgingly impressed, and Naganara continued, 'They have poisoned wells and streams, killing thousands of humans, animals and plants. The fields lie fallow, because once they have been envenomed with the powders especially concocted by me, nothing will ever grow there again. Charitable organizations run by my Hatakas regularly send out poisoned food for the poor or cut off their own flesh and serve it raw to them.

'Poorhouses and orphanages have been burnt down. Religious institutions have been bulldozed to the ground. Doctors butcher their patients at my instigation and kill foetuses in the womb, or poison suckling infants with creams and lactation aids sold by pharmaceutical companies we now control.

'Himsa and Adharma have control over the world, and there is nothing anybody can do to stop it. The rot has set in too deep!'

'You are far too complacent for your own good,' Himsa barked irritably. 'Let me refresh your mind about the veshas you were breeding. As I recall, the Kritya put paid to all your efforts.'

'It does not bother me. The arakshas no longer need to be fed on the blood of veshas. They are strong enough to fend for themselves.'

'Then allow me to remind you that the girl roams free. If she really is a reincarnation of Dhumorna, Yama's lost whore, then she just might be able to restore the Rodhana and send the arakshas back to hell. Adharma and I will be confined to our cage with the Narakamayas to round out the cramped quarters.'

She glowered at Naganara and continued, 'Then the Yamaduttas will be revived from their poison-induced coma and they will flay the skin off your body, cover it in honey and leave it for the flies and bees to feast on. When that gets old, they will douse your entrails in oil and roast you on a low fire, but not before tearing out your tongue, hair, nails and teeth. Even your eyes will be gouged out, and the ears, nose and nipples lopped off. There will be none in the three worlds whose state will be more pitiable than yours if you are not careful.'

The necromancer smiled, his eyes shards of ice. 'I already told you that the trio will be intercepted long before they reach the portals of Patala. That is, if they don't turn on each other. Veera told me that that the Kritya is extremely unstable and has not been able to successfully control the magic.

'As for Agni Prakash, he still remains in the dark about the nature of the charge given to him. The moment he finds out the truth about the plans of the one he serves, it will destroy him. All that will be left will be a thirst for vengeance, and he will turn on the false goddess! It amuses me to keep him alive, just so I can see that day.

'In the meantime, I will personally ensure that the Rodhana is torn down and Yama's soul is trapped within the Varudha. Luck is on our side. None among the mortals believe in the old gods any more, and their power is all but extinguished. The humans are defined by their need to consume all the things they can get their grasping hands on. Now it is their turn to be gobbled up by superior beings.

'Yama is all that remains of the old order, and he is a spent force. Once his lieutenant and the Kritya have been deposed, I will send the girl to you in chains, and Yama can breathe his last, watching his beloved breathe her last while getting buggered by his own buffalo.'

Even Himsa had to admit that it was a satisfying thought and one that was well on its way to becoming a reality.

41

From Varu's Book: Another Kill

Tragedy is hard to keep under wraps, and Amaravathi was buzzing with the news of the sudden deaths of an affianced duo. It was Sani who carried the news to his bereaved brother. One look at his grave countenance and Yama knew. His twin was no more. A tidal wave of grief should have crashed over him and destroyed him forever. But it did not appear. He should have cried out his anguish for the three worlds to hear and kept at it till his suffering consumed everything. That did not happen either. Rage should have erupted out of him like molten lava and destroyed the three worlds so that his pain became theirs as well. But it stayed down, a chastised and broken dog.

Yama felt nothing at all and wondered if his response to her passing was inappropriate. But then how exactly did one respond when a part of you just shrivelled up and died? Quietly, without kicking up a fuss. A gentle retraction and severing of all that had been entwined with another. 'Tell me everything that happened. And don't leave anything out just to spare my feelings, Sani!'

'Yami went off by herself into the woods, through the gate she believed only the two of you knew about. Nobody saw her leave. Svana must have followed her in there. There must have been a vicious altercation. He bashed her head in at that shrine she loved so much. And then he killed himself. It was I who discovered their bodies. Father sent me to look for her.'

'Nobody saw her leave? You wouldn't be protecting the one responsible for her death, would you now, little brother? That mother of yours always has eyes on Yami.'

'All I know is that mother was away at Sachi Devi's Varalakshmi Puja. Besides, there are other things for you to worry about. It is the reason I wanted to be the first to find you and warn you.'

Sani took a deep breath, preparing himself to spit out something so vile it sickened him. Yama had never seen his brother so devastated. Steeling himself, Sani spoke quickly, 'Svana left a scroll behind, explaining how he found it in his stony heart to kill his betrothed. According to that nasty little missive, Yami was guilty of incest. He said he could not marry her knowing this and yet could not live without her. That poltroon claimed that her sin merited the ultimate penalty and that he could not bear for anyone else to be the executioner, which is why he took up the task.'

His voice cracked with emotion and he swallowed repeatedly, trying to get a hold of himself for Yama's sake, reminding himself that his brother's loss was much greater than his own.

Yama watched impassively as Sani struggled to compose himself before speaking again. 'Brihaspati is livid. He has gone to Indra and is insisting that you be made to pay the ultimate penalty for the same crime. He demanded that you be decapitated and denied a decent burial. Father had to be physically held down in the sabha to stop him from attacking the preceptor. He promised that he would burn down the heavens and every one of the wicked rumour-mongers who dared to spread such scurrilous calumny about his children. Indra assured Father and Brihaspati that he would look into the matter himself before deciding on a course of action.'

He watched his brother's face anxiously, wishing he would cry, smash a few things, pull his hair out, beat his chest or bash in the nose of the one who had brought such terrible tidings. But Yama did none of those things and, inexplicably, Sani was terrified for his brother. 'Our wily monarch knows your worth, Yama. He needs you on his side. Just don't give Brihaspati any more weapons to use against you by doing something extreme. Please don't do anything hasty, Yama! All eyes are on you and so you must be prudent. Our family will never recover from this tragedy or be whole again. But if anything were to happen to you . . . I beg you, please show some restraint.'

'That is my intention as well, Sani,' Yama replied with infinite calm, and his brother felt fear roiling inside his being.

'Please don't kill her, Yama! It will not bring Yami back or help you find acceptance or peace. Even the pain will not be alleviated, nor will the void inside you be filled with her blood. You will merely be ruining your life, which has only just begun and shows such promise. Yami would not want you to throw it all away over that accursed woman!'

Yama listened politely, but he had started towards the palace and was picking up speed. His younger brother ran alongside him and bodily blocked his path. 'I won't let you do it, Yama! Your twin may have been the one you loved best, but you are the only one whom I have ever cared about. I respect and love you more than the one who bore me and I'll be damned if you let her win by pursuing this foolishness!'

'Don't make me hurt you!' Yama's voice was dangerously soft. But Sani stood resolutely before him, looking even smaller and frailer than usual before the formidable physique of his older brother. He did not flinch when Yama, who had never ever said an unkind word to him, raised his danda and knocked him aside with it, sending him hurtling.

Sani rolled painfully to his feet. Every part of him throbbed with excruciating pain, but the terrifying thing was that Yama had shown restraint. Despite how far gone he was, Yama did not really wish to harm him. 'You will have to kill me to get past me, Yama! All I can do is advise you against it, because my death would make you guilty of fratricide and you will be in a whole lot of trouble. Don't do this!'

Yama raised the danda again and Sani shut his eyes in despair and dropped to his knees. But his brother seemed to have frozen. Slowly, Sani looked up at him and he appeared to be staring into space. All he could see was a little silver bubble, but perhaps that was the sunlight playing tricks on him. Understandable, because the sun was not himself today.

Yami's dear face looked accusingly at her twin from the bubble. 'Don't be a fool, Yama! So what if I am gone? You know I wanted something drastic to happen to stop this marriage from happening, and I got my wish, though it's not exactly what I had in mind. Imagine an eternity married to that miserable little prick!

'Mercifully, death has liberated me. There are so many exciting possibilities now open to me!

'If you think that Chaya and that moron I was to marry can actually tear us apart forever, you are far more foolish than the two of them put together. Have you forgotten what we shared? It was and is something extraordinarily special and incredibly rare. Some go through entire lifetimes without experiencing anything even remotely close to it. We are among the few fortunate ones, and I am so grateful for what we shared as brother and sister. Something that magical can't just disappear because of death. It lingers and will bring us back together in some form or another!

'In the meantime, don't lose hope and, even more importantly, don't do anything to destroy the beautiful existence fate has marked out for you. Become the hero and legend you were born to be. Nothing would make me happier, and I'll kill you if you do anything to jeopardize that future!'

The bubble burst and she was gone. Yama looked around. He noticed Sani cowering beneath him, looking frightened, not for himself but for his brother. Yama helped him to his feet. 'Did I hurt you?'

'Of course not!' Sani replied, looking relieved that Yama had returned to him. They walked back to the palace in silence. Both were in better spirits, wrapped in thoughts and memories of Yami. As they approached, the half-brothers noticed that the sun's abode had been plunged into darkness. Sani frowned. A sinking sensation in his gut warned him that the day's horrors were not yet over. In silent accord, they made haste to enter.

Surya sat still as stone in the middle of an inner courtyard. His head was in his hands, and he was bathed in the subdued hues of the setting sun. The scorched remains of his replacement wife lay at his feet. Her form was intact, and her arms were raised to shield her from the deadly effulgence of her husband. It looked like a sculpture done in ash.

As Yama and Sani drew closer, it collapsed and lay in piles till the wind swept it away. All that remained of her were the shadows that had robbed their abode of its radiance.

42

A Brush with the Asra Tadanis

It was time for Agni and Minothi to get over themselves and get a move on. The urgency that had come to define their existence could be felt keenly. Nitara indicated as much, pointing to the packs that stood waiting in a corner of their cave, assembled by those incredible silver sprites. There were rolled-up sleeping bags, clothing for all weather, handcrafted shoes to allow a firm grip on the surface that had been worn smooth by time and erosion and, of course, the magic plate with the matching cup.

Agni wondered if it was the legendary *akshayapatra* Varu had told him about and coveted for herself, with the caveat that the delicious stuff it produced be completely fat-free. Gathering his pack and shouldering it along with his backpack, he followed Nitara.

Minothi joined them after taking a few moments to smooth down her long hair and plait it most severely. No matter where they went or what they did, she had to take a few moments to splash water on her face and comb her hair. It was a good thing she did not lug around a vanity case filled with cosmetic goop and trunks full of clothes and shoes. Agni was careful to mask his grin of amusement. It was bad enough that Dharami thought him insensitive.

A frown creased his face, and he did not notice the self-conscious look Minothi threw his way. He wasn't sure exactly how much time had elapsed since he saw the land spirit last, but it had to have been a considerable amount. She had been in the ruins of that castle in the valley of death, where he had battled Sudhana, but he had no idea what had become of her. While it was true that she liked to disappear without a word to him, he nevertheless could not help but wonder if she was safe and sound.

It made him guilty to think that he had forgotten entirely about her, so engrossed had he been in keeping his own backside intact and in one piece. Not only that, he had linked hands with the Kritya and taken off to realms unknown, without so much as a word or backward glance at Dharami. She would be seething, and who could blame her? Perhaps he was every bit the giant ass she thought him to be.

Minothi knew he was thinking about Dharami and felt a twinge of jealousy. It surprised her, and she wondered if it could be possible that she had feelings for Yama's lieutenant. Dismissing the thought immediately, Minothi arranged her own pack comfortably on her shoulders. Ganga had told them that the tayaka was all used up but she still wore it. The gurvi had given it to her, and the talisman had proved to be a good friend. One did not throw away something like that.

Her thoughts strayed back to Agni, who was lost in thought, probably fixating on that dead twin of his or Dharami. She did not want to be his lover, nor did she expect him to be her Prince Charming. But they shared a certain bond, which she cherished.

They had a tacit understanding of each other and the magic that bound them. It had created an affinity that was hard to describe but which transcended petty passions like love and lust.

All in all, she liked him for these reasons, but mostly she was grateful. It was obvious from the watchful manner in which he looked at her on occasion that he knew about the awful things she had done. Yet, he had looked out for her when the Narakamaya came for them, shielding her from its unstoppable relentless attack and every moment thereafter. He had never once brought up the transgressions of her past or treated her with anything less than respect. Agni Prakash was one of the good guys.

Neither of them was entirely sure about the waif who led them through the tunnel of rock that wound downwards, somewhere inside the mountain. The atmosphere was cold and dank. There were more caves where the light seeped in through cracks sealed shut by translucent ice. Dispersed thus, it bounced off the ice that coated the insides, forming charming murals of light and colour that enlivened the place considerably. Agni and Minothi followed cautiously, too tense to appreciate the beauty of the place.

The company stopped when they saw a wall of rippling ice descend through an aperture on the roof, frozen at the point where it hit the floor of the cave. It was a waterfall, its flow arrested by the elements, and the wall of frozen water marched rigidly through the stone, winding its way downwards, a solid stream with the same inflexibility, hoping, no doubt, to reach a place where warmer climes prevailed.

As they descended into a narrow, steep passage, even the dim light faded, and they were engulfed by the darkness, leaving them sightless. Even Agni's impossibly keen vision failed him, and they would have been lost if Nitara had not been lit up by a gentle glow that threw back the opaque shadows that blocked their passage. Agni remembered the Glo Worms he and Varu had loved so much. Minothi thought of hurricane lamps. Nostalgia gave their meandering a bittersweet taste and strengthened them somewhat.

With her penchant for playing the mother hen, little Nitara made them stop and rest when they were too weary to go on. She alone seemed to thrive on that serpentine journey, coming alive and looking more exquisite than was humanly possible, covered as she was by an aura of light.

Nitara's incandescent beauty was affecting because it bespoke a goodness that was not merely skin-deep. She gave of herself freely and generously to everything that crossed her path, leaving behind a piece of her heart and soul, little drops of sunshine that brightened and warmed the places it touched.

Minothi cleaved to the child, drawing in the comfort afforded by her beatific presence. Agni too found himself caring deeply about her, and yet there was something about her that made him ache. He could not put his finger on it, and the more he pushed it away, the more it disturbed him. And still they walked, following Nitara who set a punishing pace, her small feet skipping over the rock passage with surprising speed.

All too soon, the presence of Nitara notwithstanding, Agni felt an alarm bell go off. He felt a creeping unease mingled with the chill that penetrated the protective gear supplied by the sprites settle into his bones, making them brittle with cold apprehension. He glanced at Minothi and saw in her eyes that the dread had settled in her heart too, like a chip of ice that could not be prised loose and flung far away. Even Nitara's steady golden light that made her shine with an other-worldly elegance could not comfort them.

Nitara alone seemed unconcerned. She did not walk so much as flow, her presence reassuring yet separate, detached from her surroundings and them both. Her eyes gleamed with an intensity and exuberance that was unsettling. There was an eagerness to her, a hunger for the fulfilment of a deep-seated desire.

Minothi had not seen Agni look this concerned in a while and she spoke to him just to hear his voice and forget about the secret fears that were haunting her. 'What exactly is bothering you about Nitara?' she asked him in a low tone.

Agni shrugged. 'I am not sure. It could be the fact that she seems too sure of herself for one who claims she is discovering the answers to her identity as she goes along. She knows exactly what she wants, where she needs to go and how to get there. It does not matter whatever form of disruption the powers that govern the universe have in store for her, nothing will stop her. Her single-mindedness and determination are a little disturbing.'

'You shouldn't be worrying about her. Nitara is special, and she won't do anything without apt reason. I think she is incapable of lies, deceit and the rest of those horrible games people play to hurt each other. Our bigger concern ought to be what is out there hunting her. How can we protect her if we don't know what it is we are protecting her from?'

Agni had nothing to say to that. The air grew close and musty as they made their way through the tunnel, which branched repeatedly. Nitara never faltered. She just kept on walking, pulled along by a magnetic force she could not, or would not, resist, lost in her thoughts.

It was warmer now. Agni and Minothi were perspiring freely. Occasionally, they heard the sound of running water. The feeling of oppressiveness was intense. Minothi tried unsuccessfully to block out memories of her peers being buried under a pile of rubble that had trapped them without warning. She felt the panic rise in her throat.

She swallowed it quickly and addressed Agni again, 'I have been wondering, is she going to be Yama's child-bride or something? That's a little gross, isn't it?'

Agni hesitated. 'I am not sure about it, but the thing is, she seems to be an older and wiser soul than the two of us put together. For instance, take the case of the four Kumaras. Varu told me about them. They were Brahma's sons and looked no older than five, though they were brilliant rishis and enlightened souls. Vishnu's gatekeepers Jaya and Vijaya denied them entrance to Vaikunta, the fabled abode of the divine protector, no doubt because it is hard to take naked kids seriously, and got themselves cursed as a result.'

'What does that have to do with Nitara?' she asked impatiently.

'Well, the point is, we cannot be expected to understand what these superior beings get up to. Nitara was a mortal in her former life and was killed by the Hatakas sent by Naganara who sensed her to be a threat. Ganga snatched her up and raised this particular soul as the baby she never had. But that does not mean she is a little girl.

'She seems to be fast-tracking through the dictates of samskara, and that is a little odd. I am just saying that there must be more to her past than even she knows.'

They fell silent after that. It no longer felt safe to talk. Agni and Minothi felt like they had been trying to get clear of the snaking entrails of the mountain for an eternity, with no end in sight.

The complete darkness was accentuated by the fact that Nitara could illuminate only a small portion of the space that surrounded her. It made an ideal hiding place for all manner of creatures that lurked in the shadows, and they would be drawn to the three companions. Minothi was finding it difficult to breathe. Agni was remembering the same sensation that had buffeted him before his encounters with Quills and Sudhana.

Suddenly, Nitara's light grew dimmer and dimmer till it was completely extinguished. The three of them stopped where they stood. It had been dangerous to use a light for a long time now, but they had had no choice because of the steeply winding passage. But now there was no doubt that something was out there—waiting for them.

They heard it then. It sounded like paper rustling, or clothes hung out on a line flapping in the wind, interspersed with high-pitched squeaking that made them gnash their teeth together. Their eyes grew accustomed to the darkness and they could make out each other's shapes. Silently, Agni and Minothi drew close to the child, flanking her on each side.

There was a foul smell of moisture and droppings, both stale and fresh. There was something else too—an all-too-familiar metallic tang, the distinctive scent of blood. Bats. Judging by the infernal racket, there were lots of them. And they were close.

In a voice so soft it barely carried to their ears, Nitara spoke, 'They have been sent to wait for us—*asra tadanis*, the bats of hell. Murderers of blood relatives. Their punishment is to spend an eternity as bats, suspended from the rafters of the torture chambers. They die slowly, unable to quench their thirst for blood, even though they can smell it and hear it splash to the ground.

'Our enemies could not get to us while the Ganga flowed through the heavens from Vishnupada, but we are close to the land of the mortals. They have been released and ordered to stay at the portal and await our coming.'

Agni was no longer surprised when these things happened. Varu had written about those foul creatures. He even remembered the little notation she had made for his elucidation: 'They are hell's equivalents of vampire bats but far nastier because they are bigger and so much harder to kill! Plus, they are very human in that they can be complete assholes!' Agni wondered if the saliva of these tadanis would also stop the blood from clotting.

Nitara was speaking again. 'This passage opens into a larger chamber, where the asra tadanis will launch an attack. We have to get past them, though their numbers are greater than we can handle, and run the last few miles to get clear of this passage and into the foothills beyond. Once we make it to the river we will be safe. Remember—'

They never did hear what she was going to say. At that moment, the flapping and shrill shrieking reached a crescendo as the tadanis got a whiff of warm blood and came at them from everywhere, their leathery wings fluttering in a frenzied rhythm, brushing up against the arms they had automatically thrown up as a pathetic defence.

It would have all been over in seconds. Minothi shrieked as the creatures slashed at her arms with impossibly sharp teeth that cut deep furrows into her clothing and raked the skin beneath. She could feel them tearing at her hair and smelled her own blood. But she was thinking of Nitara and, in silent accord, she and Agni shielded her small body from the predatory bats. She felt something slash her cheek almost to the bone. Before she had had the time to register the sensation, dozens of them were latching on to her thighs and feet.

Agni had already released the red flames of hell and he flung them at the bloodsuckers, feeling that strangely satisfying sensation as thousands of their attackers melted under the assault, landing on the rocky passage as sticky piles of ooze. He did not even register a membranous wing covering his ear while sharp fangs almost ripped out the helix and the soft folds within. Mercifully, the creature could not withstand the heat and died as it fed, coating his ear with brown grime.

Yama's lieutenant covered them in a wall of flame, drawing it close around them. Minothi was covered in brownish gunk, and she ached from her many wounds. Paralysed with fear, she prayed for the magic to help her but the terror that flooded her entire being washed all else away.

The red flames scared her as well. She saw herself in their depths, covered in blood, looking upwards at the bats hanging by their heels, ugly wings swathed around their rodent bodies, swaddled like hideous infants. They looked down at her, dreaming of sucking her blood, as her tormentors hung her by the heels and flayed the skin off her body, little strips of flesh littering the floor below, which was crawling with writhing maggots.

All around her stood the inmates of Sivagami Math. The old ones, younger ones and the children. They stood and watched her punishment, ghoulish glee writ large on their faces as they feasted on her pain and guilt. Agni was shouting something at her but she could not hear him over the buzzing in her ears.

She felt Nitara's soft body pressed between her and Agni, a child staying close to her parents. Clutching at the lifeline, she rallied her scattered wits and pulled herself to the shore. She was covered in something indescribably foul and slimy, but the red fire was keeping the bats at bay. This time she did not look into its depths.

Agni was shouting for them to keep moving but all they could manage was to shuffle along. There were just too many bats, and a few had already made their way past the protective flames, sensing the desperation of their victims and the weakening of Yama's lieutenant. And then he tripped, dragging the two with him, and they landed in a tangled heap of arms and legs.

The tadanis were upon them in seconds, rending and tearing through tattered clothes and skin, fighting and jostling for the red stuff that flowed thickly through the veins of their victims, trying to quench their insatiable thirst. Somehow Agni got to his feet in a daze, weak from the loss of blood. There were too many of them and they were not yet clear of the mountain passage. Just then he thought he saw an opening.

Marshalling his resources, he unleashed the red flames again. Somewhere in the corner of his vision he saw Minothi. She had somehow rallied and stood ready to fight by his side. The Kritya levitated above him and seemed to be spinning like a top. High-velocity winds gathered up Agni and Nitara, negating his power, sucking them in through its funnel-shaped opening, right into the vortex of the violently gyrating gale-force winds.

Snugly ensconced in the calm within the eye of the storm, Nitara pressed close to him. Agni watched in silent amazement as the Kritya's power slammed into the tadanis and tore them apart in seconds. Their wings were ripped apart and sinewy bodies shredded, but still they surged forth, driven mad by thirst. He felt her savage joy and was feeling judgemental until he remembered the euphoria he had experienced, seeing the tadanis deliquesce in the red flames he had conjured up.

Nitara's eyes were closed and Minothi's were glazed over, lost to the power of the magic, but at least she seemed to be firmly in control.

They blew past the bats, twisting out through the narrow opening that marked the end of their journey, all the way past the fertile lowlands, and were plunged into the arms of the Ganga. The icy water and the impact from the fall nearly knocked them out but the river had them in her watery embrace and she bore them away to safety.

The bats tried to give chase, but they met their match in the sunlight and returned to the dark hole from where they had emerged.

43

A Safe Place

The pregnant storm clouds chose the inopportune moment when the trio were trying to get their bearings in the river to unloose their offspring to the dramatic accompaniment of thunder and lightning. They could barely keep themselves afloat as the agitated waters, in full tumult, dragged them away, the river's deep eddies trying repeatedly to pull them down into its depths. Nitara was in Agni's arms, and he used what remained of his strength to steer them clear of the sharp rocks that dotted the sides of the blessed river.

It was hard going, and Agni wasn't at all certain they would make it as he swallowed mouthfuls of water and inhaled more through his nose, leaving him unable to breathe. He promised himself that if he could not find the strength to save the child, he would follow her to the same watery grave. Neither could speak, but it was the calm in Nitara's eyes that saved him. She was Ganga's daughter and, while the goddess may cheerfully kill him many times over, she would never harm a hair on Nitara's head.

Minothi grabbed on to the strap of Agni's precious backpack and held on tight. She was still on a high from having rescued Yama's lieutenant yet again and nearly forgot to be terrified, especially since she did not know how to swim. But with the confidence bred on the rush of her high, she knew that death would not claim her on that day. She was sure of it and, reiterating the thought repeatedly, Minothi clung to her makeshift lifeline.

Her confidence faltered and disappeared altogether when the gushing waters pounded on her head and shoulders, landing repeated blows. The biting cold turned her fingers numb, and she could barely hold on. Worn out from her battle with the tadanis and the draining effects of the magic, she tried desperately to keep her head up. Gasping for air, she swallowed mouthfuls of water, which made her cough violently.

Feeling her grip on the strap slipping, she felt the brush of death. But still she held on, knowing that to let go meant surrendering to a fate that included death by drowning.

Eyes scanning the shoreline for an overhanging branch, a fallen log, anything they could use to haul themselves out, Agni found nothing. He had no idea where the currents were taking him, but they needed to get out of the water fast before his overburdened lungs gave out. He hoped Minothi was keeping up, since he simply did not have the strength to go after her in Ganga's unfriendly waters.

The river barrelled past the hill country, carrying them to the grassy plains beyond. It widened slightly, allowing its waters to pool, giving them a brief respite as the current slowed down. Agni saw a tiny finger of land jutting into the water and swam towards it, dragging the other two along. It was probably their last chance to get to dry land before the river plunged south.

Somehow he made it and pulled his charges along with him on to the shore. Their strength was almost completely depleted, but wearily they crawled past the prickly scrub and other vegetation till they reached the bark of an enormous tree and collapsed by it. Shivering with cold, they lay sprawled under it, too tired to even think but far too wired and uncomfortable to sleep at once. Eventually, all three dropped off, dead to the world.

Agni was so exhausted he knew he would sleep right through an araksha attack if they were to come for them then. It was his last thought as he nodded off.

When he came to a little later, the sun was out again and Nitara had somehow managed to get a fire going. Minothi was still sleeping, her mouth slightly ajar, drool dampening the patch of skin beneath her lip before drying under the sun, leaving behind a whitish smear.

Agni's ear was oozing blood and his left leg had a wicked-looking laceration. Minothi looked scarily worse. Her face was so badly scratched it was as though she had let hyenas chew on it. One eye had turned black, and an eyebrow had practically been torn off, leaving only a vicious gash behind. Her clothes were in tatters, and the tadanis had left her body a ravaged mess of cuts, bruises and deep scratches. The wounds she had sustained had turned ugly shades of indigo, and parts of them were badly swollen.

Nitara alone looked fresh and dewy as always. Her body was unmarked, though her clothes had not escaped the mauling. Agni wondered if the child's benevolent mother had something to do with her miraculous recovery.

They had lost the packs the silver sprites had given them, but Agni, who always felt naked without his backpack, had had the foresight to replenish its stores with a few odds and ends. He pulled out fresh clothes for all of them and even found the salve Taravarsha had given him. Minothi sat up with a yawn that quickly changed to a groan, and she inquired if they had anything to eat.

Nitara insisted on dressing their wounds first, and used the salve along with the juice from some crushed leaves she had plucked. Her fingers were cool and soothing, and her charges felt much better after submitting to her affections. She cooed over them, urging them to fill their bellies with the berries and roots she had foraged.

The little girl seemed distressed and was practically in tears, blaming herself for the injuries they had sustained. Agni changed the topic to get her mind off the guilt trip she had dispatched it on. 'Do you have any idea where we are or what we are supposed to do next?' he inquired of her.

She nodded by way of reply, playing with her curls, which made Minothi smooth down her hair for the umpteenth time, willing the tangles and frizz to disappear. 'I told you that Mother would help us despite everything!' she began brightly, and Agni swallowed the uncharitable words that rose unbidden in his mouth. 'We have to make our way to the Daraka forest, which is not too far from here. And once we reach the spot, we find ourselves a safe place to stay and then we wait.'

Agni nodded, and in a conspiratorial aside to Minothi said, 'As you probably know, this is the place where Shiva enticed the wives of the hermits who lived there by showcasing his skills as the lord of dance, thrusting in their faces his phallic prowess. Infuriated, the sages cursed him and his potent prick fell off.'

Minothi choked on the root she was chewing, wondering what the good ladies of Sivagami Math would have said if they had heard her discussing the male organ with a male. It made her blush. Agni was looking at her strangely, so she addressed Nitara, 'I don't think we should be out in the open like this, where our enemies can track us down. Let us start moving, before the bats and the undead start honing in on us.'

Nitara was already standing and was staring intently into space. Minothi wondered if the veils of time would part and show her the things she wished to see. She herself wanted to know what was going on inside that well-shaped head. Did she really have no idea that they had been ordered to keep her alive so that a dying Yama could be revived and make her his bride? What about the Itvaras that the pitrani had mentioned?

Minothi would have loved to ask the child about all this, but some instinct deep within insisted that she hold her tongue.

Gathering their things, they set out, Nitara taking the lead, with Agni and Minothi following close behind. They walked southwards, on the land that lay on the windward side of the mountain range they had crossed, having been dumped there rather unceremoniously by Ganga. Surprisingly, a lot of it was unspoilt territory carpeted by lush greenery. The grass grew long, and salt cedars with their pink-petalled flowers could be found in abundance. Little patches of brightly coloured wild flowers made their hearts sing.

Birdsong filled the air and everything smelled clean and sweet. The weather stayed pleasant, and they enjoyed journeying past the terrain, across which lazily meandering streams and shimmering lakes could be found. The surface of the water was clear, too clear, Agni thought, because their mirror-like surfaces revealed to Minothi the full extent of the damage done to her face, which promptly sent her into a blue funk. He was glad she could not see the bald patch where the tadanis had torn out a chunk of scalp, but unfortunately her straying fingers found that out as well and she glared resentfully at his full head of hair.

Agni pulled out a small bar of candy for Minothi and Nitara to share and was rewarded with beatific smiles from both. As usual, Varu was right—chocolate was the answer to most of the problems in the world unless it was tooth decay or a fat arse.

They walked for five days, stopping to rest for a few hours at night or when the sun got too hot. Agni kept watch during the long nights, and Nitara insisted on relieving him. Minothi volunteered as well, but her offer was politely declined because, willing as the spirit was, her flesh was too weak to resist the lure of sleep, compelling her to drop off like the legendary Kumbakarna.

Around that time, the character of the land began to change, gradually worsening, showing signs of the blight that had taken over so much of their world. Their mood became increasingly sombre as they took in the extent of the devastation done to Mother Earth.

The trio walked past ghost towns that had formerly been densely populated but which now lay abandoned and dead. The remnants of evil hung over these places, hovering over them like a mushroom cloud, a bleak epitaph for prosperous communities that had become a repository for nothing but bones, which lay in indiscriminate piles everywhere.

Nitara stood there for a while, tears pooling in her eyes, before moving on. 'The Narakamayas have been here,' Agni told them. 'Foul beasts!' he would have spat to indicate his contempt had he been that sort of guy, but he contented himself with a grimace.

'Originally, the children of Himsa and Adharma were blameless,' Nitara told them, discovering the things inscribed in her memory from another age, as though for the first time. 'The debt incurred by the sins of their parents saw the creditors come to collect from them, and they were chosen to carry out the dark deeds that had been bred by the former's predilection for violence and injustice. They were the answers to the conundrum of allowing life to breed and multiply unchecked, which would lead to the eventual destruction of the things that sustained life and, therefore, life itself.

As harbingers of death, they were shunned by everyone and became misfits and outcasts. Deciding that it was better to be feared than loathed, they threw in their lot with their mother's designs and went to war against the celestials. They were defeated by that matchless warrior Yama, and imprisoned with their parents in the Varudha, let out only to do his bidding, like a dog on a leash, which grew all the more infuriated from having been occasionally loosened.'

Agni was surprised. Varu had written pretty much the same thing, though there were minor variations regarding certain details. Perhaps his sister had had it right all along; good stories were the only things to survive the passing of the ages.

Nitara seemed to pity the Narakamayas, but Agni could not bring himself to do the same. Minothi picked up a small handmade doll that was peeking out from under a broken pot. Its owner had clearly tried to save it. Agni refused to look at the small pile of bones that lay near it. The Kritya hurriedly wiped the tears from her eyes, but not before Agni had glimpsed the rage in their depths. She was raring to have a go at the Narakamayas. He would have to warn her that their powers rendered them invincible and there was nothing in either of their arsenals that would destroy them completely.

They kept on moving and, two days later, Nitara led them into the Daraka forest. The glorious green of the plains on the banks of the Ganga seemed to be a distant memory, as were the flowers, herbs and shrubs that had beautified the landscape with splashes of their iridescent hues. Daraka was a travesty of what it had once been.

Formerly tall, broadleaved evergreen trees had been hit hard by the blight that afflicted the land and sucked it dry of life, leaving dried-out and stunted things little more than stumps, without a single leaf, vine or fern. Barks lay peeled open, revealing skeletal trunks that had imbibed the poison of the land in good faith and forfeited their lives.

Nitara led them deeper into the forest, which seemed completely devoid of life. They could hear no birdsong or chirping from the insects as they trudged across the forested pathway, choked with dead scrub, thorny brush and fallen logs and branches.

As they went deeper into the forest, skirting their way past narrow gullies and muddy streams, the rot grew worse. The ground beneath their feet had been so badly violated that it seemed highly improbable that it had once been verdant and life-giving.

Agni and Minothi were thoroughly despondent, but Nitara cheered up when she led them into a clearing that she had been looking for. It took the other two by surprise when they stumbled upon it, deep as it was within the depressing, unchanging forest. The open space was situated on an elevated plane, and they could see the dark mass of stricken trees that hunkered down, dead or dying from the poison that had consumed them.

They made camp right there. Agni was not sure if he could handle another meal of roots and berries. Minothi had a certain starved look in her eye and looked ready to chew off his arm, not that there was much meat on it. He scrounged around in his backpack and emerged triumphantly with a can of noodle soup. They warmed it over a small fire and had a humble feast, right there under the night sky on the hard woodland floor.

Wreathed with stars and lit by a full moon, the sky made for a heartening sight. Agni was staring at it and thinking of the circle of life Mufasa had waxed lyrical about in *The Lion King* when he dozed off, lulled to sleep by a partially full tummy. He woke up with a start when he heard the sound of weeping.

It was Minothi. She sat huddled with Nitara under a huge tree, which was among the many that circled the clearing, some distance from where he had been sitting. He stood there hesitantly until the child beckoned to him to join them. Slowly, Agni inched closer.

Minothi's face was buried in her hands. She could not bear for anyone to look upon her as she spoke. Nitara and Agni listened intently as the words came out of her in a torrential outpouring, fighting and jostling each other as they tumbled out, unable to keep pace with her chaotic thoughts, punctuated by rasping sobs.

Minothi talked about her mother, sharing with them her bedtime stories and the little things she had done to make her existence more bearable. Painful memories that had long been buried were prised open, and they came surging to the surface, accompanied by the blood and pus of bitter recrimination.

Minothi talked about the magic. The thing that was in her blood, which she had fought to keep locked up but which had broken free, more uncontrollable than ever before, its killing frenzy at fever pitch. She excoriated herself over and over, flagellating the self she had grown to abhor for the blood of innocents that stained her hands. Her words were dipped in acid and Agni flinched under their onslaught.

Nitara seemed to understand though, and those ancient eyes shone with compassion and her child's body held the damaged soul close, absorbing the brunt of the pain. Minothi wept as though her heart would break, and Agni was tempted to move away, unable to bear her anguish, but she soon seemed to gain a measure of relief, as though the poison was slowly being purged.

'I deserve death, not your kindness!' Minothi said between pitched bouts of crying that racked her body. 'No matter how much I try, no matter what I do, there is no hope for redemption. The terrible things I did in the past cannot be changed. Being a part of the mission to keep you safe is the most decent thing I have ever done in my life. And yet, my motives are not entirely altruistic. This undertaking is a dangerous one, and I find myself torn between the longing to kill or be killed.

'It is further proof, if any is needed, that deep down I am a beast. I always have been and will be. There is no changing any of that.'

'There *is* no changing any of that,' Nitara said emphatically, 'which is why you should stop bothering about the things you can no longer control and focus solely on the good you still *can* do. Being sorry for your sins is only the first step, but it is not enough if you are merely going to punish yourself repeatedly for them, simply because it is far from productive. You have to make amends for the mistakes you made in the past and the ones you will make in the future.

'As you said, it may never be enough. But the fact that you did everything you possibly could to set a wrong right, to redress the balance inherent in all things, will be more than enough. It has to be!'

Nobody spoke after that, and they sat that way for a long time. Minothi had finally fallen silent and laid her head on Nitara's lap as she sang a beautiful lullaby to her. Agni did not know how it had happened, but his head was on her lap too. He lay there more content than he had ever been, feeling warm and safe. It was pure bliss.

When he awoke, dawn was breaking, and he lay alone on the floor. Nitara was close though and she gave him a small smile before shifting her gaze. Minothi was kneeling at the centre of the clearing, seemingly oblivious to everything else. Her ear was pressed to the ruined surface and blackened soil and she seemed to be listening intently to a voice or song that only she could hear. Gently, she tucked her legs under her and sat with her eyes closed.

Agni could feel her magic build and he was mesmerized by its power. It took some time but slowly its tendrils spread from within the Kritya to the ruined elements that lay without in a slow merging of disparate elements. She was giving so much of herself to make the fusion happen. Agni was deeply moved, Nitara seemed to feel the same.

A bright light flared up from the depths. And then another and another till they were wrapped in a glow that outshone the tender light of dawn. The ground beneath their feet shifted and rolled as the earth's crust shuddered and stirred itself from the sickness and poison which permeated its core, to fight off the infection. Boulders toppled over and giant trees crashed down to be swallowed up by the ground, only to be regurgitated as fresh loam, rich and fertile.

Tiny saplings sprang up, little green shoots that grew roots and shot up towards the sky, branching out, trunks thickening into fully formed massive trees that towered over them, cramming the growth that took several years into seconds. They stretched out as far as the eye could see, noble and majestic, their boughs bursting with green leaves.

Vines, creepers, moss and ferns sprang up everywhere. The barren ground was carpeted by lush grass and fresh brush, soft and springy to the touch. Little buds popped up everywhere with explosions of colour snatched up from the spectrum of the rainbow and splashed anew on a brand-new canvas of earth, which had finally stopped convulsing and settled down, all aglow from its rebirth.

Everything smelled new and clean. Minothi, the favoured daughter of Mother Earth, sat still in the middle of that clearing, the architect of the magic that had restored life. It had taken its toll on her though, and she was swaying on her knees, weak as a kitten. And her face! There were new lines and wrinkles next to the ridged scar tissue and her hair lay in clumps around her. It was the price exacted by the magic, the extent of her giving.

Yet, there was an almost spiritual calm to her. She had never looked more beautiful or so at peace. Her arms were raised and were weaving intricate patterns in the air, though she was at the final frontier of her fading strength.

Boulders and planks of wood flew through the air, under her direction, assembling themselves to form a solid foundation before the walls shot up and the latticed wooden framework of the roof was filled out with straw and water reeds. And lo and behold, before Agni's amazed eyes, there stood a simple and beautiful cottage. He knew it was Minothi's labour of love for the child who had helped restore her to life.

Unsteadily, she got to her feet and made her way towards Nitara, who looked fit to burst with pride. Minothi, the Kritya, beloved daughter of Mother Earth, fell at her feet in profound gratitude. She was too weak to stand up again. Agni scooped her up in his arms and carried her into the dwelling she had built.

44

Dinner and Conversation

Minothi had been sleeping like a log the entire day, but Agni resisted the temptation to dump a bucket of ice-cold water on her head, acknowledging that she had earned her rest. He went for a long walk to clear his head and marvel at the changes she had wrought. It was nice to hear the sound of living creatures again, and he even espied a deer or two.

To his delight, he found a clear stream filled with fat fish. His father had loved fishing and would have been proud of Agni's catch of the day. After gutting and cleaning it with expert strokes, he had just wrapped the fillets in leaves and was steaming them over hot coals when Nitara joined him, nostrils quivering at the aromatic odour and the sight of the succulent white flesh. Keeping some aside for Minothi, the two of them tucked in with gusto.

'Why are you looking so pensive?' Nitara inquired of him between bites.

'It has been an eventful few days, hasn't it?' Agni replied. 'I was thinking about that thing you said about making amends. And I will admit that it sounds lovely, on paper, at least, but I can't help questioning if it really is the most practical way to deal with sin.'

'Don't you agree that it is a better option than locking people up behind bars or condemning them to an eternity of being roasted in the fires of hell?' she asked him seriously. Agni could not help thinking that Yama's bride-to-be would be locking horns with her future husband over ideological issues.

Out loud, he only said, 'As I said, the concept of soothing the savage beast with music, love and kindness is a charming one. Its efficacy in dealing with the worst sort of crimes is yet to be quantified, but I daresay a few bad apples may change for the better. On the other hand, there is evidence to show that repeat offenders are not merely escaped fragments of nightmares but a constantly recurring menace.

'There are many out there who are not at all sorry for raping children, prostituting the unwilling or murdering for gain or pleasure. In fact, all they care about is not getting caught and keeping up with their criminal activities. If they don't care about the terrible things they do, why on earth would they want to make amends?

'And even if they did, how do you make up for kidnapping a girl and getting her hooked on drugs, just to make her a more pliant sex slave? Or severing a little boy's limbs because his parents could not pay the ransom, and forcing him to beg on the streets? You can't just wave a wand to wipe off a slate stained with so much evil. I say that if the criminal is mortal, he deserves the death penalty, and if he is a guest of Yama in hell, perhaps he deserves to be kept there as long as his murderous and rapacious instincts are alive and kicking. Life is sacred, but if keeping these buggers locked up and in eternal torment means that an innocent life will be spared, then surely that is the choice we should be making?'

Those wisdom-filled eyes looked back at him and he braced himself for a lecture, but instead she just laughed as though he were the precocious child who had said something very witty. 'I am not an ideological hardliner and, as a rule, I prefer to sit on the fence because every theory ever expounded will definitely have at least a few merits going for it. In all honesty, I cannot dismiss the points you made.

'That said, I still think that force or violence should be availed of only as a last resort or not at all, because we always have choices. If we could make people see the error of their ways and show them that they are capable of being better, even the worst ones, instead of killing them outright, it would make a positive difference in a world is so cynical that nobody dares to believe in goodness any more. That is the real tragedy. It is the reason we stand here today, trying to save the humans from all that is the worst in them.

'Which is not to say that I condemn those like Yama, whose very job entails the use of an iron hand. Let me put it this way, if an unfriendly mutt were to attack you, a viable defence could be to brandish a stick or hurl a stone at it. But a better option would be to throw a few biscuits, wouldn't you say? Ultimately, though, it is hard to be definitive about these things, and we all have to go where our hearts and instincts lead us.'

Agni thought of the dogs that bit the hand that fed them, leading to death from rabies, but he let her have the last word. He need not have bothered because she laughed again, reading his thoughts with ease. 'It is just not in my nature to get into a violent kerfuffle, break somebody's bones, stick a knife in one's heart and bathe in blood, even if my life depended on it and the situation demanded that I resort to violence. Therefore, it is unlikely that I will ever do it or recommend it to others. Is that better?'

Agni grinned back, but he thought he understood why she needed protectors so badly. Those tadanis would have finished her off in seconds by the time she could make them see the error of their bloodsucking ways. But he had to admit that the world would be a better place if there were more like her and if humans had the sense to value kindness and goodness as much as they did things like brute strength, flawless beauty and cold cash.

They had finished their meal, and Agni debated consuming Minothi's share as well, but there would be hell to pay if she woke up and was told to fill her belly with fruits, so he wisely left it alone and began to clear up.

'Tell me what is really bothering you.' The words were gently spoken, but it was a command.

Agni had no wish to stir up the tranquillity of their setting with the blackness of his thoughts, so he took his time to reply, putting away the remnants of the meal inside the dwelling. Then he joined Nitara at the entrance and they sat there looking at the stars. Agni knew that there was no point in dissembling because she would see right through him.

'It is just that everything is so peaceful and beautiful right now that I would hate for it to be reduced to a battlefield. Naganara is probably assembling an army of arakshas, Hatakas and Narakamayas even as we speak. Although, truth be told, he won't need his multitudes to finish us off and raze this forest to the ground.'

'He won't have it as easy as that,' Nitara informed him with assurance. 'This land is charmed by the power of Minothi's magic and the noble intent that went into its making. It will be what it was intended to be—a safe place for those who need it the most. A haven for those who will give it the love and respect it deserves. Blood will not be shed on its hallowed grounds. I promise.'

Agni nodded, but he could not help but worry about the hundreds of acres of forestland that had only just been restored. The necromancer's hordes would be upon them, and he swore to himself that he would die to save this land. He wished Dharami were there to help him scout the area and alert him to the threats that lurked in the shadows beyond the reach of his vision.

Dharami. He had hoped against hope that she would drop in on him suddenly and drown him in a barrage of insults for his insensitivity and incapability. But as the days slipped by he was forced to acknowledge that she was in very real danger. He refused to entertain the possibility in his naturally fatalistic mind that she might be dead.

The silver goddess had ordered him to be Nitara's protector, and he wouldn't dream of leaving her alone even with the Kritya, but he wished there were two of him, so that one might go in search of Dharami. She had always been there for him, and it killed him that it was impossible to return the favour when she needed it the most.

Nitara's eyes were closed and she took his hand in hers, holding it tight. 'Dharami is a beautiful soul. I have not had the opportunity of getting to know her, and that is unlikely to change, but she seems lovely and I really like her.'

Agni was so gratified, it was ridiculous. But not nearly as ridiculous as the terror he felt when a small frown creased her brow. His worst fears were confirmed when she spoke next. 'Dharami is not in a very good place right now. I fear that there is not much time left for her.' It was out in the open now, for Nitara knew not how to lie or deceive, and Agni wished the ground would crack open and swallow him up.

'Tell me that she will make it,' he begged her, knowing in his heart that what he asked of the child was impossible; yet, he insisted that she say the words aloud, because if the words came from her lips, they would magically become true.

'For a land spirit who is bound to a world that has never had room for her, death will bring with it peace and a release from the cycle of birth and death on account of the services she has rendered for mankind. It is what she has always wanted.'

'Tell me that she will make it,' Agni insisted. Varu was gone. And whether she knew it or not, Nitara would leave him too to be with his lame boss. He was not going to lose Dharami as well. He would never allow such a thing to happen.

'Do you love her?' Nitara asked him.

'Of course, I love her!' Agni replied without hesitation. 'Even if we are not in love with each other. She is the best friend I never had. And I'll take friendship over love any day of the week, and twice on every other day.

'And don't tell me she will have to die eventually. I already know that, but it is best if it is a hundred years from now, after I am gone. Then she can mourn for me and be sorry for being mean to such a nice guy. After that, she is welcome to kick the bucket and achieve salvation for her services rendered. Tell me that she will make it. Please say the words to me. If anything were to happen to her, and I wasn't there to help—' Agni was unable to complete the sentence.

Nitara looked at him again, as if to verify something for herself. Agni held her gaze and saw something there that terrified him. But it was gone quickly and she spoke again, 'It will be as you wish. Dharami will be returned to you. I give you my word.'

They went back to looking at the stars. Agni told himself he was content. But he wasn't. He had an inexplicable urge to take back something that had escaped him. Except it was too late for that.

45

From Varu's Book: Indra's Decision

A top-secret meeting was under way in Indra's private chambers. Varuna, Kubera, Agni and Kama were present. The king was looking extremely put out, dark as a storm cloud. He had already smashed three goblets and flung his jewelled sandal in the general direction of his inner council when they were not particularly forthcoming with perspicuous gems of wisdom on how best to diffuse an execrable situation.

'Brihaspati has been riding me hard! He blames Yama for Svana's damnable deed and will settle for nothing less than his head placed on a spike in front of his home. Surya, of course, will have none of it. He insists that his children are beyond reproach and that if anybody deserves punishment, it is Brihaspati, for raising a murderous brute. Between the two of them, I have been made to feel like a strip of meat being pulled apart by two ferocious dogs!'

'The question, of course, is: To what extent are these allegations true?' Kubera inquired, popping a freshly peeled luscious-looking grape into his mouth. 'Was Yama diddling his own sister? Somebody told me that Yami was in the habit of spending the night with her brother whenever he came home from his studies or travel. I don't think of myself as a stick-in-the-mud but it has to be admitted that such behaviour is lewd, lascivious and licentious in the extreme. As the patriarch, Surya should have put a stop to it.'

Varuna swallowed a mouthful of sherbet indignantly before replying hotly, 'I have known the twins from when they were wee babes in the crib. Surya is an indulgent father but a good one. I made a visit shortly after the twins were born. He was beaming with pride and joy and showed them off to me while they slept. I am yet to see children more adorable than those two. They lay side by side, and the girl had her leg over the boy's. Such innocence and trust!

'It was a beautiful sight. As a baby, she would stop wailing only if they placed her next to Yama. She never outgrew that habit. That is all there is to it.

'I refuse to think such evil about those poor children. It is nothing but vicious gossip churned out by their stepmother, who was always ill-disposed towards those two! I am certain it was she who poisoned Svana against his betrothed and orchestrated this monstrous crime. If it were in my nature to speak ill of the dead, I would have called her every ugly name there is in the entire lexicon!'

Indra groaned aloud at that. 'I hate having folks stick their noses in my private affairs, which is why I refuse to concern myself with the bedroom antics of my subjects. That said, as an expert on the subject, I can assure you that Yama is more virginal than every one of the seraphic fresh-faced maidens in heaven and on earth. Why, I once saw him polishing his beloved danda busily, when Rambha sashayed by, her bare breasts on glorious display! She did not even get the slightest rise out of him and pronounced him to be a boor with a singular lack of taste in feminine pulchritude!'

'The seemingly quiet ones are usually the kinkiest ones!' Kubera opined sagely.

'All that is beside the point,' replied Indra, looking exasperated. 'Yama also stands accused of murdering his stepmother by our revered preceptor. But in my opinion, Chaya's death is the handiwork of none but Surya of the thousand rays, each deadlier than the next if one is not careful. We all know how hot and bothered he tends to get!'

'Agni also gets hot and bothered and burns things down when angered but that is hardly any reason to accuse him of murdering Surya's ugly wife.' Kubera devoted his attention to choosing a grape before proceeding. 'I think Sani was responsible for the murder of his mother. There is something about him that rubs me the wrong way. He is never known to crack a smile, and he seems to bring bad luck wherever he goes. See what he has reduced the family to? We should use this as an opportunity to banish him.'

Kubera would have gone on, but Indra had removed his other sandal and was brandishing it threateningly. 'Esteemed Lord of Alagapuri, I will thank you not to shovel more shit into this foul-smelling mess! At this point, I don't care about who was screwing whom and who murdered whom. All I want is for all this muck to be shovelled away so that we can have peace.

'Having said that, we know for sure that it was Surya who killed his wife. That does not mean I am going to give the order for the sun's execution and plunge the three worlds into darkness. It is better if we go along with Brihaspati's hare-brained notion and mete out some form of mild punishment to Yama instead. I can't be bothered to find another lokapala when we already have a perfectly good one.'

'There just may be a way to resolve this to everybody's satisfaction,' Agni said thoughtfully. 'We can banish Yama from Amaravathi so that Brihaspati is satisfied, but we can disguise it as an honour. That way Surya will not complain either. As for Yama, I think he will be too distraught to care anyway. It will solve not only their problems but one which has been confounding us as well.'

Kama picked up the thread of the conversation smoothly. 'What Agni means is that you can appoint Yama as the ruler of Patala. Do you not remember our last meeting? We discussed the copious outpouring of disturbing complaints regarding the current rulers of the nether regions. Himsa and Adharma seem to like the job a little too much and, even by the standards of hell, the punishments they mete out are sadistic in the extreme. But it gets worse, they have a reputation for rank corruption and grievous injustice.'

'That is not a bad suggestion at all, Agni and Kama.' Indra was looking grave on being reminded of the horror stories that had been pouring out of hell. 'Reports have been coming in about how that terrible twosome is unwilling to release reformed souls. In fact, they are sending out their awful offspring, the Narakamayas, into the world of man along with the worst offenders to recruit more and more souls for them to toy with and corrupt past the remotest possibility of regaining lost grace.'

'They have grown powerful as well, my king!' Agni spoke up. 'They have been raising an army. The worst offenders are exempted from punishment as a reward for participating in every type of perversion, debauchery, caprice of libertinage and whatever other form of vileness concocted by the flinty hearts and tenebrous minds of Himsa and Adharma.

'Those who seek redemption by allowing remorse to cleanse their souls are treated the worst. If they persist in making the attempt to return to the path of virtue by refusing to yield to the temptations of vice or joining the ranks of infamy, their families and loved ones on earth are corrupted and they are forced to watch these poor souls get mutilated in the torture chambers or, worse, see them morph into one among the loathsome hellions themselves.'

'As I mentioned in the last meeting, there is not one among the thirty-three crore devas who volunteered to preside over the realm of the damned and scour off its godless rulers,' Indra added morosely. 'If I were to march in the forces of hell, the asuras will throw in their lot with them and together they will make mincemeat of the celestial army. It is simpler to give the task to Yama who has proved his mettle as a fine warrior. He will march on to Patala and imprison Himsa and Adharma before taking up his duties as the new ruler of the netherworld.'

Indra was beaming with satisfaction. The more he thought of the solution posited by Agni and Kama, the more he loved how this was playing out. 'Brihaspati would consider such a position demeaning, inauspicious and worse than death. But Yama can keep the most evil of evil souls in check until they are ready to be released into the cycle of samsara.

'Surya cannot complain because Yama gets to wear a crown and sit on a throne, even if both are made out of skulls! Moreover, he will have the respect of the gods and mortals alike on account of the dreaded task he has undertaken.'

Only Varuna looked troubled. 'It is a harsh sentence to be meted out to poor, blameless Yama. He has only just lost his beloved sister and we are adding to his suffering by driving him away from Amaravathi. He is used to the benevolent rays cast by his father, but now he will be relegated to darkness. Moreover, Himsa and Adharma cannot be destroyed forever, their power can only be contained. While Yama is more than up to the task, he will have to deal with an eternity of being at the receiving end of their malice and ill will. Is he never to be free of the shadow?'

They were all discomfited by that, but Indra spoke bracingly, 'It is a better fate than decapitation. Moreover, if Yama is here, it will only be a matter of time before Brihaspati does him in. Patala is a safer place for now. Besides, he can always ride to battle with us, so that he does not feel too left out. I see no reason to lose my finest soldier just because our preceptor has an axe to grind. My mind is made up. Yama will take up his new duties immediately.'

They all nodded. Kama spoke up quickly, 'Why don't we find him a bride once he has subdued the armies of hell? It will be a well-deserved reward and will no doubt ease his suffering and brighten his life!'

'That is not a bad idea. We don't want him to go mad with grief and unleash the fires of hell and the fury of the hellions on heaven or earth. A wife is just the distraction he needs. Sex or, at least, the prospect of sex, is the best medicine for grievous injury. But I am sure there won't be too many fathers who will be willing to send their daughter to hell. In addition to that, not many would dare to incur the wrath of Brihaspati!'

'I will offer the hand of my daughter Dhumorna,' Agni replied. 'She is a lovely girl and has a fine character, but since she emerged from the funerary smoke, those annoying pandits who dapple in the so-called sciences involving horoscopes and astrology have pronounced her unfit for marriage and condemned her to a loveless existence.

'Yama has many good qualities and will make a fine husband. If he successfully carries out the tasks assigned to him, and if he is willing, she can depart with him to Patala.'

'Excellent! I approve of this match, and may it prove to be fortuitous for the devas.' Indra clapped his hands. 'It is settled then! And if anybody brings this up ever again, I'll have him or her locked up in the torture chambers of hell for eternity. And they can moan and groan while the flesh is flayed off their backs!'

46

First Blood

People had started trickling in from everywhere, it seemed. How they had heard about 'the safe place' was a mystery but it could be put down to a nose for survival. They came mostly on foot, with little more than the clothes on their backs or a few paltry possessions in small, battered suitcases.

They had left everything behind—homes, jobs and a lifetime of things accumulated. Without exception, they spoke of the horrifying creatures that had driven them from their villages. Monsters that had driven them to madness or simply killed without rhyme or reason. Their lives had been torn apart and there had been no reason to stay, with so much lost and so many loved ones gone.

Agni wasn't sure he wanted this many people cluttering up this slice of paradise and turning it into yet another dumping ground for their filth. To his surprise, they treated the forestland, which they had christened Punyaka, with the level of reverence that met his stringent standards.

Quietly, they established a little settlement a good way off from the cottage and simply blended into the forest, like they had always lived there in harmony with the birds and animals. Agni and Minothi decided there was hope yet for the humans.

They were not the only ones to gravitate to Ganga's daughter though. Stranger beings emerged under the cover of darkness. Agni had been on the lookout when they turned up in droves—frail, emaciated-looking dead things, cobbled together from discarded skins and twig-like bones, empty sockets staring blindly at him as they tottered into the clearing.

Agni raised the danda in warning, but Nitara had materialized at his elbow. 'Don't hurt them! They too come looking for refuge and we must not turn them away.'

'What are they?'

'They are those who refuse to feed and preserve the bodies that have been robbed of the rightful souls. A lot of them have had their identities taken over by those who sought to subvert them for dark purposes. They learned to sin, sometimes under duress and sometimes because they had learned to like it.

'But they have responded to my summons and come looking for a way to help themselves.'

She would say no more. Agni looked at the ragtag band of Hatakas and wondered if they had actually infiltrated the encampment on the necromancer's orders and stood waiting for his command to attack. Of course, he would not need such elaborate strategizing to decimate them if he so chose, given that putting an end to the lot of them was akin to swatting a mosquito.

The newcomers kept to themselves and ignored everybody else, including each other. Everybody was happy to return the favour.

Occasionally, in the dead watches of the night, a few would slink over to their dwelling and wait until they caught a glimpse of Nitara. Those starved, empty eyes would then drink her in like drunkards finding a bottle in the midst of delirium tremens. It made Agni uneasy, and he discussed it with Minothi, who shrugged and said, 'She feels it is better that they are here rather than elsewhere raising hell with the necromancer! So it may not be a bad thing they are here. Your problem is that you tend to be an elitist who can't bear to share Nitara with anyone.'

Agni decided he liked angst-ridden Minothi better than New-Age-Buddha-wannabe Minothi. Needless to say, they were all drawn to Nitara. It was clear that the newcomers, human and otherwise, worshipped her. Yet, they never intruded on her space, content with the occasional smile or kind word as she walked past, lost in thoughts of her own, keeping increasingly to herself.

The humans naturally did not take to the Hatakas. Many had lost their loved ones to them and the arakshas, whom the eroding of the Rodhana had released into the world. Tension simmered underneath, but it was Nitara's presence that prevented it from coming to a boil. 'For the moment anyway,' Agni mused to himself. If there was one extremely unfortunate thing about his beloved countrymen, it was an appalling tendency to forget about the tolerance that had made the country great and instead dwell obsessively on ideological or cultural differences so that they could get into ugly fights and kill each other over it.

Fortunately, there was something about the place that seemed to have a quelling effect on pettiness, so Agni left them all to it, hoping for the best. Minothi was still too weak to reconnoitre the place with him, and so it came to be that his old friends Chandu and Suri were summoned. They came and stood by his side, massive and forbidding as always. None of the others, not even Minothi, could see Chandu with his coat of purest cream and the honey-coloured Suri.

Minothi lost her composure completely when the hounds interrupted her slumber and licked her face in a friendly fashion, responding to Agni's gentle prodding. She hurled filthy expletives at him, launching them like acid-laden projectiles, and threw in even more insults at his sainted mother and every one of his forebears for good measure, in a manner ill-befitting a Kanya and Kritya.

But Nitara could see them, and the impossibly huge beasts went to her at once, allowing her to scratch them behind the ears or tickle their tummies, though Chandu had once knocked Agni over and pinned him down by the jugular with a massive paw for the exact same offence.

Since they were bigger than horses and many times faster, and since their dispositions had been suitably improved by Nitara's presence, they let Agni and his charge clamber on to their backs. Together, they explored the length and breadth of the land.

To the north of the forest was the beautiful valley skirted on three sides by the mountains whose bowels they had clambered out of after their encounter with Ganga. The forest ran for miles to the east and ended in a patch of wetlands, forming a boundary between Daraka and the river meandering past, pockmarked with sedge and lush mangroves. To the west lay a set of hills, an array of steep peaks, towering cliffs, dagger-tipped boulders, rocks and sudden drops that made for perilous climbing.

It was a natural barrier, and Agni reckoned they would have been protected from that side if they had been dealing with a regular army and their tanks. Since they were not, he would have to live with the uncomfortable fact that they were vulnerable on all sides.

In an uninterrupted stretch to the south lay vast grass-topped plains, their monotony broken by abandoned fields of paddy and wheat and the occasional riverine island. Chandu and Suri were a huge source of comfort for Agni, especially when the hopelessness filled every cell in his body to overflowing and left him saturated with its bitter taste.

In the past, he had been called upon to put the occasional escaped araksha behind the Rodhana. The last time he had tangled with them, there had been two, and he had nearly died. Now, there were scores of them on the loose. Sudhana had nearly finished him off as well, and there were six more where he came from. Agni remembered Veera and choked on the bitter taste that the memories of the Hataka always left in his mouth. The necromancer had raised an army of those creatures.

Only a child, a weakened Kritya and Agni himself, with his far-from-impressive track record, stood in the way of the hordes from hell. He leaned against the reassuring bulk of Chandu, trying to feel better. They had spent the day exploring the wetlands and had crossed it to find themselves on the banks of the river. Riding atop Chandu's back, the journey had been a short one.

Agni had woken up that morning with a sudden urge to do what he just had, and he supposed he had been hoping to see the silver goddess. Nitara and Suri joined them, though he had requested her to stay back with Minothi. 'It is safer for you if I am by your side,' she said by way of explanation.

'My safety is not important. You are all that matters. It has been too quiet. The necromancer will not give up on his attempts to kill you. His creatures are gathering for an attack. I can feel it in the air. They could be lying in wait even as we speak!'

'Let them come!' the child replied cheerfully. 'The sooner they make their move, the sooner we will be done with all this, and you can finally let go of that breath you have been holding in for so long.' Agni stared at her when she said that. Was it his imagination or had she grown taller? He did not want that at all. It was like watching his child grow up and then be forced by societal obligation to get her married to some chump.

'What makes you think I want this all to be over? You make it sound so final. Once you have done whatever it is you have come to do, return to us and we'll keep watch on this side of the Rodhana together. Just to make sure that none of this happens again.' He said the words hesitantly but with increasing conviction. The silver goddess would not be thrilled with him but Ganga would definitely like his idea better. Besides, Nitara deserved to have a choice in the matter.

She did not say anything for a while. Instead, she stretched out, her head resting on Suri's coat, her expression one of contentment. 'Humans are lucky creatures. It's a pity most don't realize it. There is very little time allotted to them in this universe, which is why they are free to make of their lives what they will. Instead, those confused souls waste it on so many trivial things. They look at their little ones and miss their childhood. The gods look at them and feel exactly the same. Isn't that funny, and more than a little sad?'

Playing with a blade of grass, she continued, 'I have even less time than the average mortal, which is why I intend to squeeze whatever fulfilment that can be had from it. Isn't that far more satisfying than the pursuit of pleasure or happiness?'

Sensing that Agni would have preferred it if she quit the non sequiturs, she looked directly at him and spoke again, 'You will always be special to me, Agni Prakash. More so than anyone else. I'll never be too far from you. That will be true even if you can no longer see me or even feel me in your heart. Remember that, even if you forget all else.'

Chandu growled then, drowning the terrible anxiety Agni was feeling at all the talk of a life cut short. It was a deep, menacing sound from low in his throat. It made the hair on his forearms rise and they stood bristling with static electricity. Suri got to her feet, shielding Nitara from whatever it was they had sensed. Within moments, Agni saw them too.

They emerged silently from behind the trees, the reddish hue of the skinless flesh catching the rays of the setting sun. Agni wondered how he had missed them and allowed them to get so close.

Their battle cry was a high-pitched whine that lacerated the eardrums. Agni clamped his hands over his ears, they came away slick with his blood.

Time slowed down, and Agni's heightened senses took in every little detail of his surroundings. He saw a patch of violet blossoms trampled underneath a clomping pair of feet with impossibly long and curved claws. The smell of the river, fresh and clean, competed with the odour of blood and decay. He felt the battle lust of his hounds, second to his own.

He summoned the red flame and sent it spinning in arcs against the Narakamayas, who were so close he could see the maggots, permanent tenants on their rotting bodies. It slowed their headlong rush. Chandu had got a hold of the twins, dragging them into a shallow stretch of the river, and was savaging them as water splashed around them in steady jets.

Agni kept the flames in place as he placed Nitara on Suri's back, taking the time he did not have to be gentle, and yelled at her to deliver the child to Minothi. The hound responded at once.

Agni hurled the red fire at them, keeping it steady, making every bit of expended magic count, trying to buy Suri time, feeling the familiar delight as flesh caught and turned to ooze. Two of them had been turned to mush, and he kept the fire up, hoping the torrential waters would bear the ungodly mess far away from them on its swift currents.

He had been so intent on finishing off the two, he nearly missed the other three that were closing in on him. By then, Vyadhi was close and so were Krodha and Sudhana. Hefting the danda, he struck at them, feeling its power as it smashed through soft, rotting flesh and brittle bones. A hooked claw fastened on to his shoulder and tore it open nearly to the bone.

Debilitating nausea hit him. Vyadhi. Struggling to stay conscious, he wrapped himself with a wall of red fire, forcing the trio to step back. He collapsed on the grassy bank, stained with his blood as he fought for control. Vomiting in a copious stream, his head cleared somewhat and he sprang to his feet, cold determination giving him added impetus.

Agni fought the three that had closed in on him. Weaving and dodging, he refused to back off but raced into the heart of the attack. He directed the red flames at Sudhana's head and it caught on fire. The creature spun drunkenly away, back towards the river.

He buried one end of the danda into a maw that gaped open, and watched the head explode into bloody pulp. Wrenching the danda free, he plunged it into Krodha's unprotected eye. The heat of the magic melted it down in seconds, and he directed it downwards till the torso collapsed on itself, making a sickeningly squelchy sound.

Hopped up on savagery, Agni struggled not to make the same mistake he had done earlier by expending all his power in one superhuman burst. Quickly he drew it in, allowing himself a few seconds to breathe and recover.

Just as he got his second wind, Agni noticed that they were all back on their feet, grown strong on the magic he had hammered into them, the magic that had exacted a piece of his heart and soul, mind and body. Solidified on his life essence, they were getting ready to attack again. Four of them were on Chandu now, and he watched in anguish as the valiant hound went down.

Tiredly he saw that Suri had not left with Nitara as instructed, but stood watching with her some distance behind him. Noticing Chandu down, Suri charged into the melee, leaving the child unprotected. Wild with despair, Agni released the red fire, and it spread out, a solid wall to stop their charge, driving them back towards the river.

He drew on every ounce of strength left in him, digging deeper and deeper for all he had to offer, insecure in the knowledge that it would never be enough. All that was left to do was fight without giving in, even if it meant hollowing himself out till there was nothing left.

Blood trickled down his nostrils from the effort, and his shoulder throbbed with a ferocity to match the Narakamayas. The wall of flame wavered and slowly began to dissipate, faster, till there was nothing left. Agni crumpled, his iron will no longer enough for what was needed.

Through eyes that were seeing black spots dance dreamily in front of him, he saw a bizarre scene unfold before his eyes; he was convinced he was hallucinating. Hundreds of tiny black snakes spat out by the river wrapped themselves around the Narakamayas, crawling through every orifice they could find, while others coiled around the legs of the fiends, dragging them into the river.

Massive caimans, nearly twenty-five feet long, fed on the twins, their gimlet eyes cold and empty of emotion. Gigantic fish with armoured scales and serrated teeth, with deadly looking spikes on their backs, lashed at the remaining offspring of Himsa and Adharma, bloodying the waters as they made short work of them.

Schools of tiny fish with sharp fangs dragged Sudhana into the depths, their lips masticating endlessly as they feasted on him. The crystal-clear water was a roiling mess of wriggling bodies as predator fed on predator and turned the water red with their feeding frenzy.

Chandu and Suri were watching with magnificent disdain. Within moments, the water had turned calm and all signs of battle had been cleansed by the flowing water. Even the blossom patch had been restored. Only Agni's bleeding shoulder was an indication that there had been a deadly fight moments before.

'Was that your mother?' he asked Nitara, and she nodded sympathetically, already busying herself with bandaging his injured shoulder and applying the fast-disappearing salve she had pulled out from his backpack.

'They cannot be destroyed, so Mother will hold them captive in her depths till it is time.' She would say nothing else, and Agni did not press her. Nor did he add that it would have been nicer if Goddess Ganga had been quicker on the uptake and spared him that awful experience with Vyadhi.

Minothi materialized from the gathering gloom and stood at his side, looking grim as Sudhana's maggot-infested visage. She glanced at his shoulder and whispered, 'They are here! The necromancer's army is gathered on the plain. I think they are waiting for the darkness to descend completely on us before they attack. We must hurry!'

47

An Army Born of Black Magic

A wild wind rolled across the plain and the lush grasses rippled in response. A veritable sea of greenery under the sun turned inky by the darkness, quivering in fear of the violence that stood poised to be unleashed over it. Dust clouds stirred up by the movements of the army bred on the dark arts swirled across, searing the eye.

When they settled, they could see the lead forces of that accursed army silhouetted against the night sky. Ragged figures in dishevelled clothing, skeletons with their torn and bloodied flesh, provided glimpses of the horrors contained within. Ghosts and spectral apparitions were charging across the flats, numbering hundreds of thousands. It was a nightmare, numerical and otherwise.

The elderly and the children had gathered within the confines of the forest home Minothi had built, huddled together in hopeless silence. Every able-bodied man and woman stood on the perimeter of the forest. They had been hard at work under the supervision of their leaders over the past few weeks, digging trenches, setting traps and getting a few paltry defences in place. Agni did not have the heart to tell them it would do them no good against the army they were up against.

A few hundred defenders stood ready to defend the place that had given them succour. Even the reformed Hatakas stood with them, ready to fight their own kind. Agni and Nitara stood further afield with the dogs. Minothi was with them. It would all be over too soon. There were simply too many of them. The dark wave of muscled, corded bodies drew closer to them and they could do nothing but watch helplessly.

There was none of the organization you would expect from a trained army. These creatures would merely fling themselves at them, uncaring of life or even death, and they would all perish. Agni could use his weapons but they would not be enough. He could keep sending them back to Yama's hell, of course, but without the Rodhana they would merely escape again.

Minothi seemed to have read his thoughts. 'You and your pets better sit this one out!' Her tone would have been jaunty except it cracked with fear and ruined the effect somewhat. Quickly, she shut her eyes and mind to the panic that assailed her, feeling the magic gather in a powerful rush.

Drawing it close, she allowed the power to build to cataclysmic proportions before releasing it like a fusillade from a deadly firearm. Powerful winds ripped into the army, throwing them back with their ferocity, tearing their bodies into pieces and scattering them too far away to regroup. Deadly acid rain burnt through the tortured flesh of their enemies and horrifying screams rang out as the fiends revelled in the pain and nourished themselves on it.

The defenders watched mesmerized. Weapons dropped from nerveless fingers as they stared at death coming at them with full force. Forked lightning struck the advancing hordes, burning many to cinders, and the grassland became a graveyard. And still they came in relentless waves.

Agni ordered the defenders to retreat. The army born of black magic was almost upon them. But not a single one of them gave ground, steady in their resolve. They no longer had the need for the crude weapons they had fashioned for themselves. Instead, they simply took each other's hands so that they might face it together. Tears stung his eyes. It was always the little things that got to him.

Minothi was kneeling by his side, eyes closed, trying to gather together her magic one last time. She did not see what happened next.

The ground beneath their feet shook as massive tremors rippled through from where they stood on the grounds of Daraka into the vastness of the plains beyond. The earth exploded, and chunks of it were ripped out and hurled heavenwards in a geyser of blood and gore. Yawning chasms opened up across the plains, swallowing up the things born of base intent and condemned to hell by dint of their misdeeds and inequities into their fathomless depths before closing the gap and sealing them inside.

More cracks and fissures appeared as the necromancer's creatures tried to flee, the cracks widening and spreading in random directions, cutting off the escape routes and consuming them all. Hundreds of thousands of them disappeared into the earth, hunted down by a force they could not see.

Soon the plains lay barren and empty. Then the aftershocks rippled across the plains once more, and the abysses and deep chasms were closed over. Trees and grass shot up in their former places as life was restored to the land. Once more there was a sea of green and they could hear the sound of living things.

Agni grabbed Minothi by the shoulder. 'She was right! Nitara said that this would always be a safe place and your magic would keep it safe from the bloodshed. Now they are all gone—the Narakamayas, the arakshas and the Hatakas! We pulled off the impossible! Now all that is left is—'

He stopped suddenly. There was no sign of Nitara. Suri was gone too. Minothi was looking dazed. Quickly, he scrambled on to Chandu's back. 'Take me to her at once!' The noble beast merely stood there, melancholy eyes fixed immutably on him.

He struck him hard with the danda, but he would not budge. He attacked Chandu repeatedly, nearly breaking his arm in two with the effort, but still the hound would not obey his command. Minothi was weeping in silence.

Agni had given up on Chandu and started running, determined to find her even if it killed him. Minothi followed. Chandu did too, his deep-set eyes unperturbed. On and on he ran deep into the heart of the forest and then to the foreboding west. Again and again he lost his balance, but somehow he got back on his feet and kept on running, his backpack bouncing on his back. Minothi kept up with him, determined to save him from himself.

He would have liked to keep on running but Agni could no longer keep up the blistering pace. Yama's lieutenant walked and the Kritya followed. Later, they never knew how long they had walked without the remotest idea of where they were going. Suri was faster than Chandu, and it would not have taken her long to disappear. On foot, there was absolutely no way for them to catch up.

But Agni Prakash would not give up. He was like one possessed. Driven by the madness that consumed him and the need to find and protect his charge at all costs, he just kept on walking, long after it should no longer have been physically possible to do so. When even that was no longer an option, he crawled on all fours, barely recognizable as human.

His clothes had been reduced to filthy rags. There was no longer any trace of the ridiculously good-looking fellow he once had been. In his present state, the meanest beggar would have looked like Prince Charming in comparison.

He refused to stop to eat, sleep or rest. All that mattered to him was to find Nitara again and never let her go. Days disappeared into each other. The mission given by the silver goddess no longer mattered. His entire being was focused on Nitara, the child who had made her way into his heart, and whose absence made him want to tear it out just to stop it from hurting.

It was like losing Varu all over again. No girl should be forced to marry some guy even if it was preordained by fate or foretold by a prophecy and the rest of that garbage. His life's mission would be to track her down and keep her safe with him forever.

'Not that I have done a brilliant job of it so far,' he cursed to himself. 'How could she have disappeared without my knowing?' But like she herself had said, it was not the worst thing in the world to screw things up, provided you were willing to do whatever it took to set things straight again. Even if it meant killing yourself.

He refused to think about the fact that she had left of her own free will. Without a word to him. That perhaps she had made her choice and there was nothing to it but for him to accept it with all the grace he could muster.

Minothi followed as closely as she could. She was not consumed by his need, but Agni had been there for her after she had fallen apart, and it was her turn to return the favour. Sometimes, she would fall by the wayside, collapsing from exhaustion. Minothi would rest and eat what she could find. Chandu kept watch by her side. She could still not see him, but she could sense him. A stolid presence who always led her back to Agni, carrying her when she could no longer walk.

Agni had wandered deep into the Siwadri Range. Once more they found themselves in a place where Mother Earth had been sucked dry of life, in a forested valley rimmed by fanged peaks that towered menacingly above them. The rank odour of decay assailed their nostrils. Vines crawled over everything, sucking the life out of all the other vegetation save the noxious weeds that grew in virulent patches.

Skulls, bones and decaying bodies lay strewn about like a macabre explosion of confetti. An ashram of stone stood framed against the dead sal trees. Veera stood there, a faint smile on his lips, his orange-gold eyes glistening in anticipation as he flicked back his hair, elegant as ever.

Minothi gasped in shock when she saw the exquisite creature unwind herself from behind Veera and stand before them. It was Trishana, lovely as ever and unchanged, except for the golden eyes—like her lover's. They were fastened on her, and Minothi drew back, aghast at the strength of the pure hatred she saw there. There was no sign of Suri.

'You are too late!' Veera informed them. 'The girl came here of her own accord and turned herself in to the master. She decided that he was far superior to the likes of Mr No Balls here and the psycho bitch with him.'

'You are still a virgin!' Trishana trilled, and Minothi shrank back when she heard the hateful tone. 'Now, how did such an unhappy state of affairs come about? Don't tell me you are still honouring your oath as a Kanya after murdering the rest of the sisterhood! I think a more plausible explanation is that this pretty boy here is as impotent as Veera always said he was. Or else you are just so ugly that he'd rather make time with mistress palm and her five daughters rather than lay a finger on you!'

'What happened to you?' Minothi whispered, trying to tell herself that this thing cackling evilly with Veera was not her best friend. She was trying hard not to judge her for not coming to Nitara like the others. Trishana glowered at her.

Agni was not in the mood for banter. 'I am not interested in anything you have to say. Step aside before I make you—'

'Not even this?' Veera asked mockingly, flinging a sack at them. It split open and disgorged its stinking contents. The smell was so bad that Agni and Minothi drew back in revulsion.

'That is all that remains of that precious land spirit you wanted so desperately to bang but couldn't because you are no man and she was no woman. She kept calling for you though, confident till the end that you would come for her. Stupid little c—' Agni threw himself at Veera, knocking him over bodily.

The two of them were grappling like wild beasts, tearing into each other like maddened monsters. Minothi doubted Agni had the strength to take on the Hataka. She moved to go to him but Trishana had closed in on her. They circled each other warily.

'I am not going to fight you,' Minothi told her quietly. 'We have to save Nitara from the necromancer. She is innocent! Don't let that monster hurt that child! I was in the worst possible place and would have died there had she not come for me. We will find her together, and then she will do the same for you. It's a promise!'

Chandu was barking and Minothi tried to drown out the sound. Agni and Veera were still at it; they were evenly matched since both were driven by a madness that made perfect sense to them alone. Neither would back down, and they wrestled back and forth, looking all the while for a weakness to exploit.

Without warning, Trishana jumped at Minothi with a knife. Her magic responded of its own accord. The roots of a nearby tree broke through the barren ground and wrapped themselves around Trishana, holding her fast. 'Why would you hurt me, Trishana? Why?' Minothi was weeping. 'I will not fight you! No matter what! Do you know how many nights I spent sleepless and wretched, crying for you and praying that you had survived, despite everything we were led to believe?

'You were the sole occupant of my thoughts, and with every fibre of my being I hoped that you would not be harmed. My only wish was that you had somehow found the love and happiness you wanted!'

'I hate you!' she spat out. 'Those were the things you wanted for yourself. Apparently, you are quite the special one, blessed with the magic and all! All along, you planned to get all the things that rightfully ought to have been mine by hook or by crook. Don't deny that you were always jealous of me! Never once did you think of sharing the gift with me but kept it your little secret! Then you used it to escape the math and find yourself a nice boy!

'I, on the other hand, gave up everything for love, and in return they did things to me nobody would dream of doing to a rabid dog! And all the time you hoarded that precious magic of yours and did not bother helping me. The things I have done! The things I have to keep on doing because all that is left is the anger that has to be fed all the time to stop it from burning me alive! Once, everything about me was beautiful. Now, there is nothing but sewage in my veins, and I can't bear for that to be seen on my face. So I do the unthinkable. That is the only way to pretend that all is not lost to me!'

'Listen to me, Trishana. I had no idea about the magic or how to use it! How could you think that I would have allowed those things to happen to you?'

'Don't you make excuses! I was happy when Veera abducted you! It was my hope that all the things they had done, they would do to you as well. Then you would no longer be the special Kritya but just another used-up whore!'

Minothi recoiled again as though she had been struck. Her former friend tore herself free of the roots and came at her again. This time, the magic did not respond in time but Chandu did. His enormous body barrelled into the Hataka, tossing her aside. Latching on to the creature that had once been Trishana, he ripped out her throat in seconds. Minothi watched the black dust, which was all that was left of her friend, hissing and spitting as it dissolved into the rot that was so much a part of the place, and wept, lying sprawled on the ground.

Gingerly, she got to her feet, and when she saw Agni, she wept harder. He was no longer the sweet boy she remembered. His face was contorted with bestial passion and a rage so all-encompassing it seemed to have corroded every other aspect of his personality too. He was no longer the warrior who was always humane, no matter how bad things got. He had become a demon that had to kill to fulfil a deep-seated urge.

He had used the red flames to burn Veera's physical form till it had melted off his body. Then, for the first time, he had used Yama's power not to capture, but to destroy. Brandishing the danda like a cudgel, he smashed the remains of Veera's body till there was nothing. Reduced to black dust, the Hataka tried to elude his grasp, but Agni drew it back with the noose and, holding it trapped within, struck it repeatedly with his danda, channelling his rage and pain till the ground beneath his feet split asunder and the heat of his wrath turned it to nothing.

Still he went on with the manic rage till Minothi went up to him, terrified though she was, and took him in her arms. Roughly, he brushed her aside, his eyes glazed over with the unholy passion that had him in its thrall, failing to recognize her. He lurched into the ashram. Suri had materialized like a wraith and stood with Chandu, both eerily quiet.

With unerring instincts, he threw open the trapdoor and rushed headlong down the stairs into the black void of the tunnel. Minothi followed him down as he worked his way past the tortuous path, stumbling and weaving in the utter darkness. It was bitterly cold and it knifed their bodies, but Agni scarcely felt it.

He made his way blindly till he reached steps cut into the rock, winding upwards. Sensing her presence, his nostrils flared like a dog's, and he clambered up on all fours. Throwing open the door, he found himself in a cavernous semicircular cave. Nitara lay naked at the centre, and the necromancer was crouched over her, feeding, his chin red with her blood.

Emerald-green eyes noted the intrusion and he casually waved his arm. Bands of ice fastened themselves around Agni and Minothi, holding them in place, burning into them like a tongue of flame. Leisurely, he returned to his meal. Agni struggled like one possessed, but to no avail.

The necromancer took his time and, for the longest time, fed till there was nothing left. He rose drunkenly to his feet, giddy with ecstasy. Naganara had beaten the odds to win. Despite their best efforts, they had not been able to stop him. Now all that remained was to finish off Yama's lieutenant and the Kritya, slowly, of course. He would savour her another day. Then he would repair post-haste to Niryana.

The force of the explosion shook him and he was unable to complete the thought. Trying to locate the source, he looked below and saw only a gaping hole where his belly had been. She rose from his abdominal cavity, which lay splattered on the floor. He watched through green eyes burning with pain as she took form before his very eyes. Growing tall and supple, her body matured with the swell and curve of the feminine form.

Every one of the souls he had painstakingly gathered over the years tore loose from him, crowding the cave with their presence while she rose over them in a billowing cloud. Multitudes of orange-gold eyes stared unblinkingly at her till the light was extinguished from every single one of them, gathering steadily from within and without. He heard her call out to them by name, giving them back their identities, restoring to them all that had been taken from them.

They had ambushed the living, fed on their bodies to replenish their own and stolen away their souls, to be handed over to the necromancer. Then those souls too would be as lost and tormented as them. Maddened by hate, they too would turn against the living, and on and on it had gone in a vicious cycle, till the humans had almost completely been destroyed.

Yama's bride called to them, drawing them to her, so that the debt incurred by the evil they had wrought could be repaid with service and sacrifice. In return, she promised them the full restoration of their lost pride, dignity and honour until they eventually earned salvation and peace. They would be the Itvaras, builders of the Rodhana, and it would be through their untiring efforts that evil would once again be contained.

They swirled away into the darkness, and before Naganara's very eyes, the barriers of hell were resurrected as the Rodhana formed itself on the blood, bones and sacrifice of the Itvaras, the condemned ones, their act of contrition the formidable foundation upon which it came into being.

Naganara saw his own body disappear into the Rodhana, and he found that it was not intolerable. It had been his plan to consume her but she had repaid his brutality with kindness. In fact, he had never been happier than when he chose to hearken to her irrepressible call. Giving up everything to be a part of her design was not the worst thing that had happened to him. Consecrating his soul to be used in service to the three worlds was by far the best thing he had done. Finally, he shut his eyes, completely at peace.

Agni and Minothi saw it all. When Yama's lieutenant saw the bride, he screamed in anguish. It was Varu who stood before him, his twin, and architect of the Rodhana. The girl who had lived for her stories and disappeared into one, never to return. Agni could not bear it.

'No, Varu! If you leave me this time, I'll kill myself and follow you all the way to hell and then I'll kill him too!' These were the words he had wanted to say to her, to make her stay, but he could not bring himself to say them aloud. She barely looked like the girl he remembered. There was something ethereal about her. An iron sense of purpose so like his own seemed to drive her, and she had sworn allegiance to forces greater than his love. Worst of all, she looked fulfilled.

Varu looked back at him and smiled. 'Remember,' she mouthed and then disappeared, her body disintegrating into little fragments, as the last sections of the Rodhana fell in place and the gates of hell were sealed and barred, no longer visible to the living.

The cave was plunged into darkness. Agni and Minothi had long been released from the bands of ice and they dropped to the floor. He was sobbing hard, and there was nothing anybody could do to comfort him.

He quieted only when a familiar pair of hands wrapped themselves around his form, warm and soothing, the way a mother would a devastated child. If he had not been so distraught, he would have realized that it was Dharami, brought back to the land of the living in fulfilment of a promise.

48

Yami

They were all gathered in Taravarsha's hut. Minothi and Dharami were telling the aged healer everything over plates of her delicious stew, while Agni lay wrapped up in sheets on the paai, still insensible to the world. He had passed out in the cave and had been brought here by the former land spirit and Minothi.

As for Dharami, her form had been restored to her, and she was a lovely little thing, though in a rustic sort of way, Minothi thought grudgingly. Nitara, or Varu, had kept her promise to Agni. Dharami had been allowed to retain a portion of the earth magic that had been hers to wield as a land spirit, but she would no longer have to live with one leg in the land of the living and the other in that of the dead.

She was worried sick about Agni's plight but seemed at peace with herself. Minothi decided not to disturb her tranquillity by discussing her thoughts on the little stunt Yama's consort had pulled on Agni. Yama's lieutenant, her twin, was unlikely to be delighted with the consolation prize that had been left for him.

Agni thrashed under his sheets, and Dharami promptly forgot the food she had not been able to eat for centuries and repaired to his side and held his hand. Minothi took another helping. Worrying about things on an empty stomach, or even a half-full one, tended to give her a headache.

Meanwhile, far away in another dimension, Agni Prakash wanted to vent his rage and yell blue murder at the silver goddess. But his resolve crumbled the moment he laid eyes on her. This time she was seated on a lonely rock, and he was by her side. On all sides there was nothing but water as far as the eye could see.

Though his anger had dissolved, Agni was not happy about being deceived and waited for an explanation. But there was none forthcoming. She was not robed in her usual shining raiment but in simple white. Her blue-black hair and exquisite eyes were accentuated much better this way, and Agni could barely breathe as he looked into that opaque gaze that revealed so little.

'What is the meaning of all this?' Agni asked her, needing desperately to understand. 'Why was Varu returned to me, only so that she could be taken away again?'

'Yama's wife was called Dhumorna. She was the daughter of Agni. In a former age, her betrayal nearly cost her husband his life. As penance, she gave up her life by way of damage control. The Rodhana came into being, forged on the strength of her sacrifice. Her ashes were given to me for safekeeping, and I promised to keep them safe till it was time for the two of them to be reunited.'

'What was the need for such an elaborate charade? You had to have known her true identity! Why didn't you say anything to me?'

'The truth does not necessarily bring comfort or understanding with it. It would not have been of any use to you, to her, or to the rest of the three worlds. Maybe she sensed it too. Perhaps that was the reason for the form she chose to take.'

Hearing her words, Agni felt the rage and bitterness build within him. 'You are Yami, aren't you? Yama's sister who was reborn as the river Yamuna. The truth does not serve your purpose and so you concealed it from us, manipulating us into serving your needs!'

She arched an eyebrow when his voice rose. 'Despite what you think and the claim you believe to have on her, Yama's consort's path towards salvation was always going to be a solitary journey that had to be undertaken alone. The choices made were similarly personal, no doubt arrived at after much introspection and the discovery of hidden truths that can be found only by looking within.'

His voice shook with the emotion that boiled over. 'I'll grant that you bandy words with consummate skill. From the very beginning, you have used them to good effect, bringing me under their hypnotic influence and convincing me to do your bidding. I refuse to be your fool any more. There is no denying what you did.'

'You give me too much credit. All I can say is that your twin and my brother's wife made the final decision all by herself. Remember that!'

'Remember.' It was the last thing she had said to him. Suddenly, he was exhausted and no longer had the energy for either anger or sorrow, so he let it go, allowing it to seep out of him and disappear into the water that surrounded him.

'What has become of her?' Agni asked. If her story had reached its natural conclusion, then it was time for him to close the book and move on.

'She sacrificed her body in order to invoke the magic of the Rodhana, using it to bind the other bodies and souls that were ordered to her will. Once that was done, her status as an immortal allowed her to return to her former life as the consort of Yama. It is to be hoped that they find the eternity of happiness that was formerly denied them.'

Agni hoped for the same, he supposed, but he could not resist saying, 'She will always be too good for Yama. He is lucky to have her.'

'It is unlikely to make you feel better, but I feel the same way about my brother's wife.' Agni had to smile at that. Belatedly, he realized that she had lost her twin too and seemed to be handling it with a lot more grace. It made him a little shamefaced, but she rose quickly to his defence. 'I have just had a lot longer to come to terms with the whole situation. With time, you too will learn to accept.'

'What happens to me next?' Agni wanted to know.

'Whatever you wish. It is your life, isn't it? You can make of it what you will.'

'That is good to hear. I intend to take the longest holiday known to man.'

'Please do that!'

'You are only saying that! All too soon, you are likely to summon me because there is some earth-shattering need for the use of my magic!'

'You can't be sure of that,' Yami replied with a dazzling smile.

• • •

Agni woke up with that image in his head and found himself on the paai in Taravarsha's house. Dawn was just breaking. Minothi and the healer were asleep. Dharami was nowhere to be seen.

He pulled out the book. It was time for the last chapter.

49

From Varu's Book: Dhumorna

Everybody was feeling sorry for Dhumorna. She was engaged to the sun god's son, who just happened to be an incestuous, murderous brute. As fitting punishment for his crimes, he had been banished to Patala. The older folks murmured thus and rued the fate of the girl with the inauspicious horoscope.

The younger girls felt sorry for her because her betrothed did not seem to care for her at all. During the engagement ceremony, he wore a funereal expression and did not even bother to look at his bride-to-be. Dhumorna had received no visits or presents from him. Of course, he had been ordered to battle, but it was hardly an excuse to ignore his fiancée.

Dhumorna, herself born from funerary smoke, had never been happier. She took one look at Yama and fell head over heels in love with him. It was as though she knew everything there was to know of his heart and soul long before they had uttered a single word to each other.

Nothing would convince her that he was guilty of the terrible things he stood accused of. Instead, it made her tender towards him, protective even. Whenever it was possible, she slipped away to visit Surya's abode, armed with goodies and gifts for the entire family. Some would have found her familiarity a tad inappropriate, but whenever she waltzed in, she brought hope and happiness in her wake, endearing herself to them all.

Dhumorna and Tapati became fast friends, and Surya himself was charmed by his future daughter-in-law. She pestered them all for stories about Yama and never grew bored of the subject.

Stories trickled back to them about the feats of valour Yama was performing on the battlefield, seated on a massive buffalo with wickedly curved horns. The bovine hooked their enemies before throwing them aside, utterly broken. The indefatigable duo held out against the sheer numerical superiority of the forces that swarmed against them and, together with the handful of the celestial elite, hurled back wave after wave of the maddened arakshas.

It was reported that a goddess arrayed in silver had changed the course of the waterbody over which she presided, releasing it into the furthest reaches of hell so that it may scour the place of the grime that infested it.

At the end of that legendary battle, Yama prevailed over every one of his enemies, and imprisoned Himsa, Adharma and their children within the Varudha. Shiva was so impressed with Yama's prowess that he blessed him and gifted him with weapons to round out his arsenal.

Having redeemed himself with deeds of unmatched valour, and his lustre restored, Yama was once again revered by the celestials. In a lavish ceremony, he took Dhumorna to be his wife and the newlyweds returned to their home in Patala. His grandfather Twastha presented them with a beautiful palace to alleviate the gloom and doom of the netherworld. He also built him a golden sabha, where the fates of the mortals would be decided based on their propensity for good or evil.

And they all lived as happily as it was possible to be within the confines of a topsy-turvy and utterly-screwed-up existence.

• • •

And that is as far as I have got, dearest brother of mine. It is nice to think of the two of them living together in near-perfect happiness amidst the hellfire, isn't it? Yama will go on being wise and just, macho and sexy, packing off all the goody two-shoes to heaven (sometimes I think the holier-than-thou types ought to be sent off to a place where they are slapped silly for being annoyingly virtuous, but that is a book for another day) and whipping the arakshas into behaving themselves.

Dhumorna will provide the ray of sunshine that hell so desperately needs. The way I see it, she is not the sort of girl who has the stomach to watch sinners go skinny-dipping in vats of boiling oil or have the skin flayed off their backs. Like the bard said, she is just too full of the milk of human kindness. As Dad always says, the road to hell is paved with good intentions. Since she is already there, can you imagine the kind of havoc she is capable of wreaking? It would be just like her to believe in the power of hugs and kisses over whips and chains to help reform the bad guys.

The plot demands that she screws up royally, gets herself and Yama into a whole lot of trouble and has to sacrifice her own life to make up for being a dumb-ass, but I haven't the heart to tear apart the lovebirds with missiles of violence, betrayal and malicious intent yet. That kind of stuff gets intense and painful and makes me all weepy. Yama has only just found happiness in Dhumorna's arms after losing Yami, and I don't want him to get screwed over yet again.

So for now, I thought I'll leave them happy as can be in their palace in Patala. Though Yama will lose Dhumorna, and get himself cursed, for good measure, things work out eventually when Dhumorna is reborn as a mortal and reunited with him after she succeeds in erecting the Rodhana and finishing off his enemies for him.

Now that you have reached the end of my yarn, be sure to buy me a gift (I like diamonds) to show your appreciation for my awesomeness and be sure to tell me that you loved my epic saga even if you hated it (we artists have sensitive souls)!

Finally, thank you for taking the time to read my lengthy manuscript all the way to the end. In case I haven't said it already, you are and always will be my favourite person in the whole wide world!

Ever yours,
Varu

A Note on the Author

Anuja Chandramouli is a bestselling Indian author and New Age Indian classicist. Her highly acclaimed debut novel, *Arjuna: Saga of a Pandava Warrior-Prince*, was named by Amazon India as one of the top five books in the Indian-writing category for 2013. *Kamadeva: The God of Desire* and *Shakti: The Divine Feminine* are her other highly successful books, and all three are being translated into Hindi, Marathi, Gujarati and Bengali.

An accomplished orator, Chandramouli regularly conducts workshops on creative writing, storytelling and mythology in schools, colleges and other platforms and also helps youngsters in the rural belt of Tamil Nadu improve their spoken English and writing skills. This happily married mother of two little girls lives in Sivakasi, Tamil Nadu, and is a student of classical dance and yoga. She is currently hard at work on an awesome new adventure with Yama's lieutenant.

Email: anujamouli@gmail.com
Twitter handle: @anujamouli
Website: www.anujachandramouli.com
Facebook: https://www.facebook.com/authoranujachandramouli/